I0602201

Mirrors of Infinity

The Dimensional Alliance 2nd edition, Volume 3

Bonnie K.T. Dillabough

Published by The Infinite Publishing Alliance, 2021.

MIRRORS OF INFINITY

First edition. January 12, 2021.

Written by Bonnie K.T. Dillabough.

Also by Bonnie K.T. Dillabough

The Dimensional Alliance 2nd edition
The House on Infinity Loop
Infinity on Fire
Mirrors of Infinity

Watch for more at https://dimensionalallianceheadquarters.com.

Table of Contents

Mirrors of Infinity

By Bonnie K.T. Dillabough
Third book in The Dimensional Alliance Foundation Trilogy

Dedicated to Mimi and Grompi: They stepped up to the plate and raised two lost little girls and dared us to dream, to work, to be kind to others and to believe in ourselves.

Acknowledgements:

Acknowledgements of help in this book wouldn't be complete without my amazing cover artist, Richard McKenzie, who really knows how to bring my visions to life. Thank you, Richard and Dee McKenzie, his very supportive wife and a fan of the books.

And I couldn't have done this without my beta reader's group, including, Carolyn Hardy Greiner, Delia D. Michael, Jennifer Dillabough, Barbara Angst Gilbert, Jeremiah Maluse, George Samuel Dillabough, Luz Rives, Cindi Jones Erickson, Lynnette Dillabough, Maria Gurriere, Angela Bryner, Maureen Briscoe Burrows, and Cathryn Leow.

And most importantly, George C. Dillabough (Chief Bodyguard, hubby, sweetheart, cook, beta reader, and care-giver). Without whose love and support I wouldn't even be alive to write these books. Thank you, Papa Bear, for being who you are, my true love and eternal companion.

Prologue:

Jenny was dreaming. She was sure of that. And she was pretty sure that this was ok with her. She didn't remember why, but she knew that waking would be painful and she wasn't ready for that.

She was in a beautiful garden. It was still, without a breeze or sound. The leaves on the soaring, ancient trees that surrounded it didn't stir. She could imagine birds or forest animals but saw no sign of anything like that. She made a slow turn on the spot, taking in the perimeter of trees and foliage. This garden was huge, like the garden she had visited once in Victoria, Canada. And it was meticulously kept, but not stuffy. There were few straight lines. The path that wound here and there throughout was formed by edges of aromatic herbs and low-growing flowers.

She walked for a while, simply enjoying the peace of the place, not thinking, not wondering; just being in that moment. She had a feeling something momentous was about to happen, but she couldn't fathom what that might be. Her mind was adrift, completely out of touch with any kind of reality.

She passed a grouping of lilac bushes taller than her head and inhaled the sweet smell. They reminded her of...what? The lilacs were of every shade from pale white to pink to lavender and even a deep purple that was almost black.

As she rounded the lilacs, a small clearing came into view. There were steppingstones, inlaid with brightly colored polished stones, rounded like those you might find in a riverbed. The path of stones led around a small clear pool of water a dozen paces across. Why did the thought of a clear pool now bring her such a feeling of sadness and regret? Near the pool, seated on a small stone bench was the person she had once seen in this place, what seemed like ages ago.

The woman stood. She wore a simple dark teal tunic, embroidered with flowers around the neckline, and a flowing brown skirt. Her long brown hair glinted with honey-colored highlights and her deep green eyes were warm and kind. She held out both hands to Jenny with a sweet smile.

It came to Jenny. She remembered this woman. "Miriha?" she asked in wonder. "Now I know this is a dream." Jenny grasped her outstretched hands and was pulled into a warm hug.

"Yes, my dear Jenny. You are dreaming, and yet, this is as real as anything you will know in your life. Come and sit and let me give you a gift. You have a very long road yet before you and I am afraid it will be rocky, often dark and, yes; even painful, but not always and not forever. You have many loving friends and family who will support you and give you the strength you need to complete your part."

From a pocket hidden in the folds of her skirt she drew out an interesting box about the size of a small matchbox. It was made of silver or maybe platinum? Inset into the lid of the box were tiny jewels of indefinable colors, similar to a crystal a friend had once given to her to hang in a window. Those colors shifted in relationship to the light around them.

Miriha touched a small button on the top of the box. The box didn't open, but it began to sing. Music unlike anything Jenny had ever experienced wafted out of the little box. But it wasn't just music. Listening to it formed pictures in her head. She didn't really understand them, but they were interesting. Random scenes, some she recognized and some she didn't rotated through her mind as if viewing multiple video screens all in the same room.

"Miriha, what is this? It is beautiful and I am sure precious. But I know enough of you to know you don't just give gifts for entertainment or without purpose. What are we experiencing here?"

"Insightful as usual, Jenny," Miriha said, delight showing in the lights of her green eyes. "This is a weapon for your arsenal, although it will not directly harm anyone. As you attune yourself to it, it will begin to show you things that will be useful to you. This takes time and practice. You can use this both in the waking world and in your mental exercises.

The images and the music are transmitted directly to your mind. You cannot control the images, but each image has meaning and may help you to sort through your options quickly. Often the images seem random, but as you gain experience with the quibox, you will find yourself putting the images together more and more intuitively. The images will not tell you what to do. They will allow you to see more clearly the reality of the choices before you.

There is nothing magical or mystical about this. It simply shows you images created by things you may have only noticed subconsciously and allows your mind to extrapolate the patterns which will show you possibilities. It does not predict the future, nor will it give you answers. You will learn to interpret the series of images and use the information to form your own conclusions.

You were not ready for this before, or I would have given it to you sooner. Even now, it may not feel immediately useful, but I promise you, as you continue to practice with it and give it time and attention when you are able to spare it, it will expand your ability to choose well.

Choice, after all, is the greatest power of any being and to make the best choices, you need to have good information to base them on. This is why those who would restrict the reasonable exercise of choice are considered truly evil. They not only restrict choices; they restrict the availability of good information that is necessary to make good choices in the first place.

The right to choose is not to be confused with the necessary laws and guides that are put into place in any developing culture. But growth only can occur when we are allowed to choose our paths and the twists and turns that occur on our journey. I have always believed this to be true, but it is only when I achieved this level in my progression that I realized how vital it is to the development of the mind and heart and the eventual ongoing happiness of each soul."

She touched the button on the box and the sweet ambient music ceased and the images faded.

"I don't know what to say, Miriha."

Miriha extended the tiny box to Jenny and Jenny took it from her, holding it and feeling the weight of it in her hand before stowing it without thinking into her MDP. She often forgot about the wonder she had first felt when she discovered the MDP and what it could do. It had become a tool that she honestly took for granted most of the time. Since the scientists of the Alliance had created the flesh-colored bands that camouflaged the MDPs so effectively, she didn't even have a visual to remind her that it was there.

And here it was in her dream. Was it a dream?

Jenny sighed. She looked into Miriha's eyes, so understanding and so empathetic. If anyone knew and understood what Jenny was dealing with, it was Miriha, as she had been the Gatekeeper before her death. Her death; Jenny had to ask.

"Miriha, how is this done? I know I asked you this before, but I still don't think I understand. Aren't you, well...dead?"

"That word is such a misnomer, Jenny. Although it is true the physical form of my previous state was destroyed, which happens soon or late, I am and always have been Miriha. Before I took on the tangible humanoid state I was blessed to experience, I was still me. I have since shed that form and I am still me. When I have accomplished what I must do to progress, I will achieve a yet more glorified form and yet I will still be who I am.

You, the person who is Jenny, are not defined by the boundaries of your current mortal state. You always have been. You always will be yourself.

The stage you are experiencing at this time is vital to your movement forward in your progression. The things you do, the choices you make, they matter to you and to those whom you are able to influence for good.

I cannot make it much clearer than that, nor is it my place to be more specific. I can see so much more than I ever could before my transformation. But I cannot see all things or know all things. I only hope to guide you. Do you understand?"

Jenny nodded. "I think so, but I'm sure I will understand more as I go. You have been so kind and generous. Will I remember this when I awake?"

"Perhaps not at first, Jenny, for such is the nature of dreams, but this isn't a regular dream and you are not a regular person. When you do remember, remember this: You are loved, and you are so much more than you realize. And now I must go, and you must return."

And blackness enveloped Jenny again for a time.

Chapter 1: Awake

Jenny awoke in darkness. She had no idea where she was, and she didn't remember how she got there. She only had vague memories of chaos and some deep sadness that she just couldn't touch right now. Her head hurt and she reached up to touch what felt like a cloth bandage wound around her head, padded in the back. When she touched the padding, she winced.

She was lying on what felt like a camping cot with a thin pad on it, a small, flattish pillow under her head. Her muscles ached, as if she had been lying in this one position for a long time. When she went to turn over, she realized that she was bound to the bed by a wide band of cloth around her chest. Her hands and feet were free, but the band was firm around her chest and would not allow her to move.

Since she didn't know where she was and due to past experiences with kidnapping and torture, she hesitated to call out. On the one hand, she needed some time to think and evaluate her situation. On the other, she could see or hear nothing, and the fact that her head wound had been bound was somewhat encouraging.

Of course, that might have only been because whoever had bound her to this bed needed information from her and the binding of the head wound had nothing to do with kindness. Either way, she was in no position to do anything about her current situation. Perhaps she could contact Elizabeth and get her to take her out of here, but would she be putting her dear adopted sister into danger that way? Perhaps she should contact Tarafau.

Her lack of recent memory, however, was daunting. It wasn't like she had amnesia or anything. She knew who she was, and she remembered that she was on some kind of mission for The Dimensional Alliance in her role as the Gatekeeper, but the details were fuzzy and something told her that whatever the plan had been, it had not gone well. And for some reason, she felt that this might have been her fault.

She decided that she should contact Tarafau. She tried to shift into the mode that allowed her to communicate across dimensions, but the ache in her head made it nearly impossible to take herself into the detached state of consciousness that allowed her to do that. She dutifully did the breathing exercises that had become second nature to her and realized that it just wasn't happening. She had become so very reliant on that newly acquired ability that she took it for granted as something she just did. This was disconcerting, for sure, but Jenny didn't panic. Panic wasn't in her nature.

Rather, she decided to focus just on doing what she needed to do to completely relax. It might have been that the blow to her head that had caused her so much pain was also the reason for her, hopefully, temporary memory loss.

At that point, however, this all became moot. A blinding light shot through an opening in the room that faced her on the bed. It was like a curtain had been drawn and she realized that the painful light was sunlight. So, she had simply been in a darkened room, but where?

The stolid female figure that stood silhouetted in the light stood for a moment, very still. Jenny assumed she was evaluating her patient.

"You are awake. This is good," she sent mentally to Jenny. *"It has been days, and we were beginning to despair that you had been permanently damaged."*

"Where am I? What happened? I don't remember much." Jenny despised the fact that her mental voice sounded a bit whiny to her. It wasn't the first impression she wanted to make.

"You are on the Groga home world in the town of the home of Anwhal, Groga-ha and lieutenant-governor of this place. This is the city, Melek. I am Freia, his wife. We met before; do you not remember?"

"No, I'm sorry. Did I know you well?" Jenny's mind was racing. She was on the Groga home world and in the home of a prominent Groga military man? This hadn't been on the list of possibilities that had first run through her mind upon waking.

"We had only just met before...I am not sure if I should tell you all that has happened so abruptly. Head injuries like yours occur often in battle and lost memories need to be re-introduced gently. For now, let's see if you are able to sit and take some strengthening broth. I know your mind is probably swimming with questions, but please know that you are in no imminent danger. You are an honored guest. Allow me to untie your safety band.

When you first came here, you were thrashing and calling out aloud in an unknown language. I was fearful your injuries would be made worse. When it is loosened, I will help you to sit up very carefully. I have treated too many of this type of injury and I can tell you we must go slowly if you are to be returned to health. Are we agreed?"

"Yes, Freia, I agree."

Freia carefully loosened the wide band from around her chest. Slipping an arm under her shoulders and supporting Jenny's neck with the other hand, she gently and slowly helped Jenny sit up. It was surprisingly difficult and painful, but she was able to get to a sitting position on the low cot-like bed. Freia had left the door curtain only slightly open, but enough that Jenny could now see that the small room around her was humble in its furnishings: a simple stool, some shelves that were empty for the moment, a little table at the end of her bed and what appeared to be a washstand. Jenny realized her clothes had been changed, perhaps more than once, in the days she had been unconscious.

Someone, she assumed it was Freia, had cared for her fastidiously while she had been there, helpless, and very ill. She felt somewhat dizzy and definitely disoriented. She was more than just far from home. She was in an unknown dimension on an unknown planet, among people she had once thought were the enemy. She only remembered vaguely her association with the Dimensional Alliance and something about the Insenium, but details and faces were fuzzy in her mind.

She didn't remember ever having such a pounding headache in her life. The back of her head felt like a horseshoe being pounded on an anvil. The pain extended from the back of her head, down her neck and spine behind her shoulder blades.

"Now, be still for a moment. I will check your bandages and then I will get you some broth that is warming on the stove. I have been drip-feeding you as you slept, dribbling the broth into your mouth to keep you from suffering from thirst or hunger."

Jenny nodded and then regretted the movement. Wow! How could a simple nod hurt so badly?

Freia carefully unwound the bandage and removed the padding. Jenny realized, with a shock, that at some point her head had been shaved. She knew that earth surgeons often did that for brain surgery and realized that the wound would have been impossible to treat with all of her curly blond hair getting in the way. One shock after another were mounting up. She dreaded what yet awaited her as she regained a clear knowledge of what had brought her to this point. She attempted to steel herself for this, but realized that her mind and emotions felt as limp and unresponsive as cooked pasta.

Freia was very gentle as she probed the wound which stung like fire.

"It is healing faster than I expected. You were struck from behind by a rather large rock thrown from close by. I don't think you were the intended target, but that didn't make it any less effective. It doesn't show any signs of wound rot, as we treated it immediately, or at least as soon as we could get you away from there. Anwhal had given us strict instructions to protect you and care for you in case there were, um, complications."

Jenny wondered vaguely what kind of complications there might have been and how her care had been entrusted to this kind Groga woman. She didn't ask. Something in her, something she couldn't quite put her finger on, told her that she didn't really want to know, at least not right now.

Freia cleaned the wound and then dabbed on some kind of salve that smelled a lot like the tea tree oil she had used in her soaps and shampoos at home. The smell was strong, and she assumed the ointment was a lot like the anti-bacterial ointments she kept in her first aid kit at home.

As Freia completed re-bandaging her head with fresh bandages, Jenny sent, *"Freia, thank you so much. You have a gentle touch. And I know you have labored kindly to care for me while I was unconscious. I want you to know that I am forever in your debt."*

Inscrutably, Freia replied, *"I have a feeling we will be much more in your debt than you in ours before all is finished Jenny. My husband has great hope for what you will be able to do for our people now that we actively seek our freedom. You have but to ask and we will do as you desire. This has been hundreds of years coming and our people are finally ready. The Dimensional Alliance, which we had considered our enemy for so very long, is now our ally. We will serve them and you as you need us to."*

Jenny was flabbergasted. There was no other word for it. What could she possibly have done to gain this kind of allegiance, this kind of fervor? She didn't know what to say, so she just said, *"Thank you so much Freia. I will do what I can and for now, I just need to get well enough to continue my mission, that is, as soon as I remember exactly what that mission is,"* she concluded with a weak laugh.

Ooh! That hurt!

"I will take these dirty bandages to be cleaned and return with some broth. Please stay still. Don't lie down yet, but as soon as we get some broth into you, I will give you something for the pain. It may make you sleepy, but right now, sleep may be the best medicine of all."

Jenny remembered not to nod, but waited patiently, staring off into space, not thinking about much of anything. Freia returned quickly with a mug of broth. There was no steam coming off of it, but the mug was warm in her hands.

"Do you need help with that? Just sip it slowly. Your stomach isn't ready for much more than that. This broth is one my people have used for healing for longer than our memory extends. It is very high in the nutrients your body will require to heal itself, for after all we can do, your body does most of the repair work."

Jenny obediently sipped at the rich, warm, and tasty broth. It was a deep brown color, and she thought she detected a taste similar to shitake mushrooms.

She had noticed that many planets used different kinds of fungi for food. She had no idea why humanoid species seemed to be so similar in their requirements, although Lova had warned her during her training that some species reacted differently to certain foods and when you were new to a dimension, it was important to be careful with the native foods.

Lova? Planets? It seemed that there were some things that had not been lost to her memory, and this gave her hope.

In this case, she had not had any recourse for her food choices, so she was grateful that, so far, her body had not reacted badly to any of the food they had been feeding her even while she was unconscious.

Before she realized it, she was surprised to find the mug empty. Her tummy felt warm and full and satisfied.

"Thank you, Freia," she said, holding the empty mug out. *"That was delicious. You must give me the recipe someday."* It was something her mother might have said, she realized. It was amazing to her how often she heard her mother's words coming out of her mouth.

"Thank you, Jenny. As I said, it is a traditional food for my people. I would be glad to teach you to make it when you are well. For now, I must give you this."

She handed Jenny a smaller cup of cold liquid. *"Drink it down quickly. It is not so pleasant as the broth,"* Freia advised.

Jenny complied, shooting it down like she used to do her mother's old family cold remedy. Freia was right. It tasted pretty nasty. But since her tummy was happy with the broth, it didn't make her feel sick to her stomach.

Almost immediately warmth spread throughout her body and the pain in her head faded. Freia was also right about the sleepy part. Her eyes soon drifted closed and she felt rather than saw Freia gently easing her back into a sleeping position, the pillow comfortably under her head. She felt a light blanket cover her and then she didn't think or feel anything at all.

Chapter 2: Apocalypse Looming

Tarafau paced back and forth on the long balcony of the Sanglarka lodge overlooking the valley and looking beyond to the snow and ice-covered mountains in the distance. He had always thought this a peaceful place, but he knew no peace at this time.

Jenny was gone. Burt was dead. Yes, the rebellion had begun and the Inseni on the planet seemed to be well subdued. Yes, the secret science lab with its wizards had been successfully sabotaged by the Mookookie and many of their current projects were in ruins, to the perverse delight of the scientists who Emperor Peril had called wizards. Yes, the slaves and Groga and Mookookie were busily setting the planet to rights, cornering and sequestering the captured Inseni, those who had capitulated quickly, which was actually most of them but at what cost?

It was true that no Alliance troops had been involved in the fighting. They had reserved those for battles to come, if needed, but their role was yet to be determined. Jenny and Burt's instincts had been good. The Inseni on the planet had been little more than "front men" for a much larger plan. All of this time the Alliance had been so convinced they had found the true enemy, and it had all been smoke and mirrors.

Elizabeth had returned from the chaos of the Insenium revolution brimming with self-loathing. She hadn't protected Jenny. She hadn't protected Burt. She hadn't even been following orders at the time she had helped Jenny set all of this up. No one had known about their little side plan. Jenny's bodyguards were furious, both with themselves and, to be frank, with Jenny.

Everyone had thought they had impressed on the young Gatekeeper the absolute necessity for her to be kept safe. They thought she had understood how important it was for her to be held in safety while they implemented the war strategies they had so carefully planned out.

It had been nearly a week now with no mental contact from Jenny. There had been no choice but to contact the alternate Gatekeeper, Anela, and bring her to the Sanglarka headquarters. For now, she was staying in Jenny's suite in the lodge, guarded by the three bodyguards, Lyra, Nona and Mynn, who were now taking turns sleeping on a cot in the bedroom.

Interestingly enough, Anela's key was not activated as the official Gatekeeper key. They had tested that and were both relieved and frustrated. Relieved, because it probably meant Jenny was alive somewhere, if possibly not well and still in potential danger. Frustrated, because there were certain things Anela would be unable to do without the authority of being the official Gatekeeper.

They would continue to intermittently test the key, but Anela said she would probably know if the Gatekeeper key activated and named her the official Gatekeeper.

Tarafau had tried to reassure Elizabeth that, although he was not pleased she had not confided in him, he did understand. Jenny had something about her that made others want to do as she said. It wasn't a conscious thing on her part, and he was convinced she was unaware she even did this.

Elizabeth had confessed she hadn't known the full extent of Jenny's plan, but had acceded to her requests for transport to the little thicket on the far side of the Inseni palace. She was now beside herself. He had sent her home, not in disgrace, but to the loving ministrations of her mother. She would return in a few days.

In the meantime, the rest of the team was still reeling from the loss of Burt on top of the disappearance of Jenny. Of course, they lost team members from time to time, due to injury or accident. In addition, the entire earth council was still trying to recover from the loss of Ingot and the disabling of Myla. Liliath was at Alliance headquarters, reorganizing and bringing her new team up to speed on what was going on with the mission to prevent the Insenium from plunging the multiverse into war on a scale that none of them could fully comprehend.

Liliath was competent and would be a great leader, but the timing of the disaster at Alliance headquarters was particularly bad with the new information that now disrupted everything. Not that they hadn't put plans into place in case there was more to this than Emperor Peril and his apparent schemes, but now they had a new force to reckon with. This creature Gall, who was evidently also Inseni, but not of the same race as Peril and his people, was truly the element that had been missing from their plans.

Gall appeared to be the true power behind Peril's throne. How they would get more information, Tarafau had no idea. But for now, they were all focusing on trying to figure out what had actually happened on Peril's planet. Tarafau was soon to meet with some of the Daringi who had participated in aiding the revolutionaries, and he needed to have his head on straight, as Lizzie would have said.

New agents were being prepared to move forward with Burt's mission as soon as they could be briefed and placed in key places. They had taken advantage of the scientist's lab planet to launch their nearly imperceptible but powerful communications satellites that would allow communications within the Inseni dimension via the Dimensional Alliance communications network.

They had placed a temporary gate to link the Alliance gate network to the portal in space just off of the scientist's planet. However, it was unclear how long that resource would continue to be available. There were no planetary defenses, and Tarafau was unsure how much Gall valued the tech these scientists had come up with for Peril. He wasn't even sure if Gall knew about the card that Bob and the Alliance scientists had been so concerned about.

It was so frustrating! There was so much he didn't know. Part of him wanted to slam his fist into something, anything, to express his anger and frustration, but the part of him he had so long disciplined to the contrary kept him from expressing himself that way. As a young man his temper had been fiery and quick. It had taken a long time before he realized how little expressing that anger had helped him and how much it hurt those around him as well as his chances to have a happy life.

When he had first met Amenia, he had been attempting to master that side of himself. She wouldn't allow him to court her, after he had expressed that desire, until he got it well in hand. It seemed to take forever, but the incentive of a lifetime with Amenia had been the one thing that could keep him on track.

He couldn't think of Amenia and not smile. She was truly the light of his existence and after hundreds of Earth years he couldn't imagine his life without her. Her patience, kindness and brilliance never ceased to delight him.

He brought his thoughts back to the issue at hand. He WOULD find Jenny and would find her safe and undamaged. He only hoped it would be soon. Unless he was mistaken, there would be no easy fix to this newest challenge and none of them would be safe until they had defeated the inimical forces of this new face of the Insenium.

He was so engrossed in his thoughts that he actually jumped slightly when Arvid planted himself in front of him. *"Earth to the big old cat!"* he sent gruffly. *"Is there anyone in there?"* he asked pointing to his head. *"I'm not sure that there is. Your people have arrived. Lova is setting them up in the dining room, which is convenient, since lunch is nearly ready. You'd better get in there. They're a pretty morose bunch, from the look of them."*

Tarafau entered the room wondering what his people would have for him. Their instructions had been to not participate in the battle except to defend their lives. The agreement with the slaves and Groga who had wanted to rise up against their masters was that they wished to fight their own battle, rather than be "rescued" by outside forces.

Only the Daringi warriors who had agreed to those terms had been sent. Their only job was to help the Groga and slaves participating in the uprising get from one dome to another, waiting in reserve until called upon. Jenny, Burt, and Elizabeth had done a tremendous job in coordinating all of that in the short time they had been given.

The Mookookie simply rode along with agreeable slaves or Groga as part of their clothing or equipment. All in all, it had been timed very well and had been going as planned, with fewer casualties than one would expect in such a revolt, mainly due to the element of surprise. Then, Gall had appeared and with him, troops that none of them had expected.

They still had no idea how he had done that, as he hadn't appeared to have used the portal in the Inseni palace. The Alliance strategic and logistics teams had planned so carefully with the information they had been given. The victory should have been cleanly decided based on what they thought they had known.

However, although they had won the day by the time Gall had abruptly withdrawn his troops on his departure, it would be a long time before things were normal again, if they ever were.

He stood before his own troops now, who had not yet taken their seats, standing at attention to honor their commander. He felt himself a sham. The intel he had provided for his men had been faulty. As a result, they had lost eighteen of his valiant warriors out of the two hundred he had sent. Two hundred of his Daringi, when given the proper coordinates, could move thousands of troops in a matter of minutes, assuming those troops were well organized and prepared for their journey.

To the naked eye, the process would have looked like an army melting away row after row only seconds apart and appearing in those same ranks on the other side of the journey equally as rapidly. To many it would have seemed a lot like magic at work.

Desminda had been the commander of the operation and their part had gone well, notwithstanding the unexpected appearance of Gall and his troops.

"*Be seated, my friends. Thank you for your prompt response. You may not have heard. The conflict had more casualties than you may realize. The Gatekeeper, Jenny Japhet, is missing and Burt Scout, our operative for the Insenium mission, has been killed.*

One of the missions we will soon undertake is the rescue of The Gatekeeper as soon as we know where she is. In the meantime, I need your report of the most recent mission. Please be candid about your experience. Any small detail or nuance could be important. Arvid has a lunch prepared for us and we can be free to talk as we eat. Lova has activated the screen to allow us to keep track of everything you say so we can use this report for future strategy sessions.

As soon as we are finished, you may return to your homes and families on standby until we are ready to use your gifts again."

Tarafau noted both concern and relief on the faces before them. With the exception of Desminda, they all looked so very young. He couldn't ever remember being that young. He was betting Desminda felt the same.

Tarafau let them take turns around the table, Lova and Desminda adding questions and repeating certain points that seemed particularly relevant. He watched the tension go out of each one of them as they finished their own report.

As a result, they knew a number of new things about this new addition to the Inseni threat.

All of the reports of those who witnessed the appearance of Gall and his subsequent murder of Burt agreed that it was clear that Emperor Peril was emperor in name only. There were none of Gall's troops in the square or in the capital city, for that matter, but gangs of them had been seen in nearly every other dome, apparently randomly slaughtering slaves and Groga alike, hauling them from their homes, men, women, and children. The status of their victims seemed to be entirely random, chosen for sport.

The women were not ravaged and there was no plunder evident. Gall's troops were all male and all huge, like their master with a single large eye in the middle of their forehead. They wore no armor, but scarlet uniforms similar to earth battle uniforms, but with no apparent rank or other adornment. The word "gangs" was repeated more than once during the reports, as the soldiers didn't appear to have a command structure. They weren't even congenial with their own people. More than once, arguments had broken out for no reason anyone could fathom, and more than once the argument escalated to the violent death of one or another of the combatants.

They appeared to be brutes, delighting in only one thing, killing and destruction. In one dome they had burned every home in the little town, sparing the mercantile and other businesses on the town square.

The destruction was all so random that, try as they might, the Daringi troops could see no pattern. It was like every gang had their own agenda. Then, with no apparent signal any of Desminda's troops could discern, they simply marched out of town and disappeared outside of the dome.

There were no threats given, no ultimatums, and no reason for the sudden attack. Some of them had been killed by the villagers who had the courage to try, and the gangs had left the bodies of their fellows as if they were so much garbage.

Once they had continued around the table with their reports, each adding to the information, the young man who had begun, Lanari, stood again, to Tarafau's surprise. *"Sir, there is one more thing, an aftermath, so to speak, that you must know about..."* He hesitated, shifting from foot to foot, like a little boy caught in childish mischief.

"Understand we didn't realize it until things had calmed down and we had been ordered home. Remember the little folk, native to the Inseni world? Well, we had also been transporting them to allow them to participate in the revolt, mostly on our clothing. Jenny had given them an order to multiply. They followed that command admirably, so much that there was no keeping track of all of them. They are friendly, at least to everyone who is not Inseni, but there is a problem."

He looked at his fellows, as if for encouragement. It became obvious to Tarafau that he had been "elected" to bear this news. This didn't bode well. They had possibly drawn lots and he had lost. Tarafau nodded in what he hoped was an understanding way and waited.

"You see, the Mookookie really like Jenny. They think she is some kind of angel or something. She told them to multiply and never actually told them they needed to stop. Of course, they have their entire planet to spread out into now, with no fear of being hunted.

The people of that world, the slaves who have decided to remain and the Groga, who are still there, look on them as little heroes. They have taken to leaving out food for them and even taking some of them as pets when they can be present as new Mookookie are budded. So, that is a good thing, right?"

"The point of your report, Lanari?" Tarafau said, puzzled by this long drawn out explanation that didn't seem to have anything to do with why they were here.

"Well sir, some of our people accidentally bonded with some of the little creatures and..."

"WHAT? You know they bond for life? Like Linklings? Were you not briefed on this?"

"Actually, no sir. We were only told to transport them, sir, and to treat them kindly. But there is a problem. You see, we ended up bringing many of them with us when we went home before we realized the...um...multiplication problem. They won't stop multiplying until Jenny herself tells them to do so. Their cycle is a few weeks apart, so we have a little time, but the thing is they multiply up to twelve at once. We have presented this, uh, difficulty to the council and they are considering it, but we really need Jenny...Um...We REALLY need Jenny to help us with this."

"You're telling me they are on our home world and multiplying?" Tarafau said, a little more forcefully than he intended.

"Yes, sir. We didn't know. We didn't understand." The young man sat, his head hung low, and his compatriots mostly sat looking at their hands folded before them on the table. Tarafau was admittedly shaken by this.

One more reason Jenny must be located alive and safe and quickly he thought. Not that they weren't all frantic to find her already. It was no use to berate the young man or to rant about this new complication. For now, he would have to stay focused. Losing Jenny was only one big issue among dozens of big issues that were necessary to address.

"Another incentive to find her and as quickly as possible," Tarafau sent. *"In the meantime, we can't let this distract us. As of this moment, every warrior who has volunteered for this mission is effectively on standby. Be ready. Thank you for your reports. Enjoy the amazing meal Arvid has prepared for us and then report home. You have done well. I am proud to lead such brave and diligent warriors in this mission. Desminda, do you have anything to add?"*

"Only this. We've stirred up a nest of zap-stingers here. I doubt Gall has any desire for any kind of alliance or negotiations. As I perched on a rooftop in my bird-form that day, I could feel waves of evil intent wafting from Gall like the waves of the sea in a storm. There is no doubt as to the danger he represents, and it is unlikely there can be any peaceful resolution. My warriors and our people are committed to seeing Gall eliminated and his people either pacified or removed in a way that they cannot ever threaten the multiverse again."

Tarafau nodded in agreement. The flame that had been lit in the last few days was now a bonfire, and it would engulf the multiverse if they didn't hold firm to their resolve. Like the Daringi, troops and resources all over the multiverse were being put on alert and readied for the assault in whatever forms it may take. The Dimensional Alliance that had always been an advocate of peace and freedom was about to be tested to its limits.

Chapter 3: Coming To

Jenny sat up in bed with a start and regretted it instantly. She lay gently back on the small pillow of her cot and willed the stabbing pain to subside. Breathing carefully helped. Freia had stopped tying her to her bed, and she was allowed to sit up for a bit to eat, clean up and take the medicine, which was now being prepared at a lower dose. However, it still meant she slept a lot, which worried her.

First of all, she was anxious about the war with the Insenium although so much of that was still fuzzy. Her dreams had been filled with pools of water, one in a forest by a river and another in a beautiful garden. No actual people appeared in either dream, but she had a nagging feeling that this meant something important.

Try as she might, however, she still couldn't figure out why both pools seemed so familiar as if there were memories attached to them, some of them wonderful and some of them painful. It was a lot like having a tender tooth in your mouth that you couldn't help but probe with your tongue.

The room was no longer completely dark. Freia had taken to leaving one of the window curtains open during the day. It was on a shaded side of the building, so the light was not quite as intense as the light let in when she entered through the door curtain.

Evidently the climate here was very mild. Jenny only needed a light blanket at night and none through the long days. Freia came in twice a day to change her bandage and several times a day with broth, usually followed by the bitter medicinal tea. Generally, the pain was beginning to subside, except when she forgot and sat up or moved quickly.

The bright light of the curtain being drawn away from the door into the room didn't hurt as much as it had before.

"How are you, Miss Jenny? Your healing is coming along. Do you think you might be up to walking to the outside of your guest hut to sit in a chair in the sunlight? I will gladly support you and you can take it very slowly."

"I would like that, I think," Jenny agreed. She had given up the habit of nodding yes or no lately as it often caused her pain. *"It would be a nice change from lying in bed here."*

"First, we must change your dressings and then you can sip your broth outside and enjoy the sunshine."

Freia went quickly to work, removing the old bandages and setting them aside, then gently cleaning the wound, which stung, but wasn't quite as tender as it had been. Once again, she put the ointment on the wound and covered it with clean padding and then wrapped a clean bandage over that. It was good her head was covered in the bandage, Jenny thought, as by now her head was probably covered with blond stubble. She dreaded to think about looking in a mirror.

When she had asked, Freia had told her that she had bruises under her eyes, but those would fade. There might be a scar on the back of her head, but that would eventually be covered with hair. She was much more concerned about how the inside of Jenny's head would heal, and Jenny had to admit she felt the same.

When she was finished wrapping Jenny's bandage, Freia drew back and looked directly into Jenny's eyes. *"I will be able to see better when you get out into the sunlight, but your eyes seem to be responding well. Are you still dizzy while sitting?"*

"No, not as long as I don't move quickly," Jenny admitted. She hated being so weak and sickly. Only once before in her life did she remember being this way, and it was before her tonsils were removed. The infection in her tonsils and adenoids had been so severe that she had been in the hospital for over a week before they got it under control enough to be able to operate.

"This is progress. Your wound has finally closed and is beginning to scab. It was not as deep as some I have seen. At least we don't think it cracked your skull, just rattled your brains around in there a bit. Based on past experience I would say you will be all right, but I do expect it will take a while before you can do the things you are used to doing.

Assuming your memories aren't completely lost, you should start to remember some things as we get you out and about more. Now can you hold onto my arm and get up slowly? Never fear. I will support you."

"OK," Jenny agreed, *"Let's do this."*

She reached out and, holding onto Freia's proffered arm, she slowly stood. For a moment, she almost sat right back down as the dizziness returned, but she took some careful breaths and steeled herself. One careful step at a time they moved across the room and out the door into brilliant sunlight, which made Jenny squint.

Just outside the door, as Freia had promised, was a wicker-like chair with padded arms and a low footstool. Next to the chair was a small wooden table, and on the table was a covered mug of Freia's nutritional broth. Jenny would have expected herself to tire of having the same meal day in and day out, but she knew her tummy really wasn't up to anything more complicated.

Her view from the chair wasn't what she expected. Before her was a very comforting scene. Birds, Jenny assumed they were like chickens, pecked in the short dark green grass and the yard was surrounded by a fence of split rails. Surrounding the fence were tall bushes that served as both a hedge and apparently a food source as they were covered in some kind of bright yellow berry. To her right, the yard opened up to what looked like a vegetable patch.

It was quiet except for the chortling back and forth of the feeding birds. The broth was still warm, and Jenny sipped at it contemplatively. So, here she sat, eating with the chickens in what might have been any small farm on earth, completely separated from the battle that was potentially raging across the multiverse.

"Will you be all right here for a few minutes?" Freia asked, after looking again into Jenny's eyes. *"I have chores to see to. I may send someone to check in on you from time to time and you can go back to your bed, if you tire of sitting."*

"I will be fine here, Freia. You have already done so very much for me, and I appreciate that it is taking you away from other things you need to do. Thank you. I will enjoy sitting in the sunshine."

Freia nodded and left, hurrying off past the little garden.

Jenny put down the empty mug and breathed out a big sigh. It was so peaceful here at this moment and she took that as a gift, if a potentially fleeting one. Then, suddenly she felt a small warm hand on her cheek. As she carefully turned her head, sitting on her shoulder was Chidwi! How could she have forgotten about her little friend?

"You are truly awake, dear Jenny? I was so afraid for you. I have been here with my reflection turned off as I was when we were in the Inseni city. Something large and hard crashed into your head after..." Chidwi trailed off. Jenny didn't remember the little Linkling ever reticent to say what she thought.

"What is it Chidwi? What is it you don't want to talk about to me?" Fear began to well up unexpectedly in her gut. *"What are you not telling me?"*

"I mustn't tell you. You must remember on your own. It will be hard. But I am here. May I touch your head? I may be able to help the inside part, as the Groga woman doesn't seem to know how to help you there. She has been very kind, very gentle and has cared diligently for you while you were helpless. This says much for her. I have not shown myself. I don't wish to startle them or keep them from helping you."

"Thank you, Chidwi. But I feel so helpless. All of the work...all of the work we did."

"Yes, yes," Chidwi said. *"For now, don't think. For now, don't worry. I will put my hands on your head. You must be calm and breathe. You know how to do this."*

Jenny took a deep breath and Chidwi, oh so gently, laid her tiny, warm hands on the top of her head, away from the padding that covered the wound. Jenny immediately felt warmth creep from the crown of her head clear down into the soles of her feet. It was like hot fudge dripping down the sides of a sundae. As the warmth filled her body, she felt every muscle release gently. The throbbing in her head eased and then, from her toes spreading upward into her body it was like she was filling up with a white light. Not a glaring light, but crystalline and warm.

Once again, a crystal pool came into her consciousness and by the pool sat...

Burt! Oh, my goodness Burt!

From calm and peace, she went into pain and sheer agony of soul in a single instant.

She saw him again in her mind's eye, standing straight and defiant of the giant, Gall. Once again, she heard the soft and fervent, *"Jenny, I love you. I always will."* And then he exploded in a shower of burning sparks.

"No!" she shouted at the top of her lungs. "No! No! NOOOO!"

She put her head in her hands, her head now aching again as before, the throbbing and thundering. "Burt! No! How could you go? How could you leave me? How could you have waited to tell me?"

The words came out between huge wracking sobs, her shoulders heaving and tears running down her face.

Freia came running around the corner, her eyes wild. Her son, Grephan ran behind her, a club in his hand.

"Jenny! Jenny! What is wrong? We thought you were being attacked!"

But Jenny could not even make the attempt to answer. No words came from her now, just horrible heaving sobs. She was bent double in her chair, her hands clutching the sides of her head. Chidwi, in her shock, had not turned her reflection off, so there she was on the back of Jenny's chair, in full view.

When the Groga saw Chidwi their reaction was dramatic and unexpected. They both fell to their knees and bowed, their faces hidden in the grass of the yard.

"Honored one," Freia finally got out. *"Now we know that Jenny is more than she appears. We promise, wise one, that we have done her no harm, nor do we intend any. Please forgive us for not recognizing one of your disciples."*

Jenny's sobs continued, although she was aware of the drama playing out by her. She wanted her sobs to stop. She knew this was a turning point, vital to her mission and yet...Oh BURT! Even when Sam had been cutting that butterfly into the flesh of her arm and she thought she would die she hadn't felt like this. It was as if her entire being was turned inside out, raw, burning and so very empty.

To her astonishment, Freia began to sing in a chanting rhythm much like the Hawaiians do. It was slow and low pitched. Jenny could almost hear the ukuleles softly strumming in the background. She heard the shuffling of feet to that rhythm and looked up.

Freia and Grephan were no longer alone. Several men and women and even some children had joined in the singing. Even Chidwi was crooning along and as they sang; they danced a slow shuffling dance with their arms linked together. The steps were simple, and the mood of the dancers was solemn and reverent. The music had begun softly, but now more and more voices chimed in, rows and rows of dancers wove in and out in a pattern that was entrancing.

Jenny realized that, although tears still streamed down her cheeks, she was no longer sobbing. Her head had begun to throb again. Chidwi, without being asked, placed her little hands back on the crown of Jenny's head and as she did so, the dancers stopped, and the singing faded. As one, they all bowed toward Jenny and Chidwi.

Freia stepped forward. *"Honored one, please accept our offering. To you and your disciple, Jenny, we pledge our devotion, our lives, and our service. Ask what you will, and we will obey."*

Chidwi's mind voice was so very gentle. *"Children of light, we accept your offering and your pledge. Please rise and do not bow in supplication anymore. I am not the being to whom that kind of obeisance is required. All I require is that you listen to Jenny and learn from her. She has much to teach you.*

But for now, she needs rest. Freia, your ministrations will still be required, but I will heal the inner pain as I can. This will take time. A loved one for whom Jenny cared deeply has passed beyond the veil and her soul is bereft. Please continue as you have begun.

There will soon be much for you to do. When Jenny is ready, we can begin preparations to rid the multiverse of the curse the Insenium attempts to inflict upon us."

The group of Groga nodded reverently and all departed with the exception of Freia and Grephan.

"Please help Jenny back to her bed and give her some more of the medicine you have been administering to her. In the morning she will need to try sitting in the sunlight again, but for now, her strength is depleted, and she must sleep. I will stay with her and call you when she awakes for more broth and medicine. Thank you."

Freia helped Jenny stand from her seat and both she and Grephan helped her into the quiet, darkened hut. Grephan gently lowered Jenny to a seated and then a reclining position and left. Freia was ready with a cup of the medicine. Jenny gulped it down gratefully and closed her eyes. But she didn't drift off to sleep right away.

"*That was amazing, Chidwi. Why did they react that way to you?*"

"*This story is a long one, Jenny. The short version is that the Linklings lived on the original Groga home world before they became a violent race at the prodding of the Fleistians and Inseni. They had been a rural people, mostly farmers before that.*

Some of them got it into their heads, because of our powers of healing, soothing and being able to turn our reflections on and off, that we were some kind of deity or at the least magical beings. We never did convince them otherwise, but at one point when the violence was at its height, we fled through a portal that came out on Miriha's world.

When Tarafau and Lizzie first visited Miriha, Lizzie was chosen to bond to Ynni. Ynni was with child at the time. She birthed in Tarafau's grove. Ynni gave birth to twins. This was the foundation of the Linkling tribe which lives in his grove, of which I am a descendant.

The Groga have evidently kept legends of the Linklings alive in their lore. This may be helpful. For now, however, may I suggest that before you sleep you do your breathing and begin to recondition your mind? I have mended some things that were damaged. Do not try to communicate across dimensions at this time. Some healing must yet occur. I will be right here with you Jenny, and no one will disturb you."

"*Thank you, Chidwi. I am so grateful that we bonded that day. Was it only weeks ago? I feel as if we have been together forever.*"

"*Linklings believe that when we bond, which is fairly seldom, it is because there was always a bond there. We believe in the immortality of what you would call the soul. You have always been and always will be. We believe that you and I knew each other at an earlier time.*"

"*That might explain it. I have certainly learned that there is so much more to life and the multiverse than I ever expected.*"

"Indeed, and now what I expect of you is to do your breathing and rest. There will be many opportunities for the advanced version of this conversation. You and I have all of the time that there is."

And obediently Jenny began her breathing exercises. Her heart still hurt, but it was manageable as the medication had begun to take. There was time. Was there? She didn't know, but she would take the time that was given her. She couldn't give up yet.

Chapter 4: Dungeons and Dragons

Liliath finished her report to the main body of the Dimensional Alliance with a shake of her head. The voting had been unanimous that they do everything in their power to prevent the incursion of this new threat. The thousands of delegates could never be held in one room, so the meeting was attended via various communications devices tied into the Dimensional Alliance Communications Network. Voting was done electronically, even by those who attended in person.

She was nearly overwhelmed with the responsibility that had been placed on her by the untimely death of Ingot and the maiming and permanent loss of hearing of Myla, which had made him incapable of flying and had completely disrupted his ability to balance.

Their system of government allowed for replacement of one or all of the Chief Councilors out of a pool of pre-approved candidates. Each dimension was allowed to put forth a new candidate on a rotating basis, so that at any given time no single dimension could dominate the political structure.

The rule was that new councilors had to be chosen from one of the dimensions that had not been chosen in the previous 3 replacements.

Generally, barring death or disability, new Chief Councilors were chosen every five years. The Chief Councilor would retire from the post, the 2nd Councilor would rotate into that position, the 3rd Councilor would rotate into the position above him and a new member of the Chief Council would be chosen. Most of the time, this meant that during their term on the council, each Councilor served a total of 15 years.

They had been nearly to the end of the cycle and Ingot would have retired, something he had been looking forward to with great anticipation. He had missed his family intensely, not taking leave unless necessary. He had taken his responsibility very seriously, and Liliath had learned much from him over the years.

Each Councilor was provided with room and board and any necessities they might require, but it wasn't a plush life by any extent of the imagination. True, Liliath's quarters were more than adequate; meant to accommodate those of her kind comfortably. There were servants employed by the Alliance who took care of cleaning and maintenance. There were excellent healers on staff in the headquarters building infirmary, if they were ever needed. The cooks were nearly as good as Arvid and well trained in preparing food for any of the many species who frequented the building.

That being said, she and her fellow Councilors didn't have a salary or any additional compensation besides the needs that were attended to here in the Dimensional Headquarters Building. And to Liliath's thinking, that was completely appropriate. Although she acknowledged that their system of government was by no means perfect, she had seen few that compared with it, considering the resources they had been able to acquire over the thousands of years they had been doing this.

They didn't tax the member dimensions. Each was asked to give of resources as needed and as they could afford to do so. In some cases, this meant abundance and in others, a seeming pittance was all they could give. None of the donated resources was "owned" by the Alliance. It was merely offered to aid the combined efforts of the dimensions, thankfully accepted, and used prudently.

As she contemplated the current situation, she knew there were a number of facts that needed to be faced. First, her new councilors were just that...new. They were both very capable beings, well-educated and well-versed in the needs and logistics of keeping the Dimensional Alliance Gate Network secure and functioning, one of their primary responsibilities. Or at least they were as knowledgeable as anyone could be. Not even their most competent and intuitive scientists truly understood how the whole thing worked.

There was, for instance, the issue of the conservation of energy that must have somehow been addressed to even make it possible to pass from one gateway to the next. Theoretically, it should have been impossible to open and pass through a gateway without the forces on both sides of the gates being balanced somehow.

Not something she needed to focus on right now, but it was a continuing fascination for her and all of those who pursued the sciences to contemplate. Mervin had been researching this for hundreds of years and kept running up against one dead end after another. Liliath thought he would have resigned his position to devote all of his remaining time to pursuing the path of those original scientists if he thought he could. For now, they still had his attention, but she couldn't help but wonder if...no...WHEN they finally defeated the Insenium, if they would have Mervin much longer.

She had avoided the crowd in the council assembly room by ducking out a door designed for that purpose behind the podium. She heaved a sigh when the elevator doors opened into the private council room reception area. The white-furred receptionist sat in her usual place. She had survived the explosion that had killed Ingot and injured Myla with only minor injuries by ducking under her large, official-looking hardwood desk. It was comforting to see her there.

"Good afternoon, Chief Councilor," she sent with a smile. *"There is no one in the private council room yet."*

"Thank you, .Gissah. Please let my councilors know that I need their presence as soon as they can get away from the assembly hall."

.Gissah nodded cheerfully and got the look of concentration that meant she was communicating mentally over a distance. It was one of the reasons they had hired her for this position; her kind could mind speak to specific people over impressive distances. Not like Jenny, across the dimensions, but she could reach nearly anyone in the Dimensional Alliance Headquarters building. She only knew one other person who could do that, and she was not available.

Liliath entered the private council chamber where she had already spent nearly ten years working with Ingot. It still seemed surreal to her. The maintenance people had cleaned up the debris and repaired the walls and ceiling, reinforcing the ceiling and replacing the lighting with a new style that simply emanated from the ceiling material. It would be unlikely to fall on anyone's head ever again.

The room was the same, but again, not the same. Her special chaise had been placed in the preeminent position on the dais. Her two councilors' chairs were just chairs. They were both humanoid bipeds, although one was covered with sleek, shiny reddish brown fur and the other was almost reptilian with slick skin that somehow managed to always look wet or oily. However, when he clasped hands with her, his palms were as dry as her own.

They were both extremely competent individuals from completely different backgrounds. Rilian was a well-beloved leader on her planet. Her furred species reminded Liliath of an Earth creature Lizzie had once told her about. She called it an otter. Rilian's species, the Kaylats, were not aquatic, however, and much larger. Rilian was easily over six feet tall.

She was sharp and highly intellectual and versed in the sciences, although that was not her field of expertise. She was a professional mother. In her species that was as respected a title as the highest politician or celebrity in their culture, perhaps more so. Her children were long since grown and now she mothered her people, working in her community. In this case, she had been serving as a standing representative in the Dimensional Alliance Council before being chosen as first councilor.

Rilian was a good choice, Liliath thought. She was a stable being with a practical attitude and the respect of most of the other members of the Alliance Council. She had won Liliath over at their very first meeting and Liliath had often consulted with her on various issues after Ingot had chosen her as councilor.

Balth, on the other hand was a bit more quicksilver. He listened to all sides of an issue and then quickly formed an opinion, which he would stick to doggedly unless someone could give him a well thought out reason why he needed to change his stance. He was short, and a little round, his tummy covered by a black tunic. He would have probably come up to Jenny's shoulder. His eyes were the most brilliant green and his slick skin the color of a ripe peach.

The three of them, side by side on the dais, were quite a contrast, as were their personalities. But experience had taught Liliath that she could work with them, and that was vital at this juncture.

Once they had settled into their seats, Liliath began. *"So, we have mobilized the dimensions, and all have agreed to contribute to the cause as they are able. This is a good first step.*

Now we must deal with the prisoner. I admit I am at a loss of how to deal with him. He has made claims and they contradict witnesses. But the little complication is that we have no way of discerning which to believe. We know for a fact that it wouldn't be the first time that the Insenium had placed a red herring in the mix. Is he who and what he claims to be?"

"So far, with the exception that many people saw him die, all of the evidence he has presented has been credible. He feels trustworthy to me. Mind you, I never worked with him before or saw him other than in passing. I am not familiar with his mind," said Rilian, spreading her four-fingered hands wide. *"I am still uncertain."*

"The original was known to be wily and cunning," Balth said, *"but he wouldn't use such guile on his friends. However, if the being in the dungeon is a copy, he is a good one. Many witnesses vouched for the fact that previous to his death a copy was created out of seemingly thin air, so not a clone and not any technology that we are familiar with. The DNA print, as analyzed by our lab, is identical to the original. There are no radiation markers or other telltale traces in the blood to say the being in our dungeon has been tampered with.*

That being said, he has been throughout the dimensions on assignment, after all, so even if we had found unusual markers, we might still not have conclusive evidence of tampering. I am still undecided. Shall we invite our scientists in to see if they have found anything that will be useful in making this decision? If the prisoner is indeed who he says he is we might want him out of there and back on assignment. There is, after all the Gatekeeper who needs to be found and rescued."

"As you say," agreed Liliath. *"This is only one of many priorities we need to address. So, I would have some suggestions from either of you of how we may test the prisoner to determine his status, so we can move forward."*

"Who knows him best?" asked Rilian. *"Perhaps we are not the ones who should examine him. Perhaps there is someone who knows him well enough to be able to tell if he is lying."*

Liliath considered this. Her first thought was Tarafau, but he was embroiled in dealing with the rest of the aftermath of Gall's attack and preparing his people for the next level of warfare with the Insenium. Of the council members, Ingot had been closest to him, taking him under his arm as a young agent in training years ago. But with him gone, there were few besides Tarafau who knew much about him.

Except...

"Let's have the scientists in for a moment. Is Mervin here or is he off planet? I want him included in this discussion. I just had a thought, but I want to ask Mervin a few things first. I know Mervin wasn't in Alliance Headquarters when we first brought him in, so now is a good time to brief him."

The others nodded in agreement and Liliath gave the order to .Gissah. It was only a moment before she replied, *"Done, Chief Councilor. Mervin actually just got into the lab about an hour ago from visiting with the Inseni scientists. He is eager to see you as well."*

The scientists sauntered into the council chamber in what couldn't have been more than two minutes. They were almost humorous looking, the white lab coats contrasting with the jeans and assorted colorful t-shirts. Without the lab coats and seeing them on the streets, most people wouldn't have thought much of them. However, these were some of the most brilliant minds across the dimensions.

Argent was absent. He had taken the death of Ingot harder than any had expected of the old curmudgeon. He had returned to his home planet to clear up Ingot's estate and comfort his many living family members.

Liliath had only been able to send her condolences via messenger considering the urgency of the current situation, not to mention the fact that dealing with the newest developments had taken all the strength and time that Liliath had. Her heart still ached from the loss, but she knew she didn't have the luxury of taking time out to grieve. It would have to wait. And what made it worse was that she was sure that when that time came, assuming she survived all of this, her list of those to mourn would have grown considerably.

"*Your timing couldn't have been more perfect,*" Mervin said as soon as they walked in the door and before any of them could seat themselves. "*We transported the rest of the Insenium scientists to your home dimension to work with Cornelium, Liliath. They bring with them a wealth of knowledge that not even their masters ever got out of them.*"

He would have gone on, but Liliath cut him off more abruptly than was usual for her. "*Mervin, that will have to wait. There is an issue that we have been dealing with secretly since the revolt, and we need your input. The other scientists are well aware, as we have briefed them, and they have been working with us.*

Don't look at them like that, Mervin. They haven't exactly had time to tell you since you have been back, and we were not transmitting any of this information for fear of it being intercepted by the wrong people.

How well do you know the Dimensional Alliance Agent, Burt Scout?"

Mervin shook his head, confused. "*Burt? He used to spend most of his off hours in the lab. He even has his own workspace there. I would say he and I were friends. I'm still reeling from his death. He will be greatly missed.*"

"*Hmm. So, you would say you know him pretty well?*"

"*I would say so. Tarafau asked me to take him under my wing, since he had such a curiosity about 'sciency stuff', as Burt liked to call it. He could never get enough of 'dastardly alien tech'. Even the rest of us lab rats have taken to calling it that. Or DAT, as Bob had shortened it. He was a good kid; bright, quick and a real smart aleck. We will all miss the heck out of him. Why do you ask?*"

"Did you read the report of the uprising and the appearance of Gall to the assembly in front of Peril's palace?"

"I did. I remember it coincided with the disappearance of the Gatekeeper."

"Did you see the part where the witnesses swore that just previous to his assassination, a duplicate Burt popped up in front of him?"

"Yes, I saw it, but I have a hard time believing it was more than a store front dummy or a hologram. No way they had time to clone him. The best they might have done was to make a stand-in by some kind of surgical techniques. Or at least, that's my opinion lacking any information about tech to the contrary."

"So, what if I told you that we have what appears to be, according to DNA testing, Burt Scout, being held in the high security detention area in the basement of this building?"

"I'd say, 'let him loose'!" Mervin said, his fists bunched in frustration. *"What are you thinking?"*

"We're thinking that the Insenium has fooled us, including Burt, more than once so far, and we aren't willing to take any chances."

Mervin took a few slow, deep breaths. *"OK, I get it. What do you need from me?"*

"We would like you to have a conversation with him. Observe him. You know his little physical quirks and natural body language. You've shared inside jokes and you know a lot of the same people. No copy could be so perfect, or so we think, that they could fool someone who knew him well. It is the one test we haven't been able to run, and perhaps the most important one. We don't think anyone besides Tarafau knew him better than you did."

"OK, I'll do it. The rest of these can brief you on some of our newfound tech resources. See ya in a bit. Tell security I'm on my way." And he stomped out, obviously not looking forward to a chat with his friend under these circumstances but determined to do the job quickly and get it over with.

Liliath turned on the overhead screen and tuned it in to the security cameras in the cell wherein "Burt" was being kept.

He looked up directly at the camera. Evidently there was a very tiny electrical sound that Burt could hear whenever they had activated it. She handed Balth and Rilian each the headphones with the translator software in them, so they could listen. Liliath spoke passable English, as many of her kind did. She knew Mervin would talk to his friend vocally, as he usually did.

Burt waved with a saucy grin. That would have been very typical of the real Burt, she had to admit. He was a canny agent, and things like surveillance cameras weren't new to him. If it was the real Burt, he would understand why they were doing this and she would inevitably apologize and just as inevitably, he would forgive her. But it still bothered her that the Insenium could sow such distrust among them at a time when their solidarity was vital.

The door opened in the cell, but Burt didn't jump to his feet, rather he called out. "Hey Merv! Have a seat." Burt had been reclining on the cot provided in the cell and had pointed to a plain chair that louvred out from the wall. Merv sat with folded arms, his long legs sprawled out in front of him, a reflection of Burt's own casual pose.

"So, Burt, how'd you get into this mess? Personally, I think it's a silly way to get a vacation when you could be out on some warm beach with an iced lemonade and a pretty girl. I thought I taught you better than this."

"It's just a bit of hocus-pocus courtesy of our friends in the Insenium. Somehow, they gave folks the impression that they killed me good and proper and made a duplicate of me, not something remotely possible, as there can only be one of me.

As far as the killing part goes, my little buddy, BaaGah is a suspicious little bugger. He had stationed himself as a shield over my entire torso. Something he calls, 'hardening the spaces'. It makes a flexible shield that is nearly impenetrable but can't be detected in a body search.

I didn't try to talk him out of it, since I knew my little big-eyed friends hadn't been very forthcoming about pretty much anything. Besides, I couldn't feel it and they couldn't see it, so as far as I was concerned it couldn't hurt. Turns out it was a smart thing to do. When Gall came on the scene, I was pretty sure the jig was up. I knew Jenny was along for the ride, so whatever happened would be reported right away, which meant it was time to roll the dice, so to speak.

I let him talk, but I reckoned without him being so quick on the draw. Fortunately, BaaGah had another little trick up his, well, sleeve isn't the right term as he doesn't have arms most of the time...let's just say he had a few tricks he hadn't shown me yet.

It turns out the little guy is a master of 'the spaces'. He makes 'beam me up Scotty' look like hocus pocus. Somehow, he drew both of us down through the stone steps of the palace. We waited there until nighttime, when the commotion was over, and everyone was elsewhere picking up the pieces. The palace was deserted; every single one of Peril's cronies and minions had gotten out of Dodge.

We walked into the throne room like we owned the place. But there was a bit of a sticky wicket. I remembered the stupid amulet Peril had tricked me into putting around my own neck. I told BaaGah about it and before I could say anything else, he simply swarmed up my shirt and ATE IT!

I would never have thought of it. He ate it and BURPED! What a sound and what a stench!

I decided not to take a chance of going through their portal, which just would have probably landed me back where I started, at the Fleistian gate, so I sent a message up through the communications link and one of Tarafau's people came and grabbed me and brought me here, where I was immediately handcuffed and thrown, without comment, into here, where they took a hair sample, a skin sample and a blood sample.

I tried to explain, but no one seemed to believe me or want to hear anything about it. So, that's my story and I'm stickin' to it."

He drew a deep breath, folded his arms, and looked straight into Mervin's eyes defiantly, his cocky grin still in evidence in the corners of his mouth.

"Nothing is ever simple with you, boyo. By the way, don't I owe you $10?"

"That's $40 and you know it. Don't be trying to pull that with me, buddy."

"Just testing. I'll pay you on payday."

"Which is when, exactly?"

"Dunno. I haven't had one yet. So, where is BaaGah? Did he survive all of that mayhem?"

"He's tucked away in the spaces of the shield over my MDP."

"Show me your MDP, Burt."

"Oh, I get it! Why didn't I think of that?"

Burt ripped away the flesh-like shield that covered his MDP and there it was; the one thing the others could never have duplicated. The emblem of the Dimensional Alliance was clear on the little black armband.

Liliath knew that a typical earth gesture at this point would have been a palm to the forehead. Why hadn't any of them thought to ask him about the MDP? Had they become so casual about their use of such amazing technology that they forgot they were even using it? Of course, the flesh armband that covered the MDP might have blinded them to the idea, but she had to hand it to Mervin. His scientific logic had singled out the one thing that would definitely have set the real Burt apart from any fake anyone would have decided to make of him, regardless of their methodology.

Mervin stood and turned to the camera. "Well?" he said, shrugging. "That's as good as it gets. Can he go now?"

"Both of you come up," Liliath hissed, not unkindly. It was just hard to get her mouth around the English language.

Mervin knocked at the door and Burt stood and bowed to the camera.

"Welcome back, Burt. We need to talk." Liliath said with a rueful shake of her head. He wasn't going to like it.

Chapter 5: The Spaces of the Mind

Jenny sat in the sunlight, Chidwi, once again behind her with her hands on her head, directly on the healing wound. It was still sore to the touch, but Freia said that it was already looking much better and much sooner than she would have expected. Freia attributed this to Chidwi, and Jenny felt she was probably right. Who were these Linklings, really?

Their pale green fur and long dark green moustaches combined with their intense blue eyes surrounded by white circles of fur were almost comical. Their lithe monkey-like bodies were small and light, almost as if they had hollow bones like a bird. They crooned and sang, but they could also screech and howl in pain or grief or warning. She had yet to see one angry but had a feeling that might not be something she ever wanted to see.

They had a very advanced understanding of manipulation of matter and the science of the mind. Chidwi's mental abilities exceeded even those of Liliath. Jenny somehow got the feeling that the Linklings looked upon other beings as not exactly inferior, but very adorable, like a parent watching the first steps of their toddler. Chidwi was never offensive at all, but somehow Jenny felt like she was watching her just like that adoring parent of a small child, proud of her accomplishments and yet knowing how very much farther she had to go.

She could wobble carefully on her own now to the padded wicker chair the Groga had provided for her. They had placed a woven mat in front of it and a small table next to it, to hold small snacks they laid out for her throughout the day, mainly consisting of slices of some kind of amazing citrus type green fruit and a somewhat pungent but tasty cheese, along with a salty crisp cracker bread. She would nibble at it as directed and then had a tasty soup for her other meals with the same cracker bread.

She was beginning to worry that she might gain weight with all this sitting and eating, but both Freia and Chidwi assured her that right now her body needed the extra calories to give it the energy to repair the damage done to her by that rock or paving stone that had been flung at her from behind that fateful day that...no, she wouldn't think on that. She was now aware of it and the pain was still there, but with Chidwi's help, she was choosing to not dwell on it.

Burt was dead. He was gone. No weeping or mourning would bring him back. From time to time she still dreamed of the little crystal pond by the Merced River, and that seemed to help somehow. The virtual time she had spent there with Burt had been so pleasant; more than pleasant.

Why hadn't she ever had the guts to tell him how she felt about him? Perhaps because she hadn't been completely sure of her feelings until that last crucial moment. "I love you, Jenny. I always will," still rang in her mind. It was both like a knife to her heart and a joy that made her heart sing.

She had always wondered why her aunt had never married. She should have been more diligent about reading the journals Lizzie had left behind. Had she ever been in love with someone? Had she ever felt the grief and mourning of losing someone like this?

She was feeling a little stronger every day. Each evening a group of villagers gathered in the area in front of Jenny's sitting place to sing and dance for her and Chidwi. Jenny wasn't completely sure if she would have received such a reception if it weren't for Chidwi's presence.

She was charmed and a bit puzzled by the Groga. How could they be such ferocious and seemingly uncaring soldiers and yet, such a delightful people in their own environment? She knew she would never forget the lessons she learned here. How often had she judged another person or group of people based on only seeing one side of their personality or the action from a single person or small sampling of that community?

Look at her relationship with Sam. She had never even imagined that someone like Engoza had lurked behind her smiling mask and cheerful demeanor. In Jenny's experience, most people considered themselves a good judge of character. She had. Now she realized that the whole 'judging' thing wasn't quite as simple as it seemed.

She realized Chidwi had removed her hands and now sat crooning, almost as if she didn't realize she was doing it. Jenny couldn't decide if it was an instinctual trait or purposeful, but it was pretty soothing, and she frequently did it after a healing session.

She found herself drifting into her breathing patterns without even thinking about it. Now Chidwi's little hands rested gently on her shoulders. Everything faded and Jenny found herself standing on the drawbridge of her mental fortress. The guard looked at her quizzically, as if not sure who she was and then his face cleared, and he bowed.

"Pardon, your grace. For a moment I didn't recognize you. Are you well?"

"Well enough to go on with. I've just had a bit of a hard time."

He nodded and saluted, gesturing her through the raised portcullis.

As she walked into the town square before her, it felt a little odd to be here by herself. So much of the time she had spent here had been in the company of Amenia, Elizabeth or Liliath. For a moment she felt a little shiver, as if she stood in a ghost town that should somehow be filled with people, instead of a place she had created for herself to organize her thoughts and learn about her mental abilities.

She passed by the library and the communications room. She didn't think she was ready for the communications room yet. She knew she had worried and probably frustrated her teammates, and they were undoubtedly none too pleased with her at this point. She knew it to be heartless of her, as she also realized they were probably worried about her. She wasn't generally a secretive person, although somewhat private in her thoughts and about her life in general. However, she had been pretty sure that if she had told them of her plan, they would have been more than a little vehement about her not doing it.

As Burt used to say, "Do what you need to do and then take the consequences." That wasn't usually her modus operandi, but in this case, she had felt so strongly about it that she had to act.

So, she avoided communicating with her team for one more day, confident that by tomorrow she would feel better enough to 'face the music' as her dad would have said.

She wasn't exactly sure even what she was doing here or why she had decided to come here. While it seemed obvious that she needed to be here to finish the healing process, she wasn't really sure why she had chosen to be here now. Out of the corner of her eye she noticed a building that she hadn't seen here before. It was white and square of several stories, with a glass and aluminum front.

Out of curiosity she entered. The automatic sliding glass doors opened into what was obviously a hospital waiting room. There were no patients waiting, just a receptionist, a rather chubby lady in a white uniform and wearing a nurse's cap.

"How may I help you?" she asked in a crisp professional voice.

"Um, I'm not sure. I suppose I have a wound on my head that could use some help."

At that moment, Jenny didn't have a clue what this was about. Why a hospital? Both Liliath and Amenia had taught her that the buildings inside her mental fortress always meant something important related to the development of her abilities, but a hospital? How could a hospital that only existed in her mind make a difference in a physical wound on her head?

"The doctor will see you now," the chubby nurse told her, with a clipboard in her arms. "Follow me, please."

She turned and Jenny obediently followed. They went down a corridor to an open door. The nurse stopped in front of it, placing a folder off of her clipboard in a file pocket on the wall. "Please have a seat in here. The doctor will be here in a moment." She turned and left.

Jenny obediently went into the typical patient's room and sat on a chair. She looked around. There were no windows. The room was equipped with familiar things like the blood pressure monitor and a drainboard and sink laden with various medical instruments. There was an examination table and a rolling stool. All perfectly normal, except that none of it was actually real.

The one thing that both Liliath and Amenia seemed to agree on was that the benefit of the buildings and objects in this place was always real on one level or another. So, Jenny didn't follow her first impulse to just fade back into reality and get some sleep.

The doctor who entered was tall and skinny with black hair and wire-rimmed spectacles. "I'm Dr. Conrad. I hear you are wounded."

"Yes, sir. I was hit on the back of the head with something. It is being treated by Freia, a Groga." That sounded somewhat lame to Jenny's ears, but the doctor didn't even blink.

"Ah, yes. She does good work. So why are you here?"

Jenny was flummoxed. Why was she here? Why did this hospital with this imaginary nurse and doctor and her as the only patient even exist in her mental fortress?

"I'm not really sure. Can you tell me?"

"A wise question. Let's take a look. Hop up onto the examination table, please."

So, Jenny hopped. He pulled out a curious, very odd instrument with a ball on one end and a handle on the other. He placed it in the bend of her elbow and ran it up and down between there and her wrist on her inner arm. He looked into her mouth and her eyes. He gently pulled on earlobes and wiggled her nose like a doting uncle, all with a completely passive face. Jenny half expected him to grin at her, like he was pulling her leg, which he actually did.

"Hmm. Ah. Yes, I see," he mumbled as he continued to examine her feet and thump her back from the base of her spine to her shoulder blades. He had her wiggle all of her fingers and stick out her tongue.

"So, doc, will I live?"

He looked at her quizzically. "Live? Of course, you will, even if you don't. Don't be silly."

He opened the folder that the nurse had left on the door and scanned it carefully, then closed it and said, "You have a small blockage. I see it a lot in people who are making great strides forward. It is caused by self-doubt.

This would be difficult for anyone but the patient to cure. Fortunately, it isn't a fatal case. The blockage is being dissolved by frequently applied poultices of love, patience, forgiveness and understanding. Don't pick at the scab and you will recover."

Jenny looked at him in amazement. Which hat had she pulled this guy out of? How was any of this helpful? She looked at his grave face and waited for someone to say, "Gotcha!" She nodded, equally as gravely and asked, "Is this visit covered by my insurance?"

He nodded. "You're always covered here, Jenny. I thought you knew that."

At that moment, the kindness of his tone almost undid her. "Why am I here, really?"

"You are experiencing mental growing pains. Most people don't notice them. Your instincts are better than many. You have a great mind and a kindly spirit. Much of this burden you carry must be supported by others, and you have always been self-sufficient and independent. You need to get used to the idea that you aren't in this alone and allow others to carry their share of the burden."

He pulled out a prescription pad and began to scribble on it and handed it to her. "Take this daily and don't pick at the scab."

And he turned and walked out of the room. Jenny just sat there, stunned. She opened up the folded piece of paper and in a messy scrawl she read just one word: "Forgive".

When Jenny looked up, through the tears blurring her eyes, she was standing in front of the observatory. The piece of paper fluttered to the ground. She would have no trouble remembering what was on it. As it hit the ground, it disappeared, but the word on it was seared into her mind.

She wondered why she had been transported to the observatory, but she knew that often things she didn't understand here made sense in retrospect. She entered the room with the huge telescope in the center and looked at the screen. Sprinkled across it were question marks in all colors and of all sizes, in different fonts from plain to decorative.

Questions? Like she didn't have enough of those. She wished she wasn't there alone. Then, one by one, the question marks faded from the screen. As the last one faded, one word appeared: "Forgive".

"Forgive who? For what? I don't understand. Of all the things going on out there, with everything I hold dear hanging in the balance, why is this important?"

"Forgive Jenny," was now on the board.

Now tears began to flood her cheeks in earnest.

"That can never happen. I let them all down. I went behind their backs. I've ruined everything. And Burt is DEAD! Why didn't I stop him? Why didn't I see this coming? What good are all of these awesome and amazing abilities if they can't protect the people I care about? Who's next? Tarafau? Bob? Elizabeth? My parents? The entire earth? How could anyone have ever entrusted something this important to someone like me?"

She collapsed on the marble floor of the observatory and just sobbed and sobbed. She had thought she had sobbed before, but it was nothing like this. It wasn't just her body, but her entire soul shook.

Shook? She realized it wasn't just her; the entire observatory was shaking, things falling off of shelves, the telescope swaying in its metal brackets.

"Stop it!" she yelled at the top of her mental lungs. She idly wondered if she was also shouting aloud in her little hut, upsetting Freia and Chidwi.

But at her shout, the shaking stopped. She straightened from her heap on the floor, gulping deep breaths of air and shaking as if she had the chills.

What was she doing? She remembered the kindnesses of all of those who had supported her through her first steps in the responsibilities as Gatekeeper. She remembered the acceptance of Chidwi, such a great honor. She remembered the words of Miriha in that dream near the crystal pond, "You have many loving friends and family who will support you and give you the strength you need to complete your part."

"Forgiven," the screen now read.

All of the others had forgiven her? Could they?

"Forgive," the screen said again.

"Forgive myself?"

She pondered this. Could she ever? So many people depended on her. So many people she had let down. How could they forgive that, or she forgive herself?

She wasn't ever sure how long she had sat in that one place. In this place a second could take forever or the other way around. She sat there, all bunched up, her arms around her knees and her head laying on them, just breathing. As she calmed, she realized that she might be worrying about the wrong thing.

Her mom had been a very practical lady, kind, intelligent and caring and yet, she never seemed to let anything stand in her way. She always said, "There is only one way to fail. You can't fail unless you quit, so don't."

Since when was Jenny a whiny, sniveling quitter? Since when did she hold massive pity parties for herself? Was the death of Burt more of a loss than the lives of those who started this war had already taken? Was it any sadder for her to have lost a dear, a very dear friend than that thousands, perhaps hundreds of thousands would live the rest of their lives in slavery to the Insenium? Was this war she was fighting worth the price or not? If it was, how dare she quit just because it had just gotten really, really hard?

Every military person involved in this had emphasized to her that this was going to cost lives, many, many of them. How were her feelings about the loss of Burt any more devastating than those of the Groga, or the slaves, or the Mookookie?

She stood and looked around her. The screen was blank. Forgive? It was blank because there was truly nothing to forgive. She hadn't failed, yet. She had made some very human mistakes, mistakes that she wouldn't likely make again. The only way she would fail is if she quit and she wasn't going to do that.

None of this made her miss Burt less or feel less pain at his passing, especially after that revelatory pledge of love. Her heart would hurt for a long time, but she could manage. Tonight, she would sleep and tomorrow she would begin the fight anew, only this time, she truly understood the price.

Chapter 6: Found

Tarafau gave Amenia one last hug, breathing in the scent of her as if he could somehow carry her with him that way. Elizabeth joined in after a moment.

"Please keep your dad out of trouble," Amenia breathed as she released them both.

"I thought he was supposed to do that for me," Elizabeth replied with a twinkle in her eye.

It was good to see that twinkle back. It had been a very hard several days. Tarafau knew he was needed at Headquarters, but he also knew that he couldn't leave his daughter in that state even knowing that Amenia would work with her. He knew Elizabeth was no longer a child, but she was his youngest and so much like her mother.

He had stayed in touch with the Alliance Council and Sanglarka, of course, but there was nothing at this point they couldn't do without him. He had no illusions that he was irreplaceable, but he also knew he had skills and resources that could mean the difference between success and failure on many fronts. He couldn't feel guilty about taking care of his family when he got the chance, however, else why was this even important? Even in the large scale, it all added up to the individual choices each of them made.

So, he squeezed both of them one more time, an arm around each, and he and Elizabeth faded into the Sanglarka lodge entryway.

The lodge was mostly silent. The only sound came from the kitchen, likely Arvid working on their noon meal and the murmur of voices in the situation room. Tarafau stopped into the kitchen first.

"How are you, old dwarf?" he asked when he saw Arvid was indeed perched on his kitchen stool, chopping vigorously at a pile of fresh vegetables and scooping them off into a large pot already simmering on the stove beside him.

"Probably about the same as you, old cat; too much to do is a good thing when you have too much to think about."

"Indeed," agreed Tarafau. *"But at least we have Burt back, when we thought we had lost him forever. I am hopeful that Jenny is still out there and will soon contact us. It concerns me that she hasn't even contacted Amenia or Liliath. I would have thought if she was able, she would have done so by now. It makes me think that she has been injured or..."*

"She's a tough one, our Jenny," jumped in Arvid, before Tarafau could finish the sentence. *"I'll not believe she is gone until I have physical proof. We must hold onto that. We must."*

Tarafau nodded at Arvid's emphatic tone. He too would hold onto hope as long as it took to determine Jenny's true state.

"So, what are they up to in the situation room? I heard some buzz from the lobby."

"Same, same...Coordinating resources, troops, and strategies. They've been in a bit of a frenzy since the revolt in the Insenium capital. Bob has some new findings on the MDP situation, and Burt is mapping potential scenarios as to where Jenny might be found if she remains unable to communicate.

Gariel is beside himself that they didn't see this coming. The new element is disconcerting, although, in my opinion, not all that surprising. It had been doubtful from the start, based on Burt's intel, that there wasn't more to this than anything Peril might have come up with."

"Agreed. He had 'puppet' stamped all over him, in hindsight. So, I'll see you in the situation room in a bit? Looks like you've got most of the vegetables in the stew. I don't smell rolls rising, so I'm guessing the soup is in its infant stages."

"Yep, I'm nearly done. I'll be ready for the briefing they will be holding in about 10 minutes. By the way, hello, Elizabeth. Glad to see you back." And with that, he went back to chopping vegetables with perhaps more vigor than was entirely necessary.

Lova, Gariel, Burt and Brendan looked up from their conversation as Tarafau and Elizabeth entered. Their faces were serious, but they smiled when they saw them both. Tarafau knew that Elizabeth's trauma had been as much on their minds as any of the long list of other serious items they had been considering.

Lova stood and greeted Elizabeth with a long hug. *"Welcome back, Elizabeth. It's good to see you here. We had hoped some time back home would be helpful. Are you ok?"*

"Good enough," said Elizabeth, stepping back and smiling sadly. *"I'll be a lot better when we locate Jenny and find her well."*

She stood next to Burt who grinned his best Burt-grin for her. He knew of her time at home to recover from the trauma of losing him and Jenny. Tarafau knew Burt had a kind heart and he treasured him for that.

"As will we all," agreed Lova. *"And you, Tarafau?"*

"The same. We have a lot to consider and much to do, but Jenny is a huge priority for me and my family, as for all of us. I am so glad to see Burt back with us. I read your report before we came. I find it interesting that Gall knew that Peril was about to praise you in front of all of those people and turn you loose. I also found the solution to the medallion issue brilliant. Is BaaGah with you now?"

"BaaGah is here. I couldn't go anywhere without him if I tried. Not that I would. He's become not just an ally, but a friend."

From Burt's shirt, like a magician's trick, suddenly BaaGah appeared, seating himself on Burt's lap.

"BaaGah is Burt's buddy. Your buddy too? BaaGah likes it here. Nice peoples. Lots of good food."

Tarafau and Elizabeth couldn't help but smile. Elizabeth reached out and gently stroked BaaGah's head.

"Hello, BaaGah," she sent. *"I am Elizabeth, and I would be happy to be your buddy. I hear you and your people, the Mookookie, did so much to help in bringing down the Insenium capital a few days ago. Thank you so much for everything you have done to help us."*

"BaaGah likes 'Lisbeth. 'Lisbeth buddy. BaaGah likes to help Burt and his buddies."

To everyone's delight, when Elizabeth sat down on the chair next to Burt, Noony now also showed herself. The two Mookookie looked like nothing more than two spaghetti squashes side by side with huge mouths and round eyes that were crinkled in amusement and satisfaction.

They all laughed and BaaGah and Noony laughed with them, their wide mouths open and their big tongues lolling out. This made them all laugh even more. You could feel the momentary relief in the room from this humorous respite, like gentle rain hitting a scorching sidewalk.

"So, what do you have for us?" Tarafau continued to Lova. "I know you have a meeting scheduled for any minute now, with the Council, I presume?"

"Yes," Lova replied. "Liliath will be signing on any minute now. I'm glad you got here. And here's Arvid, so we're all here."

As if cued, the big clear screen appeared before them, Liliath standing in the foreground and her two councilors seated just behind her. It seemed odd not to see Ingot and Myla there, and Tarafau's stomach did a little swoop as that sadness threatened to invade again. Tarafau tamped it down to be dealt with at another time. For now, he needed his wits about him.

Elizabeth with Noony on her lap smiled with delight when BaaGah also crept into her lap purring like a cat. Elizabeth delightedly stroked his bald head, which was also his body. The two Mookookie were snuggled contentedly next to one another.

The others were leaning slightly forward in their seats, focused entirely on the screen in front of them. Tarafau wondered how many of them were feeling as he did about the strangeness of it all.

"Greetings, Earth Guardians. We have much to discuss. First of all, you should know that the planet we thought was the Insenium capital is fully in our hands, including the planetary base of their scientists. The slaves who have chosen to remain on the planet due to the previous destruction of their home worlds by the Insenium, are in the process of electing and forming a representative government in conjunction with the Mookookie, who have given their enthusiastic assent to this arrangement.

This planet will now serve as a base for the Alliance in the Insenium dimension. It will unfortunately and inevitably be under attack, however, if we don't put our plans into action soon. So, we will need our space fleet to be deployed immediately."

Brendan nodded at this. Tarafau knew that he had been expecting it. They had finally worked out how to deploy his fleet into a different dimension, thanks to some fancy footwork by Bob, Merv, Cornelium and the Alliance scientists. They were confident that they had prepared as well as they could. It was time to test that theory.

"In addition, we will be establishing a gate on the Inseni planet that will be connected to the Alliance Gateway Network. This will allow us to utilize Tarafau's troops elsewhere with the aid of the Mookookie, which will be crucial if we are to maneuver quickly within that dimension. When the war is over and assuming we are victorious, we will be presenting the Mookookie planet to the Alliance Grand Council for official admittance into the Alliance. The Mookookie have been more than helpful in all of this and it is our desire for them to be recognized as useful members of the Alliance."

BaaGah and Noony bounced enthusiastically on Elizabeth's lap, to her obvious delight.

"In the meantime, the scientists the Inseni had labeled 'wizards' are being extremely helpful. They have helped us pinpoint several additional planets which have been populated by the Insenium, including one that sounds particularly interesting. We are theorizing that this may be the base for Gall and his people. It turns out they are one of two separate races that evolved on their original planet before it was destroyed. The two races went their separate ways for the most part. Peril's empire was merely a puppet state for Gall and his people who call themselves the Great Insenium and their people are the Norgoth.

These are our true enemies and the ones behind the plot to control the multiverse. Now we need to find out as much as we can about their resources and strengths. Fortunately, we now have some new agents."

And she laughed! Watching a dragon laugh is always a somewhat surreal experience, especially when you don't know why she is laughing. Her huge jaws lined with large pointy teeth were opened wide and her shoulders were shaking with mirth. Tarafau was glad it was a laugh, as he had also seen her angry and that was a fearful albeit inspiring sight.

"*The Mookookie are coming to our rescue there. They managed to go into the 'spaces' upon many of the big Norgoth thugs before they left for their own worlds. They are in direct communication with our other little friends who are now in your midst. The only issue we have right now, which might not necessarily be a bad thing under the circumstances, is that Jenny never gave the Mookookie the command to stop multiplying. They refuse to hear from anyone but her, insisting that they would know if she wasn't alive.*"

"This is actually good news," said Burt, his eyes and face solemn. "*BaaGah is seldom wrong about this sort of thing. It gives me hope. It also means that on Insenium planets, the Mookookie population continues to increase.*"

"*Truly said,*" Liliath agreed. "*In the meantime, we are still searching for clues. So far, none of the reports we have received have given us a single one. The only thing we do know is that Burt felt her presence just before Gall tried to eliminate him. Speaking of which, we also have no idea what happened to the duplicate Burt. Obviously, we thought we had found him. Sorry about that misunderstanding, by the way.*"

"No big deal. Just chalk it up to the power of prestidigitation and misdirection. Now you see me, now you don't." Burt replied, almost like his cocky self, for a moment.

Liliath continued, "*Bob's work with the origin of the MDP technology is starting to bear fruit. Through Fidget, he has actually made contact with the little nano-beings that inhabit them. As it turns out, they are friendly to anyone associated with the Alliance, and Bob is working with them to make MDPs a more useful tool in conjunction with the two cards we now have, courtesy of the 'wizards' of the Insenium. As a result of the collaboration between what we will call the 'Nanoites' and Bob, we have discovered that the technology of both the card and the MDPs are similar and the Nanoites seem to think they can potentially activate the cards in a useful manner at some point.*"

"*However, the technology is still very dangerous, should the Great Insenium ever get their hands on it. Therefore, the Nanoites have basically buried the cards in a way that only they can do.*"

One of the things we were able to acquire from one of the dead Norgoths was some viable DNA. The Nanoites have those samples now programmed into their warning systems to assure the Norgoths never get access to the MDPs or any of that associated technology. Should they attempt to enter an MDP, they will immediately be destroyed. It turns out the Nanoites have defenses we were not aware of.

We are no longer storing any technology that is under development anywhere but in a private MDP that is only keyed to Mervin, Bob and Argent. We are also making it policy that none of them be in the same place at the same time under any circumstances until further notice. For this reason, Bob will be transferred to Adelle's Science and Technology Team on Earth to work from there, with full encrypted communication with the other science teams. Merv will remain at Cornelium's lab with the same arrangements while Argent heads up the Alliance Headquarters Science team. We hope these precautions will keep us from giving the enemy any more help than is possible."

Tarafau nodded. It sounded like the current Alliance Council definitely had their collective act together. This was comforting. There was always a concern that at some point their government would fall into one of the many potential traps of greed for power that had destroyed so many planetary governments over time in the multiverse. So that was one less worry on his plate.

"I don't have much more to report at this time. Still no contact from Jenny. I will go into deep mental relaxation later today, hoping to hear from her. We have great hope as the alternate Gatekeeper's key has still not activated.

So, I will let you get back to work. Keep us updated on any progress on anything that is on the priority list. Thank you, once again, for your dedicated service...Liliath out."

The screen went dark and then disappeared. They all leaned back as if pulled by a string.

As he pulled his eyes away from the screen, Tarafau's eyes were drawn to Burt's face. Although he too was relaxed back into his seat, something had changed. He hadn't made a sound, but there was something far away and almost holy about the look on his face. Tarafau didn't want to touch him or interrupt anything that was happening there, but all of a sudden, he noticed Elizabeth, sitting next to Burt, her hands stilled on BaaGah and Noony's heads, looking at something he couldn't see. Then, one by one it was like a virus of unfocused looks of transport and joy on every face.

Then he heard it. *"Tarafau? Can you hear me? It's Jenny."*

Tarafau imagined that anyone walking into this gathering would be very concerned. All these adults staring joyfully into space as they heard the sweetest sounds they could have imagined. Jenny's mind voice sounded as if she was standing right in the room with them.

"I have only recently learned to do conference calls like this. I admit to being a bit surprised to see Burt among you. He was on my contact list and I had not removed him yet. Are you sure it's him?"

Liliath's mind voice cut in. *"Yes, Jenny. It is truly Burt. We have confirmed it is not a duplicate. Please continue."*

Jenny's mind voice continued. Did Tarafau detect something like breathlessness in her tone?

"In this conversation I have connected with all those at Sanglarka, the Alliance Council, Amenia, Bob, Mervin, Cornelium, Gariel, and even Fidget. Over time, I will connect with all of the Earth Guardians to give them the same message, but this group needed to be the first.

I don't have a lot of time, but I wanted you all to know that I am all right. I was injured, but I am mostly healed. I couldn't have contacted any of you before now. I would like Amenia, Elizabeth and Tarafau to take note of the coordinates of where I am right now. I am on the Groga home world. And before any of you get all worried and excited, I am doing well, and I am in no danger. In time I will arrange for a few of you to visit me here, but there are things I must do first. Just don't assume anything and please take no action until you hear from me. We know a lot less about the Groga than we thought.

Some of you will be receiving personal visits over the next several days while I make preparations for the next steps we need to take. It is both better and worse than we thought it was, and I can give no further explanation until we can meet at the Groga home world. I just didn't want any of you expending any unnecessary effort in my behalf. I'm sorry for the concern I may have caused, but I'm not sorry for the choice I made, as it may make all the difference in this fight. So, I guess, just stay tuned. I won't leave you out of the loop, I promise.

Take care and know that I love you all. See you soon."

With that, she was just as suddenly gone as she had come. They all just sat there, silent, stunned and more than a little confused.

Chapter 7: Shift

Jenny stood, Chidwi sitting lightly on her shoulder. She wasn't as shaky on her feet as she had been, but she knew she would need to sit again soon. She hoped her abrupt appearance for her teammates hadn't caused any new issues for any of them, but she kind of felt it was like pulling off a bandage; it needed to be done quickly for the least possible shock and pain.

She had quickly done each of the separate teams as well, stopping in at the Puerto Rico and Switzerland gate groups, basically with the same message each time. Now that she had broken the ice, so to speak, she would go back and make individual contact, but not right now. Now she had the Groga to reassure and to begin some things that would hopefully prepare them for friendly contact with the Alliance.

Freia walked stolidly on one side of her and Grephan on the other, ostensibly as an honor guard, but she knew it was mostly to catch her if she collapsed. She tried to imply a stately stroll as opposed to an invalid's barely functional gait. She wasn't sure if she was pulling it off, but she needed to give a good impression and weakness wasn't in it.

She willed herself to look to the left and right, nodding and smiling to those they passed as they moved toward what might be the equivalent of the village square she had experienced in the Groga dome on the Inseni planet, tagging along with Burt.

After the revolt, the Groga had split into two separate camps; those who supported the revolution and those who still wanted to be part of the Insenium. There were no hostilities or confrontations between the two groups, although that might change, depending on the outcome of this particular struggle.

Like the square in the dome, they approached a wide open space among the shops and residences they passed through on their way. There was a large raised platform stage at one end and the square was beginning to fill with curious Groga of all types; merchants, farmers, governmental leaders, soldiers and even children.

As they got to the platform, Anwhal greeted them. He was in uniform as before, and beside him was someone Jenny assumed was a city official.

"Welcome, Jenny, and your honored companion. I would like you to meet Governor Milhem, our leader. He is in alignment with the things we discussed with you, Elizabeth, and Burt. He has asked that you speak to the people this day if you would."

"It is good to meet you, Governor, and to see you again, Anwhal. I would be happy to speak to your people and Chidwi would also like to speak as well, if that is alright."

Governor Milhem smiled broadly. He was short for a Groga, with round shoulders and a bit of a paunch. Jenny guessed that public figures were often a little less than fit, especially if they spent most of their time at a desk.

"My people would be delighted to hear from your honored companion, Miss Jenny. I will introduce you when all are assembled. In the meantime, would you take a seat on the dais, please?" He offered Jenny his arm and she took it gratefully, hoping she didn't show that she was fading fast.

Thankfully, there was a speaker's podium on the stage which would give her something to hold onto as she spoke. It would also serve as a perch for Chidwi so all could see her clearly when she took the stage alone, as was Jenny's intent.

When she had broached the idea with Chidwi, she had agreed placidly. The Linkling seemed to have no fear, which made Jenny a lot more confident when she remembered that Chidwi was always in it with her to the end.

The crowd assembled was huge and as Jenny took her seat, butterflies began to rage in her stomach. This reminded her of her valedictorian speech. She had nearly thrown up before heading to the podium that time. She hadn't actually thrown up, but her stomach was still queasy even when the crowd had applauded enthusiastically as she had sat down. She was fine in small groups, but crowds like this were intimidating and she wasn't sure that would ever change for her.

She guesstimated there were close to ten thousand people in the crowd and these were only the people in this village which was not the capital city of the Groga planet. According to Freia, they were separated into cities and towns and training camps, but not into any kind of states or countries. They were simply the Groga.

Hundreds of years ago, according to Freia, the Groga had been conquered by the Fleistians. At the time they had been a rural people. The Fleistians had been on one of their planet discovery expeditions, and when they had found the Groga they had taken one look at them and decided to co-opt them as slaves.

They had easily subdued their people and began a project to train the best suited men as warriors. Over time, that meant most of the men. The women, in the meantime, did the farming and other tasks necessary to supply an army, not to mention that the strongest of them were forced to bear children of the strongest and most able warriors.

This breeding program did not focus on intelligence or talent in any other field; simply how many naturally strong and fierce soldiers they could obtain.

The Groga never saw anything of the Fleistians other than their masters in the training of more soldiers and the small force of trainers that stayed with them on their planet. It had never occurred to them that they were actually more numerous than their masters.

Domination and enforcement had never before been a part of their nature. They had humbly and obediently done the will of the Fleistians, raiding and enslaving others at their master's bequest, because they knew their families were held hostage for that obedience, although the Fleistians had never specifically said so.

The Dimensional Alliance had finally subdued what they thought was the Groga's attempt at dimensional domination and had nearly destroyed them on their world. The Fleistians, to preserve the services of their armies, had moved them to this new planet. For many years, the Fleistians allowed the Groga to increase their numbers again, serving only to fight from time to time in the quarrels between the Fleistians and the Cindu, and the Groga had no longer been a focus for the Dimensional Alliance, as they considered them defeated and no longer an issue.

Then the Insenium had virtually taken over the Fleistians and once again the Groga were employed to plunder as much technology as they could find and supply the Insenium with slaves.

Unknown to both the Fleistians and the Insenium, a story had been passed down amongst the Groga that the time would come when their masters would be overturned and they would once again become a peaceful and happy people, freed from the compulsion to murder, torture and enslave people for whom the Groga had no enmity.

There were a small number of them who had finally succumbed to the violent philosophies of their masters, embracing the life of raiders and slavers. These were generally shunned by the majority of the Groga people.

Now, here was Jenny, and they had seen how Burt and Jenny and the allies of the Dimensional Alliance had organized and supported the revolt by the slaves and Groga in the Inseni capital. Anwhal had been training his soldiers behind the backs of the Insenium, that they would only have to wait a little longer before they would be free and wouldn't have to do the will of evil masters to protect their families.

When Burt and Jenny had shown up that day in the military training dome, Anwhal had known that the time had finally come. He had a strong feeling that these could not only be trusted, but they had the ability to plan and execute that plan successfully. He also knew that by siding with these strangers he would not only be putting the entire Groga population in jeopardy, but it would put him in conflict with those Groga who had bought into Fleistian and Inseni policies and philosophies. This worried him so much, but he knew that this was more than about losing Groga lives. It was about saving Groga souls.

He feared deeply that if they continued to serve the Insenium, the time would come when all of his people would finally be degraded to the point that they began to enthusiastically embrace those wicked philosophies, and the Groga as a people would descend into complete and willing barbarism.

This is what Freia and Anwhal had expressed to Jenny during her days of healing. They would sit by her bed when she was awake, and finally by her chair when she was able to sit and talk to her earnestly about their hopes and desires for their people. And as they did so, Jenny found she had learned to love these people. Of all the things she had expected to happen during this war, this was definitely not one of them.

So, when Milhem stood to introduce her, she calmed her heart and focused instead on what she was about to say, on the people to whom she was about to speak, like all beings everywhere, not perfect and not always lovable, but of great worth and potential. This would be her message. She could do this.

She stood, Chidwi perched comfortingly on her shoulder, and for a moment she gazed solemnly around the huge gathering. Then she took a calming breath. *"Groga people,"* she broadcasted, *"My name is Jenny Japhet. I come from a planet called Earth. I am a representative of the Dimensional Alliance and all free beings in the multiverse. I am here to offer you an opportunity to join us as free beings who value families, liberty, and the hope for happiness.*

I will not lie to you. This is not a gift I can merely hand to you. Freedom never was without a price. But I can offer you the support and resources of billions of freedom loving planets throughout the multiverse. We do not yet know the full import of what we are up against, but I can tell you that we are committed to this fight.

Your people were once a happy, productive, and peaceful race. It is my hope you can be so again. Your past can be put behind you. Your future is in your hands. No one will force you. No one will blame you for the past or hold your service under evil masters to your account. The only thing that will matter going forward is your desire and commitment to become what you were always intended to be."

She paused, scanning the crowd. The faces were intent and most appeared open and receptive. She took courage.

"You must ask yourself the question; 'Is it worth the sacrifice?' Because there will be necessary sacrifices. There will be difficult times, perhaps more than any of us can imagine, but you won't be taking the risk alone. Every one of my compatriots have made the commitment to put their lives in jeopardy and to risk annihilation if necessary, to send the message to those like the Insenium and the Fleistians that we will not lie down and accept their domination and tyranny. Will you make that commitment?"

Jenny was unprepared for the response. One person, far in the back, began a rhythmic stomping. It was picked up by another and another. Within moments, the stage began to quiver under the relentless stomping from the crowd. They didn't say a word, but then they began to beat their chests in an opposite beat to the stomping rhythm. Stomp, thump, stomp, thump!

Instinctively Jenny held up both hands high over her head, looking into those intent faces as the rumbling continued. Jenny realized that Milhem and Anwhal were also standing and joining in solemnly. It appeared this was a kind of ritual. Suddenly Anwhal held up one fist. Every fist in the assembly shot into the air, and the stomping and thumping stopped abruptly.

She had no words. Fortunately, at that moment, Chidwi stepped onto the podium and all went silent. She raised her hands above her head in imitation of Jenny's gesture. *"My dear Groga friends, I am Chidwi. I am Jenny's companion and friend. I wish to thank you for your kindly care of her after her injury while aiding in the revolt against the Insenium. I wish to thank you for your response to her words. Jenny is wise for her young years, wise beyond any expectations, including her own.*

Your people have entered onto a new path, but you don't even know what that path is.

Do you think that Jenny's invitation is to fight? Is Jenny inviting you to mortal combat?

I tell you NO! She IS NOT!"

Jenny could not remember hearing any of the Linklings ever use such a forceful mental voice. She could see the shock on the faces before her, as if they had all been doused in ice water.

"This will not be your battle. Your battle is of a different sort, and it will be far harder than picking up your weapons of war and marching forth to conquer. That will no longer be your path.

How strong are you really? How brave are you? A true warrior's heart is not measured by their victories in battle. A true warrior is measured by their integrity, their courage, and their devotion to what is right. Your new path will test your mettle, but you will accomplish more on it than you ever did with a weapon in your hand.

So, I ask you? Will you learn? Will you discover the true potential of your race? Are you willing to throw down your weapons of war and become a truly free people? Will you trust that this thing which goes so counter to what you thought you knew will actually give you the freedom you seek?"

There was no stomping this time. One by one, like a wave of grain in the wind, they knelt hands to heart in silence, including Anwhal and Milhem.

Jenny was stunned. Chidwi had truly spoken what was in her own heart, but she hadn't known how to tell them this. She had been having some dreams that she could never remember on waking, and this seemed to be the essence of them. She had thought she would have to ease these people into these ideas and wasn't sure of how this would finally go over.

Now here, kneeling before her, was the entire population of this Groga town. How did that happen? Something about their attitude toward the Linklings, Jenny was sure. She was pretty certain it wasn't anything she personally had said or done, at least not to her knowledge.

She once again took a calming breath and sent to them. *"Please don't kneel to us. We are not your masters. We are only here to help you however we can and to get your agreement. This must be accomplished with all the Groga on your planet, and when we can, we will draw the rest of your people who have been sent to other worlds, to join you. Chidwi is a great teacher and a good friend. She has agreed to have several of her family come here and make a home with the Groga to support them on their new path. Please stand and don't kneel to anyone. That should be reserved for the Creator of All Things."*

Chapter 8: Mookookie Rising

Elizabeth and Burt stood in one of the farming domes on the former Insenium capital planet, now once again the domain of the Mookookie. Before them were assembled former slaves and their new compatriots, the Mookookie, thousands of them.

The newly released slaves had erected a platform for them to stand on, so they could look out on the crowd and they were easily seen. Earlier that day they had met with the leaders of this town as they had been doing across the face of the planet. Things were changing, and rapidly. There had been some disputes of how to handle the newfound freedom and many of the slaves, those who were able, had returned to their home worlds.

Now, the newly formed community had all opted to continue in the domes where they had started, the difference being that they could now travel freely from dome to dome. The transportation network that had been put into place by the Insenium was going to have to be expanded, as commerce and trade began to happen in this new economy.

Elizabeth had explained to the main leaders the Daringi economic model of exchanging hours instead of currency, and they had agreed that this would be a good plan, but infrastructure had to be put into place to make that possible.

In the meantime, they had agreed to simple barter for the time being. Now Elizabeth and Burt were going from dome to dome to aid in uniting the various beings now represented by the new government. They had been chosen mainly because of their bonding with two Mookookie, BaaGah and Noony, and Elizabeth's ability to transport them easily between the Alliance and the Mookookie planet, which they called Krim.

This was the last stop on their tour. Jenny had checked in just this morning with the news about the turnaround of the Groga, and they were very encouraged. One of the goals Burt, Jenny, and Elizabeth had discussed before the revolution was the idea that taking the Groga completely out of the fight would hamper their enemies in a major way. Or at least, that was their hope. It had been a bit of a conspiracy just between the three of them, as none of them had told the rest of the Alliance agents or Guardians about their idea. At the time they were worried about security and the fear that the enemy would catch on too early and they would prevent them from getting to the Groga.

It had definitely come off better than they had hoped, but they had no illusions that the easy part was behind them. They knew things were about to heat up in ways they couldn't possibly anticipate. This made them all nervous, but, as the youngest of all of the representatives of the Alliance, they also knew they were fortunate that, in retrospect, their elders had not only approved their plan, but applauded it.

Now, the next step involved the Mookookie and the Daringi. Mookookie who had been unwittingly transported by Gall's minions to their various planetary and potentially dimensional holdings were able to communicate through the spaces with their fellows on Krim. Burt and Elizabeth, with the help of BaaGah and Noony, had organized a group of Mookookie to act as relays with these new Alliance agents. Slowly they were creating a map of coordinates of the holdings of the Insenium, and it was looking pretty grim.

Burt sent to the assembled Krimians, *"Elizabeth and I must leave you soon. You have the basic building blocks now of a great society if you will choose to use them. You have elected wise leaders. Trust them, but also hold them accountable.*

Your continued freedom will require diligence and vigilance. Your planet and that freedom are still in danger. Leaders of the Daringi, Elizabeth's people, will be coming to help you prepare to defend yourselves. The struggle isn't over yet, but it will be, and unity will be vital to your success.

Our hope is that we will triumph over this threat that is over all of us and when that is done, all will be free to live their lives according to the dictates of their desires and their public conscience. None of us need to do this alone and our people have committed to make any sacrifice to do this. Are you with us?"

The response was deafening. The Mookookie had sprouted legs and arms and were doing the most amazing little dance. Elizabeth had the biggest grin on her face, and Burt once again appreciated the beauty of the Daringi people.

Burt was amazed at the reception they had been given in every dome, by every group. But he realized when he had initially toured the domes, only the Inseni were their enemies, not any of these people.

None of them had bought into the Inseni idea that this was all for their own good. They had never considered themselves anything but unwilling slaves, so when Burt, Jenny and Elizabeth had begun stirring the fire, they were ready tinder for the spark that had been set to them.

They stepped off of the podium and were swarmed by the crowd, pats on the back, hand-shaking and hugging. Noony and BaaGah were enjoying all of the attention. Most of their Mookookie friends continued the energetic dance, and some joined in with enthusiasm and delight on both sides.

Let them celebrate, thought Burt with a sigh. It's about to get really hard and they'll need every bit of that positive energy.

He wished, as he had so many times before, that somehow, he could wave a wand and make it all better. But he knew it didn't help him or anyone else to think that way. Elizabeth had been such a help and fired by her intense loyalty to Jenny, he knew he could count on her to do whatever it took to give the Alliance the edge they needed. Tarafau and Amenia had given her a strong work ethic and the desire to maintain freedom for all beings. And, in spite of the huge difference in their ages, Elizabeth was emotionally and mentally a match for Burt and Jenny. In her culture, she was considered very much the same stage as the 'twenty-somethings" of Earth.

They made their way through the crowd to their vehicle. BaaGah and Noony had retracted their limbs and blended into Burt and Elizabeth's clothing and rode along. Once inside the vehicle, the villagers made a path to allow them to pass through to the dome entrance.

As they exited, Elizabeth let out a long sigh. *"I had no idea how much work this would be. I don't know what I thought we would be doing, but all of this educating and rallying and endless meetings to attend is exhausting. How do you do it?"*

Burt grinned. *"I like people and I like helping. This is the best part of my job, interacting with amazing new cultures and different beings with all their diversity. And seeing this culture changing and developing right before my eyes is exhilarating."*

At that instant, as Elizabeth nodded, they both heard Jenny's mind voice, *"Burt? Elizabeth? How is it going?"*

"You weren't riding along?" Burt asked, somewhat disappointed. *"It's going great. Better than expected, which makes me a little worried. I keep waiting for someone to throw a monkey wrench into the works."*

"They will. Count on it. But for now, we can shore up the defenses. A contingency of Tarafau's troops has already arrived at the capitol dome and will be deployed in units to each of the outlying domes, to set up the training camps. I did let the Mookookie know that they can stop multiplying for now, but we may decide to do more of that later. They are very helpful.

Have you distributed that map of coordinates to Tarafau's people yet? Thanks to Bob's MDP research, we have a plan that will allow them to transport troops in large numbers when we are ready to begin the coordinated assault."

"I sent the list of coordinates to my dad earlier today. He should have distributed the list to all of the commanders of the Daringi forces by now. Glad to hear your voice. Wish you were here with us," said Elizabeth wistfully.

"Me too, but for now, we all need to be where we are. All of the rest of the team are working long hours to begin to bring a plan together. The Linklings are also deploying, some here to the Groga home world and the rest to the various coordinates we have received. Due to their abilities to read minds, we should be able to get plenty of intel without putting them in any danger, as they will go in with their reflections turned off."

Burt had loved Jenny's explanation for Chidwi's abilities to be invisible. As it turned out the Linklings were all of a mind to aid the Dimensional Alliance in every way possible, short of actual violence on their part. They were still incensed at the attack of Miriha's town and that their relatives were potentially killed or at the very least shut off from the gate system by the sealing of the gate there. It turned out they were better allies than he would have previously imagined.

"So, what are your next steps, Jenny?" Burt asked. "I know you are doing a lot of rallying of the Groga. How does that work, really? Are you experiencing any resistance?"

"Only at first, but the Groga leaders are behind the plan and were convinced surprisingly easily. They are going to concentrate their efforts on defenses. Their top military minds are gathering to discuss ways to fortify their cities against the Norgoth and the Inseni. Meanwhile, the general populace is just digging in and getting to work, stockpiling supplies, and setting some really interesting booby traps. They won't be caught unaware or unprepared.

They seem to be clear about the risk they are taking. So far the Norgoth, the Fleistians and the Inseni don't seem to realize just how far this rebellion has reached. When they discover the Groga are no longer theirs to command, however, it could get pretty nasty. I have been completely honest with them. I didn't want them making these commitments blindly, just because of whatever pull I seem to have with them."

"Then we're good for now. We have a lot of different troops from different dimensions, all preparing to support the effort. It will be easier when we know more about this enemy and exactly what we're up against. I'd just as soon not have any more nasty surprises. The last ones were enough for me to go on with," Burt agreed.

"Very good. Now, where are you two off to this time?"

"We're headed to the capital. I think the two of us are stuck here for a little while yet, while we try to get all of this mess sorted out and everyone prepared. We know the Inseni won't leave this situation as is, the nasty bug-eyed, baby-faced, shark-toothed, jerks that they are; not to mention their slime-eating, cyclops friends, the Norgoth."

"You're absolutely right," said Jenny. *"It looks like the Groga are going to agree to accept some Daringi consultants to help them do their preparations. I have the General of the Groga armies, the ultimate Groga-ha with me pretty much constantly now, but Tarafau says 'the girls' are anxious to get back to me, so I will have them here soon as well. Try as I might not to have an entourage, it looks like I'm stuck with it."*

Elizabeth cut in, *"And a good thing too. The only thing I regret is that I'm not right there with you. I feel so much like I've let you down..."*

"Don't you EVER say or think that again, Elizabeth! You're always there for me when I need you, and I promise I'll let out a holler when I need your assistance."

"A lot of good that did for you during the revolt," Elizabeth said, her face sulky and her eyes downcast. *"We all thought you were dead. The one thing about those abilities of yours that always gave me comfort was that you would be able to ask for help no matter what happened and then you got yourself knocked on the head..."*

"OK, OK, I get it. But it all worked out and what's the likelihood that will happen again?"

"Hello?" Burt chimed in, *"isn't this YOU we're talking about? You went from mild-mannered blog writer to superhero in less than a year. Do you have any clue about how important you are to us?"* he hesitated for a moment, *"to me?"*

"That's a discussion for another time, but I get it and I'm sorry for the scare I gave everyone, but not for what I did. It needed to be done."

"That didn't make it any easier. All I'm saying is that I'm good with you having as big an entourage as possible if you can still get the job done, OK?" Burt knew he sounded a bit pugnacious, but darn it all, he didn't know what he would do if he lost Jenny, not that she had yet mentioned his final words before disappearing with a flash of light. He was pretty sure she had been saddened by his apparent death too. What a pair they made.

"Let's not argue, folks," chimed in Elizabeth, holding up both hands. *"We've got enough opposition to be going on with here already. Let's save it for the 'bad guys' as Burt would put it."*

Burt realized he was flushed, and his fists were balled up like he was ready to punch something. He relaxed them and said, *"Elizabeth's right. Truce?"* and he grinned his most charming grin into space, as Jenny still hadn't learned how to make a physical representation of herself during these communications unless it was in his dreams. His dreams. He didn't want to think about that at the moment.

"Truce," Jenny agreed. *"And with that, I have to run. I have a session with the Alliance Council yet and a meeting with their version of the Joint Chiefs of Staff later today and I haven't prepared anything yet."*

"Goodbye, Jenny. Be safe." Elizabeth said, blowing a kiss into the air before her.

"Bye, Jenny. Keep me posted." Burt said with a wave and a grin which faded when she didn't reply. She had obviously already moved on.

Elizabeth looked at Burt with bright eyes. *"You love her as much as I do, don't you?"*

"I don't have words big enough, but I'm not sure she sees me as more than a friend or teammate. And I don't know if she ever will."

Chapter 9: Oh, What a Tangled Web

Sam stretched and sat up in her bed in her room in the Fleistian fortress. It was nice to be home. Servants for her every whim, Groga soldiers at her command and her very own unique mount to traverse the dimensions with.

Her parents had not been pleased, however, with her venture into the Dimensional Alliance Headquarters. They had warned her that any further misadventures would cost her. Lately, it seemed like nothing she could do pleased anyone. She had been severely scolded and barely escaped more serious punishment. Her protestations of good intentions hadn't impressed her parents much.

She had imagined coming home victorious, acclaimed by the court and her people as a great and canny warrior. Instead, she had been publicly humiliated for her immature spur-of-the-moment, egotistical stunt. Stunt! Like she was just doing it for attention. Like she didn't totally shake up things in the Alliance.

She sneered at the very thought of them and couldn't help but gloat to know that their spies reported that the leadership of the Alliance had been busted apart with the death of Ingot. How could they possibly put it off like it was some kind of childish prank? They had grounded her like some Earthling teenager. Ziggin had been quarantined in one of the stables underground, and she wasn't allowed to go anywhere near him. Evidently he couldn't transport out of there, due to some kind of new tech they had installed since the last invasion by Tarafau's people.

Not that he would be able to go anywhere, anyway. He was probably an outlaw to his home world and sought after by their agents.

In the meantime, everything had been turned upside down. It turns out her parents hadn't chosen very wisely themselves. The Inseni Emperor had been deposed in a wild revolt by the slaves and even their Groga. This was unthinkable. Upon hearing this, her father, King Namal, had brought the command of the Groga into the fortress to stand and report.

They seemed clueless about the revolt and protested their undying loyalty.. Namal rousted some of his own troops and a few trolls to oversee them.

Gall had come to visit, and it had been horrible. She was present to watch her parents grovel in terror after Gall had subjected them to some kind of shock torture, electrifying the thrones on which they sat while they writhed in agony. She found herself wondering how he did that and whether she might be able to get ahold of that kind of technology. She had heard that Gall had killed Burt; a bright moment on a dark day.

Gall had pretty much ignored Sam, for which she had been grateful. He had announced that they were no longer to report to Emperor Peril, but that he was the Overlord of All and they could address him as Overlord or Lord Gall. He also told them he had retuned their gate to go directly to his command post on a world he called Xatal.

Her mother had burst into wracking sobs when Gall had finally left them. Her father had slapped her and screamed at her to stop to no avail. She had fallen into a heap on the dais floor in front of her throne and would not be moved or consoled for over an hour. That shook Sam more than just about anything. She had never seen her mother like that. "It is the end!" she screamed, over and over, "the end, the end, the end..."

Her father had dismissed her when her mother had finally subsided, still whispering, "the end" continuously. Her father had simply told Sam to go to her room and stay there until he called for her.

She felt like somehow, they blamed her for the visit from Lord Gall, but she couldn't see how. And for the first time in her life, she didn't think of her parents as grand, regal, fearless monarchs. For the first time, she saw true fear in them, and it made her sick. Especially after their chastisement of the week before. It grated on her like the incessant buzzing of an insect.

She threw on some clothes and pushed the buzzer for her servant. Moments passed...Nothing. She buzzed again...Nothing. She buzzed for her guards. In both cases, her guards and servants lived in the apartments right beside hers, and they should have been there nearly instantly. But the guards didn't respond. Now she was truly irritated. She was hungry and needed news. Being restricted to her room was exactly that. She waited, but whole minutes passed.

She pressed both buzzers over and over, first in anger and then in panic. Were her parents so angry with her that they now intended to starve her? Surely not!

She attempted mindspeech, *"Mother? Are you alright?"*

...Silence.

"Father, may I speak?"

...No reply.

Now Sam wasn't just worried, she was afraid. What could have happened to keep her parents from at least acknowledging her attempts to communicate?

Was this some kind of test? Was this more punishment, what Jenny would have called "the silent treatment"? Hmmph. Jenny. She didn't want to think of that insignificant twit right now. She would get hers. Sam would see to it. She realized she had stopped thinking of herself as Engoza a long time ago. And Sam she would be until she was sure that Jenny had been permanently dealt with, dishonored, repudiated, tortured, and finally killed. This was all HER fault; all of it.

As she paced back and forth in the living room of her huge suite, she got angrier and angrier. She let it build up in her. She was furious. Not at herself. Not at her parents. She was furious with Jenny and those self-righteous prigs of the Alliance.

Who did they think they were, after all? Who gave them the right to "guard" the multiverse like it was their personal property? Who gave them the right to set the rules for the rest of them? Them and their vaulted freedoms. Who were they to stop the valiant efforts of those who would create order in the multiverse?

It was vital that no system be left out to challenge them. It might take many years, perhaps eons to establish lasting dominance, but it would be worth the sacrifice when everyone was exactly equal, completely the same. It would mean the end to pain, conflict, and desertion.

Parents, for instance, would no longer be able to choose how to treat their children, there would be laws and oversight. Bosses would not be able to promote someone over another person without approval from the government. No one would be able to charge more for their goods, or less, than anyone else. People would no longer be allowed to take risks that might harm them or another person. Art, literature, and invention would all be regulated, so that no one would ever be insulted or passed over; complete and utter equality in all things.

And what if it took wars and strife? What if it meant that some brilliance would be dimmed? What if it meant that technology would be slowed? People would no longer work for reward or kudos. There would be no competition, no need for envy. And no one would be troubled with ever having to make decisions. That burden would be taken from them.

Every being in the multiverse would be governed by the same rules and all would comply or die. There WOULD be order!

But for now, Sam was hungry and frightened. What could she possibly have done that would have her completely abandoned? Why wasn't anyone answering her mental calls for help or even just communication?

For the first time in her life, living in the massive Fleistian fortress, she wished for a window. She felt utterly alone for the first time ever.

As time passed, she fumed and continued to buzz her buzzer and call out mentally to anyone who might answer her until finally, when the day was half over, she couldn't help herself. She prepared herself for a conflict with her parents, but she couldn't continue in this condition.

She walked past the tapestry scenes of violence and war without even seeing them. She pounded on the locked doors of her servants...nothing. Her guards...nothing. She passed no one in the corridor, but on this floor, that wasn't unusual. She practically ran down the several flights of stairs to the main floor, still not encountering a single being. While she strode forward, nearly running now, she continued to call out; those mental calls becoming more and more plaintive.

She entered the cavernous hall that traversed the full width of the huge indoor complex; torches flickering dimly, as if they were running out of fuel. To someone who hadn't grown up here, this would feel foreboding, as it was designed to do.

It was so far from one torch to another that the light from one torch didn't quite overlap with the light from the next set of torches. As she hurried, her heart was in her throat. How angry would her parents be with her for breaking her restriction? They would consider her weak and childish for coming to them this way.

They obviously didn't want to see her. They were ignoring her, punishing her for being such a great disappointment, and now she was about to make it worse.

She nearly turned back. But the eerie stillness, the lack of a single guard which should have been stationed under every set of torches along this path, the lack of sighting a single soul from her room to this point had her in a panic. When she finally neared the throne room, she gulped and straightened the cloak she wore for audiences with her parents. It would never have done for her to come dressed casually before her parents where anyone might see her. Taking a deep breath, she strode forward at a more measured pace, trying to appear composed and respectful of the royal presence.

But when the raised dais with their thrones finally came into view, there was no royal presence, no guards, nothing.

She turned and ran in the only direction she could think of...out. As she pelted back the way she had come, she noticed that some of the torches had flickered and gone out. Not good. Not good.

She reached the outer doors and there were no guards standing there. She pushed the huge doors open with an effort. No guards outside the doors. What could possibly be happening?

As she stepped from the entrance and finally could see around her, she fell to her knees...Nothing. In the distance was the Groga city and encampment, dark smoke rising in massive clouds above it. In the nearly dark, it was all the more ominous, as the clouds were lit rosily from below by low flickering flames, like the coals of a dying fire.

What had happened here? Had the Alliance decided to take vengeance? Had the Cindu decided to eliminate them finally? Whoever had done this was very thorough. She doubted a single one of her people had been missed by whoever had removed them. The silence of the inner fortress, the absolute lack of discernable life, was more frightening than anything Sam had ever experienced.

Where were her parents, her people? How could she possibly have been overlooked?

She sobbed and screamed until her voice gave out and her strength with it. At long last, she passed out there on the ground and for a long time, she knew nothing.

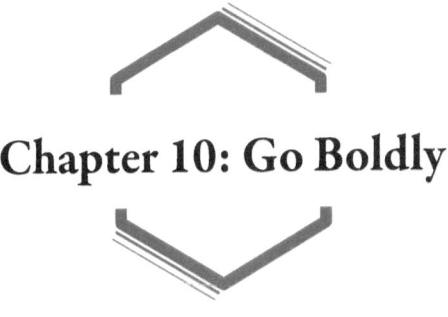

Chapter 10: Go Boldly

Brendan subconsciously tugged at the waistband of his uniform. It felt a little strange to wear one after all of this time, something he never thought he would do again. But then, he would have never imagined standing on the deck of a starship in his lifetime, either. This was nothing short of miraculous in his mind.

Not that he hadn't dreamed of it, wished for it, for sure. From childhood he had imagined himself in space; fed on a diet of Star Trek reruns and binge-watching Star Wars at every opportunity. He had watched broadcasts of every shuttle launch and footage from the space station with intense fascination. Now, here he stood, surveying the activities of the bridge crew as they prepared for launch through the dimensional gateway situated light years away from Dimensional Alliance Headquarters.

From what he understood from his briefings, natural dimensional portals didn't just appear on planets. It was impossible to say whether they were numerous or not, wormhole theory notwithstanding. These were not wormholes as Earth scientists understood them.

Interdimensional gates occurred as naturally in space as those on planets did and were seldom discovered due to the fact that space travel was not as common in the multiverse as space operas and science fiction would have you believe.

For one thing, it wasn't generally a necessity. Earthlings had an innate natural and driving curiosity that had led them to the verge of space exploration, but even then, it had a hard time finding its way into the budgets of the various countries that pursued it. But, according to the Alliance scientists, there were some cultures in the multiverse that had thriving space fleets and where inter-galactic travel was as common as air traffic was on Earth.

The Dimensional Alliance Headquarters was situated on just such a planet. Not far from the city was a shuttle service that would take passengers to and from a massive space station that was as busy as any of the airports on Earth. It was easy to ignore that fact on the basis of the massive Gateway Network that was the center of attention there. Compared to interdimensional gateways, space travel was somewhat cumbersome, but the network only extended between dimensions, not between planets within a galaxy or universe.

Brendan admitted he had gotten spoiled by interdimensional travel, casually stepping from one universe to the next like going from one room to another in his house. Space travel, like air travel on Earth was time consuming and required many more resources to do it well.

He had undergone his rather rapid training from the space station, a massive complex capable of hosting the entire fleet docked around the various airlocks. It was one of two space stations, one for commercial and civilian use, and one for the military fleet. This fleet was largely for defense, as the beings on the Alliance planet were not a warlike culture, at least not in living memory. However, there were some space-going races that had challenged them in the past. There were no conflicts in their galaxy at this time, but they maintained a space fleet on the off chance it would be necessary in the future.

At some point in the distant past, dimensional scientists had discovered a gate in space. Brendan would have loved to have known the story behind it, but his training had been rather cursory, and his instructors had admitted that much of the history and science of it all had been lost. A study for another time, he mused.

For now, the gate presented an opportunity since they had been able to establish a similar gate in orbit around the planet where Emperor Peril's "wizards" had resided. So, at this point they waited for "the word" to be passed that it was time to launch.

Thanks to the combined efforts of the Mookookie and their Daringi counterparts, they now had space/time coordinates for many of the Inseni worlds within that dimension. They were still researching which of the planets contained the standing Norgoth government and the elite forces of the Great Insenium, a necessary part of their stratagem, but before they could put it all into place, they needed more intel about how far the Norgoth threat extended and how many of their troops might have been inserted into other dimensions.

Currently their strategy would be to destabilize the Norgoth government and military, with the hopes that this would at least curtail further incursions into new dimensions. However, this did not address the issues of any dimensions where they already had a foothold. The multiverse was massive, beyond imagining. It was unlikely they could rescue them all, no matter how extended the conflict or vast the resources of the Alliance. So, for now, they needed to concentrate on what was within their reach.

Brendan had a strong feeling that even if they were able to eliminate the immediate threat, the conflict resulting from Gall's plan for domination of the multiverse would extend beyond many of their lifetimes. This didn't make him any less determined to continue the fight, but he realized that many things would be different.

He had been and was still a Gate Guardian, but, if this conflict continued for years, would he need to find a replacement Guardian for his gate? Probably. If he were honest with himself, if he got to choose, he would choose the starship. Either way, this was an opportunity beyond anything he had ever thought possible in his lifetime. It only made him sad to think of the devastation ahead of them if they were going to protect the innocent from ultimate evil.

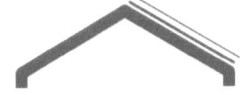

Chapter 11: Promises to Keep

Jenny stood beside Anwhal in the village square where she had instructed "the girls" to meet her and Chidwi. The Daringi forces all had the coordinates to this place, and a delegation would be arriving shortly after her bodyguards to meet with many of the leaders of the Groga. Those assembled here had all committed to the resistance of the Insenium and could be trusted according to Anwhal to help the Groga people accept the Daringi and other Alliance representatives as allies.

Chidwi was perched on her shoulder with her reflection turned on, as she generally did these days. There were others coming and going in the square and they nodded and smiled at Jenny and Chidwi as they passed.

The air shimmered slightly in front of her and Nona, Lyra and Mynn faded into view, each with an accompanying Daringi with a hand on their shoulders.

"Reporting as requested, Jenny." Mynn said immediately, the three of them snapping to attention.

Jenny assumed she was trying to impress the officials that surrounded her. *"Stop that,"* she sent privately to them with a grin, *"None of that military stuff here. I saw enough of that as a kid growing up to last me a lifetime."*

"Yes, Jenny," they sent nearly in unison, without appearing to relax the tiniest bit.

Jenny rolled her eyes and introduced them to her companions. Each nodded in turn somewhat solemnly, and Jenny sighed. She would have to learn to deal with this, but she couldn't help but remember the shopping trip she and her bodyguards had indulged in, which now seemed such a long time ago. It would have to do for now, but she knew she would need to have a bit of a "sit down" with the girls later when they could be alone.

Their Daringi transport officers faded away and just behind that, several Daringi in muted robes appeared, each bowing slightly to Jenny and her entourage. *"Welcome, my Daringi friends. I will introduce you to our company in a moment, but for now, let's retire to the village inn to a room our hosts have set aside for us to eat and discuss what needs to happen moving forward."*

They nodded and the entire group moved off to a large inn at the edge of the square. Mostly traders and merchants stayed there, and it had a large great room and some private meeting rooms able to accommodate a few dozen people depending on how it was arranged. The one the inn-keeper had set aside for this meeting was set up with chairs arranged in a loose circle, per Jenny's request.

They waited for Jenny to sit first and her guards arranged themselves behind her, declining seats for themselves to Jenny's discomfort. Oh well. For now, it would have to do, but she didn't want any of the others to think her pretentious. The rest sat in no particular order, which was what Jenny had hoped for. She remembered Bob telling her that Merv said the round table wasn't so much about King Arthur being wise as it was that he needed a table quickly. Nevertheless, a circular meeting format, as Ingot was fond of, was perfect for diplomacy, as none of the participants could take any visual precedence over the others.

Anwhal stood and introduced the various members of his party. These included the mayor of this town and mayors from three other towns, a couple of military officers, and a teacher who all seemed to hold in great regard. Jenny stood in turn and introduced her group.

Anwhal then sent to the group, *"I don't want to sit here for days trying to figure things out, so I will summarize our purpose today and let our new friend Jenny tell us where we go from here. Time is not our friend at this point, so we can't be hashing and re-hashing every detail.*

We are here because we are finally being given an opportunity to end the tyranny of the Insenium over our people once and for all, as we support the efforts of the Dimensional Alliance to rid the multiverse from the Inseni not only for our people, but beings throughout the multiverse.

These people want to help us get our lives back, but they are not here to tell us what to do, how to act or what to decide. That is up to us. Each of us here has heard what Jenny has to say, and we have agreed as one to commit to her cause. The beings she has brought before us today are here to teach us and support us in our decision to once again become a free people. There will be more coming, but first they need to know of our commitment to learn and to support this effort."

His fellow Groga nodded somberly and placed a fist to their chests. Jenny knew this was her cue.

"Fellow beings of the multiverse, I must tell you that this is very humbling. I am but a young woman and not a career politician or public figure even in my own world. Regardless, I have been put in this position and I will serve."

She gestured toward the Daringi and then toward the Groga, taking all in with a sweeping gesture.

"Those of us seated in this circle, including my dear friend, Chidwi, all come from different dimensions. And at one point or another, our people have been enemies. But now we find ourselves with a common cause. The Daringi have put aside contention to come here, and you have also put it aside to have them here. As we gather in town after town and city after city in our plan to eliminate the Inseni threat, more Daringi will come to counsel and advise your leaders on how to prepare for the adversary who will come.

Gall will not willingly allow the Groga to change their allegiance. Nor will he simply shrug his shoulders and move forward without you. As a people you must choose your path and it will be difficult regardless of which one you pursue. For now, we have a strategy that should give you the best chance to survive this with the fewest possible casualties, but we cannot promise your safety.

It will be vital that we glean as much information as possible from those of you who have worked closely with the Inseni in the past. This will help us to not only defeat them in the long run, but better protect your people.

As you know, we are not asking you to actively fight in this war. In fact, what we want from you is exactly the opposite. We do not ask you to fight for us against the Inseni and potentially against your own who will be fighting for them. We simply want you to defend yourselves, if necessary, and aid us with the information you have that may make the difference between victory and defeat."

All in the circle nodded solemnly. *"Then we are ready. Anwhal has the list matching up the Daringi with the Groga mayors and captains. I will leave you to it."*

She stood, and nodding to each with a gentle smile, left the room, her bodyguards behind her.

She had been given rooms in the inn. Freia came each evening now to check on her wound, but she said it would soon not need bandaging. The stubble on her head now reminded her of a honey-colored version of Chidwi's fur. Chidwi had told her it was very becoming and that she should let her body fur grow as well. Jenny wasn't sure the Linkling wasn't serious about it, but she laughed and was glad mirrors were scarce in the Groga culture.

If she was honest with herself, the lack of comb-able hair was more of a big deal than she wanted to admit. She had never taken a lot of time on her appearance, preferring neat and clean to stylish. But now that she was in the public eye, she couldn't help but think she was less than imposing to look at. The bandage no longer encompassed her head, front and back like a wool hat. It was now more of a band around her forehead, reaching around to the wound on the back of her head.

She also wondered if Burt would be so obsessed with her if he could see her this way. Not that she had enough time on her hands to worry over this much. She couldn't talk to Chidwi about this sort of thing. Human dating was a great puzzlement to her. And she didn't dare say anything to Elizabeth about it, considering how much time she spent with Burt these days. Not that Elizabeth would say anything to Burt, but she also didn't want to color that relationship.

She got to her room that was conveniently on the main floor of the inn. Technically, it wasn't a room they usually rented out. It had been intended to be a guest room for visiting relatives of the inn-keeper, but the inn-keeper's wife, Lida, had insisted, saying she was grateful to have the honored one and her disciple stay under their roof. Jenny hadn't argued. The idea of climbing stairs at this point was tiring just thinking about it.

Jenny closed the door and sat carefully on the bed with a sigh. Chidwi hopped down from her shoulders and stood behind her on the bed stroking the back of her neck, starting at the base of her skull and down between her shoulder blades. She barely felt it as Chidwi continued. It amazed her how such a light touch seemed to give warmth deep into the muscles of her neck and back. As Chidwi continued, Jenny did her breathing, focusing on simply being. Later she would mindspeak with her various contacts in the Alliance, but for now she just needed to let it all go. It had been a long day arranging the meeting she had just left.

In no way had she ever imagined herself in this role, and now she was learning as she went, one day at a time. Each evening before bed she took out the little jeweled box Miriha had given her that came from another dimension Jenny didn't even begin to understand.

When she had awoken from her unconscious state, the little box had been in her MDP however, so she couldn't doubt that the experience had been real.

All of these were part of her life now. It was so bizarrely different than her life before she inherited the little house on Infinity Loop, that she sometimes felt that her previous life had been a dream she had awoken from to find herself in the midst of conflict and constant movement toward...what? That was the big question. Where was this all heading?

And the thing with Burt? In her old life would they ever even have met? Could she afford to invest herself in anything but a friendship with anyone? Both she and Burt were in danger; the recent past had proven that. Either one of them could be injured or killed at any time. Dared she commit herself? And would he even want her now? She ruefully touched the fuzz on the top of her head. She just couldn't face any of that at the moment.

Chidwi tapped her cheek with a finger. *"Jenny must breathe. Jenny must relax."*

Jenny realized she had been tensing, lost in this disconcerting train of thought. She put it aside and focused on her breathing. She only had about an hour before she had to move on to the next stage of her journey.

She relaxed into Chidwi's ministrations with a sigh, willing herself to blank her mind and tune into Chidwi's crooning. It wasn't any cadence or music pattern that Jenny was familiar with and yet, she often found that she was humming along. She assumed it was a part of the link she had with Chidwi that she could harmonize with Chidwi's music perfectly, as music had been such a small part of her own education.

Finally, she realized that Chidwi's warm little hands had ceased their stroking and Chidwi had climbed onto Jenny's lap, looking into her eyes with her sweet smile. *"Jenny is better now?"*

"Yes, Chidwi, I feel much better. I think we must go out to meet the others. We have a bit of a journey yet today. Anwhal said he would get "the girls" settled in, so I'll check on them and we can leave."

There was a light tap on the door. It was Freia. *"I need to check your dressing before you leave, if that is alright."*

Jenny nodded and Freia went to work, gently unwrapping the band from around her head.

"I think we can leave it unbandaged today and just start wrapping it at night," she said as she gently touched the wound. *"It has scabbed nicely and is healing much more rapidly than I ever expected to see. I am sure this is because of the treatment by the Honored One. In a week we may be able to leave off the bandage completely. I would recommend you wear a hat, but I am concerned it might rub on the wound, so I brought you a kerchief to shield it from the sun."*

"And to cover my horrible hair as well," Jenny sighed. *"Thank you, Freia. I don't know what I would have done without you and your family to care for me."*

"It has been our honor, Jenny. Never did we think we might have the opportunity to care for a disciple like yourself. The entire Groga people are forever in your debt, regardless of the outcome, because you have brought us the chance to make things right again. Thank you."

"You're welcome," was all Jenny could think to say.

Freia finished her task, carrying out the soiled bandages. She wasn't giving Jenny the potion for pain anymore. Jenny had told her that she would gladly take the healing broth and the herbs for healing, but she was handling the pain with breathing and mental pain control techniques Lova and Amenia had taught her. She didn't need her senses dulled at this critical point in her mission.

They left the room; Chidwi once again perched on her shoulder. In the common room of the inn at a large table were seated Lyra, Mynn, and Nona, along with Anwhal and his son, Grephan. They all stood as Jenny entered the room. She was still having a hard time getting used to this, but she realized that telling them to stop wasn't working, so she smiled and nodded at them.

"Where to now?" she sent to the group.

Anwhal answered, *"We are joining my battalion on their way to the capital city. The word has spread quickly of what you are doing, and the ultimate leaders of our planet have gathered every authority amongst us from villages to cities. We will be meeting them in two days, so we will need to pick up the pace. My troops have found sturdier transport, but I'm afraid the ride might be a little bumpy."*

Up until now they had not had to travel long distances. She had been ensconced into a little market cart pulled by a farm animal the size of a large goat. The little cart had fairly good suspension as it was intended to haul delicate goods to market, but even on the main roads it was a little jarring. She understood that the roads between here and the capitol were not all well paved, and for her head that was a concern.

Jenny decided to take a chance. *"Anwhal, if it will not be offensive to your people, I have my own transportation that will be smooth and allow me to easily keep up with your battalion without compromising my wound or the pace they need to keep to get us where we are going in a timely manner. Is there a private place outdoors where I can show you?"*

Anwhal considered. *"We can go into the assembly area for the local troops. It is currently empty, as the contingent here will be accompanying us and they are assembling on the square."*

Jenny knew she had to be careful about this. Exposing these people to "dastardly alien tech" might be a mistake, and it's hard to put the genie back into the bottle once others have seen it. However, right now, they needed every edge they could get and time was the real enemy at the moment. She also knew that the soldiers had seen alien tech on other worlds during their time serving the Insenium. She probably wouldn't have considered it, but the previous night, as she had viewed the fleeting images from the little jeweled box, she had seen herself in one of the hover cars surrounded by Groga troops.

They walked down the street, greeted with nods and waves by the townsfolk. Small children delightedly pointed out Chidwi, laughing when Chidwi waved back, crooning at them. At length they entered a side street that led to the barracks and training area of the local militia. It was quiet, not a single lingering soldier in sight. They finally paused in a fenced off area that served as the training ground. Jenny waved the rest back and invoked one of the hover cars out of her MDP. It would hold up to 6 passengers comfortably.

Anwhal didn't flinch, nor did he display any surprise as the vehicle unfolded itself, seemingly appearing out of thin air before Jenny. Grephan's eyes widened slightly, but he didn't betray any more than that.

"The Inseni have similar vehicles. No one on our planet will probably think much of it. Though we have not been allowed the use of such technology, we are aware of it. Because we have been under the thumb of one dictator or another for so long, we really don't have any sciences of our own."

Jenny nodded. She realized that the Groga were in an awkward stage. It wasn't like exposing a primitive culture to advanced tech. The Groga were fully aware of tech beyond their own. Perhaps this wasn't the kind of tech pollution she needed to be worried about and it might give her the ability to keep up with the timetable set before her.

"So, you think it would be alright for me to ride in this to your capitol?" Jenny asked.

"I cannot foresee any problems with it, unless it requires fuel that would not be available here."

"OK. Then I will meet you with my guard and Chidwi in the square. When do you wish to leave?"

"My troops are ready to go. They're waiting for us. Do you require anything from the inn?"

Jenny lifted the flesh colored armband from her MDP so all could see.

"This is a tool I use to store my belongings. It is keyed only to me. No one can invoke anything out of it but me. I keep it hidden so as not to expose it to curious eyes. I have everything I need as do my guards."

She replaced the armband, which immediately looked as if it blended in with her skin.

"I would appreciate it if you do not tell people about it. At some point, after this is all over, we can discuss possible exchanges of ideas and information, but I can't promise this technology will ever be able to be shared with your people. It is not my decision to make."

Anwhal nodded, saluted, and he and Grephan turned and left. Jenny felt that Anwhal understood, but she was also pretty sure he wouldn't leave it at that. There would definitely be discussions in the future.

Chapter 12: Indiscretions

S am gazed around herself from her elevated vantagepoint on Ziggin's back. She had only been on the Norgoth capitol planet once before on a short trip with her father, King Namal. She had gone along as his "page" more to observe and learn than to serve her father. He had a body servant for that. So, she had tagged along to various places as Lord Gall's chancellor had shown them the might of their empire.

She had been to this particular spot when they had been taken hunting. There was a beast that roamed this forested area that was much prized for its horns and bones, as well as its hide, which was like plated armor. They had camped at a type of hunting lodge. But this place, although not far from there, was somewhat isolated by a tall thicket. She had discovered it to her delight at one point when she had an opportunity to explore while her father and the chancellor were off hunting.

The thicket was like a circular wall of trees with a strange winding path that led into the center of it. It was quiet and generally unused by anything but small forest creatures, much like the rabbits of Earth. The inner part of the circle of trees was about 20 paces in diameter and would be a perfect place for her to camp while she decided what to do.

Once she had rounded up supplies from the fortress, she had passed the coordinates of this place to Ziggin. Like her, he was happy to take his leave of the eerie, silent fortress. Gathering the supplies had been puzzling. Although everyone had disappeared from the fortress, no one seemed to have taken anything with them. Tools had been left as if dropped where they were being used. Food had burnt into the pans on the stove in the main kitchens, bread in the oven turned into charcoal. Most of the torches and lamps had burned out.

She was glad she had kept the backpack from her hiking club days as a souvenir, as it had flashlights and other supplies that would come in handy.

Her first impulse when she had finally gotten out of panic mode was to go to Overlord Gall and ask for his protection from the Alliance, but something made her rethink this. After all, although she really wanted to blame Jenny for all of this, she didn't have any idea what had happened to her people. There had been no sign of a struggle, which puzzled her. She knew her parents had installed tech that would have kept Tarafau or any of the people from his dimension from porting into the fortress.

Whatever had happened hadn't involved that particular little dimensional trick. She honestly didn't see how it was possible for it to have happened. True she had been isolated in her room, but even then, her guards and servants had been available to her the night before she awoke to her world turned upside down.

So, it had to have happened in the middle of the night. She knew there were always guards at the entrances and watch was kept on every floor at night. And had she gotten just accidentally skipped over? Had she been left there alone intentionally? None of it made any sense that she could tell.

She dismounted from Ziggy (as she now called him, mostly to irritate him). She was now grateful for her experience in the Earth hiking club. She quickly set up a tent large enough for herself and Ziggy and put together a shielded fire pit. She was marginally sure there were no flights over the forested area here, something about not disturbing their hunting grounds. The Norgoths did have aircraft, large dirigibles that served as transport for goods and people between the multiple cities on this planet. The cities were huge. There were no tiny villages except those in the farming belt. Even those small enough to be called towns were bustling with activity and were usually only stop-overs between cities.

As one would expect from Inseni, everything was rigidly regulated even in the farms. The industrial areas were more like a military compound and nothing went in or out of them without inspection.

The number of inspectors employed by the Norgoth was unbelievable. There were food inspectors, industrial inspectors, school inspectors, vehicle inspectors, clothing inspectors, weapons inspectors and the list went on and on. The inspectors were a branch of the military and went armed, prepared to enforce what they did with lethal force when necessary.

This was actually needed very seldom. The Norgoth were so regulated from the moment of their birth (inspectors in every birthing chamber) that for most of them it never occurred to them to do anything but precisely what they were told to do. The occasional infraction was immediately and severely punished, and it would never have occurred to them to try to circumvent their restrictions. The majority believed fervently that it was all for their own good, and those who didn't feel that way prudently kept their radical opinions to themselves.

Sam snorted. As regimented as her life had been in the Fleistian fortress, it was nothing like this. And she admitted she had gotten used to a looser lifestyle as an agent on Earth. Although she was sure the Insenium was correct that the multiverse needed to be put in order, she wasn't quite so adamant about it when it applied to herself. Being able to make her own decisions in the pursuit of her mission had been exhilarating. She was careful to walk the fine line between melding into her role as an Earthling and trying not to do too many things that compromised her beliefs.

Deceiving Lizzie and Jenny hadn't bothered her, though. The ruse was part of the role she had to play to get what the Insenium and her parents wanted.

Ziggy was poking around in the little thicket, possibly looking for something to eat. She thought he would probably be able to digest the dark blue-green leaves of these trees, as the green might have been an indication of chlorophyll, but she couldn't be sure. In her hiking club she had been taught the principles of surviving in unfamiliar circumstances and testing possible food sources when you weren't familiar with local flora.

She had brought some freeze dried fungi from her home planet, but it wouldn't last long. She knew that while she had been here as a teen that none of the food she tried had been difficult for her digestive system and the food she had eaten in Ziggy's community hadn't bothered her. This led her to believe that Ziggy could eat pretty much anything she could eat and that most of the local flora would work for him.

"Hey, Ziggy! Are you hungry? Let's eat and we can gather some food later. I just want to settle in here good and tight and then we can go exploring."

Sam was quite sure that riding Ziggy around the countryside would get her unwanted attention and might be dangerous for both of them, but she had a few new tricks up her sleeve. She had discovered she could extend her camouflage to anything she was touching, so she would be able to potentially take Ziggy with her without anyone being any the wiser. Of course, the camouflage wouldn't keep someone from noticing if Ziggy stepped on their foot or brushed up against them, but for now it would have to do.

Their agreement was that a specific rhythmic squeeze from Sam would be the signal to return here to their base camp. It would still be risky, but Sam needed to gather some intelligence and she didn't want to have to do it without her arachnid friend. He was a quick getaway for her and hopefully no one would guess their current camp easily.

They ate quickly. Ziggy had been somewhat sullen and quiet, not generally answering Sam unless she persisted. He was very stung by what he perceived as betrayal on Sam's part, but she didn't let it bother her. She got that a lot and she was fairly used to it by now. Her casual attitude to the supposed commitment of "friendship" came naturally to her. Lizzie and Jenny had actually been her very first forays into this very foreign concept. For some reason they still seemed to tug at her, a fact she found irritating.

Sam took a moment to focus her mind. The little camouflage trick wasn't something just anyone of her species could do. You had to have the gift, and the gift needed training. Fortunately, her mother had passed this on to her, and she had been diligent in training her daughter. Sam admitted that at the time she hadn't been all that enthusiastic about it, but she was grateful now for her mother's persistence.

She didn't fool herself that her mother had trained her out of motherly devotion. She simply wanted her daughter to be superior to any of the other children in the realm. Sam had not been trained side by side with her peers but had still been entered into all competitions with the clear understanding that she would win or face the consequences.

Sam had won nearly every challenge they had given her. It gave her no pride or feeling of accomplishment however, only relief that she wouldn't be punished for failure. When she had discovered she could do something that none of her peers or even her father could do she was tempted to brag about it, but her mother had told her that it was a good thing to have some surprises in reserve and it was enough that the two of them knew she could do this amazing thing.

So, she mounted Ziggy and the two of them, now conveniently camouflaged, went to one of the few small villages close by to test her disguise and see what useful news might be floating around.

It turns out it was market day, so there were many people milling around in simple clothing, men and women dressed very similarly in breeches and plain loose-fitting shirts in muted colors. After years on Earth, the conservative simplicity was almost grating to Sam. She and Ziggy headed to the outskirts of the town and found a place for her to "park" him away from prying eyes.

Sam strolled about among them, having already "borrowed" the appearance of someone she had passed on the road before she had settled Ziggy in his hiding place, and now no one would have given her a second look.

It was a bit odd adjusting to the single eye that was typical of the Norgoth, but her gift allowed her to adjust quickly to anything involved in creating a new persona.

She milled around with the rest from booth to booth in the marketplace, fingering cloth or perusing hand-crafted household goods and furnishings, never staying long enough in one spot to get anyone's attention. She spoke the language fluently, having been encouraged in this by her parents. They had discovered early on that she had a talent for this. As a result, she also spoke Groga, French, English, and German.

Mostly she just listened to the conversations of those around her, only joining in when someone spoke to her first. "Did you hear about the revolt in Emperor Peril's domain?" One tall dark-haired man said to the short red-head beside him as they looked at a simple set of hand-crafted tall shelves on display.

"Yes, of course, where have you been? The word is that Peril is no more and good riddance," he said, spitting on the ground. "Should have wiped the whole bunch of them out eons ago. A waste of a good planet if you ask me. I hear the Dimensional Alliance has a finger in that pie.

The only reason I even care is whether they raise the conscription rate. I've got two sons eligible and I need them for harvest time, not haring off some place to serve in the military. But Overlord Gall has the right of it, I suppose. After all, we can't ensure order in our own realm if there are insurgents instigating rioting and disgrace among the populace of the law-abiding and orderly."

"Yeah, they should mind their own business. That's what I say."

At another booth they were talking about recruiters who were coming through the farming community more frequently. "It'll be a rough harvest if they deplete the numbers of workers too much," one grey-haired woman complained grumpily. "And the Overlord has increased the farm quotas, so we planted more. Even if they don't take any, it will still mean long hours with every worker we have."

Her friend merely nodded, tight-lipped.

One conversation in particular caught her attention.

"They're going to go straight to the heart of the Dimensional Alliance very soon," a stocky merchant confided to one of his customers. "There is a recruiter at the village square grabbing every strong looking youth they can find, trained or not. They're going to do to the Alliance what they did to the Fleistians. Namal and his little queen got it good. Serves them right for falling down on the job and not taking care of business."

The man turned to Sam who was standing there in shock. "You buying or eyeing miss?" Sam realized she was no longer fingering a piece of cloth, but had it bunched tight in her fist. The memory of the torture of her mother and father on their thrones came back like an electric shock.

"Just checking to see if it wrinkles easily. It won't work for what I have in mind." And she sauntered off casually, realizing she needed to get herself under control.

What they did to the Fleistians? Got it good? Were they talking about that day in the throne room when Gall tortured her parents? What did he mean and how could she find out?

She returned to Ziggy in his hiding place. *"Let's see some countryside,"* she told him with what she hoped was an off-handed way. She didn't want to betray her worries to her arachnid friend. His loyalty to her had eroded seriously after having been imprisoned by her parents and she didn't need to strain it, at least not yet.

She had no illusions that she was doing anything other than using him, and she thought he was beginning to suspect this. Oh well. Not sure what he could or would do about it if she left him high and dry at some point, which was entirely possible if he became an inconvenience. She couldn't think about that right now, however.

She camouflaged them once again and they went off in the direction of a large city she knew about. She needed more accurate information, and this little farming town wasn't the place to get it. They dropped by their encampment in the thicket for a meal and then left down the main road that led to the city she had stayed in with her father on one of their expeditions what seemed like forever ago. She needed intelligence, and she needed it now.

What had happened to her people, and what did it have to do with the planned assault on the Alliance? Time to get down to business.

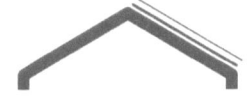

Chapter 13: Laying a Foundation

Burt was worried. Things were going too well. So far his mission with Elizabeth had gone off without a hitch. Experience told him that things were seldom this easy. So far they had visited every dome and met with all the individual dome councils of combined Mookookie and former slaves.

All of these were currently calling themselves "Krimians" which boded well for their solidarity. Daringi and Alliance troops had been stationed in every dome and they were training the general populace in basic defense skills. They had discovered that some of the slaves had been warriors in their own right in their respective cultures, so these had been given responsibility for assembling local militia for each dome under the direction of their Daringi trainers. This was temporary while the Krimians were creating the infrastructure for an organized planetwide military organization.

A main military training facility had been established in the capitol dome city. The unity of this people was spectacular considering that they came from such disparate backgrounds and cultures. Over time, living together as slaves, they had even begun to assimilate common traditions and cultural similarities. Most of them were discarding the imposed styles and colors that were so prevalent with the Inseni, and the schools had been reorganized as places of learning instead of political indoctrination.

Even with the threat of war looming, they devoted time and resources to creating small parks and playgrounds for the children. It was a joy to visit the domes and see their progress toward some kind of normality. As they passed people on the street, they were greeted with smiles and waves and sometimes bows (something Burt tried to discourage).

He should have been turning cartwheels with joy, but the niggling doubts in his head kept telling him he was missing something, and he really hated that when it happened, since those doubts usually had some foundation in fact. What was he missing? His compatriots had often said that he could pay attention to minor details with his eyes closed. He felt a shiver go down his back and the hair on his arms was standing up.

Elizabeth, matching stride for stride as they went down the main thoroughfare of what was now being called "New Horizon", appeared to also be lost in deep thought. She had become a welcome companion in all of this, and he knew her to be a thoughtful and intelligent person. She also seemed to "get" him, something that not many people ever did. He could see why Jenny loved her so much. The two of them were adorable together, both so different in build and coloring but so very alike in temperament and ability.

The street they were currently on was in one of the industrial domes. The Inseni had separated the communities of slaves into certain types of workers and the inhabitants of each dome had a specialty appropriate to the function of that particular dome. In this case this dome was devoted to the higher tech operations such as manufacturing transportation and equipment. Right now, they were focusing on creating adequate transports from one dome to another to allow more interaction between domes as a free society.

It turns out the Mookookie were actually quite agile of mind and hand, and took great delight in learning the manufacturing techniques the other Krimians had been trained in. They also were very knowledgeable based on their understanding of the spaces and of their planet's resources. They had come up with some rather brilliant ways of bringing ore deposits out of the ground without mining or other invasive technologies. As a result, a very pleasant partnership was springing up in the industrial domes all over the planet.

Because of the Mookookie ability to sprout appendages at will in whatever number or size was required of the tasks before them, they became quite amazing line workers in the factories. When the humanoids had tried to discuss fair wages with them, the Mookookie had laughed in their faces.

"What need have Mookookie for such things? Is there not food to eat? Is there not fun to make and to do useful things? Do not make things hard or complicated. Spaces provide all we need. We all buddies here, right? Do things together? Have fun? Monies not needed. It is a thing of your peoples, not Mookookie."

Burt couldn't help but smile at the thought. What far-reaching effects had radiated out from that one small act of kindness in a dark cell on a dark planet. BaaGah had become such a good "buddy" and he could barely imagine his life without him. He wasn't sure if this was a thing like the Linkling's bonding as Chidwi had with Jenny, but he had discovered that the Mookookie were intensely loyal friends and could be counted on much more than he would have expected based on his first encounter with BaaGah.

At this point, he only knew that the new society that was being founded in Krim was beyond any of his hopes or expectations. These people who had been so thoroughly exploited and oppressed were determined to create a free society where every being had the opportunity to become their best selves.

They all knew that there might be hard times ahead, and many of them had perished in the revolt that had made this possible. But they had already been through so much that they grieved and moved on, feeling that they did more honor to the fallen by creating something amazing out of their sacrifice than dwelling on the unfairness of it.

And now he had to do the part of all of this that he hated the most. Jenny was so good at this. She stood in front of large crowds of people with such confidence and eloquence. On the other hand, having to speak in front of crowds made him physically ill. He wished he could carry it off like she did.

They reached the square where it appeared the entire population of the dome had assembled. He shook his head. Nothing to be done for it. They expected him to encourage them before he traveled on, and he would do his best.

He stood at the slightly raised podium and looked out at the sea of faces. There was hope there. There was determination there. He could feel it coming off of them in waves. He didn't have any special mental powers like Jenny, but he felt like this would have been obvious to a blind man.

"Krimians, I commend you! Your efforts to rebuild a broken society from oppression and tyranny to freedom are already beginning to pay off. Optimism is the rule of the day and this is a good thing. I have no intention of dampening those feelings. They are good and right.

However, I wish to remind you that your fight may not be over. You have among you the resources, the abilities, and the spirit to make all of this work. It is worth defending. You need not build a warlike culture, but you must be aware that something worth having is worth defending. In this you will not be alone.

As you know the Daringi and others from the Dimensional Alliance have chosen to make their home among you for a time as they aid you in strengthening your defenses and training you how to secure your claim on this planet alongside the Mookookie who were here before any of us. This may yet require significant sacrifices on the part of the Krimian citizens. I cannot promise an easy victory. I cannot promise a fast victory. I can promise, however, that we will not quit on you as long as you do not quit on yourselves."

He stopped, looking out again into the eyes of those he could see. There wasn't a sound or stirring. They all stood as if frozen in that moment.

"Thank you," he finished simply and stepped away from the podium with a mental sigh of relief.

Suddenly it was as if a wall of sound hit him. They cheered for him, for what he said and for what they all felt.

"Well said," Elizabeth sent with an impudent grin. *"Jenny couldn't have done a better job."*

"Liar," he retorted. *"But thank you."*

"Are you impugning my honor?" Elizabeth shot back with mock horror. *"Shall we duel, as is your Earth custom?"* She held her quarterstaff in the guard position and arched her eyebrows in challenge.

Burt shook his head. *"Now how would that look to our allies here? Besides, I don't think I am up to having my tail whipped in front of all these people. Your father trained you much too well for me to fall for that."*

They shook hands with as many of the people who could reach them. BaaGah had been hanging out with his Mookookie friends but now he strode over, his legs fully extended, his round ball of a body-head bobbing along beside them. *"Peoples like Burt and 'Lizbeth. Mookookie too. Lotses of peoples. Lotses of Mookookie. BaaGah is having fun with buddies. We go another dome now?"*

"Not this time, BaaGah. We're going to Alliance Headquarters to talk to the Council. Remember Liliath?"

"Ah, yes, BaaGah remember big lizardy person with nice smile."

Burt wouldn't have said it in exactly that way. Liliath was pretty imposing when she smiled. If you saw that smile out of context, you might not know it was a smile. When a dragon shows all of her teeth, you'd better have a quick exit ready. But BaaGah was right about one thing. Liliath was as kind a being as Burt had ever met. She had been a supportive mentor throughout Burt's career as an Alliance Agent and he always looked forward to time he spent with her.

He was still getting used to the idea of her as the Chief Councilor, but her new fellow councilors were congenial beings and had accepted him gracefully once they were sure he was who he said he was.

BaaGah retracted his limbs and blended into the skin like armband over Burt's MDP. Noony had been riding along in Elizabeth's quarterstaff, a place she enjoyed because of the texture of the spaces in it. Burt waved one more time to the crowd and Elizabeth placed her hand on his shoulder.

Within a heartbeat they found themselves in the reception area of the private council chamber. The receptionist waved them forward. Burt wondered, as he often did when he and Elizabeth made their mysterious and abrupt departures from among the Krimians, whether they were creating some myths that would perpetuate within that budding culture. "I hope they get my name right," he thought, thinking of Mervin and his history with King Arthur of legend.

The three councilors were obviously in a mindspeech conversation when they entered, and Liliath held up a hand to them, so they waited a few moments.

The council chamber hadn't changed much. When they had repaired it after the explosion that killed Ingot and wounded Myla beyond healing, they had kept the original configuration of the room, only changing the lighting to be something less likely to fall from the ceiling and hit someone on the head. Burt was glad they hadn't decided to redesign the room as it held many happy memories for him.

Finally, Liliath turned toward Burt and Elizabeth.

"Welcome to you both," she sent, nodding in their direction.

"We were just finishing up some business that involves the two of you interestingly enough. We are sending some trained cultural and social structure experts to continue what you started with the Krimians. You may return there at some point in other capacities, but for now we need you elsewhere."

Burt didn't know whether to be relieved, excited, or concerned about this.

"Oh? So, what's going on?"

"Not to worry, Burt. It's a temporary adjustment. You've gotten Krim well in-hand and the Daringi and the Krim council are going to take it from here. Your efforts are not only well appreciated; if we were the kind of organization that relied on ranks for authority, you would be up for a promotion. But your skills are unique, and we have reached a crucial stage with the Groga planet. We need you and Elizabeth to help there for a bit. Jenny has her work cut out for her and although she is doing an admirable job, and although she might not agree, she needs a support staff.

Of all the agents in the Alliance, you have the most context and history with this kind of work. She needs eyes and ears in addition to those who are accompanying her. You and Elizabeth are uniquely qualified for this assignment. Can we count on you?"

She tilted her huge draconic head to look directly into his eyes.

"Of course," Burt said, standing a little taller. His instinctive urge was to shift his stance, using body language to express his willingness to stand for Jenny, the Alliance and all it stood for, but he maintained his casual pose. He had long since disciplined his body not to telegraph his thoughts. It was important in his line of work to only express what he wanted people to see and hear.

"Yes, Liliath," Elizabeth echoed stoutly. *"We are here to serve as you need us."*

"Very well. Please take a moment to debrief with Gariel at Sanglarka and then send a message to Lizziebot through the network that you need the coordinates of wherever Jenny is. Lizziebot is generally stored in Jenny's MDP, but thanks to Bob's work with the Nanoites, the communications network now works from within the MDPs."

"Bob and DAT! What will he come up with next?" Burt chuckled. *"OK. We're off. Anything else?"*

"Just this: Jenny is a very capable being. She is coming into her leadership abilities and should not be coddled further. I am concerned that our joy at her progress and constant encouragement may be similar to what happens when you help a dragonet out of its egg. They will never be as strong as when they do it themselves. She is fast becoming a powerful mind and as her powers expand, if she doesn't also develop the necessary social leadership muscles, she could miss fulfilling her potential and the Alliance needs her to become everything she is capable of."

"So, what does that mean exactly, 'not coddle her'? I haven't noticed any coddling. For heaven's sake, how much does she have to go through? If anything, she insists on putting herself into risky situations without support. I'm sorry. I don't get how anyone could say she is coddled."

"She is indeed stretching herself beyond what is comfortable for the rest of us to observe. That much is true, but I want you to remember your own training and some of the interesting positions you have placed yourself in over the years. Jenny is of an age with you and has a lot more in her than any of us may realize.

I'm not saying not to support her, and I'm not saying not to protect her from danger. I'm saying let's not limit her decisions. She has a natural instinct beyond most humans at this stage of development and it will only continue to grow if she is allowed to make decisions and make mistakes."

Burt realized with a start that he was having an argument with a dragon. He had seldom seen Liliath really agitated, but the one time he had seen her truly angry he had nearly wet his pants.

"Sure, Liliath, I'm sorry. I guess it just concerns me when she goes haring off without the rest of us knowing what's going on."

"She and I have had a pointed discussion about that as well. She promised me to be more communicative in the future." Liliath said dryly. *"Are we good?"*

"Of course. Elizabeth and I will head to Sanglarka and I will remember what you said."

As Elizabeth put her hand on his shoulder to take them there, he heard Liliath send in her softest voice with just a touch of amusement, *"Remember. You DO taste good with ketchup."*

Chapter 14: Being Groga

Anwhal took a deep breath before calling a halt to the marching troops behind him. They were making good time toward the capitol and he knew his soldiers could push hard when the need arose, but he also knew it was important to be seen approaching the various villages and allowing them to move the message forward that Anwhal was coming and he was not alone.

The column halted and immediately settled into parade rest, awaiting the order to set up camp. He was proud of them. They represented to him what it really meant to be Groga. These men were not blood-thirsty or cruel. They were well trained in the arts of war, but they would have been just as happy to settle somewhere with their families and live a quiet life. Up until now, that hadn't been a possibility for them.

Neither the Fleistians nor the Inseni had a concept of a retired soldier. They used their forces until they used them up or until they were killed in battle. The enslaved Groga soldiers were only sent away from the battlefield to breed some unfortunate Groga woman and never allowed to stay on the scene long enough for one of their children to be born.

It was a constant focus of Anwhal and the commanders he had personally trained to prevent these men whom he so admired from going hard-hearted. This was a continuing struggle as their Inseni and Fleistian masters seemed to have no emotions other than cruelty and domination.

Anwhal had developed a training program for the Groga force that hid his actual intent. He had learned that their overseers were really only interested in the scheduled training exercises. Mealtimes were ignored as were maintenance times when the soldiers repaired clothing and equipment. Therefore, he kept the military training exercises completely businesslike.

His soldiers knew that during those times they needed to be accurate in their execution of every command, more than for the reason that this would save more lives in actual combat than anything else they learned.

During mealtimes and maintenance sessions, however, Anwhal kept the traditions of his people alive. He was even able to convince the Inseni that their ritual music and dances were "war chants and warrior posturing". In actuality, they told of the honor, service, and loyalty of a manly heart.

Since neither the Inseni nor the Fleistians would put themselves to the trouble to learn the Groga language, this ruse was easy enough to get away with. So, the chants they marched to in formation were uplifting and kept his forces on a higher path than their tyrannical masters would have them pursue.

This is why, when the opportunity finally presented itself to potentially free them, he didn't hesitate.

His men dispersed to their several tasks to set up camp for the evening. Jenny and her guards disembarked from their hover car and strode over to greet him. Jenny was looking much better the last few days, as their schedule was much less demanding during their travels, especially when she was able to ride comfortably in her out worldly conveyance.

"I have some good news. Burt and Elizabeth will be joining us shortly."

"Lord Burt? The ambassador of the Alliance? I saw him die. That is not possible."

"You saw, as I did, an illusion designed to confuse the enemy. Gall was also deceived. Burt is quite well and ready to assist us in our cause. According to the Alliance Council, this is only the beginning of advice and support that will come your way as we are able to make agreements with your government and get the consent of your people to join us in our endeavor to liberate the multiverse from the Inseni threat.

They are prepared with foodstuffs and supplies for the journey, so they will be no additional burden on your resources. Burt has been assigned as an ambassador and a consultant for the potential upcoming conflict. He has the confidence of the Alliance and will be in constant contact with our assembling forces, so he will know as much as is possible about what is going on in the Inseni dimension."

Anwhal nodded. This made sense. It was Burt who had made the arrangements for the revolt that was the first step in acquiring the final freedom of his people. Elizabeth was from one of the races who had at one time made it necessary for them to flee the original Groga home world, but now the Daringi understood that the Groga had fought under duress and were willing to work with the Groga to obtain freedom and peace.

It was ironic that they now found themselves on the same side, but stranger things had happened. Jenny, for instance, had been a key person in routing his people from her planet not so long ago and yet, here she was, championing the cause of Groga freedom and learning Groga customs. She had even begun to learn the basics of his language. Although she primarily still used mindspeech to communicate with his people, she could now use key phrases vocally. Considering the short time she had been with his people, this was nothing short of amazing to him.

"Will they need tents?"

"No, they are fully equipped. They use the same storage technology you saw me pull my vehicle from. They will be subtle about it. We aren't trying to hide anything from you, but we also don't wish to cause a distraction from the issues at hand. Fair enough?"

"As always, Jenny. If you and the Honored One will come with me, I will see to it that you are settled in your usual accommodations. Freia will then see to your needs and check your head. I hear it is healing surprisingly rapidly, although, as I think about it, probably not that surprising when the Honored One is aiding that healing."

Jenny had tried to get him and his people to simply call the Honored One, Chidwi, her given name, but they could not bring themselves to think of her in that way. The legends of his people still spoke of the wisdom and goodness of the "Honored Ones" and this generation would not be the one to become casual with the respect owed to them.

Probably the deepest shame of his people was when the Fleistian contingent had raided the world where the former gatekeeper had lived. They had encountered Honored Ones in the trees beyond the village. They had not harmed them, but the Honored Ones had chittered and scolded from the treetops in that plaintive wail of theirs. For that reason, more than anything, the majority of the Groga people had disowned their brethren who had comprised the Fleistian forces.

None of them were proud of the part they played to protect their families from the depredations of the Fleistians and Inseni, but they were horribly shamed by the actions of this group of Groga soldiers.

They had strayed far from their training. They had embraced cruelty and barbarism to the point that what they were forced to do by their masters no longer seemed to bother them. These were fortunately the minority, but their force was still large enough. The headquarters on Fleist housed nearly a billion between the soldiers and their slaves.

The Inseni, on the other hand, kept a contingent isolated on another planet in their own dimension. Anwhal knew nothing about their numbers or whether they had succumbed to the culture of the Norgoth. The forces on Emperor Peril's planet were still fairly large, potentially a million or so more than held by the Fleistians and they had left that place to return here, to their new home world.

As promised, Freia met them at the headquarters area of the encampment where the tent for Jenny and her bodyguards had been erected before any of the others. Freia escorted Jenny and the rest inside the tent where she would check on Jenny's wound and make sure they got fed and rested.

Grephan joined Anwhal as he supervised the setup of the remainder of the camp. Not that he needed to do much more than encourage his men. They knew their jobs and were quick about it. They knew the sooner everything was in order, the sooner they could get food and have the opportunity to rest and enjoy one another's company.

He was proud of his son. He hoped the time would come when he could engage in some occupation besides warfare. They all educated their children privately, as their masters didn't encourage formal schooling. If it didn't apply to warfare or producing needed food and supplies for those armies, it was discouraged and potentially even punished.

Their women had ceased doing traditional decorative needlework on their clothing, nor did they embellish any of the furniture or construction of their homes with anything that could be called creative or artistic under the reign of the Insenium. This had been considered a waste of precious hours when they could be producing what was needed in the Inseni plan to dominate the multiverse.

In addition, family lines had become blurred due to the aggressive breeding program of the Insenium, which had become stricter and more cruel than their lives under Fleistian rule.

His own father had been killed in a raid only a few days before his son was born. Anwhal hadn't been there for the birth, of course, as he had been preparing for another raid. It was unusual for them to have many casualties because most of the raids were against dimensions without any real defenses. They simply invaded with no warning in huge numbers, completely overwhelming their victims. Most of the time those they attacked were exactly that; not foes that had done any wrong against them, but simply the victims chosen by their masters for the next raid.

The first time there had been any real opposition was in the final raid launched from the Earth base. For a change, they were the ones surprised by overwhelming numbers of trained warriors. They had lost nearly three thousand on that terrible day. These were of the Fleistian contingent; Groga who had been absorbed into the cruel attitudes of their masters. Anwhal grieved for their choices. For him, there was a big difference between fighting to protect their loved ones from harm and doing it for the pure joy of killing.

Or was there? Since the revolution Anwhal had been absorbed in the thought that they could have done this long ago had they been willing to make the sacrifice to expose their own non-combatants to the horrors of war. This was the decision they were making now. This was the commitment they would make by choosing not to fight for the Insenium and the Fleistians. How many innocents would die? On the other hand, were their own any more valuable than those they had callously slain at the command of their masters?

Unfortunately, there was nothing any of them could do about the past. They would pay the price now as they might have done in the beginning. They would no longer allow themselves to be used as an indiscriminate weapon to raid and enslave the innocent.

The slaves that were rewarded to them for successful raids lived among them. They had long since stopped treating them as such, but that didn't compensate for the fact they had been brought here against their will initially. Most of the various people who had been brought there originally as slaves had been with them for several generations. They had created lives for themselves here. Some of them had gathered in villages of their own, but the majority lived mixed among his people, no longer looked down upon or treated any differently than any Groga citizen.

Considering that his people had been used as a weapon, they were a surprisingly peaceful people among themselves. He hoped that wouldn't change if this war extended beyond generations. He had no illusions. His grandchildren and great-grandchildren might find themselves still fighting this war that he and his band had begun with the revolution against Emperor Peril.

A scout came running. *"Commander, there is a delegation approaching from the capitol. They bear the standard of the High Groga."*

"Bring them to me in the command tent. Please notify the Gatekeeper and the Honored One that we desire their presence at this meeting."

The scout nodded, turned on his heel, and ran off to do as he was told.

Anwhal straightened and ceased his inward turmoil. There was work to do. His course was set, and he would not agonize over what he couldn't change.

Chapter 15: Spaces Expanded

Bob was glad to have Ignatius back by his side, although the bird had chattered nearly constantly since Bob had picked him up from Alliance Headquarters. He had evidently decided that now that he had mindspeech he would make up for lost time. He told Bob stories about the different scientists who had all made over him the entire time he and Bob had been apart.

The bird had been terribly spoiled, and it didn't look like that was going to change. Adelle and the rest of the Science and Technology Team were already making much of him, and he seemed to accept it as his due. Bob had to admit Ignatius was charming and entertaining. They had installed his special perches in the break room and at Bob's workstation and had insisted on a special open cage for him in Bob's personal quarters.

It was good being back on earth, and the countryside surrounding the observatory was breath-taking. Adelle had taken great pride in showing him around the facilities, including her little farms, one in the countryside with the usual farm animals and the one in the lowest basement, lighted with artificial light. Adelle had created an aquaponics system to raise fish for eating and fresh vegetables. Root vegetables were raised in the outdoor gardens and stored in a specialized refrigeration unit or freeze-dried for storage, but the rest of the vegetables for the table were harvested fresh each day.

She raised a variety of tilapia, catfish and trout in the tanks that fed and watered her plants. She raised the worms and duckweed that she used for fish food herself. Her energy was provided by a combination of solar and wind power. She told him, "When the sun isn't shining, the wind is usually blowing, so it works well for us."

All in all, she had a fairly self-sustaining system, which was a good thing, as isolated as this spot was. Of course, there was a gate there as well, so supplies, even in the worst winters, were never really a problem. Notwithstanding that groceries were generally a doorway away; Bob had admired the self-sustaining system Adelle had put together. And it was really nice to have fresh food pretty much on demand.

Bob continued to work on his theories about new ways to expand what they could do with their MDPs. Working with the Nanoites through Fidget had been exhilarating. It was different from a lot of the work he had done with robotics, but the principles he had learned while working with AI had come in mighty handy. The other scientists were fascinated with the research and they spent a part of each day discussing potential uses and companion technology that would allow them to leverage this new information, for peacetime uses as well as for warfare.

The easy accessibility to the animals on Adelle's home site was a great bonus. Bob was sensitive to the idea of random animal experimentation, one of the reasons he had confined himself to the study of robotics and AI for most of his career. However, due to the help of the Mookookie, they now knew that at least some organic beings could survive the transfer into an MDP.

Fidget had been able to return many times into Bob's MDP and retrieve air samples and the team had analyzed the samples. The Nanoites didn't require an oxygen rich atmosphere but, having come with Fidget into the atmosphere of Earth and Cornelium's lab, they reported that it did not have any negative impact on them. Therefore, they were willing to use oxygen generators provided by the Alliance to add oxygen to the atmosphere in the MDP satellites that orbited their planet.

Also, the Nanoites were interested in exploring potential interaction on other planets as ambassadors of their kind. They especially wished to establish a colony in Dimensional Alliance Headquarters. They were so tiny as to be invisible to the naked eye; therefore, even the smallest room in the Dimensional HQ building would host millions of them. Mervin had come to the conclusion that this was a topic for further consideration, as, although the Nanoites appeared to be harmless, he wanted to understand more about their culture and their goals before acceding to this request.

The Nanoites didn't seem to have a firm grip on the concept of time, but they seemed to be willing to be patient. Those dwelling in Fidget found it a congenial environment, so they were content to wait and to confine themselves to the robot for now.

Bob really had no idea how many of them were contained in Fidget. Fidget was equally clueless. *"Lots and lots, as BaaGah would say,"* he had replied when Bob had asked him at one point. *"I have no way of accounting for them. They are very active and vary somewhat in composition from one to the next, similar to the specialization of cells in organic beings. I assume the variations serve a purpose, but they don't seem to be aware of what that might be."*

So, Bob continued to move forward. Recently they had successfully transferred a mouse into an oxygen-prepared MDP and retrieved it alive. There was great rejoicing over the tiny creature that scampered into its habitat apparently unharmed but not willing to stick around for more adventures.

They had graduated to rabbits and chickens with no adverse effect. The next step would be human testing, and if that worked, Bob had a strategy that he thought would increase their likelihood of success in the coming conflict exponentially. Tarafau's people were key to making it work the way Bob had envisioned it and there were volunteers arriving later today to see if they could make it work.

Liliath had been both excited and cautious about the potential for success and potential epic failure. *"I know we are short on time and I know this doesn't appear to have a down-side, but we have made way too many assumptions in the past. Please do your evaluation of this very carefully. There are so many elements here that must all work together for this to be successful. We have no desire to expend lives unnecessarily, though a certain number of losses are inevitable.*

Based on the intel that is coming in through our Mookookie agents, the Norgoth have appropriated not only many planets in their own universe but have extended their domain into multiple dimensions. We must be careful to make no more assumptions based on misinformation. It is unclear if they plan a new push in the near future, but, from what we understand, they are actively recruiting from their own people as well as forming new forces based on the slave population.

You have our support in this line of consideration, but we can't afford large losses at the onset, as this will likely not be a short battle with a convenient outcome. We have to be in this from the beginning with the intention to persist until the job is done."

Bob agreed with Liliath. He had always been a careful "tinkerer", following proper experimental protocols for safety and as few errors as possible. Through the Alliance communication network, he had conferred with Mervin, Cornelium and Argent. They encouraged his line of reasoning and supported him in his progression through the various tests and experiments necessary to reach the optimum conclusion one way or the other.

He had discussed it with Jenny also, as he respected her quick mind and her ability to make logical conclusions. Merv had said it was one of the things he most admired about the human race, their ability to go beyond the dogged course of logic and spring beyond the process to conclusions that worked.

He had gifted both Mervin and Argent with the two newest robotic siblings of Fidget and Lizziebot. Merv had been openly delighted. Argent had thanked him gruffly and said he would see how it worked out. Bob knew him now well enough to know that this was as enthusiastic as Argent ever got about anything. Merv had christened his new bot, Guinevere on the spot. Argent, on the other hand, simply called his, Bot1. Bob wondered if this meant he hoped to eventually have a "Bot2" to add to his assistance.

Bob chuckled and shook his head. Like Burt, he had spent a great deal of his career working on his own in the quiet of his own mind. Now he was part of something so big that it almost broke his mind considering it. His hope was that once they had resolved the current situation, however long that took, that he would have the time to explore peaceful uses of his newfound knowledge and understanding.

The two Daringi arrived just before lunchtime. The rule in Adelle's lab was that lunch was an informal affair, but that everyone assembled for a good breakfast and supper. This meant that even the most intense of them were required to take at least two breaks every day to, as Burt would have put it, "hobnob with their fellow wizards" and get some outside stimulation.

In Adelle's lab every work area was supplied with several constantly running cameras, recording every step of any process to preserve it for future study and to allow the other Alliance scientists to have input. Bob had ignored the cameras as he worked, remembering what a key part the video feed in Cornelium's lab had played in his discoveries. He had made a mental note to himself to establish video cameras strategically in his home lab.

Bob met Adelle in the break room to greet Elgyra and the two volunteers he had brought with him from Ungoli. He had been sent there to recruit two strong, healthy Daringi to help with the next step of their research. Although Bob knew that this stage must come, he knew that there were always potentially unintended and unexpected risks anytime you added organic beings into the equation.

Elgyra faded into the room exactly on time, with two young Daringi in tow.

"Please greet Lutha and Gremmel, my friends. They will be helping us with the next stage of this project. They are aware of the risks and come willingly and without hesitation to aid in our cause."

Bob and Adelle shook hands with Lutha, a female built very much like Desminda, warrior braids in her hair and Gremmel, a tall slender male with the scholar's knot of the Daringi university. It proclaimed him as a teacher and scientist.

"We are excited to meet you and to have this opportunity," Gremmel sent with a wide smile. *"We had to draw lots at the end because so many wanted this chance to be part of something so amazing. Elgyra has briefed us and we are ready to begin."*

Lutha nodded in agreement. *"We are rested and ready,"* she affirmed.

"For now, let us sit and eat. It is lunchtime here. While we eat, we will brief you on protocol in my laboratory and then we will get you settled into your quarters. After that we will begin. All preparations have been made to work as quickly and safely as is possible. You are welcome in Starlight."

After they had eaten and the two volunteers had been oriented to procedure and protocol in Adelle's lab, they took a short tour of the facilities. The Daringi had been impressed with the beauty of the Alpine countryside and had listened intently as Adelle had explained the various aspects of her self-sufficient lifestyle. In turn, they had compared it to their own culture. It had been an enjoyable exchange, but Bob admitted to himself his own impatience to begin was beginning to wear on him.

Finally, after showing them to their quarters, the two of them had reported that they had no need to linger there and were anxious to begin.

As they settled into the chairs provided in Bob's work area and were greeted by Fidget to their great amusement and interest, Bob slid the sleeve of his lab coat up his arm to expose his MDP. *"This is our new laboratory. There are several things we intend to explore at this time. One of them is the ability of an organic being such as a human or a Daringi to enter the MDP, which has now had a balanced oxygen atmosphere and proper pressurization added to it. Once there, we wanted to determine if a Daringi can actually sense the coordinates of the MDP area in question. We have the complete agreement of the Nanoites who inhabit these spheres to do this. Lastly, we want to determine if each MDP has different coordinates and whether it is possible to create a coordinate map of the known MDP spheres.*

I have several MDPs currently keyed to me at this time for the purposes of this experiment. Each of them has been optimized for the transport of beings amenable to an oxygen atmosphere and Earth-type pressurization. Is this clear?"

The two nodded and Elgyra smiled encouragingly.

"Very well. We will proceed as follows. Fidget will precede you into the MDP to observe you and aid you if aid is necessary. He will be recording your visit there. We will do one of you at a time and then make some decisions at that point. We have a theory, but we don't want to prejudice either your experience or the experiment itself."

"I will go first," Lutha volunteered. *"I'm not being brave, but we drew straws,"* and she grinned wickedly at Gremmel, *"And I won."*

As Bob had explained, he touched the MDP to Fidget and the little bot folded in on himself and disappeared into the simple plastic-looking little bracelet on Bob's arm. He then nodded solemnly to Lutha who stepped forward and extended her hand to touch the bracelet.

Her eyes sparkled with excitement and she also folded in on herself. Bob and Elgyra had agreed that they would need to spend at least as long as someone could normally hold their breath inside the MDP. This would limit the danger to the subject and also give them some moments to orient themselves to their environment.

Although Fidget had previously tested the atmosphere and pronounced it safe, Bob was taking no chances, so when Lutha disappeared he held his own breath as long as he could and then invoked the MDP to bring Lutha back out.

She appeared before them with an amazed look on her face. *"That place is huge!"* she exclaimed as soon as she had taken a breath. *"Breathing is fine, and I didn't feel any ill effects. May I go back in?"*

While she had been enthusing, Bob had also withdrawn Fidget from inside the MDP. *"All systems go, boss."* He said as soon as he was clear.

Elgyra was examining Lutha, listening to her heart and taking other measurements.

"Can I go again?" Lutha sent like a little kid on a carnival ride. Bob understood it wasn't immaturity or taking the venture lightly. He felt the same breathless excitement going forward. If he could pull this off, how many lives could it save?

"Yes, but this time Gremmel will go with you and I will leave you in slightly longer. Did you experience any difference in gravity? That was one issue we weren't able to determine at this point."

"*It wasn't much different than my home planet. I feel slightly heavier on Earth, though. The air seemed fresh enough. I didn't have to hold my breath in there and didn't feel the kind of pressure you feel under water, so I believe the relative pressure in there is about equal to here. Do you know how the builders of the MDPs accounted for the mass differential like we find on opposite sides of a wormhole, for instance?*"

Bob shook his head resignedly. "*There is so much we don't know about this technology. By all the physics I understand, it shouldn't be possible for the portals to do what they do. Equalizing what we might think of as pressure on both sides of a portal is beyond anything our scientists or those of the Alliance know how to do. But I'll just go on with the idea that if it works, we don't need to try to fix it.*

It well may be that it is part of the natural properties of this type of portal and that the original gate builders simply capitalized on it."

Elgyra shook his head in agreement. "*We still don't understand how the species on our planet can traverse dimensions as a natural gift. For all we know, it could have something to do with the water we drink or the kind of light we receive from our suns or the rings that surround our planet. But the mysteries of the multiverse are what make pursuing the sciences so much fun.*" And he grinned at his own whimsy.

"*OK,*" Bob continued, "*Here are two chronometers set to Earth time in Switzerland. You have the coordinates for us here and now? Good. I want you to try to retrieve the coordinates from the MDP sphere when you get there and see if you can then transport on your own back to these coordinates. We will then see if the chronometers on your wrists match the time here. Clear?*"

Lutha and Gremmel nodded. Bob touched the MDP to them one at a time. As they folded into the tiny dimensional portal, he took a deep breath. Five minutes could be a very long time when you were...

Suddenly Lutha and Gremmel stood before him! Ignatius squawked and Bob hooted in joy, doing a little jig on the spot. "*Yes! YES!!! It works! Look out Gall, we're comin' for ya!*"

Chapter 16: Adjustments and Assumptions

Jenny entered the command tent with her retinue, which seemed to be expanding at what seemed to her an alarming rate. She understood the reasoning of the Alliance Council regarding her need to surround herself with credible advisors, and she knew both Burt and Elizabeth had more experience and understanding in these sorts of negotiations than she did. Burt had dealt with so many diverse cultures on his many missions for the Alliance over the years and Elizabeth was a trained diplomat and negotiator, something she had decided on early in her education based on Tarafau's involvement with the Alliance.

In addition, both Burt and Elizabeth had recently been a key component in the reorganization of the people of Krim following the revolution, not to mention orchestrating the revolution in the first place.

Jenny, by comparison, was what her generation on Earth would have called a "newbie". So far, she felt like she had been propped up by those around her, gaining experience more rapidly than she could take it all in.

On the one hand, she was grateful for the support she had received in her unplanned roles, first as a Gate Guardian and now as the Gatekeeper. On the other hand, she had always been a very self-sufficient person, and having to rely on others was uncomfortable for her.

Therefore, when Burt and Elizabeth had appeared just outside of her part of the encampment, she greeted them with very mixed feelings; not only that her entourage was growing, but also it was the first time since her accident that anyone had seen her in her damaged state. Thankfully, her head was nicely covered by the colorful kerchief wound artfully around her head every morning by her faithful attendant, Freia.

Jenny realized she kept acquiring extra parents and, in this case, a bonus mom. But Freia, although she loved meeting Jenny's needs, did not cosset her. She insisted that Jenny stretch herself a little more every day now that the wound was healing so well.

"Sunshine, good air, good food and regular exercise, a little more every day and you will soon be as healthy as any of us. No more lying about, especially when you must spend so much time enclosed in that 'contraption' every day."

There really was no word for contraption in the Groga language and Jenny sensed that mindspeech was translating her intent as it often did, ignoring the actual vocabulary used. Jenny nodded and thanked her for her kindness and support.

"You came to us at great risk to yourself to do something for us we didn't have the gumption to do for ourselves. All of us agree that you have set an example each of us should follow. You don't spend a lot of time talking about what to do as much as you show us by your actions what real courage and commitment look like. If I had a daughter, I would want her to be just like you."

She smiled at that memory and entered the tent feeling ready for whatever was about to happen. Freia had been right about one thing especially; she was committed. As Brendan would have said, she was "fair dinkum"; as Burt would have put it, "all in".

Inside, several Groga were in vocal conversation with Anwhal and his officers. Jenny caught the words, "war", "fight", and "coward". She had been studying with Grephan as she rode in her hover car. She and her bodyguards had been intensely engaged with the young Groga and had taken to teasing him in his native tongue to his delighted confusion. She had decided that she would be more credible and perhaps less intimidating if she could converse with these people as one of them, rather than relying on mindspeech as a crutch.

They turned as she and her group entered the tent and Jenny met their eyes, not in a challenging way, but as an equal who was worthy of their respect. She didn't know if they were buying it, but she needed to begin as she meant to go on.

Anwhal introduced them. *"Jenny Japhet, Gatekeeper of the Dimensional Alliance and Chidwi, Honored One; allow me to introduce you to the High Chancellor, second to the High Groga, Merdahl by name. He is accompanied by his staff members and clerks. They are here to discuss the details of how you intend to teach us what we need to do to free our people from the tyranny of the Great Insenium and their Fleistian minions."*

"I am honored to meet you," Jenny replied. *"Shall we sit?"*

Merdahl nodded curtly, and they all sat in the chairs that were arranged around the planning table, which had been cleared of the usual maps and other items they used in their battle planning sessions. As they sat, Jenny waited patiently. She had determined not to be the first to speak and to spend most of her time listening intently. She noticed that Anwhal had not introduced any of Jenny's party, nor had he given names to any of Merdahl's group. She assumed this was proper protocol for this type of meeting in the Groga culture.

Anwhal stood once all were comfortably situated.

"Jenny, I know you have questions and now we have those in authority to properly answer them. Merdahl, I would like to start with your report on the current line of thinking among our leaders, and then we will open it up for discussion and questions on both sides."

He sat and Merdahl arose. He was shorter than most Groga she had met, but still sturdy and square. Unlike the Groga soldiers, his hair hung down past his shoulders in many small braids like many Groga men she had met who were not in the Groga military. Female Groga also wore their hair in braids, for the most part, with the exception that they often braided beads and ribbons into theirs.

His hair was a pale brown and his eyes were dark, as most of his kind. They weren't quite black, and although the irises of the Groga were definitely in different colors, you had to see them in sunlight to be able to discern one color from another. He wore no uniform and didn't appear to be dressed in anything that labeled him as aristocracy or high rank.

"Gatekeeper and Honored one and Alliance guests, I carry greetings from the leaders of our people. For the first time in many generations, we are beginning to hope for an end to our servitude to masters who would have us become as twisted as they are. We are not without concerns however, and we would not want to once again find ourselves as pawns in a game of conquest belonging to someone else." He paused, and as if expecting a negative reaction to this last, he held up both hands before him.

Jenny did not allow herself to react. She was pretty sure no disrespect was intended, and she would hear him out before coming to any conclusions. Liliath had stressed in her nightly training the importance of clear communications in her role as the Gatekeeper. She had emphasized that good communication began with good listening.

When she didn't react overtly, Merdahl continued. *"We have no reason to either trust or distrust you at this point. Anwhal made the only logical decision he could make considering the circumstances he found himself in.*

Either way, we do have more than one option here. Please allow me to present them logically, so you understand our thinking on this situation and then let us discuss the implications of those choices. The High Groga wanted you to have an opportunity to hear us out before you arrived at our capitol to set the tone of further discussion. Are we agreed?"

Jenny said nothing but nodded her assent without looking around to see the faces of her team. She knew they would follow her lead on this. She had yet to speak with Burt or Elizabeth in person before now as they had arrived moments before the breathless messenger had relayed his message that the High Chancellor was coming and where they were going to meet.

She had only had cursory mindspeech discussions with them before Elizabeth and Burt had arrived. She had not expected to find herself in negotiations with the Groga before they got to the capitol with the exception of the ongoing briefings she had pursued with the various local leaders as they passed through cities and towns on their way to the capitol.

Merdahl looked a bit relieved at her agreement and plunged on, *"The first option we have is to fall in with everything you have said and potentially end up simply trading one master for another, blindly doing everything you tell us to do and ultimately finding ourselves simply the fighting arm of another entity, once again sacrificing Groga lives and culture for no reason we can discern.*

The second option is to cut ties immediately with you and go back to our masters like a penitent dog to receive our chastisement for a poor decision and hope for mercy from a known entity that is not prone to mercy or forgiveness in any form we have ever experienced.

The third option is to reject both sides and try to stand to one side while you destroy one another, hoping there are no victors on either side.

The final option is to join with you in your fight as equal partners and participants, with a say as to our part in all of this. This would imply that commitments are made on both sides and both of us benefit from the relationship."

Jenny was impressed with the logic of the case he was laying before her. From her standpoint, it gave her hope that they could indeed form an alliance, however temporary or permanent it became. The contrast between this man and his well thought out conclusions and the preemptive and haughty attitude of Peril was almost comical when she considered that Peril (and the Alliance for that matter) had assumed the Groga to be unreasoning brutes.

"As you can see, we have given this much thought and there have been many discussions that went late into the night ever since Anwhal reported his decision to join in the revolt. As far as we know, Gall does not yet realize we had any part in it.

We have had no communication from them, and we must assume they believe we were defeated and may yet be held captive by the Alliance. They would base this on our last encounters with your people, which did not go well for us or them.

Understand, I do not apologize for any of that, nor do I expect any apologies from the Alliance. We were both working under false assumptions. Your people thought we were working at our own design and we only knew of you what our masters told us, which was nearly nothing. Our orders were always exclusive of any information they did not think was relevant for us to know in order to accomplish the task at hand."

Again, Jenny nodded, and he continued, *"Because of this, I respectfully request we begin anew. Let us both be direct and honest in our goals and desires and see if there is anything for us to agree upon here. Is that fair?"*

Jenny nodded. *"I agree, Merdahl. My introduction to the Groga people was skewed both by past impressions of my leaders and my own encounters that were not what they appeared to be. One of the things I am learning in my position is that we often make judgements based on misleading information.*

We need to be able to reevaluate our assessments when it becomes obvious that what we think we see isn't always the truth we think it is.

Having lived with your people for a time now, I must say you are nothing like what I pictured you to be. I find the Groga to be intelligent, kind, hard-working and respectful people. You are nothing like the mindless brutes I was first exposed to from your world.

I now realized that these are those who have broken off from you, and I am saddened by their current state.

I know each of us get to make choices and that they could have chosen a different way, as Anwhal did, but it is not my place to judge. We do, however, need to deal with the situation we find ourselves in as it is instead of what we hoped it was.

It is the opinion of my leaders and I that the most effective thing your people can now do to help us rid the multiverse of this looming threat, is to withdraw the Groga completely from the conflict. Without the numbers of your forces, we believe the Norgoth and the Great Insenium will be greatly hampered in their attempts to dominate, enslave, and terrorize the multiverse.

This probably does not mean, however, that you will not have to fight. I doubt seriously the Insenium will simply shrug and say, 'Oh well, I guess we'll have to manage without the Groga.' They think you are malleable and subservient in your bones. They have no idea of your true courage and determination.

In addition, they also have a false impression of your capability and intelligence. They have chosen to see you as mindless brutes based on the behavior of a small segment of your people.

I see this misinterpretation a lot on my home planet. People assume when a fraction of a group of people behave a certain way, that all of them must be alike. This is a big mistake, one I am guilty of myself, especially when it comes to the Groga.

The Inseni appear to be so caught up in themselves and their self-supposed superiority that they have failed to notice, and will likely not admit it if they do, that the Groga are more than cannon fodder to be used up at their convenience."

The delegation, including Anwhal and his adjutants, nodded somberly. She noticed that they had brought a clerk with them who was assiduously taking notes, his eyes narrowed in concentration, a pen, similar to a fountain pen, flying across the stack of papers before him, each sheet being laid carefully aside as it was filled for it to dry.

Anwhal stood. *"Jenny and I have discussed this at length, and I believe she is right. The very thing that makes the Norgoth and The Great Insenium, arrogantly presume they can pay no heed to the Groga as a people will be their undoing. We do have some time to prepare to resist them, something they will not expect.*

We are also in contact with the slaves and Mookookie on the Inseni former capitol planet. They now call that planet Krim. They are also ready to actively resist, re-enforced by allies of the Dimensional Alliance. I understand the need for this, as these people are not by their nature warriors.

In addition, the Mookookie have managed to infiltrate the Inseni planets and are actively working as intelligence agents for the Alliance. This means we should be able to accumulate more relevant information and may actually have some warning before the Great Insenium decides we are a threat and move against us.

I have expressed the opinion to Jenny that the Groga can probably manage without any assistance, other than in helping to plan, and in the initial preparations to prepare for an assault. The consensus of the Mookookie agents is that they have decided on sending ground troops as opposed to attacking from space.

However, the one request I made to the Alliance is to potentially have a space fleet in readiness in case they change their minds. To prevent the Norgoth from changing their strategy, we have not blocked the main portal to allow them to easily send troops through. However, when they arrive, we hope to have some rather nasty surprises lying in wait."

Burt cleared his throat. Jenny and he had not had an opportunity to discuss a strategy for this meeting, so she hoped it wouldn't be a mistake for him to speak.

"You seem to have this mostly in hand, but I would like to offer a tiny bit of help in the 'nasty surprises' department, if I may. You may have heard reports of our encounters with your troops on Earth and the planet you raided a while back from the Earth portal you erected in the Amazon jungle?"

A few of Merdahl's contingent nodded grimly.

"Ah, so perhaps you would like to have access to some of the technology and stratagems (including some we didn't get a chance to use at that time)?"

Merdahl nodded again. *"That might be, umm, helpful indeed. To whom am I speaking?"*

"I'm Burt; a Dimensional Alliance Agent. I'm here to support Jenny."

"Very well, Burt...Of Earth?" Merdahl acknowledged, as Burt nodded. *"I believe our leaders would like to hear more about this. I assume this is not an offer of troops? No? Good. One of the things I was to make clear to Jenny and her staff was that we prefer not to have off-world troops involved in any of this. No bases. No establishments of any kind. We will not make the mistake again of becoming dependent on outside forces to handle our problems. We have learned our lesson in buckets of blood and regret. No more."*

"We respect that," Jenny agreed. *"And I must say that this is my desire as well, that the Groga once again become the independent and respected people they are able to be. May I suggest perhaps a small embassy at the capitol with a specifically limited number of beings in it at any given time so that you can stay in communication with the Alliance?"*

"We shall see. A lot will depend on whether there is even a Groga people left when all of this is done." And he raised his hand to stem the protest he could see on her face. *"If that were to happen, it would be the results of our own past actions and no responsibility of yours. We will go forward with the intent to vanquish our enemies and reestablish our culture and our independence. But we would be as foolish as before not to be aware of the potential consequences of this decision."*

No one jumped in to speak. They all sat there for a few moments considering the discussion so far.

Anwhal finally stood again. *"What are your orders, Merdahl? Are you returning immediately, or will you proceed with us on our journey to the capitol?"*

"I must return," Merdahl said with an earnest sigh and a nod toward the stack of papers lying before his clerk. *"The High Groga is anxious to get our assessment based on this conversation. I know there is much more to discuss in detail, but for now we will make preparations to receive the Dimensional Alliance envoy and decide the best way to notify the people of the decision that lies before us.*

We are adamant that every Groga get a voice and be allowed the opportunity to decide whether or not to support this action. If there are only a small number who dissent, we will find a safe place for them to abide until the conflict is finished. If the majority choose otherwise; we still don't foresee what that outcome would look like, but we must be prepared for all contingencies."

His clerk hastily gathered his papers, folding them carefully into a leather-like folio and wiping his pen, stored it into a small wooden case that went into the pocket of his vest.

Chairs scraped back and they all followed Merdahl and Anwhal out into the light. The ball was rolling. Jenny couldn't see the ending from where she stood, but she knew she wouldn't quit on these people or the Alliance or the people of Earth. She squared her shoulders and moved forward, the only thing she could do.

Chapter 17: Mango Tango

Juan hadn't wanted to leave her here without him; Luz knew that. However, she also knew that, although he trusted his team implicitly, there were simply some things he needed to handle on his own. One of these things was the meetings that took place in the security and privacy of Sanglarka. Alliance officials had still not shaken off the betrayal of Guaray. They needed to know exactly who were at the meetings to eliminate the possibility that the private Alliance communications network might be compromised.

Luz had told Juan that it wasn't much different than as if he stepped out of the house for a moment, gate travel being what it was and that if anything happened here, she would have Mustapha let him know right away. Juan had simply hugged her. "You're right, of course," he admitted. "If I can't trust you to handle anything that might come, I don't know who I could possibly trust in your stead. Just be careful, mi amor."

"Of course, you silly man. Now go. You know Liliath will be there and punctuality is important to her."

He kissed her fervently without another word and turned and stepped through the portal to the L.A. gate, where he would then go through the gateroom to the Sanglarka gate. For security reasons, only the official Gatekeeper gate could allow anyone to go to Sanglarka. There would be guards there to inspect him and be sure he was who he said he was, based on the Guardian Key he had around his neck.

The outside of Jenny's little hacienda-style home looked like any other of the homes on Infinity Loop but the inside of the gateroom office and the gateroom itself was bristling with Alliance Troopers, handpicked by Gariel.

Luz sighed and entered into their large, bright, airy kitchen with its terra cotta tiled floors and immaculate white walls and cupboards.

On the large marble topped island in the center of the kitchen was her tablet. On it was her to-do list along with inventories, accounting data and other things necessary to run her mango orchard business. Deeper in an encrypted mini drive were the necessary parts of their true business for the Alliance. Her tablet, although it looked like any other tablet you could buy online or in an electronics store, had been "souped-up with DAT", as Bob would have put it.

She grabbed the tablet and placed it into a special holster she had made for it. On her other hip was a holster of another sort. Anyone meeting Luz for the first time would think her the ultimate homemaker and hostess. Her home was always clean, the meals she prepared for her guests were delicious, and on top of that she ran a successful mango orchard with distribution of her fruit throughout the coastal towns of the main island of Puerto Rico.

However, from a purely superficial standpoint, they would have missed so much else about her. Besides being an avid reader and textile crafter of crochet, knitting, weaving and embroidery, she was also skilled in the martial arts and an accurate and deadly marksman. It was also her secret triumph that she had once defeated Arvid, his quarterstaff versus her kali sticks. It had been a private workout with no witnesses and Luz had been discrete about it, never telling anyone. As far as anyone else was concerned Arvid remained undefeated and she was ok with that.

She never went out into the mango grove or anywhere outside on the property unarmed. First of all, because the surrounding jungle was alive with native animals, many of them serious predators, and secondly, she knew that their particular gate was more vulnerable than many of them, such as Adelle's lab high in the Swiss Alps or Sanglarka, also surrounded by mountains, or even Brendan's gate deep in the forests of New South Wales, Australia. Even though their compound was in the inland jungle, the island was relatively small, and they were less than an hour's drive from several large coastal towns. Their elevation wasn't high enough for any real protection from an aerial assault.

Luz had always been a firm believer that it was far better to be over-prepared than to face the consequences of a lack of foresight. So, she also strapped on the special harness that gave her easy access to her kali sticks on her back and went out her front doors. Although this was her habit on any normal day, she was especially adamant that all her hired hands also were armed and well-versed both in martial arts and projectile weaponry.

She waved to Aliki, on his way to his workshop, where he and Leland continued to assemble the necessary supplies and equipment and vehicles into the MDPs they were preparing for the various Alliance forces. She enjoyed having Aliki and Leland on the property. Both were of a cheerful and optimistic mindset and evening meals were entertaining as both had some amazing stories to share.

They came and went through the gate office to the various dimensions that were supplying the Alliance in the war effort, but anyone watching would only see them going to and from the hacienda, seemingly unencumbered. Anything they acquired on their several trips each day was conveniently stored in their MDPs. Since all of the Earth gate guardians had taken to wearing the flesh like armbands to cover them, you wouldn't have noticed the MDP even close up.

The skies had cleared from the storms of the day before and a warm light breeze stirred the leaves of the mango trees only slightly. The trees in the grove were well-spaced to allow the harvesting equipment ample room for the safety of her workers and the proper picking of the fruit. Her workers picked in teams, one operating the harvesting machine and the others using "picking sticks" to reach mangoes as far up as they could reach. In addition, mangoes in the top of the trees were picked by an individual in a cherry picker unit and dropped to deep pads where the others on the picking team would gather them and process them into the harvester.

As the containers were filled with the processed fruit, they were hauled off to a waiting truck and then to the harvest barn where they would be packaged for distribution.

Mangoes were tricky to work with. They grew on long stems, hanging down vertically. The picking sticks grasped the stem a few inches above the top of the fruit and cut the stem while still holding it. The worker then took the fruit to the nearby specialized harvesting machine.

At the machine, the stem was snapped from the mango and the mango was immediately put under running water that washed the acidic sap from the fruit. Even missing the tiniest drop of sap would damage the fruit, making it useless to sell.

On top of this, the sap was very dangerous to human skin. You could generally tell an amateur mango picker from the acid burns on their arms or legs. For this reason, even in the hottest weather, the pickers wore long-sleeved shirts and long pants and washed their hands frequently under the streams of water constantly flowing in the harvester.

Luz's workers had one of the lowest damage and injury rates of any crew she had ever seen, and she gladly paid them top wages. Of course, their main purpose was as a security team for the hacienda and its precious gateway. Her workers didn't know this, but Luz was aware of the speculation that occurred amongst her crew. She was a government spy. Juan was fleeing a government hit squad; and on and on...

She didn't mind it. The little mystery added a bit of spice to their days and kept them alert and ready for action. She had provided them with workout facilities, but for the most part the work in the grove kept them fit and muscular. To all outward appearances, they were simply hired hands. But to Luz they could be the one thing that stood between inimical forces and the gateway she and Juan had committed to protect.

Currently within the gate office in the basement of the hacienda there was a constant guard of at least four armed troopers, but that didn't prevent anyone from attacking from outside. Aliki and Leland's shared workshop was even more vulnerable than the gate and crucial to the war effort.

In addition, in the library of the hacienda, Mustapha manned the communications network that coordinated communications related to the war. He had a couple of Alliance Agents also stationed there with him and the ability to completely fry every piece of equipment if it became necessary to prevent the compromise of the Alliance communication network.

But it was a beautiful day and Luz was determined to enjoy it as she could. She checked on the harvesting which generally ran like clockwork, but in large part because she took an active interest in the work, often pitching in alongside her harvesting crew, "just to keep my hand in" as she told them.

As she worked alongside them, she focused on drawing them out, listening while they talked about their families, their interests, local sports teams, not to mention their inner circle clean joke competition. There were several types of these, groaners, belly laughs, puns, and riddles. At the end of the week she would award them points and once a month they would add up the points to crown a new champion in each category.

Generally, the harvesting season lasted about six months out of the year, between September and March. During that time, it was a daily routine, picking, processing, packing, and shipping the mangoes. It was physical work, but with her crew it was also happy work. All of them loved what they did, and Luz was glad to pay them well for it, especially considering their additional duties.

Each of them pulled a night watch at least a couple times a week, rotating through the schedule. At one side of the main gate, which was shut at twilight, there was a watchtower capable of comfortably housing two guards. There were floodlights powered by solar charged batteries at each side of the gate in addition to infrared video cameras at intervals along the wall. The video feeds were monitored from inside the hacienda by Aliki, Leland, Mustapha, Luz or Juan in shifts day and night.

The video cameras had been added as part of the additional security required by the Alliance after it was determined that there was a small possibility that Sam might know where they were and what they were doing.

"Hey Victor!" Eduardo called from up on the cherry picker. "How much money does a pirate pay for corn?"

Victor looked up and scratched his head. "I dunno, Eduardo. How much DOES a pirate pay for corn?"

"A buccaneer!" Eduardo shouted down and the cherry picker wobbled with his guffaw.

Victor groaned. "That was pretty corny alright. But I think it was only a two pointer," he remarked to Luz. "He's behind on points. I'm guessing Diego has the lead again this month. The one about the monkey and the parrot still has me chuckling."

"That was a good one for sure," Luz agreed with a grin. "But this one might make it into the groaner pile. It was punderful to say the least."

Victor rolled his eyes and Luz patted him on the back. "How is Catarina? Is she over that cold?"

Victor's eyes always lit up when he thought about his newborn daughter. "She is fine. Aliana is a good mama. She treated her as her mother had done for her when she was little, and all is well. She got better pretty fast, for which I am grateful. She is growing so fast. She turns her head to look at you when you call her name now. It makes her smile."

Later, when they were out of the grove, he would show her the latest photos his wife had taken. He went down the mountain for a couple of days every week. He missed his little family, but the pay was good, and Luz made sure that his family lacked for nothing. She was like an extra auntie to all of the children of her workers. She and Juan had discovered early on in their marriage that she was unable to bear children. So, she expended her maternal impulses in behalf of other children and found herself finally at peace with it.

Once a year she held an "unbirthday" party for the families of her workers with music, great food and, of course, presents which she took great delight in purchasing for each member of those families. And at Christmastime they all attended a parade and pageant in the local coastal town together, followed by a nice meal at a favorite restaurant and presents for all.

Jorge and Vittorio worked beside her and Victor, breaking stems from the mangos on a special tool at the back of the harvester and immediately plunging them under the constant stream of water that continued to run over the mangos as they moved down an open conveyor belt and dropped onto a foam cushion at the end of the harvester. At the other end of the harvester, Augusto and Manuel slid the cushion out from under a layer of mangoes at regular intervals so they rolled off into a draining area below. From time to time they would stop the progress of the belt to load the accumulated mangoes into boxes on a pallet which would be hauled with a small tractor to the storage area. Carlos and Sebastian had just taken a load a few minutes ago.

For her and her crew, this was just a normal day during harvest season. All of them took Sunday off to attend various religious services or just spend time with their families. On those days, Juan, Luz, and the other Alliance Gatekeepers in residence took turns at night watch and watching the video feed supplemented by humanoid Alliance Troopers. All in all, the increased security wasn't as stressful as Luz had originally feared it might be.

The work had a soothing rhythm to it, chatting and joking and even occasionally singing as they worked. Luz was content with this part of her life as anyone could be, she mused.

Suddenly a shout from the direction of the harvest barn brought them all up to complete alertness. It was definitely a shout of alarm and was followed by a loud wail. Each of the workers carried a "shouter" with them, a simple device with a single button that let out a high decibel screech. These were only to be used in a serious emergency. They served two purposes, first to get the attention of all the workers and second to pinpoint the location of an incident. The shouter would not be turned off until help arrived. Where predators were concerned, the high pitched wailing sound also served to frighten them off, all but the largest and loudest of them.

The harvester was not turned off so the water could continue to circulate and prevent the mangoes from being spoiled. The cherry picker descended. Before it could reach the platform it rested on, the others had already dropped whatever they were working on, including their tools, and had pelted down the little road that led to the harvest barn.

As she ran, Luz pressed the little button on the armband that lay next to her MDP. This would alert Aliki, Leland and Mustapha that something was wrong. They would be able to track her via one of "Burt's Bugs" as they referred to the little nanobots they had each agreed to host during this crisis. Their first priority would be to secure their particular areas and workspaces and then to come to her aid. They had drilled in this early on and found they could secure their stations and be out the door in a matter of a couple minutes.

Part of that security was to put any DAT into their MDPs and to remove the power supplies from anything else, as well as employing the shielding and locking mechanisms for each of their areas. She knew that her team was well trained, but she also knew from experience that you couldn't plan for everything. The one thing she did know is that Sanglarka had also been immediately notified of a breach in security, which meant she could depend on help coming within minutes.

She didn't dwell on this. She was running flat out. Her workers had immediately let the fastest runners get ahead while three of them paced Luz, one on either side and one behind. The main road leading to the harvest barn was level and led to a loading yard in front of a large metal building, roomy enough to be able to pull the large cargo trucks in at night and still store hundreds of reusable crates holding the harvest of the day. Each morning the trucks went out and delivered mangoes while the others got a start on the next batch of harvesting.

As they neared the building, suddenly the wail of the shouter cut off. Behind the cargo trucks on the loading dock, a scuffle was in progress between about a dozen hefty men and her security squad. How these men had gotten through the gates without detection was a mystery that Luz had every intention of discovering.

"Don't kill all of them!" she broadcasted in mindspeech while shouting it vocally. She wanted the attackers to hear this and if, as she suspected, they were from off world, she was pretty sure they would understand what she was saying. *"We want at least a few of them alive!"*

The attackers, realizing reinforcements were near, renewed their attack with a frenzy. Evidently, they had come in without any type of projectile weapon, or at least they weren't using them at the moment. Some of them wielded clubs, and some had a sort of flail made of chains. Luz couldn't fire on them, as good a shot as she was, without the potential of hitting one of her own men.

As one of them turned so she could see his face, her heart sped up. In the center of the forehead of the intruder was one large green eye. These were obviously not from around here.

Leland and Aliki pounded up behind her. *"All is secure!"* Aliki sent to her. *"Who are these Mea Uli? How can they even be here?"*

"I don't know, but we're about to find out. Staffs out, my friends. We don't want to harm our own. Let's flank them. My team, to the right. Leland and Aliki, you're with me."

Luz pulled her kali from their sling on her back. She knew Aliki must be pretty angry. "Mea Uli" meant "black animal" and was considered a great insult among his people. Aliki nearly never swore, so there must be more to this than she realized, but her curiosity would have to wait until later.

The intruders had the dock workers backed up to the metal sliding harvest doors on the dock. Her men were holding their own, even as out-numbered as they were. Carlos looked injured, however, and Sebastian had a cut under one eye that looked as if it had come from a blow with a heavy fist.

Luz and her companions had their kali staffs out and were striking out with them, back to back. The dock was wide enough to allow them some movement, but fortunately it did restrict their attackers as not all could get to them at once.

Luz, Aliki and Leland raced up the side stairs on the left as her security team ran up the stairs on the other side. It was only six steps to the cement dock platform, and they ran up two steps at a time. Out of the corner of her eye, she noticed that instead of staves, Leland had a knobbed shillelagh in each hand.

"Alliance Aboo!" Leland shouted.

"Ou te fasioti oe!" shouted Aliki at the same time.

Luz had no battle cry, so she beat a quick tattoo on the metal door beside her which rang out with metallic booms, much like a kettledrum.

This got the attention of the brutes that had surrounded Sebastian and Carlos. At the same time her team shouted "Muerte!" from the other side of the dock. As the intruders were attacked from both sides they turned from Carlos and Sebastian. This was a mistake they soon discovered, as the apparently beaten security men immediately attacked them from behind. At this point, other than the fact that these attackers were tall, about six and a half feet, and heavily muscled; the odds had evened out considerably.

Luz took on the first man she came close to. The arrogant and disdainful look of her opponent would have angered a less experienced fighter, but Luz actually smiled her most winning smile at him. She could see the shock in his one eye, the single eyebrow raised as high as it would go and she didn't hesitate to thrum his upraised arm with her kali sticks, even getting in a good whack at his elbow.

Now her grin became wicked as she ducked under a swing from his oversized club and thrust both sticks point first into his gut. Spinning around the arm that had instinctively clutched his stomach, she sent a rapid rat-a-tat to the bend of his knees. He couldn't turn fast enough, and she attacked his ribs from behind under the upraised arm with his club in it.

Meantime, she could hear the battle around her, almost as something faint and far away. To her, every step in this horrible dance was in slow motion. Her dance partner was slow and clumsy compared to her quick and nimble footwork. The sticks never stopped, striking again and again at the most tender and vital parts of any humanoid body. It was as if his body had become a drum and she the percussionist. As she swung around again from his back to his club hand side, she swung with all her might at the man's elbow.

With a cry he dropped his club and turned to face her, which was a mistake. This whirling, encircling move was much like a ballerina's pirouette. Only instead of graceful arms artfully outstretched, Luz held pain in her hands. Once again she struck at the ribs on the other side of the man's body. By this time, he was in pain and enraged, flailing out a large fist, but he never made contact. She thrust one staff hard under his raised arm directly into the armpit and as the pain bent him nearly in two, she followed through with a forceful blow to the back of his neck. He fell like a ripe mango onto the ground, still as death.

Luz sincerely hoped she hadn't killed him; not out of any compassion on her part, but she really did want to know why these brutes were here on her plantation and if there were more on the way.

Panting, she looked quickly around her. Several of the brutes were either on the ground unconscious like their fellow or still fighting against greater and greater odds. For, as each foe was downed, the defenders instantly ganged up on an intruder who was already in a ferocious fight. At this point it was two on one and, in one case, three on one. She was about to join in with Sebastian and Carlos on a particularly large specimen when she heard shouts from behind her.

Down the harvest road pelted a large group of Alliance troopers with Mustapha and Juan at their head. When the brutes who were already outnumbered noticed the reinforcements rushing toward them, they immediately raised hands in surrender and plunked themselves down in a submissive seated posture on the cement floor of the dock.

Juan vaulted, pushing up with one muscular arm onto the dock. "Mi amor, are you ok?"

It touched her that his first concern was always for her. She let him pull her into his arms. "I think we managed. Fortunately, I don't think we killed many of them. Shall we take them into the harvest barn and see what's going on here?"

Already the troopers were securing the prisoners, those who were conscious. Victor rolled up one of the three large metal doors and some of the troopers began dragging the unconscious ones inside.

In the meantime, Mustapha was seeing to the wounds of Carlos and Sebastian. "Nothing too serious; nothing broken, but I think they should spend some time in the hot tub and then get a massage. Fortunately, I am trained in such. I will be glad to take them back to the hacienda in the golf cart to see to this, if you would like."

"That would be very helpful, Mustapha. Thank you for your prompt action."

Mustapha put both palms together in front of him and bowed slightly. "I am grateful to be of assistance, milady Luz."

He was always so very humble and somber, Luz reflected. On the surface he often appeared stern, but the mask hid a gentle heart. Although, like all gate guardians, he was trained in martial arts he preferred to not engage in violent acts but was well versed in the healing arts using natural methods.

Aliki and Leland, on the other hand, were both still bouncing on the balls of their feet as if looking for someone else to fight.

"And THAT!" Leland, snapping his fingers, shouted at the backs of the prisoners as they trudged before the troopers into the barn, "for whatever pit ye crawled out of!"

He and Aliki high-fived one another and turned to Luz, still flushed from the battle.

"Thank you both for your assistance. I don't think we could have held them long enough for help to arrive without you."

"Ah, no, lass, ye could of taken them on with one stick behind yer back. Never mess with the mama bear. That's what I'm sayin'."

"You are tamaitai taua for sure," agreed Aliki.

"I'm sorry?" Luz inquired.

"It means warrior woman in Samoan and with such a smile on your face, as if a sunny dandelion suddenly developed poisoned thorns without changing its sunny disposition."

Luz ducked her head, embarrassed by what was obviously high praise from these two. "Thank you for your kind words. Now we must see to these alien dogs and find out what their orders were, although it appears to be pretty obvious who they are taking their orders from."

They turned and went into the shade of the harvest barn, currently only lit by the windows high up on the fifteen foot high walls. It was somewhat cooler than outside, but not by much. Large fans circulated the air so that it wouldn't get so hot as to impact the fruit they stored there.

The prisoners were sitting cross-legged against the back wall of the barn, staring straight ahead with their huge single eyes in various colors, their jaws set and their faces like so much stone. Troopers stood at parade rest facing them, one trooper per prisoner. The four unconscious ones lay on the ground next to their comrades, one trooper in front of each while one trooper checked each for pulse and breath.

At the fourth one he looked over his shoulder at Juan, shaking his head. "He didn't make it. Blow to the face, crushed his nose into the brain. I'll dispose of him after we take blood and DNA samples."

Luz and Juan exchanged looks. "No," she replied to his unspoken question. "That one isn't mine."

"We'll put them into the back of the maintenance truck and haul them to the gate. I think maybe our scientists and security team at Alliance headquarters would probably like a chance at them. The infirmary will hopefully be able to revive them.

As for this bunch, if our trooper friends would be kind enough to keep an eye on them for the moment, I will check with headquarters and see how they would like to handle this. My first impression is, based on descriptions from Burt, Elizabeth and Jenny is that these are probably Norgoth, which means somehow the Insenium once again have access to Earth."

Juan had every right to be concerned. They had sealed the Fleistian portal in the Amazon basin months ago and had it guarded night and day by the flying robots they had discovered in one of the five MDPs that had come in so handy during that conflict. These little bots could camouflage themselves and were tied into the Alliance communication network. According to their surveillance, the area around the portal remained deserted the entire time since they had cleaned it up.

In Luz's opinion, this could only mean there was another undiscovered portal that was not in the gate network, but how this was possible, she had no idea. She sighed. Like a multi-headed beast of legend, it seemed that every time they chopped off a head, two would grow in its place.

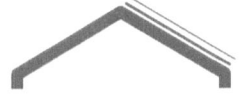

Chapter 18: Dripping in Reality

S am slung her pack on her shoulders. It was a familiar motion; one she had done many times on all of the hiking trips she had gone on with Jenny and the hiking club. That self-righteous, pig-headed, too cute for her own good, freak! She ground her teeth, a habit her mother had abhorred.

And where was her mother now? What diabolical plot had Jenny enacted on her kingdom? Was it revenge? Was it a military tactic? Were her people prisoners somewhere on Earth or on the damnable planet where the Dimensional Alliance made their headquarters? If they thought eliminating the Fleistians would prevent this dimensional war, they were sadly mistaken. She would see to it.

She marched along down the road leading to the closest large city from here. She had left Ziggy behind in the little thicket, cautioning him to be careful not to be seen. She couldn't take him with her to do what she needed to do.

Ziggy really had nowhere to go, and a tiny corner of her mind almost felt bad about leaving him there, especially after she had promised him so much to persuade him to free her. She wasn't so sure she would be back to get him anytime soon.

More than likely, he would be stuck there. But this was what she did, wasn't it? Use them up and drop them.

But she couldn't worry about this now. This needed doing, and she wasn't going to quit until she had leveraged every possible advantage to seek out Jenny and destroy her and her fellow Alliance freaks. At no time did it ever enter her mind that there was the remotest possibility she might be mistaken. No. Jenny was to blame. This was obvious. Who else could it possibly have been?

She had altered her appearance slightly to match a female Norgoth she had passed on the trail. Changing her appearance frequently was a favorite tactic of hers. It prevented anyone from tracking her with any success. It was vital that she blend in as closely as possible with the beings and culture she found herself in. She needed to find a way to get close to the seat of power. She had a plan, but it would be tricky, and she was running out of time if she wanted to be there for the final power play between the Alliance and the Great Insenium.

She encountered none of the tiny, big-eyed Inseni she was most familiar with. They had been the main contact with the Insenium for her parents, but even then, they visited seldom to oversee the Groga encampment. From time to time, King Namal had been invited to visit the "true" capitol of the Insenium ruled by Overlord Gall and it was inevitable that Sam would be taken along with her father to give her the opportunity to see and be seen by their Inseni masters, although Sam would have never considered calling them that in front of her father.

It had been a sensitive topic, to say the least. Once the Inseni marched in and basically took the Fleistian kingdom without firing a shot, King Namal had been harder and harder to get along with; not that it had ever been easy. Her mother had learned the hard way not to mention it.

He had taken her into the anteroom behind the throne dais and closed the doors behind them. When they had returned, she had been very quiet for a long time and never even hinted she knew what the Inseni was from that time on.

As Sam tramped along the road, she saw Inseni heading to the town she had just passed. She amused herself by changing her appearance from time to time as she saw an interesting face here or there. It was almost an unconscious impulse which, at this point, she didn't try to control.

Her father had often chided her for that. "You are squandering your potential with these frivolous pursuits. You must learn to control yourself. This lax behavior will lead to unhappy consequences for you and for your people."

Sam had listened, nodded somberly, and completely ignored him. What was the use of these cool abilities if they couldn't be used to amuse herself?

She loved to walk. Her long legs ate up the miles easily and this particular road was straight, even and level. She could see the city she was heading for coming closer and closer, and the air, unlike Los Angeles where she had spent so many years, was clean and refreshing.

Clean air had been one of the reasons she had looked forward to her hiking expeditions every month. She would often brave the L.A. traffic to head out to the coast and go walking out on a beach where the sea air was fresh. There were no oceans on her planet, albeit many streams and lakes. The salt air was a novelty to her.

As she neared the outskirts of the city, she settled on a particular appearance, locking it mentally into place until she chose to release it. Once she had assumed a physical aspect, she could maintain it indefinitely without having to focus on it and she was also able to call back previous personas at will.

She realized she was hungry and stopped at an inn for some food and potentially some information about what she might be getting into here. While rummaging through room after room of her home fortress as she had prepared for this venture, she had found stashes of her father's wealth in two denominations, the fiat currency of their own domain and the currency of the Inseni. She realized that Fleistian money was pretty much useless now, but the Inseni money (and there was a lot of it) could be very handy to get what she needed to get into the right places to make her plan workable.

The persona she had chosen was that of a well-to-do merchant she had passed on the road a mile or so before she got to the outskirts. Her long black hair was braided over one shoulder. She was tall, although not quite as tall as Sam was in her Sam or Engoza personas. Her clothing: a long flowing tunic with leggings that felt somewhat like Earthly corduroy and high-topped boots that overlapped the leggings up to her knee were of soft greens and browns. Around her neck she wore a medallion, which Sam immediately removed in case it had some recognizable house emblem.

Sam chose a table along a wall that faced the entrance. She wanted to be able to see those who were coming and going from this place. She had chosen it because it looked like a well-used traveler's stop. It was amazing what you could learn about an area by just listening in a place like this.

The Inseni, although they were capable of mindspeech, didn't use it much amongst their selves. This meant Sam had been able to pick it up easily as a child visiting the area with her father. There did not seem to be dialects or any recognizable accents among this people. The strict laws and upbringing of this people were evident in the lack of defining regional customs or traditions you often saw on other planets.

As a result, Sam didn't stand out at all in this crowd. Muted colors (albeit not the milksop pastels of the Inseni of Peril's realm) were evident everywhere, including their architecture and décor. Sam had admittedly quickly become enamored with the bright colors available on Earth. When she had gotten her first car, it was the red one she chose. All of her clothing had included bright color accents as well.

The server returned with her meal and Sam tuned into the conversations around her as she ate.

"My son went to see the recruiter last week and good riddance. It's about time he made himself useful. You know the families of recruits get a cash bonus as soon as they complete their training? I sure hope he doesn't mess it up. I could use a new..."

"Business is good since the conscriptions began. We have tripled our sales of basic equipment. I have to order in more knapsacks and boots. People want to equip their young ones well to be sure they make it through their training. It's brilliant that the government requires the families who can to equip their soldiers. I'd better order in more water skins as well..."

"How long will you be gone? We've only just been betrothed, and now you're leaving? Oh, Renar, what will I do without you?"

This last was from a young lady seated across a table from a square built young man. She clasped both of his hands as she spoke. He merely shook his head and looked down at the table in front of him, not willing to look into her pleading face.

A sampling of other conversations proved Sam's previous assumptions to be correct. The Great Insenium was gearing up, and they were conscripting actively from among their own people. She wondered why. She would have thought that between their elite guard and the Groga they had ample resources.

She knew there were other slave populations besides the Groga who were conscripted for supplemental forces. Something was definitely afoot. She took her time eating her meal, which was the common meal for the most part anywhere you went on this planet. She suspected it would be duplicated in every society formed by the Great Insenium.

They adored consistency. Being the same as everyone else was the goal of every loyal member of the Great Inseni Empire. Standing out was not just frowned upon. Those who chose to be different were not only shunned, depending on the type of aberrant behavior, they were often imprisoned or enslaved and, in some cases eliminated entirely and publicly in the most gruesome way possible.

Attendance at local executions was mandatory to every citizen, and every effort was made to be clear about why they had to be eliminated as a danger to the entire Inseni society. The constant indoctrination of "safety in sameness" was begun in the cradle and continued to the grave in one way or another.

When she could no longer dawdle at her table without appearing suspicious, she tipped the server moderately, as over-generosity was considered unusual behavior. She headed back out onto the street, which led to the main thoroughfare. The streets were broad with areas for walking on either side of the street, but no curbed sidewalks. The entire area was paved with a concrete type substance. Walking areas were designated by a six inch wide stripe.

Wheeled vehicles were both of the two wheeled type, similar to a bicycle and the multi-wheeled type with 4 to 8 wheels depending on the length of the vehicle and were powered by people pedaling them. There were even some that were simply pushed or pulled by people, similar to a handcart as the pioneers often used to traverse Earth during one point of United States history.

Sam knew they had the technology to have motorized vehicles, if they desired, but Gall preferred to use that level of tech only for his war machine, which ultimately took the majority of the goods and resources created by his people.

Sam had to admit she missed her little Smart Car. She didn't miss the rush hour traffic, however. She could have rented a small personal vehicle either of the two-wheeled or four-wheeled variety at a local public transport area, but she preferred to walk for the moment.

It gave her a chance to review her plan in the quiet of her thoughts as she walked and also to get an idea of the temperament of the city. For although sameness was the goal, she had noticed that the mood of a place changed based on what was happening and how it was slanted for reception by the masses. Crowd mentality definitely had to be taken into consideration.

For now, there only seemed to be the usual bustle of people getting things done. Sam had to hand it to the Great Inseni, they were productive. There was no such thing as a "four day work week" among them. They would have been appalled of the very idea of three days of unscheduled and unproductive time in a given week. Their weeks were six days long, but the principle still applied. There was no such thing as idle recreation. The closest they ever came to that were the competitions between the military units for best maneuvers, marksmanship, and combat skills.

Even with those competitions, the crowds that observed them did so silently, never cheering or applauding as that would have singled an individual out for their accomplishment, which violated the doctrine of sameness. There was also no grading in schools. It was strictly pass and fail. You continued at an educational path for a specific time until you succeeded. If, within that time, you did not succeed, you were simply "reclassified" as a candidate for a craft or manual labor.

The only show of public pride that was encouraged was pride in the fact that they were not prideful and that their form of government was superior to all others. They didn't even consider it a government for that matter. The Inseni simply were what they were and were led entirely by Gall and his minions. This didn't prevent maneuvering to rise in that power structure, however. Toadies and sycophants abounded, carefully dancing the steps of the dance before them.

This was a very dangerous path for any to take, so only a few ever attempted it. More heads were removed for taking a wrong step than in any other thing under Gall's reign. There was no concept of a trial or any adjudication other than Gall's will. You were either guilty or not and if you were, you paid the consequence and, assuming he didn't just kill you outright, you never had any inclination to make that particular mistake again. So, at least outwardly, none gave any sign of any discontent or disagreement with any of the clearly outlined policies of their culture.

Rewards from Gall's hand were always subtle and never trumpeted by the recipients. These consisted primarily of a step up in the hierarchy, but were never presented as such. That would have been prideful and therefore unacceptable. These rewards were humbly accepted and then life continued as if it had always been that way.

Compliance and obedience were taken for granted, so when someone succeeded at something, it was only what was expected. Sam admitted to herself that she had enjoyed the bit of the spotlight she was able to bask in with her job in the media as she stalked Jenny. She was praised highly for her skills and had been up for a promotion, a concept previously foreign to her. The praise she had received earlier in her college career had been equally invigorating. They had no idea she wasn't just another twenty-something, moving forward in her life, with little experience or understanding.

Her professors had petted her and praised her extensively for her accomplishments. Had she been able to be honest with them, she could have told them that most of the concepts they were teaching were juvenile and beneath her, but she played her part and just missed the valedictorian by only a few points, losing once again to Jenny smarty-pants. One more thing added to her growing list of reasons to hate Jenny.

She arrived at the gathering square, one of several throughout the large city. This was a place of instruction and oftentimes public executions. There was no "market-place" or "town-square" as other cultures would describe it. This was strictly for weekly town meetings broadcast onto a large screen suspended over a large platform at one end of the area. There were also no seats. There was no need for such softness here.

Elderly or disfigured or any other helpless individuals were simply "euthanized" quietly and were not mourned. Every person you would ever see in this realm was "normal" and ordinary. If a person didn't have the ability to stand for an hour and hear the important communications from their leadership, they weren't fit to contribute to society and were therefore useless and redundant.

For now, the square was unoccupied, and Sam's attention wandered to her real destination. It wasn't exactly an embassy, as you were either an enemy or a sworn vassal to the Great Insenium. No planet or dimension would be classified in any other way. But this was the one place she might be able to get some answers. She knew her father kept an official representative of the Fleistians there. She knew the importance of approaching Gall through the chain of command. No one had any business skipping any step in the official policy.

The building was large, but no more imposing than any of the other adobe-like buildings she passed on her way through the city. There was only one architectural style here, simple and utilitarian. There were no carvings or ornamentation on any of the surfaces she passed, and windows were just that...window glass inset into a wall; no window-boxes or shutters or even molding.

She walked up the broad steps, still in her semblance of the merchant woman. She didn't want to reveal her true nature until she was more certain of the circumstances. She met few people going in and out of the building. Several dozen planets and dimensions were represented here, if you could call it representation. It was more like they were a conduit for information, namely demands from the Inseni and reports of compliance from the dominions of the Great Insenium.

Sam's father, King Namal, had worried about her mind being polluted by the Earthlings and the representatives of the cursed Alliance. He had been right to be concerned. Sam found herself sucked in, to the point that she sometimes regretted she couldn't just stay and be Sam. Obviously, that hadn't been possible, and she often privately chastised herself for her weakness in being enticed by the flagrancy of Earth cultures.

It didn't vary much from one country to another. Of course, the cultures were varied, and their traditions were often unique on one point or the other. India had been particularly interesting, she thought. She had enjoyed her part there as an Indian street vendor, haggling and hawking her goods to passers-by. Playing Indira had been fun, but not as fun as playing Sam. She hadn't been sad when she had completed her mission to subvert Guaray and get him to take on a gate by the murder of a gate guardian.

She had accomplished that before her assignments of Lizzie and Jenny. Jenny had been her first true failure. Curse her soul.

She found all relatively quiet in the building and made her way to the third floor office of her people...Except it wasn't there. The door was not locked. (Locks didn't exist in this place. Street crime and thievery was virtually unknown, and no one ever got a chance to make a career of it.) She entered to find not a single stick of furniture. The room was clean and empty. The lack of dust on the floor was no clue one way or the other. None of the buildings in this place would ever be anything but spotless.

Puzzled, she retraced her steps. Perhaps the Fleistians had been given a larger or smaller space in the building. She noticed a man with cleaning supplies on a small rolling cart moving up one hallway.

"Excuse me," Sam said, stopping him with a gesture. "I seem to be turned around. Can you give me directions to the Fleistian embassy office?"

The Norgoth man eyed her up and down and finding nothing unusual about her said, "I think you must have been away for a while. The Fleistians no longer have any offices here or anywhere else. Where have you been that you didn't know this?"

Sam didn't answer him. "Thank you," she said vaguely and continued down the hallway out into the sunlight.

Chapter 19: Cha-cha-cha

They were arguing again. Jenny gently reached back and rubbed the back of her head. It was healing, but even then, these days she often got serious headaches. This was definitely the part she hated most about her role in all of this. Part of her just wanted to shout, "STOP IT!" It wouldn't have done any good, of course, but that didn't stop her from thinking it several times a day.

Their arrival in the Groga capital city had been pleasant enough. Everyone treated Jenny with respect, although she often wondered if any of that would have happened if she hadn't had Chidwi on her shoulder.

However, the past several days had been one disagreement after another. Not between her and the Groga, but between differing factions among the Groga themselves. It wasn't even about whether or not they wanted to separate from domination of the Fleistians or the Inseni, but how it was to be accomplished. What had seemed simple to her from the beginning was appearing more and more complicated.

All the Groga agreed that it was time to end their enslavement, but not all could agree on the means or whether they even wanted the help of the Alliance. To many, it seemed too much like what they had already experienced at the hands of their former masters.

Jenny tried to explain that they got to choose in the matter and as long as they didn't actively oppose the Alliance or attack them, they wouldn't be in any danger from them. The majority seemed to like the idea of joining forces, so to speak, but didn't like the idea of not actively fighting. To their warrior's minds, this was cowardice, and they had a hard time seeing where simply defending their planet would be any real contribution to the war.

Still others wanted to follow Jenny's every suggestion as part of the transference of their adoration of Chidwi to Jenny. This made Jenny uncomfortable, and she made a conscious choice to never take advantage of that.

She had gotten so used to the orderly agreement that seemed to pervade her work with her team. She knew that none of them were panderers or toadies, but Jenny now wondered how that had happened the way it had.

Mostly she just felt tired and her head hurt. Truth be told, she was still recovering from her head wound. Although the wound itself had closed over and no longer required bandaging, she still wasn't feeling completely like herself.

Both Chidwi and Freia had assured her that her headaches would eventually go away, that no permanent damage had been done, but Jenny was impatient to get on with it. She doubted she could even last through a quarterstaff match, much less tag her opponent. Sure, the likelihood she would need to was pretty small, based on the fact that she was never without one or more competent guards, but she had liked the feeling that came from being able to defend herself.

And when it came to that, she realized that in a fight she had only come off conqueror once and that had been with the very skilled help of her bodyguards. She had been so cocky about it and now she wondered what would have happened if they had not been there to support her. Sometimes she just felt like a fraud.

She came out of her rueful contemplation as Burt stood and brought his fist down on the table in front of them.

"*Enough!*" he bellowed in mindspeech. "*We don't have time for all of this petty bickering. And one way or the other, this thing is going to happen with or without your help. We are offering you our assistance to defend your planet, which you will now have to do with or without us.*

You have offended the Insenium, something I doubt they will take lightly. You don't have the resources to field an offensive, and you don't have the knowledge or tools necessary to transport yourselves about in the multiverse. You aren't even in the same dimension as these people. So quit blustering and start planning, for heaven's sake.

If you decide to defend without us, we won't stop you. We've already made that plain. We have no desire to make your choices for you or to force you to do anything. So, either step up and let's do something productive or we'll haul ourselves back to the Alliance and get on with eliminating the Inseni threat without you."

Jenny smoothed her face and tried to act as if this was all part of the plan, but she was hard-pressed to do so. She had never seen Burt actually angry and even now, she felt this was a calculated move on his part, however sincere. She hadn't expected this. She knew Burt had a lot more experience in these things and now hoped with all her heart that this wouldn't perhaps create the opposite of the desired effect.

However, the Groga paused in mid argument and all eyes were on Burt. Jenny saw shock, but not anger in those faces. These high end government officials were obviously not used to being spoken to in that way, especially by a non-Groga and a puny one at that.

"Look. I get it. You've been enslaved for a long time by beings you thought were there to help you. When you realized you were in a trap, it was too late, or so you thought, to change things without devastation to your families.

Where I come from, we experienced a similar situation. The people were being burdened and taxed by people who should have been their supporters. Finally, when they could take it no more, they appointed a leader and fought back. But they couldn't do it on their own. Allies came to their aid and after much hardship and many lives lost on both sides, they were able to establish their independence. That didn't solve all of their problems, but they were an independent nation with their own laws and leaders.

Their allies in that war remained their friends but did not interfere with their choices or afterward with their government. We want to be for you what those allies of ours were for us. We want to support your bid for liberty.

My ancestors took the counsel and accepted the resources offered by their allies. The Dimensional Alliance wants nothing to do with your government on this planet or within your dimension. Our only desire in this is to free the multiverse from the tyranny of the Great Insenium. Can we agree on that and then move forward to assist you in defending your people wherever we find them?

I know you are concerned for the Groga who still live under the thumb of the Inseni. Wherever possible, we will free them and enable them to return to you and strengthen your people by their return. Can we cease the bickering for a moment and at least agree on that?"

Jenny had not ever thought she would see a Groga show open shame, but one and all the Groga cast their eyes to the table in front of them, heads drooping. The silence was deafening and seemed to stretch out forever. Finally, Anwhal raised his head and looked into Burt's eyes as he stood there calmly, waiting for their decision.

"We have lost sight of why we are gathered here today. Burt Scout is right. We can't move forward in this without a foundation of trust. Do we trust the Alliance or not? Once they discovered where we live, they could have easily wiped us out. They have the technology and numbers to have done that, and they wouldn't have even had to touch one foot on our planet to do so.

They are willing to guard the space around our planet and aren't asking anything in return. Jenny and Chidwi have pledged their honor to us and have brought these confederates to our aid. Can our honor stand the test? Can we decide that we can be compatriots in this cause without being subservient? Will we? My brothers, we must choose."

One by one they stood fist to heart, looking directly at Burt. The High Groga, Lenwhal, stood last. *"You have our pledge and our honor in this,"* he sent soberly. *"My honest apology for our misunderstanding. Your words ring true, Burt Scout. Let us begin anew. Tell us your plan again and help us to understand the reasoning. We will listen and we will help with that plan with the understanding that we are now a free people and we will not be slaves again."*

Jenny was amazed at the power and conviction that she had felt from Burt. Although she knew he could at times be manipulative when the situation required it, she also knew that he sincerely believed in what the Dimensional Alliance stood for and he would willingly put himself in danger again and again if that meant accomplishing his mission.

"Then please sit and let's get this done. Our time is short, and we have to use our time and resources wisely if we are going to pull this off. As I told you before, we can't guarantee anything at this point, no mortal could. What we will promise is that we won't quit on you and we will put our hearts into it."

This means as much to us as it does to you. Every dimension is threatened by this and all of us are putting our lives on the line. All of us are sacrificing for this. The Dimensional Alliance has already lost many good people in this endeavor. As a famous patriot of the war I told you about in my country once said, 'We must, indeed, all hang together or, most assuredly, we shall all hang separately.' I believe this to be true in this case as well."

Burt sat. To the surprise of all of them, Chidwi broadcasted to the group, "*Burt Scout is correct. Only by every dimension uniting their strength will this ultimate evil be deposed once and for all. True strength isn't the ability to bully someone into submission or to terrorize weaker beings just because we are able. True strength is found in complete unity of mind, body, and spirit. If you will be allies and you wish to be successful, you must present a united front. It's the only thing a bully will understand, and Gall and his minions are nothing but bullies, when it comes down to it.*

My kind has agreed to be a part of this. We are peaceful and gentle beings. It is our nature, but this evil cannot be allowed to continue. For this reason, there will be one of us in each city and town. We will bond with a Groga of our choice and give counsel and help you fight when it is necessary. Once again the Linklings and the Groga will live together in peace."

The Groga seated around the long table in the huge counsel room looked stunned. Once more Jenny marveled at the influence Chidwi's kind had over these people she had once considered brutish and cruel.

"*Since we are in agreement,*" Jenny said immediately. "*Let's get this done.*"

All heads nodded and the true planning was finally underway.

Chapter 20: By Scale, Claw and Fang

Liliath looked up at the big screen hanging before her in the air. All of the members in the Grand Council of the Dimensional Alliance were in attendance. In the council chambers and senates of every member of the Alliance, beings were gathered around similar screens. Before her was every representative of every member dimension. Some of the gatherings were small. In Sanglarka, and the gates where the Earth teams resided, for instance only the guardians were present. This was typical of nonmember dimensions where their people in general had no idea the Alliance even existed. Jenny was in attendance via the connection they had put in orbit around the Groga world, along with her retinue and the officials of the Groga government.

That had been a necessary exception to the rules regarding Alliance membership. They would be working closely with the top Groga and their military advisors, as they had intel that would potentially prove vital to the Alliance effort to permanently dislodge The Great Insenium.

Those gathered in the room before her sat silently exchanging greetings and having multiple mindspeech conversations. The only sound in the chamber was the rustling of feathers or those shifting or fidgeting in their seating arrangements. Any being witnessing this gathering and unacquainted with the true diversity of the beings of the Dimensional Alliance would have been astounded at the spectrum of body types from humanoid to those not recognizable as intelligent beings at first glance.

Finally, she stood, and all rustling ceased, and every eye, for those who had them, was riveted on her.

She had known the time would come when she would stand in this place, as Chief Councilor, but she regretted with all of her heart that it was not Ingot who stood here now instead. She missed him so much and still had not finished grieving for him.

"Fellow beings and representatives of the Dimensional Alliance, I bid you welcome on this grim day. We are about to declare open war against a formidable foe; how formidable we did not know until recently and they may yet prove to be much more than we had initially believed.

Our newest intelligence tells us that we have been drawn into a conflict that may not fully succeed in our lifetimes, which for many of us are very long. The Great Insenium ruled by the beings who call themselves 'Norgoths' is a vast entity, rivaling, in some ways, even the combined forces of the Dimensional Alliance.

They are developing a weapon, not the one we thought of at first, but something so terrible as to bring every dimension to their knees. Our sources tell us that if we do not strike them soon, the weapon will be completed and our chances for success will be reduced drastically. Thanks to the teams of the Earth gates and the efforts of The Gatekeeper, as well as the ongoing support from all members of the Alliance, we have a usable plan in place. The Gatekeeper has secured the aid of the Groga.

Based on reports of our agents in the Great Insenium, they do not yet realize that the Groga planet is in rebellion. They still hold hostage a few million Groga who have been stationed throughout their domain, however.

Therefore, one important part of our plan is to infiltrate the Groga armies still held by the Insenium with Groga from their home world. If possible they will convince their Groga relations to also rebel against their captors. A vital part of our plan is to have all Groga lay down their weapons of war at the same time, thus crippling that portion of the Inseni strategy.

The Groga government has agreed to this, for which we are grateful. It is the desire of this Council to see the Groga people establish themselves as a sovereign entity and allow their culture to return to its roots of peace and productivity with the freedom to choose their path going forward. We thank the Groga leadership for their help which, although it will mean stepping back from the fight and to only fight defensively, will be intrinsic to the success of eliminating the Inseni threat.

This part of the plan will require our space fleet to be in active operation to protect the Groga home world, as we believe the Inseni will immediately divert some of their own space fleet to attempt to wipe them out as soon as they realize that they are actively in rebellion. This we will not allow.

We have located what we believe are the coordinates to most of the Inseni inhabited worlds, many of which are outside their home dimension. In the meantime, the Earth Science and Technology team, alongside Alliance scientists have developed some nasty surprises in addition to the Groga rebellion. Using a combination of Daringi abilities and the new uses of MDP technology, we can now transport huge numbers of troops, equipment, and weapons instantaneously and with pinpoint accuracy to the various battle fronts.

Fighting a war on multiple fronts is a risky and complex task, but with the ingenuity, diligence, and courage of our combined forces, I believe we can do this. The Strategy and Tactics team comprised of those chosen for that team in Sanglarka and military experts from across the dimensions are integrating the many technological advances from our various science teams in ways that frankly astound me.

Assignments have been sent digitally to every participating dimension. I know there are those of you whose personal beliefs do not allow aggressive actions of any kind. For this reason, we are especially grateful for your willingness to provide supplies and medical aid to our troops as well as to any beings potentially displaced by this conflict.

All of you should know and understand that our intent is to do as much harm to the enemy as we can with the least potential damage to those who are peripheral to the conflict. We know there will be unavoidable death and destruction, but our desire is to execute this war with the absolute least losses while still being sure to eliminate the threat.

Stage one of this war is intended to do two things: First to find and destroy their means of launching their new weapon, and second to create so much chaos and disharmony among their forces and their government as to effectively restrain them from expanding their empire further. The entire elimination of the threat will, as I have said, take much longer and we need to recognize that and accept it.

I hope with all my heart to be wrong about the length of the conflict, but we must be realistic. The scope of the holdings of the Great Insenium is vast and we don't know what new tricks they might have up their collective sleeves.

We also don't want them to know what's in our repertoire. For this reason, we will not be too specific in this briefing. Your instructions and missions as well as equipment and resources will arrive through gates via secure carriers. Please do not discuss any of this over unsecured or unapproved channels.

We try to learn from our past mistakes. It is true that no channel is absolutely reliable, but we have done what we can to vet every being involved in the transfer of restricted information.

I won't keep any of you any longer. Alliance representatives will arrive through every member's primary gateway within the next day cycle, wherever you are. It might be as easy as communicating directly over the communication network, but we hope to minimize leaks of anything but what we want the enemy to know. Thank you, my dear friends. Liliath, out."

When she cut the feed, she let out a long sigh. She had always known that her position as one of the three lead councilors held great responsibility, but she became a councilor during peacetime. In the back of her mind she had known that the people of the Alliance could potentially find themselves at war once again. But she had hoped with all her heart that it wouldn't be during her fifteen year assignment.

Now here she was, the Chief Councilor and before her time. The loss of Ingot and Myla had been such a blow, and she admittedly didn't feel prepared for this. For a moment she sympathized with Jenny. How much less prepared was this youngling? And yet she had taken on her responsibilities admirably.

Of course, neither she nor the Gatekeeper was faultless. Jenny was young and more apt to take chances than Liliath. So far, although her reasoning had been sound, the risks she had undertaken without counseling with any of those who would be willing to guide her, including Tarafau, her official Guide, were higher than any of them had expected.

Now Liliath looked out over those assembled before her. She could feel her councilors seated behind her, focusing their energy to support her and she was grateful for the choices she had made under such stressful circumstances.

"*Brothers and sisters, for so I consider you, each and every one; please attend to your people. Thank you so much for your show of support. Please send any further questions you have or any suggestions to the Chief Council communications account. I dismiss you now to your various areas of responsibility. Let us prosecute this war with a common mind and heart. I retire to the private council room for those of you who have appointments to speak with us.*"

The entire grand council stood in respect. Liliath turned and exited through the special door at the back of the dais along with her two assistant councilors. Ascending on the elevator, she sighed once again. Her work for the day was only beginning.

In the private council chamber, she settled into the chaise that had been specially made for her. Arranged before the dais were two similar chaises to accommodate her first appointment of the day. Her councilors seated themselves and about the same time, two Donalian representatives arrived from the Alani parliament of her home world. Fendal and Beren were well known to her, respected elders in her land.

"*Greetings,*" she sent in mindspeech as her two councilors were not well versed in her language. "*I have some urgent messages for you to pass on to our parliament. I had originally intended only for the Alani to supply support via equipment and resources, but I have considered and realized that Earth is not the only planet or dimension explored by our people and their legends all tell of us as formidable warriors to be reckoned with. The more I considered this, the more I realized that we must take a more active part in the fighting.*"

Fendal and Beren both nodded approvingly. "*The consensus of parliament is of the same mind. We can add shock value to the ground forces and our unique mental abilities could turn the tide of a battle. This is not the time to be retiring, nor should we allow our fellow beings to make such sacrifices without doing our part. We are relieved to hear you say this, as we were prepared to argue strongly for it.*"

"*We are all in agreement,*" Beren added. "*The voting was unanimous to approach you about this. We have ten thousand Alani troops ready and awaiting orders.*"

Liliath was deeply touched. *"Then by scale, fang and claw, let us decide the best way to deploy them."* Her mind much relieved, she began to outline her plan.

Chapter 21: Groga Going Forward

Anyone watching Burt would have thought he was thoroughly engaged with the piece of wood he was whittling as he sat on a barrel next to the door to the cottage that housed Jenny's retinue. The Groga had been generous with their hospitality. Jenny was inside, deep in communication with the Alliance council. She did this at the same time every day. He was concerned about the burdens constantly being added to her to-do list. He knew it was necessary, he just wished he could somehow carry more of the load. For now, he was on guard duty, such as it was.

Anyone thinking he was all she had, however, would be sadly mistaken. Inside were four highly trained females who could lick anything less than a platoon of armed soldiers, and he wasn't even sure about that. Jenny's bodyguards were fierce and dedicated professionals, and this was magnified by the love they had for the Gatekeeper. Elizabeth was her adopted sister and a well-trained martial artist. He wouldn't want to be the being that entered unannounced.

In addition to these were Freia and Grephan, both assigned to Jenny by Anwhal, the High Groga-ha, and commander of all the Groga forces. Their orders had been clear. Defend Jenny with their lives and honor and see to her comfort and care.

The cottage was situated just outside the walls of Groga administration, their version of a guest suite. Freia cooked all of her meals, tasting every dish herself before it was served to Jenny. Grephan took turns with Burt standing a few shifts each day outside of the cottage. BaaGah had also budded again and one of his Mookookie kids bonded to Jenny, which gave Noony someone to play with. The other Mookookie buds were assigned to each of the bodyguards to their obvious delight.

The Mookookie were pulling their weight when they weren't eating everything they could get their little hands on. They spent most of their time in the spaces in one or another piece of clothing of their "buddies" as they called the people they had bonded to. Like Burt, Jenny's Mookookie, Lolly, spent most of his time in the flesh-colored wrist band that obscured her MDP.

Despite his outward casual appearance, Burt was aware of every movement in the paved street in front of the cottage. As usual, when he was on guard duty, BaaGah was concealed as a shield over his torso, something he called "hardening the spaces". The little creature was so much more than anyone would judge by looking at the funny looking little guy. Burt was sure he still didn't know the extent of his talents. Every time he thought he did, BaaGah would spring something new on him.

Generally, the passersby were servants, couriers, and suppliers. Of course, there were military everywhere. The Groga were hurriedly preparing for war and they were dead serious about it. Not surprising since they risked total annihilation if they didn't get this right the first time out of the box.

Today the delegation from the Daringi would arrive. They would show up inside the cottage to reduce the drama of appearing out of seemingly thin air inside the council hall. A Groga delegation would escort them to the hall; where they would begin the war council. Burt expected Tarafau would be a part of the delegation as he had been appointed by his people to lead the Daringi on all fronts of this many-faceted war plan.

Burt knew that their enemies were deep in planning as well. The revolution on the Inseni capitol or what they had thought was the Inseni capitol had shaken them. He was sure the Inseni had expected a confrontation, but not there, and not by the slaves. As far as Burt could tell, the Great Inseni, the true leaders of the Insenium, had not yet determined that the Groga were involved, but that wouldn't last long. Any time now they would figure it out and it wouldn't take them long to act.

But with the help of the Daringi and the Alliance space fleet that was already hidden in a nearby asteroid belt, Burt felt assured they could do right by the Groga. The brilliant part of the strategy was that it would hopefully neutralize at least a part of the Insenium space fleet right off the bat and coordinated attacks by units from all over the Alliance would then cause chaos and instability among the Norgoths and the leadership of the Great Insenium. At least, this was what they had planned for.

They knew that even with the victories they may accrue during the coming battles. There were too many branches and tendrils of the Great Insenium domain for them to get it all. There would be constant battles for many years, potentially hundreds of years across the dimensions before this was over.

A tapping on the glass window behind him got his attention. In the window, Nona beckoned to him. It was time. Grephan came out the door, and they passed one another with nearly identical grins. Grephan had been practicing perfecting that grin when he had noticed how well Burt used it to his advantage. Burt sighed; another youngster corrupted by the enchanting draw of adventure.

"*They've arrived.*" Grephan sent. "*That was amazing. One second just the usual people were there and the next...*"

"Yeah," Burt agreed. "*They are pretty amazing, and you should see them fight.*"

"*I hope to,*" Grephan sent, his eyes alight with youthful enthusiasm. "*I am still trying to convince my father to allow me to enlist in the Groga force. I want to be a bigger part of this.*"

"*Actually, you'll probably see more action if you stick with us, Grephan. Jenny is a major target for the Insenium. She's going to need every one of us by her side.*"

"*I never thought of that,*" Grephan replied with a light in his eyes. "*You're right. I shall stay here and defend the Disciple and the Honored One.*"

Burt nodded and fired off a cocky salute in the Groga style, fist to chest.

As he had hoped, Tarafau was there with his cousin Desminda and a half dozen Daringi he hadn't met yet. He stuck out his hand and Tarafau shook it with enthusiasm, pounding him on the back at the same time. Burt tried hard not to gasp, but it was no use. Tarafau grinned at him wickedly.

"*So good to see you, Burt; I can see you're staying in shape.*"

"*I'm working on it,*" Burt replied, panting. "*I can see you're still in fighting condition. Glad to see you too. If anyone can help get the Groga ready for the coming conflict, it is you and your people.*"

"*Let's go to the council chambers,*" Jenny broke in, all business. "*The sooner we get the introductions over with, the sooner we can get down to it.*"

Tarafau raised one eyebrow. So, Burt wasn't the only one who could see the change in her. In the past week she had become laser focused on her tasks and it was taking a toll. She seldom joked with her bodyguards anymore. When she consulted Lizziebot, it was always about nit-picky details about the various combatants, and she found herself frustrated with the lack of current information. After all Lizzie had died before this conflict began and had served in a time of relative peace in the dimensions.

"*We are ready, Jenny. It's good to see you safe and functioning effectively in your calling.*" Tarafau said wryly. "*Let us see what the Groga have to say and what we can do to help them.*"

They left, her bodyguards bracketing her side to side as well as one in the back. Elizabeth walked between Tarafau and Desminda, and the Daringi ranged themselves behind as a sort of rear guard. Burt strode along between Jenny and Mynn, his eyes constantly moving, his ears alert for any unusual sound.

They arrived at the door to the council chambers un-assaulted as Burt had hoped, but not assumed; never where Jenny was concerned. His assumptions in the past had nearly proven fatal to him and to her. He would take no chances.

Perhaps he had changed as well as Jenny. He still put on his casual demeanor, but he was dead serious about seeing her safe. The only problem is that she didn't confide her plans in him as she had in the past. How could he keep her safe if he had no idea what was going on in that mop head of hers?

Her hair was growing back into soft curls framing her face. It made her look innocent and harmless, especially with those deep blue eyes of hers. He dared not tousle her hair playfully as he wanted to, however. Her playful side seemed to be buried deep within her, and Burt admitted that this was a blow to him. He would stand by her regardless, but he was afraid of what this conflict and her role in it was doing to her.

Anwhal met them at the door to the chambers. *"Welcome, honored guests and advisors. Please enter and let us acquaint ourselves. Our leaders are ready to get to work. I hope you are rested and ready to go."*

"Indeed," sent Tarafau. *"I have been looking forward to it. Jenny has briefed us thoroughly up to this point and we have come prepared first to listen and then to aide you in making the vital decisions that will hopefully mean the difference between success and failure."*

"Agreed," Anwhal bowed slightly and gestured for their party to precede him through the doors.

Inside the chamber at the huge council table were the Great Groga-ha of the Groga nation, his councilors and three other military officials in addition to Anwhal. Seats at the table had been provided for Tarafau, Desminda, Jenny and Burt with additional chairs on either side of the table for their entourage.

"We welcome the Daringi to our council of war," Merdahl began by way of greeting. *"We understand you have many things to teach us and many resources to allow us to better protect our land. We also understand that in all things, the final say about any plans that are made here will be ours. Am I correct in this?"*

"Indeed," Tarafau agreed somberly, his large hands clasped on the table before him. *"It is never our intent to force anything on you at any time. You can even refuse our help completely, if that is your final decision, and we will leave you peacefully to manage on your own."*

The Groga were large and stocky, but nearly a head shorter than the Daringi before them. They showed no signs of being impressed or intimidated, however.

It suddenly dawned on Burt he was witnessing the inside workings of an epic battle like no other before. He was somewhat in awe of this fact, considering his age and lack of any military training or experience. He put his business face on, however. He would never let any of that show to anyone.

He glanced at Jenny. She sat straight-backed, her face showing no emotion except attentive respect. Behind her, her three bodyguards and Elizabeth could have been carved from stone. Each face was intent on the events playing out before them, on hyper-alert if anything should get out of hand. Elizabeth's briefing had been that her job was to whisk Jenny away to Sanglarka if at any point anything went seriously wrong.

Tarafau's soldiers, seated behind the Groga councilors along with equal numbers of their military, were not stone. They were like jungle cats, ready to spring, every muscle in readiness. He wondered if the Groga had any idea that they could actually become jungle cats if they so chose.

As they went through the formalities, introducing one another and stating the purpose of the meeting, Burt scrutinized every face, every nuance of body language, how they presented themselves. It was what he did.

He had always had a knack of "reading" the people around him. Nothing supernatural or mystical, he just seemed to have an instinct for it. He was seldom wrong about his impressions of the people he met, and he also seemed to know the best way to approach a particular person to get what he wanted based on what he observed.

Merdahl was obviously impatient to get on with things, but he went through the motions. The High Groga-ha was doing much like Burt, apparently focusing intently on each face as they were all introduced. He particularly focused on Tarafau, immediately recognizing that this was the person to pay attention to. He treated Jenny with respect, but she was, after all very young and a woman at that.

Burt had witnessed that the Groga women were not subservient and definitely not oppressed, but they did have some very clear roles in the Groga society, and leadership in formal government bodies wasn't generally one of them.

He found it significant that the High Groga-ha was never addressed by name, only by title or "Great One". Burt wasn't clear about the hierarchy of the Groga political system, but evidently when it came down to it, the High Groga-ha had the final say.

When the niceties had been performed, Tarafau wasted no time cutting right to the issue at hand, the coming assault by the Insenium. First, he introduced them to the abilities of the Daringi, so they would have a clear idea why it was a good idea to receive their aid. He had Elizabeth transport Jenny to the house on Infinity Loop and back to demonstrate. The Groga were suitably impressed.

Secondly, he laid out several battle strategies that they could possibly choose from or even use in combination.

Finally, he turned the discussion over to the High Groga-ha. This was clever of Tarafau, as one of the concerns of the Groga was that the Alliance was here to dominate them. They were adamant they wouldn't ever go on that path again.

As Burt observed the give and take, he gained a new respect for Tarafau's abilities and how his hundreds of years of experience made him the perfect person to work with the Groga. He also realized that although he had become fairly skilled in negotiation due to his natural abilities, he could learn a great deal from this man and his respect for his friend grew substantially.

They never broke for lunch or anything, with the exception of a very few 15-minute breaks. Food was brought in by servants and they ate as they talked, barely even noticing the food that had been set before them. Everyone had some input into the plan, and he could see the Groga begin to relax in the process, realizing, finally, that their own experience and opinions were being respected and that the needs of the Groga as a people were the first priority of the Alliance representatives.

By the time they were done, late into the night, they had a solid plan that had a good chance of success with the least possible casualties, at least on the side of the Groga and the Alliance.

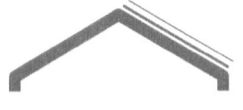

Chapter 22: Conniving

Sam halted before the stern-faced Norgoth seated at the table in the large inn common room. She had stood in line for over an hour to finally get here. She had taken on the persona of a female guard she had seen at the outpost where she had been told that recruits were being accepted at the Red Table Inn.

The soldier looked up at her and scowled.

"Another girlie who wants to be a soldier. Who puts these ideas into their heads?" he spat. "OK, kid, you know you might break a nail or stub your toe if we take you?"

Sam looked him dead in the eye. "I come from a military family. My mother was infantry. I want to defeat the Alliance."

Her simple statement seemed to take the man aback. "Fine. Name?"

By the time they had her paperwork finished, he handed her a piece of paper and she was instructed to take it to the outpost, and she would be directed from there.

Sam gritted her teeth, took the paper with the stamp on it and went back to the outpost. She altered her face only slightly, but enough to not be a duplicate of the guard but she wasn't at her post anymore. A large bulbous-nosed Norgoth slouched at the post instead. She handed him her paper, and he mumbled something about "another one".

"Go down this road to the very end. Intake is the last building on the left." He handed her back her paper and slouched once again, staring straight ahead of him as if she were now invisible.

That suited her just fine. The road toward the intake building was long and crisscrossed with many side streets. The post seemed like a small city in and of itself. Various vehicles powered by everything from pedals to beasts to engines that purred made their way down the streets in an orderly manner. Sam was unable to determine any type of stop signs, but there were no collisions at intersections, each vehicle pausing as needed to give right of way to another. She was sure there were some kind of rules to how they managed this, but she couldn't figure out what those might be.

Pedestrians made their way up and down the sides of the paved streets, obviously on one errand or another. Sam made a point of looking neither to the left or right. She had no interest in any of these. She just wanted to get started.

Finally, she arrived at the last building on the left. Like every Inseni building she had ever seen, it was plain. Simplicity and usefulness were the order of the day for the Inseni. She entered the open double doors into an entryway and got into another line, each Norgoth with a paper identical to her own, clutched in their hands. As she waited, she stared straight ahead, making no attempt to engage anyone in conversation.

Around her, however, many conversations buzzed. The young Norgoth's waiting in line were full of speculation about what it would be like to conquer gloriously in battle. Many boasted of their weaponry skills or their martial arts prowess to any who would listen. Sam mentally put them on the list of the first casualties.

Many were enthusiastically predicting easy victories over the dreadful Alliance. Sam knew better, but she wasn't here to aid her fellow recruits. She just needed to get into the military long enough to work her plan. She was confident, based on her training and past combat experience, she would rise quickly in the ranks, but there was no need to brag of this to these insignificant grunts.

She finally arrived at the head of the line, was given a barracks assignment and, when she had told the clerk there that she didn't have her own equipment or uniforms yet, he handed her a large, heavy knapsack. She was instructed to report to the outfitters at the end of the hall for her initial set of uniforms.

Following instructions, she went through another long line in the hallway outside the outfitters area. When she finally got through the door she was directed to fill in an empty space in front of one of the tables where she was measured and handed two shirts, two pairs of pants and boots. She was then instructed to go to the barracks, get her bunk assignment and change into her uniform, then assemble on the parade grounds outside the barracks.

At no time did she speak more often than necessary. She had no desire to form any relationships with anyone other than those in power to get her what she wanted. The fire in her heart raged constantly. She would find her parents and what that despicable Jenny and her minions had done with them. She would rescue them and her people, and then she would be the one to execute her former friend as painfully as possible.

She stowed her backpack in the trunk at the end of her cot, dressed, and exited the dimly lit barracks. Outside in the bright sunlight about forty or so Norgoths milled aimlessly about; talking, joking, and laughing with one another. Sam ignored them all, standing quietly at parade rest and expanding her vision of ultimate success while she waited. Something about her expression and her posture must have been off-putting, for no one approached her to chat or exchange introductions.

Finally, a Norgoth sergeant strode onto the field. "Attention!" he barked. "Form into lines ten to a line and four deep facing me." With the exception of Sam, it took a while for the recruits to sort themselves out. The sergeant stood there, his arms folded across his chest, his face like stone. When the recruits finally managed to complete the instructions, he bellowed, "Attention! Stand up straight, you good-for-nothing worms." Sam, who was already at attention, simply looked straight ahead.

The sergeant strode up and down the line, pausing to inspect and correct something on each and every recruit. When he got to Sam he asked, "Where were you trained, soldier?"

"I come from a military family. My father insisted on absolute discipline in me and my siblings, Sergeant."

"What is your name, recruit?"

"I am Sam Lastly, Sergeant."

"An odd name, but it will do. Straighten that collar, recruit."

Dutifully Sam tugged at a collar she knew needed no rearranging. But it was this man's job to find fault as often as possible, and it would not have done for her to have been the only recruit not to have received a critique.

She had decided to keep the name she called herself in the privacy of her mind. The "Lastly" part was all about the finality of her decision to eradicate Jenny once and for all for the disappearance of her parents. Why else had Sam been left alone when all of her people had disappeared? It could only have been one person who would have been that soft-hearted. Or maybe it was simply another way to torture her as payback?

The sergeant stood once again in front of the ranks of recruits, rocking back and forth on his feet, his hand on his chin as he scanned them back and forth. Finally, he told them to stay in ranks and turn on their heels to the right. This put Sam at the front of a column of nine other recruits.

"When I say 'March', you will march in step in the direction you are facing. I will call out instructions as you go to take you to the part of this post you will learn to hate. From now on, it is my job to make your lives as miserable as I can. I will push you beyond your limits.

Some of you will not make it...Many of you will not make it. The ones who do will hate me and curse me, and that will mean I have done what I set out to do. You are my worms. If I tell you to crawl on your belly, you will crawl. If I tell you to stand on your head, you will manage it or die in the attempt. I own you. Do you understand?"

There was no reply except for Sam. "Yes, Sergeant!" she shouted back.

"Only one of you? You will pay for that. When I ask you a question, you reply, 'Yes, Sergeant!' Let's try that again. Do you understand?"

The entire group bellowed their reply.

"Then, forward March!"

They marched. Sam could tell by the arrhythmic shuffle behind her that many were having trouble getting the hang of marching in step. At the end of the road, he stopped them and instructed them in how to turn in a column. After several tries and him shouting as various ones struggled with the idea, they finally made a turn to the right onto another grassy area. This was obviously not a parade ground, however. Around the edges of the large field were piles of various kinds of equipment.

He halted them in the center of the field and instructed them to space themselves out by two arm lengths to both sides and front and back. They managed this only slightly better than the marching exercise, and Sam rolled her eyes in disgust. The sergeant caught her expression.

"Since you seem to think you have a handle on this, Lastly, you will be my demonstrator today. Please step forward and face the platoon next to me."

He then ran them through a series of exercises designed to test lung capacity, strength, balance, and the ability to follow instructions.

To his evident displeasure, Sam performed each task with exactness and skill. Her father had been much harder on her in her training, she mused derisively. But her fellow recruits obviously didn't feel the same way. By the end of the series of exercises and postures, some had collapsed to the ground, exhausted and ashamed.

Those who couldn't stay on their feet were instantly dismissed with disdain by the sergeant. "Go home to your mommies," he told them. "Leave your issued uniforms and equipment on your cot."

That eliminated four of them. One of the four had been the most vocal of the braggarts in the recruitment line. Sam ignored them. Facing forward, she stood implacably at parade rest, waiting for his next orders.

"The rest of you worms will now run in formation around the edges of this field until I tell you to stop."

So they ran. The formation was ragged at first, but eventually they got into a rhythm. And they ran. After five times around the field some of the recruits were beginning to breathe raggedly. Some were gasping. Two more recruits dropped out, panting on the ground. One passed out as he ran and lay unconscious while the other recruits nearly stumbled and fell trying to avoid trampling him.

These were also sent home by the sneering sergeant. Finally, he called a halt. This time none of the recruits resorted to falling to the ground to rest. They stood there, sides heaving, some with hands on their knees. Sam was panting only slightly, although she had broken out in a sweat as the sun had risen to its apex and the temperatures had risen accordingly. She had spent all of her life running up and down the stairs of her fortress and training right alongside her father's guards from the time he decided she was old enough. His instructions to her trainers had been to not spare her because of her rank. He wanted her hard and capable, not some milksop, ladylike, lay-about.

So, this baseline training couldn't challenge her. Although she realized the sergeant knew a challenge when he saw it and would continue to raise the bar until he broke her. That was his job.

Over the next several days he did everything he could to break them without actually killing them. Well, there had been a death, but not because of the training. Two of the early boasters had gotten into a knife fight and one of them was killed. The other brawler had been put into the stockade and was due to also be executed. By the end of the week they were ten down. The remaining recruits had figured out that the only way to get through this was to work together. They seemed to immediately look to Sam for leadership and eventually that was made official by the sergeant.

"You are the private in charge of this motley crew, Sam Lastly. I charge you to expect more of them than they expect of themselves. You answer to me."

He had pinned an emblem of her new rank onto her shoulder and formed them once again into ranks.

It was over a week before they were even allowed to look at a weapon, much less touch one. Sam didn't care about that much, but in the barracks all the talk was about when they would finally be issued their blasters.

When they were finally presented to the weapons-master, he also sneered at them. "It's my job to keep you from killing yourselves or each other. I take that job seriously. We will start with hand to hand combat and will advance to dummy weapons until I think I can trust you to follow instructions."

He started by teaching them how to fall; forward falls, backward falls, and falls to either side. It was everything she could do to keep from laughing at the unintentional antics of her fellow recruits. Only a few of them seemed to have the necessary inner balance to figure it out quickly, and she began to be somewhat impatient.

She would know when it was time to make her move. For the nonce, it was important to prove to the instructors that she was more competent and knowledgeable than her compatriots. The time would come that they would recognize her worth and she could move forward with her plan.

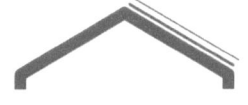

Chapter 23: Luz and Company

Luz really wished Juan would quit fussing over her. She only had a single bruise from her encounter, and that wasn't even from the fight. She had run into a crossbar on the roll-up metal door while helping drag an unconscious Norgoth into the loading bay. She had a pretty nice shiner to show for it, but Juan was treating her like she had broken a limb or something. She had wanted to be in on the questioning of the prisoners, but Juan had insisted she return to the hacienda.

The more she thought about what had just happened, the more she was certain that they were missing something. Why here and why now? Obviously, they had gotten the intel about the Puerto Rico gate at the time Jenny had first come here. Why had they waited? They seemed to have thought there was something in the harvest barn they needed. Did they think the gate was in there? They sent a small force, but how many of them might be waiting in the jungle beyond the wrought-iron gates at the entrance of her property? And how had they gotten past their security measures?

She would have to review the security footage. That much was clear. But for now, Mustapha had shut down all the communications equipment and it currently resided in his MDP. Victor had helped her search every room in the hacienda as soon as she had returned from the harvest barn. Having satisfied themselves that all was still secure here, and no one had been inside, Victor had stationed himself just outside the hacienda doors, seating himself in a cozy rattan chair on the porch.

He immediately assumed the pose of a tired worker taking a well-earned snooze. Luz knew only too well that was one of his favorite ruses. He could sit for hours in that pose, and the slightest sound or shadow would show just how alert he actually was.

She got herself a glass of her famous punch that was always chilling in her refrigerator. She sat down in her favorite chair in the living room facing the front doors. She sat her punch beside her on the little marble table beside the chair and pulled some crochet out of the basket that always sat next to her chair. She thought best when her hands were busy. As she sat there mulling over the events of the day, she recognized a presence in the room with her. *"Jenny? Is that you?"*

"You caught me, kiddo. You are getting good at this game."

"I wish I were better at other games. Are you aware of what happened here today?"

"Yes, Mustapha sent a message out to all the major players before he shut the network down. For now, I'm all we've got. Before he shut it down, however, we got the whole thing on video. Those security cams of yours are pretty high res. You totally held your own there. I loved the two stick thing. I need to learn that one next. It looks like it might be a good alternative to the quarterstaff. Of course, that will have to wait until we get a break in all of this."

"They are called Kali sticks. I learned it from a Filipino friend of mine. I like them better than the quarterstaff, and my sling back holster makes them very convenient."

"Oh my, you're hurt! What happened?"

"I ran into something with my face. Luckily, it wasn't a Norgoth fist."

"So, what do we know so far?"

"Not a lot, yet. The boys and some Alliance troopers are questioning them now. I hope for their sakes they are in a cooperative mood, as Juan is agitated. They won't like him when he's agitated. And who knew Aliki and Leland could be so ferocious? You've got to watch the cheerful ones, I'd say."

"Is this a result of my photo taking that first time I visited you, do you think?"

"It's hard to say...The more I think about it, the more I think probably not. Otherwise, why did they wait so long to do this, and why the harvest barn? And where the heck did they find a portal? I thought the South America portal was the only one, and I know for a fact that none of them would survive trying to get through that one.

But we never did find out what they were doing in the Louisiana swamp. Might they have been looking for another portal? Or guarding one? And if there, could there be other portals on Earth tuned to that same frequency, ones our gate technology sensors wouldn't detect?"

"Scary if true," Jenny agreed. *"Until the network is back online, I'm going to hang out with you for a bit. Tarafau and Burt have things under control here in the Groga capitol. I have retired to the quiet of my little cottage in the government compound, so guarded that nothing could possibly get to me without an army at their backs. Can we go to the harvest barn?"*

"I'd love to. Juan can't tell me to go home with you tagging along. Let's go."

It was such a treat to have Jenny with her. She really had grown to love her since her first introduction, what seemed so long ago. She headed out the door, told Victor she had forgotten something at the barn and to please continue guarding the hacienda, allowing no one to pass he didn't recognize.

He was surprised at these orders, as he knew he was supposed to be guarding Luz, but he didn't voice his doubts. "Yes, boss," was all he said.

Luz hurried out to the barn. The sliding doors were closed, but even then, she could hear shouting from inside. There was a trooper guard on the dock standing next to the small door that served as an entrance into the attached office of the barn. He nodded his acknowledgment of her and continued to stand his post. She walked through the office and into the main barn.

The shouting was louder, and it was obvious there was more than one trooper shouting rapid-fire questions at the Norgoth soldiers. The unconscious ones were laid face down on the concrete floor, hands cuffed behind them. It looked uncomfortable, but Luz was ok with it. Their faces were angled to one side, so they could breathe, and their chests continued to rise and fall.

At about eight foot intervals the prisoners were seated on the floor around the outer walls of the barn, their hands cuffed behind them and their legs tied in a way that attached the ropes to the handcuffs. In front of each enemy soldier was a trooper, face inches from the faces of the prisoners. They were yelling at them in a language from some dimension she didn't recognize. She realized that there were two simultaneous conversations happening before her eyes. The loud yelling actually meant nothing. It was intended to disorient the prisoners.

The real interrogation was happening in mindspeech. As each interrogator was directing their questions directly to the prisoner in front of them, there was no way to tell what they were being asked or whether they were giving any answers, but the true beauty of this interrogation was that the whole time, Burt's little bots were humming away inside each of the prisoners recording subconscious responses to the questions. The Alliance had perfected this technique after the swamp incident.

"*I thought I asked you to go back to the hacienda, corazón.*" Juan sent as soon as he saw her approach.

"*I brought a friend, Juan. Tell him, Jenny.*"

"*I'm here with Luz, Juan,*" Jenny sent obligingly. "*With the communications network temporarily down, we needed someone to see what's up. What can you tell me?*"

Juan shook his head. "*I'm not sure yet. I sent your workers back to the grove and to man the defenses on the walls in case there is a follow up and to prevent any misunderstandings.*" He sent to Luz. And he glanced meaningfully at the interrogation continuing behind him. "*I didn't think it was time for them to know yet, although this incident is making me rethink our policy of non-disclosure to the help, considering they just had a fight with a group of one-eyed aliens. That, however, is a discussion for another day.*

For now, we have to wait for the true results of the questioning. It is all being recorded on a device the troopers brought with them as the Alliance cloud is currently shut down. When I left Sanglarka Lova was preparing to send some troopers back through the Alliance gate to brief them on what we know about the situation. Can you connect Lova to this conversation by any chance?"

"Absolutely. Give me a second." There was a slight pause and then Lova's mind voice came into the conversation as well as Liliath's. *"I thought we could kill two birds with one stone,"* Jenny said brightly.

Luz continued to be amazed at Jenny's progress in her mind speaking and other mental disciplines. She wondered what other things she could do that none of them knew about yet. They had all felt so involved with her training that it felt natural for Luz to feel invested in Jenny's continued success.

"OK, so now that we're all here, let me recap." Jenny gave a succinct summary of events so far based on what Luz had explained to her and what she had already witnessed. *"So, we had just gotten to the part where Juan had said that they had to wait for the results of Burt's bugs. It's really loud in here, but I believe the captives are beginning to tire. Most of them are slumped over, but that may be a ruse on their parts. As far as the unconscious ones are concerned, can we tap into them when they are knocked out? I know it works when they're sleeping, but I'm not sure if that's the same thing."*

"They have continued to refine the process, but the answer is that it depends on whether they are unconscious due to serious brain injury or whether they are simply temporarily knocked out," Liliath replied.

"Well, based on the fact that these fellows haven't stirred a fraction of an inch since we moved them, I'm guessing they're seriously damaged. I'm not all that fussed about it, though." Juan sent with a shrug.

Luz sighed. It was so like Juan to be very businesslike, in the heat of the moment, and then to return to his usual flippant, cheerful self when a crisis had passed.

"So, how much longer will you continue to question them?" interjected Liliath. *"I would like you to make copies of the transcript from the mental extractions the moment you are finished and have someone carry them by hand to both Sanglarka and Alliance headquarters. We need to know what is going on here and whether or not we need to provide troops and support to defend Earth as well as the other fronts we are fighting in this war. For obvious reasons, Earth is a first priority and we will pull troops from other missions if necessary."*

"I think at least another hour to be sure we wear them down enough to break down their defenses so the bugs can do their job. I wouldn't put anyone through this if we had any choice. It's distasteful. If billions of lives weren't at stake, I would try a different approach," Juan said, shaking his head.

Luz loved him for his tender heart. Personally, she had seen the murder in the eyes of these Norgoth thugs and was certain that they weren't worthy of Juan's sympathy.

"Very well," Liliath replied. *"We will await your courier in an hour or so. Thank you, Jenny, for the link. I know you have enough on your plate to be going on with. Liliath out."*

"Are you alright, Jenny?" Luz inquired, concern evident in her mind voice. *"How many of these communication sessions are you doing today? As much as I enjoy your company, I know you have a lot to do."*

"I'm just fine. The head is mending and I'm not wobbly anymore and my strength is returning. I actually had a light sparring match with Elizabeth and the girls this morning. Very light and short, but it's a start. Freia and Chidwi both agree that I'm recovering better than expected. So, don't worry about me. No one will let me 'strain' myself." Jenny projected a mental sigh and Luz grinned. This sounded like her Jenny, all right.

"I'm gonna ride along for a bit yet. Can you stay in the harvest barn for a little bit longer?"

"I can, although I left the hacienda with only one guard. My other men are manning the defenses on the perimeter, so unless there are already other Norgoth we missed inside the gates; I think it will be alright for me to stay. My crocheting can wait for a bit." Luz sent this with a humorous twist to her mouth. She really didn't get much in the way of leisure most days between helping with security, offering hospitality to her current guests, and working the Mango grove and managing the marketing of her business.

So she stayed and observed. It was beginning to be obvious that their tactics were beginning to take a toll on their prisoners. One of the unconscious Norgoths started to twitch violently in some sort of seizure and then was still once again. Juan went over and checked his pulse.

He shook his head. *"I'll get one of the troopers to add him to the others as soon as they are finished with the interrogation. I don't think it will be much longer."* He nodded toward the prisoners lined up against the wall.

Luz noticed that many of them were beginning to get a glazed look on their faces and some were just constantly shaking their heads in denial; mouths shut and jaw muscles tensed visibly, as if it was all they could do to keep from opening their mouths, to scream or answer questions or shout invectives at their captors. In their place, Luz would have fallen back on her Alliance training in mental distancing, but these didn't appear to have any such tools.

Suddenly one of them started to struggle fiercely in his bonds. His eye was wild and the grimace on his face was painful to look at. He began to rear back and bang the back of his head against the wall behind him. Two of the troopers grabbed him to move him away from the wall, but he just arched his back and smacked his head violently against the floor. Again, and again before the troopers could do anything about it, he banged his head, blood beginning to pool beneath him. Then he shuddered once and was still.

"Dead?" asked Juan of the trooper who was bending to check him.

"Dead," the trooper affirmed grimly.

"OK, we're done! Stop and secure the prisoners any way you can to prevent them from harming themselves." Juan ordered.

The troopers immediately ceased their yammering at the prisoners and administered a hypo spray of a sleep drug to each of them, who went limp nearly immediately. They dragged them out to a waiting maintenance truck. From here they would be transferred to the special facility on Earth owned by the Alliance to be further observed and held until the Alliance decided on their disposition. Luz would have preferred they simply euthanized them.

She considered herself a compassionate person, but these were enemy prisoners who were so indoctrinated that they would have no hope of rehabilitation and there was no place to safely keep them unless that was a lifetime of imprisonment in a highly secure facility or banishment to a planet empty of intelligent life.

Either way, they were a drain on the Alliance at a time when they were stretched to the maximum on resources. This was no half-hearted lip-service attempt to prosecute this war. The Alliance was "all in" or as Brendan would say, "fair dinkum" in their intent to purge the multiverse of this threat.

Juan walked up to her, brushing his hands together as if to say, job completed. He reached out with a one arm hug. *"Now, corazón, can I persuade you to return to the hacienda? I think we are finished here."*

"Only if you walk with me. Jenny, we will get the download from the extraction device and will send copies to Sanglarka and Alliance headquarters as soon as it is complete. I think we're done here."

Jenny took the hint and Luz could feel her presence fade from her mind. "You look like you could use some of my nice cold fruit punch," she said to Juan with a wink.

Chapter 24: Special Delivery

B ob, Ignatius and their new Mookookie buddy, Chortle finished their rendition of "You Are My Sunshine" with gusto. "Please don't take my sunshine from meeee!" Even Fidget had joined in on the chorus, a new skill for him.

Chortle's real name was Choto, but he had this funny chuckling thing he did whenever he was amused, which was often. Bob dubbed him Chortle and, he liked it and now answered only to his new name. Chortle was one of BaaGah's buds, which Burt had insisted he take. "I think you'll find him more than useful. I've been having this idea..."

Those words were always like magic to Bob. Burt had outlined his thoughts on the matter and Bob hadn't been able to sleep three nights in a row adding it to his newest project. It was a perfect fit.

He was celebrating the completion of his "total tech attack package", TTAP for short, with the "t" or at least one of them, silent. The packs were now being manufactured and assembled by one of the Dimensional Alliance partners known for their fast, accurate, and quality workmanship where tech was concerned. He had loved demonstrating the parts that had to be manufactured to the insectoids who would be building the tech parts needed for his strategy to work. They had chittered excitedly to one another, only occasionally mind speaking to Bob to clarify a point or so. The prototypes they had produced based on his designs had been flawless.

Chortle was so proud to be of assistance in the lab. *"Chortle helps buddy Bob. Chortle is good assistant. Buddies Ignatius and Chortle rock!"*

He had picked up slang words such as "rock" with glee. He liked imitating Bob's mindspeech and favorite sayings. Bob had not considered how each Mookookie would be unique individuals, even though they basically broke off of their parent with the same DNA. They had race memory, for sure, but their personalities differed as much from one to another as any humanoid.

His highly dexterous hands were extremely useful when an extra pair was needed. He discovered that Chortle could actually alter the thickness of his fingers at will, which could be helpful in tight spaces that Bob couldn't get to.

Chortle was a delight to have around and careful to not eat those things he was told were off limits. He participated gleefully in the experiments Bob was running with the MDPs, and the others on the Science and Technology Team enjoyed him so much that they soon asked the Alliance to supply them each with one.

The request was granted but not before Jenny made sure that each of them understood they weren't to reproduce on Earth. When they were ready to bud, they would be transported to Krim where the new Mookookie were happily absorbed into their native culture.

Jenny had lifted the moratorium on Mookookie budding when Bob had explained to her the strategy he had come up with. He had met with the Mookookie "old ones" and explained what he wanted to do, and they had been ecstatic.

They wanted so much to repay the Alliance for the return of their planet to them. They and the former slaves were getting on well together, so much so that they had discovered many ways they could be of assistance to one another and it was becoming a common practice for a new Mookookie to bond with another being on Krim as a lifelong partnership.

New traditions were being formed from day to day and Bob looked forward to looking in on their culture years from now if he lived that long.

But for now, he had enough to be going on with. He had Fidget dial Lizziebot to tell her to get Jenny on the line if she was available. It often worried Bob that they were using up Jenny's youth with the huge burden that had been placed squarely on her shoulders.

He knew she was willing, or he would have been furious about the situation. Nevertheless, she was at a time in her life when she would have normally been socializing with her friends and exploring life options.

He sighed, nothing to be done about it, however. And he needed her help as much as everyone else. Her mental abilities had made her a lynchpin in this entire war. His one consolation was that she was being actively guarded by more layers than she knew about. Lizziebot had a new upgrade. She could come out of the MDP at will or whenever accessed by Liliath, Bob, Burt, Elizabeth or Tarafau.

He had taken great pride in showing off this feature to Jenny the last time they had talked. She had been suitably impressed. He now knew more about the MDPs than any of the Alliance scientists, and they made much over him.

Merv had practically strutted when he had presented Bob's finished prototype of the TTAP system in Bob's absence, via the Alliance Network, which had finally been reestablished with Earth after the incident in Puerto Rico. Merv considered Bob his personal protégé, as well he might. Without Merv's nudges in the right direction, he would still have been twiddling with his robots.

Not that he wasn't continually improving their programming as he went along. The same factory that had taken over his new project had also manufactured thousands of his bots, to his great delight. One of his daily duties was to upload software updates to the secured tech center in the science lab at Alliance headquarters, and from there to all robots that had access to the network.

With the addition of mindspeech to his robotics, thanks to Cornelium, they were much more useful and each of them was programmed with the most current information regarding the MDP research. For his plan to work, all the bots had to be up to date with the latest about the various parts and pieces that made the plan work. Both Cornelium and Merv had approved the plan as sound and after they had also gotten approval from the High Council, it was time to roll it out.

It killed him to know everything he now knew and not to be able to use it for the benefit of Earth, but he had to agree with Ingot and Liliath about this. He had given his word, and that was that. However, although none of the DAT he had used in this project was allowed to be promulgated on Earth, many of the concepts of how he organized all of this would be applicable and would not compromise either his word or the natural development of Earth's technologies.

Ignatius was starting on a second chorus of "You Are My Sunshine" when Jenny chimed in. Her natural alto voice harmonized well with the bird, even in mindspeech.

"Hello, Bob and company!" she said cheerfully. *"I hear we have some breakthroughs."*

"Breakthroughs," Ignatius agreed.

"Lots and lots," put in Chortle.

"We all helped," added Fidget.

"Indeed. The entire team has been working our collective tails off getting this together. With three separate teams each working on a separate part of the plan, and your wonderful help with the Mookookie, I think we are ready to roll it out. Could you perhaps get Elizabeth to bring you so we can discuss this? I would really like to tell you about it in person for security reasons. What do you think?"

Evidently, she thought it was a good idea. Standing in front of him, out of the blue, with Elizabeth's hand on one shoulder, was his Jenny. She definitely looked different. Her hair was a short cap of honey-colored curls and her face was tanned. Her outfit was some kind of cottony material, a soft brown tunic and breeches and laced up boots. She was still beautiful, but he could see that her face had matured even in this short time. There was a more serious set to her face, and he could see her experiences reflected in those beautiful blue eyes.

She immediately reached out and hugged him enthusiastically, eliciting a squawk from Ignatius. She laughed and skritched the back of his neck in the best spot and he closed his eyes, one happy bird. Chortle had sprouted arms and legs and was doing the Mookookie happy dance and was soon joined by Noony and Jenny's Mookookie.

"What did you name him?" Bob asked, laughing at the frolicking Mookookies.

"He's Lolly. Or at least that's what he told us when he came to be with us. But let's mindspeak. Elizabeth's English is coming along, but I don't want her to be left out."

"Gotcha. Hey, Elizabeth. Good to see you. I'm so glad you're with Jenny again. I know she's in good hands between you, the girls, and Burt. I understand Tarafau is with you all as well."

"Father is leading the Daringi delegation to get agreements of how we will proceed going forward. The Groga are adamant they want this 'victory' for themselves, but they are willing to have Daringi consultants and to use Daringi tactically for moving about, that sort of thing. They are firm on the idea that no other being will fight this fight for them.

Of course, anything that happens in orbit around their planet is fair game for us, which means that we can at least hopefully prevent the Norgoth from just bombarding the planet from space with no need to shed Norgoth blood."

"It's a bit of a fine line, but they have no space fleet and have conceded the point," Jenny put in, settling herself on a stool next to Bob's worktable. *"So, what do you have for us, Bob? You sounded pretty excited, you and your 'lab assistants.'"* And she laughed again at that. It was good to see her laugh.

The 'assistants' had settled down and Bob took a deep breath. *"We can't win this war,"* he began and held up his hand to forestall argument. *"We can't; at least not yet. This is a long term commitment, as much as we would prefer it to be otherwise. Also, Earth is back in the mix until we can locate every last Inseni portal and disable them once and for all.*

That being said, we can deal the Great Insenium a major blow if we do this right. We can disable them for many years to come and give help and protection to a lot of innocent and unsuspecting beings across the multiverse. But based on our most current intel, the numbers we are up against are more than I could have imagined possible. When the Insenium split up a few centuries ago, there were the little bug-eyed guys on Krim and a couple of other planets, but the Norgoth took a different tack.

They decided to colonize several planets that were conveniently connected by their alternate frequency portals. It appears they actually do occur naturally, as do the gates in the Alliance gate network, but their method of accessing the portals uses different technology than we do and, unlike the gateways, their portals actually occur on multiple planets.

Also, they haven't known about this technology as long as the Alliance has been in existence. Evidently, they discovered they could do this not long before the Groga started raiding under the Fleistians. Turns out the Fleistian portals are part of the Inseni portal network, which is how they discovered the Fleistians and their Groga army.

They did what they do best. They acquired the Fleistians and their Groga slave army and began raiding in earnest after what had been a long hiatus by the Fleistians. Of course, that was why the Alliance thought the Groga threat was eradicated. The Fleistians had relocated them to a different dimension, also connected to their portal.

Bringing this story up to date, the Norgoth half of the Insenium take up at least six planets and have been reproducing intentionally for all this time. Even with all the resources of the Dimensional Alliance, just getting the six main Insenium planets pacified will be Herculean. Add to that the planets already conquered throughout their network, which my sources say are several hundred, and you can see what we are up against.

Fortunately, the largest concentration of their military forces, according to what we have learned, are on just four of the planets inhabited by the Norgoth. There are others, but they are minor. If we can eliminate the threat from those four, things will be more manageable, and it will be a long time before they become as much of a threat.

So much for our reality check; now...what do we do about it?"

Jenny shook her head, her eyes large and her mouth set in a thin line. *"Are you telling me that after all of this, we can't hope to fix this?"*

"No, Jenny. I'm telling you we can't just go in and conquer, and we can't expect to see immediate results from even the cleverest plans. However, we do stand a chance if we can spread enough chaos and weaken them in their most vulnerable areas. Between all of the members of the Science and Technology teams, we have come up with some solutions that will give the best results both short term and long term.

Our biggest problem is sheer numbers and fighting a war on multiple fronts which dilutes our own numbers and resources.

To that end, right now several high-tech factories on the planets of one of our Alliance scientists are running full bore, churning out the pieces of a highly unusual and hopefully unanticipated way of doing battle. We've been dropping some hints for them, unintentionally, but I doubt that they've been paying attention, especially since the Insenium didn't have any on the ground witnesses of our previous escapades."

"What are you up to, Bob? This sounds like another one of those brilliant brainstorms that has saved us in the past." Jenny broke in excitedly.

Bob held up both hands. *"OK, look. I can't guarantee anything. There is still so much we don't know about any tricks the Insenium might have up their own sleeves, but I believe this gives us our best chance. The thing is that I took a page out of some of the subversive groups in our own culture. The only ones who know the entire plan or the entire inventory of our TTAPs is me and Merv, so we are making a point of never being in the same place at the same time. Having told you that, you and Elizabeth are way too high profile to know the entire plan.*

What I need from you right now is Mookookie. How many would you say there are right now, after your Mookookie replication program?"

"A few billion, I would guess. There could be more. What do you have in mind?"

"Every trooper commander has an MDP and most battalion commanders also have an MDP. In addition, certain entire brigades will each have an MDP issued to them. This is straining the MDP system to a certain extent, but I'm guessing I need a few thousand Mookookie willing to volunteer for a non-dangerous part of this plan. I only need them for about a week from now. It will be a short stint and I'm still working out the details of how to get them where they need to be, but Chortle has given me some good ideas about that. These are non-combatant roles, be clear about that. Can you get me the numbers I need?"

Jenny thought about it. *"Let's ask Lolly. Lolly, do you think the Mookookie will do this?"*

Lolly screwed up the face that was also his tummy in an obvious look of concentration. *"Older ones say, yes. We will do it. Ready now?"*

Bob held up both hands. *"Not yet, Lolly. I will tell you when and where and how, ok?"*

"Yes. Older ones say yes. We wait. Needs more than for Jenny?"

"For Jenny?" Bob asked, his curiosity piqued. He looked at her, one eyebrow raised in question.

"Umm...well...Let's just say I have a few things in the works myself where the Groga are concerned. And for all the reasons you just mentioned, I'm not at liberty to talk about it. Elizabeth and Tarafau are the only ones who know the whole plan besides me. As you said, sometimes we have to learn from the bad guys, if we want to win. Let's just hope between your big plan and my smaller part of the plan all goes well."

Bob grinned at her and shook one finger in front of her nose. "Not another surprise like last time, I hope," he said aloud. Elizabeth caught the joke and laughed, mischief sparkling in her eyes. Her English must be getting better than Jenny realized, he thought.

"I promise this plan is Tarafau approved, but I do believe it will take a few people by surprise. I must say it did me." Jenny retorted in mindspeech for Elizabeth's benefit.

Elizabeth nodded smugly.

"One more thing, Jenny; I need some DNA samples from those Norgoths Juan and Luz captured yesterday to give to Xao Ting. He added a nice little wrinkle to our plan to ensure long-term benefits from our short-term plans. A devious little guy. I'm really glad he's on our side. It always baffles me how so many nice people can come up with such downright scary ideas. You'd never know to look at him or listen to him that he had a talent for scheming. You've got to watch the quiet ones; that's all I'm sayin'...

I'll be in touch in about two weeks. Within a few days of my 'special delivery' of Mookookies, I will have a 'special delivery' of my own...and then we'll see."

Chapter 25: From the Depths of Denial

S am stood at attention in formation, now the official platoon leader of the recruits. It had taken less than a week for the sergeant to recognize that she was more than a raw recruit. He continued to give her more and more responsibilities. She knew that a large part of her value and the one thing that would help her get where she needed to move her plan forward was to make herself invaluable, and that meant whipping her fellow recruits into shape as quickly as their abilities would allow.

Her platoon members had begun to look to her for answers and to meet their needs rather than the sergeant. She allowed no slacking and often put them through extra drills and weapons practice to push them to their limits. Every single one of them collapsed eagerly into their beds after evening roll call. She insisted on them eating their entire ration at every meal to give them the fuel they would need to push farther and faster than any of the other recruits in the compound.

She pushed them relentlessly and they looked up to her for it. Sam had learned manipulation from the cradle and her particular skillset meant she was highly qualified to do this. If she hadn't had a specific goal in all of this, she probably would have risen high in the Norgoth army.

The sergeant did his usual inspection of the troops. He was having a harder and harder time finding anything to criticize, however. They had already weeded out the least qualified and the arrogant and now this platoon was making a name for him already with the other instructors. He stopped in front of Sam, scanning her up and down. He flicked an imaginary piece of lint from her shoulder and said, "Keep it up, rank leader."

Today they would be firing real weapons for the first time. So far they had only been using the dummy weapons, practicing holstering and un-holstering, sighting, and using the little laser lights to fire at targets which were only sensitive to the light when it hit the small circle that was the focal point for the target. They had practiced firing on the run, firing from their knees and on their stomachs.

"Forward march!" the sergeant called out, and the platoon set off in perfect rhythm to Sam's count.

When they arrived at the firing range, they were issued real weapons with instructions from the weapons master not to fire until instructed. By now, the recruits understood the consequences of not following orders with precision. Sam admitted to herself that there was a certain satisfaction in knowing that the superior performance of her platoon was in a large part due to her leadership.

At first many of the male Norgoth recruits had resented being led by a female, but they soon realized that Sam was more than qualified for her position and it helped that they knew she would stand up for them when there was a problem.

As in all groups of people each member of her platoon showed varying strengths and weaknesses and it became clear which of her fellows she would prefer to have at her side in a real conflict. That being said, this day they all performed at a higher level than the weapons-master had expected.

After their time on the range, they were sent to eat in the mess hall. Sam always entered last, to be sure that every one of her soldiers got what they needed; not out of any real compassion for them, of course. It was simply logical that she should take good care of them, as it would get her much farther along her chosen path than if she did not.

Just before she was ready to go in, the sergeant approached her. She snapped to attention.

"Rank leader, come with me," was all he said. She immediately followed without comment.

He led them to the main administration building. They checked in at the front desk and she followed him up one floor and then down a long hallway lined with offices. At the end of the corridor was a large office, much larger than any of the offices they had passed so far.

As they entered, she realized that this was a conference room with room for a good fifty people to be seated. At the end of the room was a large desk with only one chair behind it. Next to the desk was a podium. Seated in the chairs were about a dozen officer types in uniform. Standing at the podium was a Norgoth Sam recognized as the base commander.

"Come in and be seated," he said, gesturing to two seats directly in front of the podium.

They sat, and the commander cleared his throat and began to speak. "We are here to honor excellence this day. Sergeant Glur has been tracking the progress of a particular recruit who has shown skill, dedication, and diligence, excelling beyond any of her peers in any platoon in the battalion. For this reason, I have called you together to witness her promotion to corporal and to acknowledge her excellence and skill. Corporal Sam Lastly, please come forward. Sergeant Glur, please come forward also."

They stood and ranged themselves on either side of the podium. From a small box, the commander handed Sergeant Glur a small emblem. He took it solemnly and then stood in front of Sam. The commander continued. "Sam Lastly, accept from the hand of your Sergeant this emblem of Corporal. Wear it with quiet humility and continue in diligence and exactness."

Sergeant Glur pinned the emblem of her new rank to a short epaulet on the shoulder of her shirt.

Sam then turned and saluted smartly to the commander. "Thank you, sir."

"Company dismissed," said the commander tersely.

All arose and came up to Sam to bow slightly to her, evidently part of some tradition of the Norgoth army. Sam bowed as slightly in return. Nothing was said by any of them, but as each completed his bow to the new corporal, he exited the room.

When the last one had filed out, Sergeant Glur slapped her on the back. "Well done," he said, smiling for the first time Sam had ever seen. The commander then sat behind his desk, nodded to them both and returned to some paperwork lying there.

Sam knew this was their cue to leave. As they exited the building, Sergeant Glur said, "If you keep this up you will be a sergeant before you know it. You are making a name for yourself. Don't let it go to your head, however. As corporal you are now also my assistant as well as being a recruit. I expect good things from you."

Sam was unused to any kind of praise. Her parents had only noticed when she failed to make the grade or perform to their expectations.

When she arrived at the barracks, the sergeant left her after announcing her new rank to her platoon. They crowded around congratulating her. It was all she could do not to grin.

For the next few days, Sam realized that not just her status had changed. She was now required to keep records of weaponry and equipment checked out to her platoon members, but also to track their progress and make recommendations regarding their various weak points and strengths.

She also accompanied Sergeant Glur to various meetings to take notes. Often he stayed for a while at the end of the meetings to chat familiarly with his fellows. They didn't guard their tongues around the lowly corporal, so she often heard opinions and comments she would have been shocked to hear from her own Groga troops. They didn't treat her like a recruit anymore and from time to time her sergeant even asked her opinion about her platoon, the training and, of course, numbers from the various records she was keeping for him.

One particular day she discovered that she would be up on the reviewing stand as the entire battalion of fighting troops did a demonstration of parade drills for some dignitaries who were on tour of the various military bases throughout the Great Insenium. None of the recruits in training would be represented there, so Sam didn't need to be on the field with the rest.

She found herself at the very back of the stadium seating. Before her were a few dozen dignitaries as well as the commander of the camp and his cadre of officers. Sergeant Glur sat ahead of her. She had joined several other corporals on this back row and was bored to tears. So, she listened to the random conversations a couple of rows ahead of her as they were speaking loudly to be heard over the tramping feet of the demonstration on the field.

"I hear the 9th battalion is being transferred," said one officer to the officer next to him.

"Well, they earned it, after their last assignment. I hear it was pretty intense."

"Where did you hear that?" the first officer asked skeptically.

"My cousin is a lieutenant with the 9th. He was there."

"So, why was it intense? Since the recent revolt, I didn't think we had any new combat assignments. Everyone is gearing up for the big assault on the Alliance."

"You didn't know? I thought everyone knew. Evidently a certain monarch crossed words with Gall. Gall was in a bit of a mood because of the revolt and having to deal with Peril. He decided he had put up with enough and decided to send a message. He sent the 9th to eradicate them completely."

"Eradicate? Not a battle?"

"No, it was a massacre, pure and simple. The monarch allowed them into his fortress, thinking it was just some war council. They slaughtered every single one of them. Marched them outside the fortress, took them to the local Groga encampment and slaughtered the lot of them and then burned the encampment to ashes."

Sam's heart raced. This sounded much too familiar.

"So what king was that? Not on any planet I'm familiar with."

"Umm, just a little kingdom, King Naman or Namal? I don't know...something like that."

Sam felt the outrage building inside her. She recalled the glowing coals of the Groga city and feeling so alone. She remembered her anger at Jenny. She had been so sure it was her! Her mind and heart were on fire. Gall! It had been Gall all along.

She didn't even realize she was now standing, trembling in rage. As she stood there, she began to swell and grow, no longer the semblance of a Norgoth. She was now Engoza in all her wrathful glory. Long blood-red nails extended from her fingertips. Long black braids fell down her back. The long slinky robes she had worn when torturing Jenny were back and her eyes spit fire. She grew and grew. The startled corporal who had been seated next to her scrambled backwards into the row of benches behind her, speechless with what he was witnessing.

She grew and grew. Now, people were hollering and pointing at her. Even the activities on the field had slowed to a stop. She now towered above them all, four times her normal height, eyes glowing and hands emitting sparks.

"THEY WERE MY PEOPLE! MY PARENTS! THEY SHALL NOT GO UNAVENGED!"

She drew in her will. She knew she had more mental power than she had ever shown to anyone and there was this one thing she could do and now they would know. Not that it would do any good if they were all DEAD.

Suddenly a physical force emanated from her in all directions. Those in the reviewing stand simply shredded into tatters. The soldiers on the drill field were knocked back like toy soldiers swept away by the hand of an impatient child and then dissolved into dust. And then there was silence. Nothing moved. In every direction around her things were askew, toppled or completely disintegrated. Only the cement structure of the stadium was intact.

She stood there silently observing the results of the destructive power she had unleashed. She felt no sadness or shame for it. She slowly shrank to her normal size, resumed her corporal persona and ran from the parade ground shouting as if in terror, "Engoza has attacked! They're all dead!"

On the streets of the military compound, all was still. She ran through the streets stirring up ashes that once had been Norgoth into clouds around her. She exited the gates of the fort without encountering a single living soul.

People stared as she exited the gates of the fort and ran through the streets shouting, but no one tried to stop her. Instead, they were running toward the stadium to see if what she said was true. By the time they realized it had been, she would already be on her way out of town, having acquired a new identity.

But she wasn't finished. Not by a long shot. She now knew who her real enemy was. She now wondered how she had ever suspected Jenny. But those speculations would have to wait. She was going to take Gall down and ruin him and everything he had worked to build.

Chapter 26: Shout Out

Jenny approached a building in her mental fortress she had not yet examined. She could feel the gentle hands of Chidwi comfortingly on her shoulders. She was not alone and yet; she had reached a point in her development where she knew that some things she was going to have to figure out for herself. This building was highly unusual compared to the relatively normal buildings she had explored so far.

It resembled nothing more than a dilapidated Quonset hut from the old photos her dad had shown her from her grandfather's experiences in World War II. It looked battered and worn from the outside. Weeds had sprung up around it and the paint was peeling in places and where the paint had peeled, there were patches of rust.

Jenny knew that everything about each of the buildings in her mental fortress was symbolic of something, but what about this? She stepped tentatively inside and looked around. In here was an old wooden desk with a small lamp and an old-fashioned wired telephone, the receiver in a cradle and a dial instead of a keypad. Metal filing cabinets stood in a row beside the desk and there were tables with maps spread out on them; pencils, a compass, and small notebooks that lay scattered around the maps. On a blotter on the desk was a folder labeled "Top Secret".

Her hand hovered over the folder. Within this place, there was nothing secret to her. She was the master of everything she saw here, so why secret? She knew that she always ended up in one of the buildings which corresponded to a need that she didn't even realize she had; a step in her progression. Was there any reason she shouldn't open the folder? And yet, something about it made her gut churn.

Nevertheless, she knew that at this point she needed something. She knew that for the most part the majority of the plans of the Alliance were moving along quite nicely without any help from her. But something told her that what she did on the Groga home world would play a key part in the success or failure of thwarting the Insenium threat. She took a deep calming breath and opened the folder.

There was only a single piece of paper in it and it had a single word in large letters and bold print: **"Shout!"**

Jenny closed the folder and shook her head. She had no idea what this meant. She wandered over to the nearest map table. She had half expected it to be a map of the countries of Earth, considering her surroundings. However, it bore no resemblance. There was a single continent shown on the map and the names of Groga cities and towns she recognized.

A thick red arrow pointed at the capitol city. On the shaft of the arrow, the words in white, "You are here" was printed. Another arrow far to the north was labeled "battle ground" near a small village called Mortis. The name of the town made her shiver. She was sure in the Groga language it didn't mean the same as it did in Latin; death, but it seemed a bad omen to her. Of course, she really didn't believe in omens and portents, nevertheless, she didn't like the coincidence.

She had never actually paid much attention to the maps she had often seen laid out on a table in Anwhal's command tent while they had been traveling. She would want to consult with him about that, to see if her experience here had any veracity. Although she knew the subconscious mind recorded much more than anyone realized, she didn't recall doing more than glancing in the direction of the map tables she had seen.

She picked up one of the notebooks scattered around the edge of the map. Thumbing through one of them, most of the pages were blank, but at the center page was the word again; Shout! What did this mean? She took some calming breaths.

"Chidwi, are you there?"

"I am here, Jenny, always here."

"I am confused. The word 'shout'. What does it mean?"

"Ah, Jenny, I was hoping it would never come to this. Do you not remember the instruction of Liliath? A mental shout is a powerful weapon. Few of those who have mental abilities are able to do more than a weak one. But a powerful mental shout can disable everyone in a large radius around the shouter.

It does not discriminate against friend or foe. Anyone who hears it is immediately made unconscious and, in some cases, it creates damage to the minds of those who hear it. In addition, the shouter is also disabled for a time. It is a mental weapon to only be used in the direst of circumstances."

Jenny pondered this. She remembered now that Liliath had mentioned it in passing, but she hadn't been inclined to explain it at the time.

"What if someone was deaf? Would they still be disabled by the shout?"

"I believe you have to be able to hear it with your ears. The vibrations would mean nothing to your brain without the translation of the receptors in your ears."

Why did she need to know this now and how was it done? Liliath had intimated that there were things a person could do with their mind that were harmful to others. Jenny had never considered asking about it, as she had a hard time thinking about her gifts as a weapon. But there it was.

"Chidwi, this place in my mind; would it ever give me access to something that would be harmful to me or would be against my conscience?"

"I believe not. This place was built by you, every bit of it, whether you understand the purpose of something or not. If you were of an evil turn of mind, that might be different, but I know you would never consciously harm or injure another being unless it was in defense of yourself or others. So I would say that you can trust the things you find here, although they might not always be what you initially think they are."

"So how do I do a shout? What would the visualization be? I don't know when I could use it and have it be of any use, but since you say this is here for a reason, I will believe you."

"First, you must put a lock on it; a keyword that no one else would ever have access to. I don't even know if a person could use it more than a single time. I have never heard of such a thing. I am only aware of one time it was ever used by anyone I know, and he never used it again. I am not sure if that was by choice or if it can only be used once."

"So how do I do it? I assume I need to know it, or this place wouldn't be here."

"It is a buildup of passion triggered by a single word. If the passion is positive, it can stop and immobilize those in the presence of the shouter. If the passion is negative, it can kill or even destroy. You must use the unlocking word and then send a command word with all of the force of your mind and spirit. If you are not prepared for this in every way, it could damage you permanently. I might not be able to bring you back from a wound of mind and spirit of that magnitude."

Jenny shuddered. *"But I can use it to just stop someone or many someones?"*

"Yes, but keep in mind. It will disable you as well and all around you when you do it, so if you use it, you need a backup plan."

"Would it disable you as well?"

"It would indeed. I am not immune to the shout. No being with ears that can translate sound vibrations would be."

Jenny considered this. Then she had a thought. What about her Mookookie allies? If they were hiding in the 'spaces' would the shout affect them there? She knew she could communicate with them in mindspeech if they were in the 'spaces', but she had no idea if they could hear what was going on outside. Come to think of it, did they even have ears? Birds had ears that hid beneath the feathers on their heads. Was it the same with the Mookookie? It was definitely something to consider. She was just going to have to have a long chat with her Mookookie buddies.

She walked over to the antique wooden desk and opened the folder. The page inside was blank. Evidently, she had gotten whatever she had come here for and wouldn't need to return.

She faded back into consciousness, still seated cross-legged on the bed in her little cottage. It wasn't quite dark yet, but twilight seemed to be setting in. Chidwi stood behind her still, patting her on her shoulder. *"I'm fine, Chidwi. It just feels sometimes that I'm moving way too fast with my training. I'm afraid I'll make a bad judgement call. But for now, I need to see Elizabeth and Burt. Let's go out to the living room after I chat for a moment with my Guide."*

Elizabeth, Burt, and her bodyguards were in the living room playing a hotly contested game of spades. They often did so in the evenings, after a long day of planning sessions with government and military leaders. It helped them to let off steam and gave Jenny the privacy she needed to make her mental rounds of the Alliance and to continue to work on her training. Most of the time her training these days was guided by Chidwi, but it got lonely sometimes. However, both Liliath and Amenia had their hands full with their own responsibilities and couldn't be constantly babysitting Jenny.

"Hey folks, I hate to break this up, but I need to speak with Elizabeth and Burt for a bit. You're just going to have to play 'cut-throat' (what her dad had called three handed spades)."

"You got it, boss," Mynn sent cheerfully. *"I was losing anyway."*

Burt and Elizabeth rose and followed Jenny into the kitchen and closed the door. They had gotten the hint that Jenny needed to speak to them privately.

"I've been making the rounds. Can you two bring out your Mookookie buddies? This concerns them as well," she mind spoke to Lolly, and he popped out from the wristband over her MDP where he preferred to ride.

The three Mookookie each sat on the kitchen table in front of their personal "buddies" and grinned and nodded at each other in greeting. The Mookookie as a rule were cheerful and nice to be around. Jenny was glad to have Lolly, especially since the Mookookie would tentatively play a large role in her personal strategy for the coming conflict on the Groga home world.

"I've gotten new information about the situation amongst our off world colleagues. Bob, Merv and the other Alliance scientists have been making some amazing strides in their various areas of expertise. Probably some of the most interesting things he was able to tell me on my last visit is about his on-going research regarding the MDPs as a strategic tool for combat. I've drawn some of my own conclusions based on what he told me. First, however, I need to ask BaaGah, Noony and Lolly a question. How many Mookookie do you think there are since you multiplied this last time?"

BaaGah screwed up his belly face in deep concentration. Jenny knew when he did this he was usually conferring with the "old ones". Sure enough, when his eyes came back into focus and his face relaxed, he sent: *"Old ones are unsure of how to tell you. Our numbers are different than your numbers. We aren't so many as to be too many for our planet. Still, plenty of foods and plenty of stuffs. Of course, always room in the spaces too. Spaces is many manys. Lots and lots. We are many and many more than the other peoples in domes."*

He touched a saltshaker on the table. It turns out that salt seemed to be a necessary thing for most living things, and the Groga were no exception to this. They ground their salt very fine, like what her mom called "popcorn salt".

"This bottle with little tiny salts does not have as many as the Mookookie are now."

Burt let out a low whistle. *"You have been busy little Mookookies."*

"Every Mookookie does their part."

"Bob says he needs Mookookie help to defeat the bad guys. Lots and lots. Needs a Mookookie buddy to help. They will be working in the MDPs and other spaces. Can you do this?"

Once again BaaGah's eyes went unfocused and his mouth twisted as he concentrated. *"Old ones say Mookookie help. Mookookie not afraid. Mookookie strong in the spaces. Helps our buddies. Helps big, big, BIG!"*

He sprouted long arms and held his hand out wide to show how very big their help would be.

Jenny couldn't help but smile at the generosity and consistent cheerfulness of her little Mookookie friends.

"I also need the help of the Mookookie to protect the Groga people. The Groga have many, many soldiers. Are there enough Mookookie to help them as well?"

"Older ones say help and help and help!" BaaGah affirmed. *"Alliance people's get our world back for us. We help Alliance make the bad guys go away and stop, stop, stop hurting peoples and being so very, very mean!"*

BaaGah's enthusiasm was infectious. The three of them sprouted short legs and arms and did an impromptu dance on the table. Jenny, Elizabeth, and Burt couldn't help but laugh. Jenny welcomed the short relief of the tension that seemed so constant in her life now.

"So, Jenny, what do you have up your sleeve? You've been really quiet lately, mostly letting the rest of us do all the talking. In my recent personal experience with the Gatekeeper, this means you're hatching something and you're just waiting to spring it on us."

Elizabeth nodded; one eyebrow raised in question.

"You are very observant, Burt. I do indeed have a plan. It will require timing and the support of my friends and my buddies, the Mookookie. Because our space fleet is in hiding awaiting the arrival of the Norgoth fleet who intend to decimate the planet from above, I believe that following that encounter the Norgoth will realize they have no choice but to wage a ground war.

This time my plan cannot be withheld from my friends, as I will need every one of you, including the Daringi and the Groga to agree or it won't work. There are some aspects of it I must keep to myself, but it comes down to whether or not my allies trust Chidwi and me and my newfound, but yet unspecified abilities. If I am right, we can conquer in this part of the conflict. It won't stop the Insenium from any of their other conquests, but it might make them think twice about ever attacking the Groga again."

"Have you talked to my father about this?" inquired Elizabeth softly. It was clear she didn't want to offend Jenny with the question, but she also needed to know. Their last venture had cost Elizabeth nearly as much as it had cost Jenny. Jenny knew she could never put her adopted sister through that intentionally again.

"I did that before I brought you both in here. He approved it. I told him every bit of it, and he agreed that for now, I should hold one part of it back to be assured there are no leaks. If that gets out, we might never get the opportunity to implement it. Tarafau is presenting what I told him to the Groga council as we speak. If you can agree to trust me on this one part, I will tell you the rest and specifically what I need from each of you to carry this off. Can we agree on that?"

Burt and Elizabeth nodded solemnly, and even the Mookookie looked up at her with big eyes. *"Mookookie agree, Jenny. We trust our buddy."*

"Very well; this is what I want to do and what I will need..."

Chapter 27: Lights Out

One of the things Lova loved best about her little valley compound was that she was completely self-sufficient and shut out from the cares of the world around her. She took great comfort in knowing that, although she would never get kudos or credit for it, what she and her fellow Guardians did was protecting the rest of the inhabitants of her beloved Earth.

She knew that the populations of Earth were still struggling to have any real solidarity as the human race, but she had hope for them and would never give up the dream that someday the varying cultures of Earth would be able to find peace and some kind of unity, or at least tolerance for their differences.

She didn't tend to keep up much with the politics that thundered around her little valley, but she did try to not be so isolated that she lost sympathy and compassion for her fellow Earthlings.

Fortunately, her relationships with her fellow Guardians helped her to generally stay on top of things. With the help of the Dimensional Alliance she had some pretty amazing defenses here in her valley. All of the electronics and tech used in the lodge and outbuildings were shielded from electromagnetic attacks and there was an invisible protective dome to protect from fallout from a nuclear disaster of pretty much any type. They were also shielded from prying eyes and were undetectable by satellite observation or any type of device that detected heat or energy signatures.

And with the stepped-up security measures being taken at every existing gate facility, all of the other gates were now similarly protected. This was why it was a puzzle to her how the Norgoth had succeeded in invading the Puerto Rico gate. Besides Sanglarka, it had the most security measures in place on Earth. It worried her that they were able to infiltrate such a heavily guarded area.

She was extremely grateful for the quick response of Juan and Luz's people. She shuddered to think of the potential outcome otherwise. The Norgoth had been transported off world to a facility used by the Alliance for dangerous prisoners.

The prison planet was large enough to house several large institutions; some medical, and some were simply prisons where felons were held until they could be transferred to a world with no gates and no access to technologies that would allow the prisoners to ever be a threat in the multiverse again.

She admired the stand the Alliance had taken on truly wishing to allow people to make their own choices. Even when there were those who threatened the relative peace of the dimensions, they preferred to simply separate those who would make trouble for others instead of euthanizing or imprisoning them for life.

She knew she couldn't afford to assume that the Norgoth or the Insenium were done with planet Earth. They knew, from experience that Earth was a key player in all of this and they likely didn't realize that the Gatekeeper wasn't in residence on Earth at this time.

Lova wasn't so sure she was much safer where she was, but hopefully they had the Insenium confused on that point. There were agents stationed at the Los Angeles gate, but they had seen no obvious activity targeted at that location.

They had put out the rumor in Jenny's neighborhood that Jenny was away on a writing assignment and was temporarily renting out her home in her absence. This gave the agents freedom to move about the neighborhood, apparently jogging or working in the yard.

Lova retired to the gym to do her mental exercises and her stretches and work the forms for the quarterstaff and hand to hand with Arvid. The others were currently manning the situation room. They took turns these days in the workout room to be sure the communications area of the situation room was constantly manned. They had troopers on staff these days, which was a relief. It meant everyone was able to get adequate sleep and that all stations were getting needed attention.

Arvid nodded to her as she entered the workout room. He had just come out from the pool area and was drying his white wild spiky hair with a towel.

"Any news?" he asked.

"Pretty much the usual. All different forces are on full alert and battle ready. Plans in different quadrants of the planets of the Great Insenium are proceeding apace. Brendan's space fleet is hiding behind moons or asteroids in each quadrant as well as Brendan's main body, currently hidden behind the two moons that circle the Groga planet. Jenny expects the first strike to be at the Groga before the Insenium focuses entirely on the Alliance and based on all the intel we have; the Alliance Council agrees. There are no signs that the Inseni know our space fleets are in their dimension. I doubt they realize it is possible to transport a space fleet trans-dimensionally.

"I wouldn't have thought it possible myself," Arvid agreed. *"Our Science and Technology Team has been working overtime and breaking a lot of previous barriers we had thought immutable."*

"I think it is interesting what kinds of barriers come down in the mind when pressure is applied. Necessity truly can be the mother of invention, as Earthlings are fond of saying. In our case, it also helps to have some of the most brilliant minds in the multiverse working on the issues".

"I admit to having a certain amount of pride that so many of those minds originated on Earth." Lova sent with a twinkle in her eyes.

"Hmmph," Arvid snorted, but then sent. *"The Earthlings have certainly surprised many of us in that regard. You may be behind in much of the technology my people take for granted, but you tend to play catchup quite nicely. Some of your solutions have taken our best scientists by surprise. Argent is more and more impressed with your part of their team. That being said, he isn't admitting it where anyone can hear."* And he chuckled at that.

Suddenly the klaxon in the lodge went off. Even in deepest meditation, there would have been no ignoring that. Both Arvid and Lova jumped up from where they had settled down on the mat.

They sprinted for the situation room where many had already gathered. Some were running downstairs, still in their pajamas, as it had been their sleeping shift. The group parted to allow Lova and Arvid to the space in front of the overhead display.

"There has been a planetwide blackout," the trooper manning the desk explained to the group. *"Alliance satellites detected nothing that would create a strong enough EMP to do this. For now, we may be the only place on the planet, besides the other gate locations to have any power or communications abilities. One of the dangers is that the many satellites in orbit have also been affected, including the international space station.*

Although all of their communications and power are shielded, they were still affected. They are scrambling to rectify the situation, but for now they are concerned that their orbit may be affected and potentially decay and that they may quickly run out of oxygen. And they have no way of communicating any of this to their home base.

As far as we can tell, no communications on earth have been re-established. It's really quiet out there."

Lova stood there for a moment along with the rest of those gathered there and considered. *"At this point I don't know what we can do to help outside of our boundaries. Please continue to monitor all communication frequencies. Is the Alliance network still functioning?"*

"Evidently, or at least, so far. It does mean, however, that our bandwidth now sticks out like a clown in a graveyard. Should we shut it down temporarily and just communicate via gateways?"

"That is a good suggestion, but before we do, notify every gate what we are about to do and why. Let them know we will contact them in 24 hours. If any communication is necessary between now and then, tell them to send a courier through their gate."

The trooper nodded and tapped out a quick message to all receiving stations, and Lova turned to the rest of those gathered in the crowded room. *"For now, we will be in low profile mode, per Alliance emergency regulations. No lights at night that can be seen from space. No attempted signals until we give the all clear. Gariel and I will go to Alliance Headquarters' and get further instructions.*

Arvid, please hold down the fort until we contact you. Now, if you were in bed, if you can, please go back and get your rest. Even with the network down, the situation room will need to be manned. Our sensors and shields are all up as well as security cameras and will need constant surveillance. For now, go about your regular duties. Gariel and I will report back in 24 hours. If you don't see us by then, take whatever measures are necessary to protect the compound until you receive further instructions. I know I can depend on every one of you to do your duty without panic."

She looked into the eyes of each of them. One by one they nodded and returned to their duties. She noticed that none of them went immediately upstairs. They knew that Arvid kept a pot of chamomile tea constantly available on the warmer to help those who needed it to get to sleep. Tonight, that would be helpful as the worry was real. Although this worldwide blackout was very suspicious under the circumstances, it was also entirely possible that it was some sort of natural phenomenon hitherto unknown or at least not recorded in history.

Lova and Gariel stepped through the gate minutes later. All looked normal there. The upped security meant there were always guards at the gate as well as at the bottom of the hill.

They were greeted and escorted down to a waiting hover car after Lova stated their business. She knew they would send ahead to alert the Alliance Council they were on their way. There was no evidence of panic or concern as the hover car made its way down the main street. The guard greeted them at the huge double doors in front of the headquarters building and told them to go straight up to the private council room as they were expected.

In the reception area they were greeted and sent directly into the council room. On the dais, Liliath and her new councilors and several members of the Science and Technology Team were seated in a semicircle before them.

"*Welcome, Lova and Gariel. We got your message before you suspended communications. This is a grave situation. I included our scientists in this meeting as we need to explore all potential possibilities and options. Please take a moment to tell us what you know about the situation and then, I think Argent may have some things to say.*"

"*Thank you, Liliath. What we know is this: With no warning and no discernable cause, all power on Earth, with the exception of the gate facilities, has gone dark. This includes some things, such as certain kinds of battery power. Our surveillance satellites detected no blast or natural occurrence to account for an EMP that powerful.*

Most of the major governments have shielded their tech and power sources, but this affected all of them as well. All communications are silent and every powered satellite, as far as we can tell, has been shut down. We are aware of the situation of the international space station, but we are unsure if they are in any imminent danger."

"*So, our technology evidently has better shielding. Might this be the purpose of this attack; to locate our tech and the Earth gates simply because they have power, and the rest of the Earth is without?*" Argent asked.

"*That definitely occurred to us, which is why we shut down the communications network and silenced our surveillance satellites. At this point, only the gates are powered and, of course, their power source is different than the rest of earth. We've warned all gates to shut down any external power source for now, and we are taking steps at Sanglarka as well, regardless of our superior shielding. We are making every effort not to stand out in case anyone is watching.*"

"*This is good,*" Argent agreed. "*Before the satellites were shut down, we did see an unusual power surge emanating from the moon. We know the Chinese have been doing some exploration of the dark side, but they don't have the technology to do this. We are sending shielded interstellar drones via the Australian gate to investigate. They shouldn't show up on any radar devices and will also be difficult to be spotted visually as they are camouflaged to blend in with the darkness of space. When we have more intel, we will send a courier with the entire report.*

One of the biggest puzzles is how they managed to effect the entire globe, as this sort of thing usually requires 'line of sight' to work on a global scale. This screams alien interference to me. Although it behaves like an EMP surge, it may have been something beyond any technology we're aware of."

"We will make resources available to repair the infrastructure of the power grid on earth, without making our presence known. If this was caused by our mutual enemy, we will see to it that it doesn't happen again," Liliath assured them. "We must protect the Gatekeeper's gate at all costs. And we are not willing to put our Earthling friends in danger. Your assistance in all of this has been invaluable and you deserve our support."

Lova bowed her head slightly to acknowledge her appreciation. Currently she had no words big enough.

"I will want a battalion of troopers as soon as possible stationed at the Sanglarka gate to be prepared for a potential attack," added Gariel. "I believe it would take a while for them to pinpoint us in our valley, but it can't hurt to be prepared. Also, I would like to increase the numbers hidden in the gateroom in Los Angeles. They have the equipment they need to defend the gate and they have been issued Earth style National Guard uniforms to blend in if they need to leave the house during the crisis."

Lova was appreciative of the preventative steps they were taking to protect Earth and the gates. The Norgoth would not concern themselves with "technology pollution" or whether or not Earthlings were ready for any of this.

They would do what they always did. They would invade, subdue the population and be over seven billion slaves richer. Not that the Earth wouldn't put up a valiant fight, but none of them were ready for anything like this.

There were indeed some potential issues with the Alliance aiding Earth with this, but much less than the invasion and destruction that would be caused by the Insenium, if they decided to invade.

It was the primary manifesto of the Dimensional Alliance to protect all beings from those who might be taken advantage of by dimensions with superior technology. But they also believed every culture should be allowed to develop naturally without interference from other dimensions. This was the purpose of establishing the gate network with its gate Guardians, making sure there were no "accidental" or purposeful invasions. Earth's history was peppered with these, most of which were now thought of as myths and legends, such as dragons, wizards, elves, and dwarves.

Even knowing that, Lova was gratified that the current leadership felt so strongly about this and were willing to put pretty words into concrete action.

"Thank you." She finally sent. *"We'll get back home and make sure the Guardians and the troopers who are providing security are aware they will be receiving support and instructions via the gate network. If there is nothing else…?"*

"No. By all means, return. Argent will complete his report and you will be hearing from him soon."

When Lova returned to Sanglarka with Gariel, they split up to give instructions to their teams. Gariel would send couriers out immediately to the various gates, and Lova would brief her communication team on what the Council had said.

As she entered the situation room, all was eerily silent. The usual buzz of activity had slowed to anxious focus on the dead, blank screens, hoping for the slightest indication that there was some communication of any kind happening out there.

"Nothing," the trooper manning the primary station said, deadpan. He shook his head. *"I've never seen anything like this."*

"It will be ok, sergeant. Take a break. I'll take over for now. Meeting here in about 20 minutes."

He nodded and stood. Lova shook his hand. *"Thank you for your help. Please notify the others."*

"And now we wait," she said aloud in Swedish.

Chapter 28: Payback Ala Sam

By now she had lost track of how many large towns she had tromped through. This one was more of a city and the home base of the 9th Battalion. They were next on her list. She had assumed multiple Norgoth personas during her trek. She had obtained a list of the various military bases that were within walking distance. For her, that meant about 30-50 miles. She could cover the distance within a couple days with time to rest and be refreshed each time she punished the troops.

If she had her way, she would manage to disarm and destroy every military base in the Insenium, but she was limited to this one planet. So, she decided, she would do as much damage as she could.

She had acted in the first instance out of instinct and shock. She hadn't known consciously that she could do this thing. She had heard of something called a shout, but she didn't think this was that particular ability as she had not been knocked out when she did it.

This had been something primal and vicious; something she should have always somehow known was within her, and yet, something totally unexpected to her reasonable mind.

So, as she neared the city, she licked her lips in anticipation. She allowed her anger to build and build to the point that she felt she must be glowing by now for everyone to see. However, Norgoths passed her on the street without even paying any attention to the nondescript fellow Norgoth with a small pack on her back. She passed under an archway between buildings and glancing around, changed into her corporal persona, to allow her easy and unnoticed access to the military base.

Again, no one paid her any mind and she passed through the city, controlling strictly her desire to scowl and growl at every Norgoth she passed. As she finally neared the gates to the base, it was all she could do not to cut down the guard who stood, eyes glazed, watching the various people come and go through the wide boulevard that led into the base proper. In an emergency, the path would be blocked by a wide portcullis that could be dropped instantly by the guard at any time.

She was gratified to discover she wouldn't have to wait for an assembly of soldiers, as she had sometimes had to do.

The parade ground was full of rank on rank of Norgoth soldiers in their best uniforms. This was obviously some sort of ceremony. In the military these were held often and for sometimes seemingly trumped up reasons to boost morale and to give soldiers something to do besides the usual drills and training. There they all were, a complete battalion, flags flying indicating the Insenium, their city and the battalion designation.

Sam couldn't believe her good luck. The battalion flag indicated that this was indeed the 9th Battalion. Had it not been, she would have waited patiently, finding some obscure thing to do that she might appear to be busy and then attacking there first. This particular battalion was the first layer in her final plan to pay them back tenfold for what they did to her people. Her parents!

She made her way to the stands in the back of the assembled dignitaries and waited, allowing her anger to build once again. She would know when it was high enough. She listened with only half an ear while some general droned on and on about the glory of the empire. Glory! Phah! She would show them glory. The battalion stood at attention, from where she stood no more than little toy soldiers. They would pay! They would pay in blood and conflagration!

Suddenly she swelled again to four times her normal size, her disguise falling from her. She was Engoza the destroyer. She was death. She was destruction. THEY WOULD PAY!

The surging power struck from her mind like the forward wave of a tsunami. She watched with satisfaction as everyone within a thousand foot radius toppled and dissolved to fine black ash. Once again she changed back to her uniformed persona, exclaiming in a loud and panicked voice: *"She killed them all! Beware Engoza the Destroyer! She is death! Flee! Flee for your lives!"*

She imagined as she went, finally changing personas to a common Norgoth, what tales were beginning to circulate about these events. Would they think the Alliance had developed some kind of new and potent weapon? Would they think it was sorcery? What of this Engoza? Would they know she was Fleistian? Would the general public have any idea what their government was doing?

She beat herself up mentally over and over again for falling for the line "order in the multiverse". Why couldn't she see they were nothing more than interdimensional bullies? How could she have been so blinded by their flattery and impressive speeches? How had her parents been deceived? How many other government leaders of other cultures had been similarly deceived, handing over their planets without a shot having been fired? When she realized how she had been used, it fired the flames of her anger even higher than before.

She decided she needed more speed if she was to create the path of destruction she so desired. Word would get out. Security measures would be taken. This suited her just fine. Let them panic into error. Let them spread rumors and misinformation that she would gladly provide in every inn and tavern on her way. She bought one of their two wheeled conveyances as she couldn't take the chance of stealing something. This would give her the ability to make the next base in about a day with time to rest along the way and spread her rumors, the wilder the better.

The next town already had some rumors flying around, although the people spoke them in whispers to their neighbors. Rumor-mongering was considered a punishable offense in Inseni culture and by their laws. Sam went to the marketplaces, the inns and other public places and watched for those most susceptible to her message. She then would assume a new face and new rank. No need giving them a vital clue by being the same panicked corporal every time.

She fell into a pattern from town to town; spreading rumors to the common folk and then creating devastation on the military base. Each time she did it, it took less and less effort to destroy the masses of troops and others in the radius of her destruction. The idea that she might also be destroying innocents never occurred to her. In her opinion, they were all guilty and needed to be punished. Each time she fled the scene as a panicked soldier or commoner, yelling her message about Engoza the Destroyer, creating panic and disorder in her wake.

Within a week, she had destroyed five more battalions and she was beginning to feel invincible. Something in the back of her mind told her not to be so self-assured. The Inseni were idiots but not stupid. They would eventually begin to up security to the point that it would take longer to get into a place to create the most possible destruction.

Unlike the shout, it didn't seem to matter whether people were in earshot or not. Reports she had heard said that even people in buildings surrounding her target and in a 360-degree circle were turned into fine black ash. She had taken joy running through the ashes, the dust accumulating on her shoes. She didn't even bother to wash it off, as it gave credence to the stories she told in every city and town she entered.

During her last foray she had encountered a military courier and assumed his identity, including the uniform he wore. Couriers often were allowed to pass guards, even when they scrutinized everyone else. She had blithely "acquired" the message from his message bag as she had bought him a drink and slapped him on the back good naturedly.

Now with her bicycle and her uniform, it might be easier to get through security, especially since she could wave an official-looking document in their faces as she passed.

The path of destruction she had plotted out would bring her to the capitol city in a little over a week from now. Her plan for that city was a little different, but for now she just needed to keep moving.

Chapter 29: High Security

Lova greeted the courier in the situation room. She no longer greeted people at the gate in the meadow. There were troopers guarding the gateway day and night. All incoming and outgoing visitors went through an additional security check besides the one that looked like a rose trellis that arched the gateway. Their orders were that no one passed through the gateway without it, whether the guards thought they recognized them or not.

Sanglarka had been widely known for their hospitality and kindness. Now that they could no longer receive advanced notice of travelers through the gate, high security measures had to be taken. DNA scanners were now part of that security. If any of the visitors through the gate had DNA of Groga, Fleistian or Norgoth, they would be immediately anesthetized and put under quarantine in a little known area on the grounds that constituted their "dungeon". She could only remember it ever being used one time and, that was for quarantine for possible infection and the people who had been their guests in the dungeon at that time had praised their kindness and generosity.

She told the courier to wait and sent one of her troopers to gather the primary members of her team. She didn't want to waste time. These reports along with the team's recommendations would be immediately passed via gateway to all operating gates.

As they all assembled, Arvid standing on one side and Gariel on the other, she found herself grateful for the encouragement and support of her team. She had worked with people in the past, especially in the military where it was all about one-up-man-ship and rivalry. Not so with her team. She knew she could count on every single member of her team to do their part and step in to help a comrade or give that extra hand when it was needed.

When they had all assembled themselves, she asked Arvid: *"Will you read the report to us, my friend? You have the clearest mental voice here."*

Arvid nodded and began: *"The following report was compiled by Argent and approved by Liliath."*

Lova noticed the lack of titles. Anyone receiving this would know perfectly well who they were without any fanfare or formality.

"After a careful scan of the space around planet Earth we have discovered the following:

> *The international space station, due to superior shielding and automated backup systems, is functioning properly. They have not been able to communicate with Earth but continue to send signals out.*

> *From space there are no discernable signs of life or communication. During the night cycles of the planet, there isn't the tiniest spark of light, including all areas where there are active gate compounds.*

> *The biggest current problem is that the orbits of satellites and space trash are beginning to decay slightly. This will be a bigger problem the longer the planet is without power, especially where some of the larger satellites are concerned.*

> *There is nothing that we can find on the surface of the moon that might have caused this, but there is a spot where it appears something massive exploded and left debris and a large new crater where it emanated from. We have no idea why this explosion did not show up from our satellite before.*

Drone observation of Earth itself shows major cities in great chaos. Many large-scale disasters were created when passenger, military, and cargo airplanes and jets fell from the sky, killing not only their passengers but creating destruction in several large cities.

Emergency services are limited to what people can do on foot. Looting and other illegal activities have meant that local military are also out trying to keep order, but without the availability of motorized vehicles, it is taking much longer for them to get to those needing their help than could be hoped.

Power plants have been temporarily switched off to allow them to open up the power resources in stages to prevent a damaging power surge. Anything that was powered by batteries or other power sources continues to not function.

At this point the Alliance sees no option but to offer limited assistance to the people of your planet. We say limited, as we don't want the people of Earth to realize where the help is coming from. We still are of the opinion that this is not a good time to have the Alliance 'go public' as it were.

So, to prevent further panic and to give the humans hope and no reason to blame various nations for these problems, the first thing we need to do is to reestablish power and communications, preferably worldwide. For that reason, as the only representatives Earth has at this point to make any decisions, we ask you if Earth can accept these offers.

If so, we will do something we never have before done. Jenny will enter the dreams of the top scientists of every country with solutions that will seem reasonable to them to try.

Although the solutions we will be presenting to the various scientists on earth will appear to work on their own, they will not be aware that we gave it a little, um, 'boost', as it were.

When the power comes on and communications are reestablished, they will discover that the International Space Station has been sending a non-stop emergency message proclaiming that this was not caused by any technology on Earth. They continue to send this message in a constant stream to all listening governmental agencies. This should hopefully prevent any blaming or give any reason for aggression from one government to another. As far as Earth is concerned, it was a mysterious, but natural phenomenon that caused this.

We will also repower all of the orbiting satellites ourselves, to prevent any further damage on earth from them re-entering the atmosphere.

We have nothing but suspicions regarding the incident that caused this. Samples of the crater and any substances that are not naturally occurring on your moon have been taken and are being examined and tested by our Science Team.

In the meantime, although we feel fairly sure that none of the gates gave themselves away during the blackout, please continue all high security measures until power is fully reestablished.

We continue to plow through all of the data generated by our Norgoth friends from the Puerto Rico gate. Their orders had been simple: They were to discover whatever was in the outbuildings of the complex and destroy everything they saw, then to return and report. What portal they were using is still a mystery, but we continue to search the huge amounts of data produced by our mental probes.

Thank you for your attention: Argent"

Arvid finished reading and looked up at Lova. *"Well, this won't solve all the issues caused by this, whatever it is, but it does give us a direction to go. Let us continue in high security mode. I don't want to resume interacting with the Alliance communication network until the lights come back on around the world."*

"In the meantime, please distribute this report to our gate couriers and have them report back to me with any needs of any of the teams or individual Gate Guardians," Lova said.

She had learned from experience that decisive action in the face of uncertainty was usually the best course. *"Let them know there will be more instructions by courier over the coming days and as we know more about the prosecution of the dimensional war, we will be in touch. This report has been uploaded now to every tablet within the Sanglarka compound."*

The trooper officer responsible for courier activities saluted Gariel and ran out the door to notify his fellow couriers and start getting the information through the gateways as soon as possible.

Lova felt reassured at the calm reaction of her fellows. Even with the seemingly constant expansion of the crisis brought down on them by their enemies, she took a great deal of comfort in knowing that all were working at top capacity to come to the best possible solutions to the various issues caused by this war. She had hoped it would never come down to dealing with this on her home planet, but she knew they were not the only ones suffering.

Chapter 30: Miles to Go Before I Sleep

Jenny stretched and yawned. It had been a long day. She had been the only real communication that the Alliance Earth Guardians had at the moment, and she had spent a good part of the day relaying the special "dreams" to the various scientists on her list. She had discovered that her abilities had extended to a point where she didn't have to know the person well to communicate with them. She had basically connected Argent with each scientist, and he had implanted the scenario and the necessary technical information that would allow them to turn the power back on.

The scientists weren't told that the steps they were taking would actually simply trigger a mechanism that had been surreptitiously implanted within the power system to jumpstart it. Jenny could see, however, that these concepts, when followed up by tinkerers like Bob, would lead to new discoveries about electric power generation and future shielding from similar situations.

The disruption of life on Earth had been universal, with the exception of those few cultures that still lived a primitive low tech lifestyle, such as the people she had encountered in the Amazon Basin this past year.

She was pretty worn out. Although using her ability required nothing but that she be peaceful and focused, that focus actually seemed to take a physical toll on her. She had been stopping only to eat and sleep, but even in her sleep she was working, connecting various individuals for dream conversations, and trying to keep everything straight. The many requests for her "conference call" ability meant scheduling a lot of nighttime visits, as not everyone was on the same timeline.

She had finally gotten through her long list. Chidwi had gently chastised her for working too many hours, but Jenny could see no help for it. Hopefully once the various scientists and technicians had put the patches into place, the Alliance could reestablish the Earth arm of the Alliance communication network. This would lighten her load considerably, and hopefully it would mean she could get some rest.

She had made a pact with herself not to complain about all of her responsibilities, but it was becoming harder and harder. Burt and Elizabeth had expressed concern that she was impacting her immune system and had both been "mothering" her, making sure she ate and drank and rested. Her bodyguards were working in shifts, monitoring things inside and outside of the little cottage and escorting her assiduously anytime she set foot outside the door to attend any meetings that were necessary for her to attend.

Tarafau had taken over most of those duties for her as it was his expertise and resources the Groga most needed. She was grateful for that, and Elizabeth seemed to take great comfort that he was so near. So much of her life he had been coming and going between Earth and his family, seldom spending more than a few days. She had known his work was important, but it was refreshing for her to have him so close on a daily basis.

She padded into the little kitchen in her bare feet to get some of the wonderful restorative tea that Freia continued to make for her. She had assured Jenny that it had no real medicinal effect, and that she had removed the herbs that made her sleepy. It simply helped the body cope with stress. She then wandered into the little living room; cup in hand, to see what the rest were up to.

Burt was evidently at his post outside the cottage door. Elizabeth was happily chatting with the bodyguards while she assembled Nona's hair into the complex braids her people were so fond of. They smiled as Jenny entered the room, but Elizabeth's face immediately changed from light heartedness to concern.

"Jenny, when was the last time you took some time to just rest? You have purple circles under your eyes. And don't you dare tell me you have too much work to do to sleep. Mother and I were afraid of this. We knew as your abilities expanded and more of the Alliance was aware of what you could do that they might overwork you and we were right."

"I'm fine, Elizabeth. Really, I am. I was just going to have some tea and then head to bed. I came in to tell you that. Get me up at sunrise, though. I have three meetings to attend, one here and two for the Alliance."

"Will do," Mynn chimed in. *"But Elizabeth is right. You need to get more rest, or you will be of no use to anyone at all. Chidwi can you help her sleep; real sleep?"*

"I can and I will," Chidwi agreed in her soft Linkling mind voice. *"Everyone will just have to manage without her for a few hours."*

"You're all ganging up on me?"

Five heads, including Chidwi, nodded in cheerful agreement. Jenny shook her head, but she couldn't help but smile.

She took a last sip of her tea and left them to their chattering. She decided, however, to do a couple of things before retiring. She went out the front door and sure enough, there was Burt. He had replaced the barrel with a camp chair, and he was leaned back on two legs against the wall, whittling and observing.

"Hey there, sleepy head! Shouldn't you be resting? I know the girls were talking about hog-tying you the next time you got out of bed. Seriously, you look awful."

"Gee thanks, buddy. You really know how to sweet talk a girl."

"Yeah, well, there are girls and then there are girls. You belong in the latter category."

"What is that supposed to mean, exactly?"

"Exactly? Well..." and his face went from flippant to serious. "I guess that depends a lot on you, but I have made it no secret that I care for you."

"Hold on, I thought we agreed..."

"You agreed, Jenny. You decided. I just want you to know I am here and that my opinion of you has not changed. It will never change. I know right now you have way too much loading you down to spend any time creating or maintaining a serious relationship. I am able to be patient and I'm willing. I will be whatever to you that you need me to be, friend or...whatever. Was that exact enough?"

He hadn't said any of it unkindly. He wasn't angry. Jenny realized she had never known anyone quite like him. The whole thing was actually a little confusing to her. She had dated casually in high school and college, but never had any interest in a long term relationship with any of the young men she had dated...But what about Burt? She really didn't know, and she didn't have the luxury of time to figure it out.

"I appreciate your patience, Burt. I can't give you any answers right now, and I'm grateful you're willing to wait for me to figure it out. Regardless, I appreciate your friendship."

"OUCH!" Burt exclaimed, smacking his forehead with the back of his hand. "Friends? I was always told that was the romantic equivalent of the Kiss of Death where relationships were concerned. I'll take it the way I hope you meant it. But really, why are you out here?"

"I just felt like I should take a minute and thank you for everything you do. You really have become the glue that holds my part of this team together and I realized I hadn't actually ever thanked you for that."

He grinned his patented Burt grin. "Well, you're welcome, Jenny. Just doin' my part."

"No, Burt, I really mean it. When we first met, I couldn't help but think of you as a cocky kid, albeit a skilled one. Knowing you better, I realize that there is a really big heart and an amazing brain hiding behind that grin of yours." And she leaned down and kissed his cheek. "Thank you."

He touched his cheek where her kiss had landed, his face reflecting something Jenny didn't quite recognize.

"You're welcome," he replied simply, and Jenny noted his voice was a little husky.

"OK, so back to bed, as everyone keeps insisting. Be careful out here." And she turned and went back into the cottage and straight to her bedroom.

She immediately assumed a cross-legged position on her bed, to work through her usual pre-bedtime mental workout. Chidwi jumped down behind her and rested her little hands on Jenny's shoulders. Jenny wasn't sure why, but recently, the feel of Chidwi's hands on her shoulders almost instantly induced a deep meditative state. Her breathing instantly slowed to the point that someone observing her would have wondered if she was breathing at all.

In this state she got out the little jeweled box and touched the jewel in the lid that never opened. At once scenes began to pass by on a kind of transparent screen before her mind's eye. She saw scenes of devastation on her home planet, a squadron of dragons flying over a wide valley she didn't recognize, surrounded by jagged cliffs. She saw each of the Earth guardians in turn, each working on their part of their team assignments, often more than one head bent over a tablet, which she assumed had orders from Alliance headquarters. She saw a crystal pool near a river, the wide rock next to it deserted. And finally, she saw the face of her mother. She was crying!

At this she put the little box away and drifted into communication mode. She dropped in on her parents as she wished she had time to do more often and saw that they were both alive and hopefully well. Her dad had his arms around her mom, snuggled up on the overstuffed couch in their living room. It was light outside. Mom was speaking to her Dad.

"I don't understand why she hasn't answered. I've sent three letters and nothing. And now this blackout or whatever it is." As she said that, the lamp on the end table next to the couch sprung into light.

"Oh! How amazing! They got the power back on! I wonder if we have cell service. I can call her!"

Her mom reached for her cell, but it was dead and needed to be charged. Jenny doubted that even with the power back online that internet or cellphones would be functional for a while. However, assuming the Alliance network was back up, she could text her mom and let her know she was alright.

She didn't drop in on them very often, which made her feel a little guilty. Although she had automated messages going out to various people in her family, it just wasn't the same as a live conversation, but she also didn't want to give away too much. Her drop-ins were strictly one way, which felt a lot like eavesdropping to her.

Having done this, she came out of her deep state and laid down, Chidwi by her side. She fell into a dreamless sleep. The rest would have to wait until tomorrow.

Chapter 31: Tinkering

B ob and Ignatius were whistling "Oh Susannah" together. Bob often whistled as he was working on something, and Ignatius had picked up the habit early on in their relationship. He had somehow figured out how to add a harmony line instead of just whistling the melody and he was actually pretty accurate, so, in Bob's opinion, they sounded pretty nice together.

He was working on the new drone design for the TTAP that would soon be put into production by one of the Alliance supporting dimensions. He loved having complete access to production facilities without having to go through tons of paperwork and having to come up with the funding on his own.

Adelle had provided him with a private work area, unlike the ones in the main lab, for his "tinkering". This was not so much because of the promise he had made to the Alliance about not passing on "dastardly alien tech" to Earthlings, as everyone working in this lab was an Alliance agent of one level or another and all of them were completely clued in on what he was working on, but Bob had needed some thinking and working space without any distractions if he was going to carry this off.

She happily complied, giving him a place on the second floor, where no one was working at the time. The space was generally used for Adelle's computer science projects, which meant it was a "clean room", limiting things like airborne particles that could interfere with delicate operations.

He really didn't need that kind of precision for his project, but the place was also soundproof which meant drilling, shaping parts and his and Ignatius' whistling wouldn't bother any of the others who were working on equally important, but not as noisy, components of the Alliance's offense tactics against the Insenium.

Fidget was busy reshaping a tool he was going to use for the next stage of the program. He had equipped Fidget from the beginning with interchangeable tools that sprouted from his arms. Fidget was incredibly precise as long as he had a visual pattern to go by. With this specific project, preciseness was going to be key.

The prototype had to be exact, and every step of the process was being visually documented from more than one angle. The number of graphic files associated with the project was astounding, but he was leaving nothing to chance. He hoped to finish in a day or so and the factory would create a prototype and send it back to him within a few days from then.

At that point he would test the drone and, assuming it worked according to his specifications, he could give the go ahead. They had told him they were capable of producing thousands of drones in a matter of days as their factory had no human workers other than those who programmed the factory robotics and did quality control. His part of the plan would require a few thousand of the drones.

He already had the Nanoites working on improving the Nanobots he had programmed. Right now, there were over 20,000 Nanobots waiting to be deployed.

He was grateful for the experience he had gained both in the Earth military and in their recent excursions into the Louisiana swamp and the Amazon basin. He had gotten the opportunity to test some of his ideas under real battle conditions, and being the tinkerer he was, he had taken copious notes about the outcomes and performance of his drones and Burt's little bug friends. The result was that when it came time to brainstorm with Gariel when he had come to visit the Science and Technology Team, he had plenty of potential suggestions for tactics and improvements that would make the tech more useful.

Gariel had been excited to finally talk to a scientist with some real battle experience and they had continued to speak with one another several times a week via the Alliance communication network. Thus, Gariel had gotten the chance to give lots of input into the project. He had consulted with the other scientists as well. He had been very intrigued with a little nuance Xao Ting was working on that surprisingly had little to do with his usual herbs and tinctures.

Adelle and the rest had been given various assignments in regard to the MDP research Bob had been conducting and the Mookookie had shown up with a trooper carrying them in an MDP created especially for their use. They were willing helpers, and the other scientists had delighted in working with them. A few of them had bonded with some of the little "buddies", with the injunction that there was to be no new budding and that they were never to appear in the presence of a non-Alliance Earthling.

About the time Bob finished with the part he was working on he heard from the intercom: "Bob! You've got to see this! Come here. We need you!"

Bob carefully set down his tools, changed out of his clean room clothing and took Ignatius's clean room suit off of him, then perched him on the shoulder pad Bob wore to protect himself from Ignatius's claws. They could be painful when he became upset, excited, or over-balanced.

Outside of the quiet lab he could now hear excited voices all talking at once. They quietened the moment he entered the main lab area. He was afraid he might witness the phenomena of their faces splitting in two, their grins were so big.

"We did it! You've got to see this!" Dhakira exclaimed, her dark eyes showing more white than iris. She pointed urgently at the screen floating above her head. The spreadsheet displayed on the screen was toting up locations and coordinates, and they were being added to the spreadsheet so fast that the words and numbers were softly blurred.

"It's the Mookookies, those clever little buddies! They're doing it, exactly as you said. The insides of the MDPs are actual locations and we can track them. How did you ever figure that out?"

Bob shook his head. Asking a scientist where they got their ideas was no different than asking an artist or writer where they got their inspiration. It was such a combination of past experience, theory, observation, instinct and putting it all together. In this case, however, it was fairly simple, at least to his mind.

"I had the advantage of communication with the Nanoites. If their story was true and there was no reason to doubt that it wasn't, then it stood to reason that they were in a trackable dimension. We discovered when the Daringi and the Mookookie were working together that the Mookookie, like the Daringi, are able to determine the coordinates of any place they can have physical access to. We also know that, even without adjusting the atmosphere of the interior of an MDP, Mookookies can handle the atmosphere there.

Burt found that out by accident, as BaaGah had discovered the food cache he kept in his MDP storage. So, if we wanted to have access to the MDPs as a potential troop, supplies and equipment transport device in places where we don't have a gate network in place, we needed to map them. You'll notice, once the numbers slow down, that the owner of each MDP is also listed as well. This means that we can get whatever we need to a specific person without even using the gate network. Now that we can do this, I think we can have some pretty amazing surprises for our Inseni friends.

Thank you, one and all for working on this. This may well be the lynchpin of our battle strategy. I'm betting on the idea that the Norgoths don't have anything like this. When we add Xao Ting's little project..." and he winked at Xao Ting, who laughed and bowed, "we should be able to create the chaos and destruction that is necessary to bring this situation under control.

I know we still will have years of clean up to come, but for now, if we can accomplish what we set out to do with a limited number of casualties, we will have done our part and should create a safety buffer that should give us the time we need to eventually stamp out this problem once and for all."

They applauded. If Adelle would have allowed such a thing in her spotless lab, he thought they might have been throwing confetti.

"I'll get this out to Gariel to distribute the list to the Daringi captains. I've created a subroutine for the spreadsheet to make it easily searchable for any who need access. It is highly encrypted and will require a small DNA sample of skin cells to activate. Any DNA pattern not recognized as belonging to a Dimensional Alliance member species will shut down the program and destroy the file," Dhakira reported.

Bob was so impressed with her skills in computational combinatorics, which she had vastly under-stated in her original introduction to him. She was a genius when it came to taking a theoretical problem and discovering flaws and possibilities based on logic, math, and sometimes pure horse sense. She could make a computer turn cartwheels, and he loved long involved conversations with her about various scientific theories, especially where it applied to gate network science.

He had become so used to working on his own up until he became an Alliance Agent. But here were minds he could relate to in his own bailiwick.

"How's your project coming, Xao Ting?" He asked when the noise quieted down a bit. Several of them had gone to the break room to celebrate further with some food and maybe a video game challenge or so.

Xao Ting looked up at Bob. Bob was not a tall man, actually quite average in that department, but Xao Ting was definitely deceptively small. Bob had seen him take on much larger opponents during their martial arts workouts almost as if fighting in his sleep.

He leaned closer, blinking a few times. "I think we are near completion. I think our military colleagues have little respect for a weapon that doesn't make big noises and lots of flash and bang," he confided. "But we have underestimated our foe in the past, to our detriment. It's one of the reasons I wanted to take a different approach. I know it isn't considered an offensive weapon, but I believe it will do more good and make a bigger difference than the bomb they originally requested of us."

"I agree. I'm learning to look at all of this with new eyes myself. I'm learning that the element of surprise is going to be vital if we have any chance to pull this off. I don't know what the Alliance scientists have made of the analysis they did of that moon dust they sampled, but I have real doubts that the Earth blackout was a natural phenomenon, and I can't see that any of the Earth scientists we are aware of could have pulled this off. After all, if they did, why didn't they shield their own people from it?"

"I believe you are right," Xao Ting said, holding up a bird treat for Ignatius, who took it daintily in one claw, balancing effortlessly on the other foot. They totally spoiled the smart aleck bird who took it only as his due.

"So, will we be able to deploy it the way we planned? I've never seen anything quite like it and I was wondering if it required more delicacy than our current deployment mechanism will provide."

"No, I have built-in stabilizers and individual shields to prevent premature initiation. I believe we will be able to deploy as soon as we have the rest of the infrastructure in place."

Bob slapped him none too gently on the back which didn't even phase the tiny man. "I love it when a plan comes together. Let's go get some of that cheesecake before it's gone. Arvid made it, you know."

Nothing more needed to be said.

Chapter 32: Digging Out and Digging In

E d Japhet was glad his wife was at home. Inside their quiet little neighborhood, you couldn't see any of the damage that had been caused just outside of town. They'd gotten a text from Jenny that morning telling them she was alright, but the non-disclosure agreement she had signed with the company she now worked for wouldn't allow her to say where she was.

He almost wished she was ghost-writing again. She couldn't talk about her writing, but it didn't take her all over heck and its half-acre so that she was almost never home. Her little house in the foothills of Los Angeles was nice enough, but it seemed a shame she couldn't just stay home and enjoy it more often than she did.

He had stopped listening to the radio in the car. The news was all just too sad. And it wasn't just in the states, but everyone was struggling all over the world. Their government had ruled out the possibility it was an attack from a foreign power, as there wasn't a single country that didn't get blacked out.

Several smaller countries were still struggling to get the power back on, as their power plants weren't as automated as most of the power plants worldwide. Organizations like the Red Cross had been inundated with pleas for help. The United States Army Engineers had been deployed to help with the power situation, and the National Guards and Reserves of every state had been called out to help with the crisis within the states.

Based on nuclear science, there should have been a few nuclear power plants melt down, or in the process of a meltdown. Since even battery power had ceased to work, the backup generators in the power plants shouldn't have been able to keep the nuclear fuel cool enough to prevent it.

But for some reason none of their scientists could explain, all of the nuclear reactor fuel in every reactor on the planet had been at optimum temperature.

That didn't prevent trains from going off the rails or the many injuries when every automobile on the planet just stopped. It was particularly ugly on the freeways of the world, where speed limits could be up to 80 miles per hour. An instantaneous stop, even if no one hit anyone else, at high speeds caused many injuries and fatalities, even when people were wearing seatbelts. In the cases of the kind of drivers who typically tailgated the injuries and deaths were multiplied.

He shook his head. He knew his two oldest still moaned when remembering riding with him when he was in rant mode about following distance, directional signaling and paying attention while in a car. By the time Jenny had come along, he had mellowed out somewhat, but she still got the same advice when he was teaching her to drive.

He missed his kids. For forty years he had hauled his family all over the world with him, when he wasn't stationed in a war zone. The times apart were always hard on his family, but they had all been "good little soldiers" and learned quickly how to make new friends and get engaged right away in community resources and events.

He had once asked them if they had resented all of the moving and constant readjustments they had been required to make as a family. Without exception, all three of them, and his wife had adamantly assured him that few families had the opportunities for new adventures and seeing the world the way they had done.

Driving to the armory, the road was cluttered, but quiet. Broken and stalled vehicles were all over the place, but there was no traffic. One of the first things the United States government had done was to shut down all road traffic other than rescue or clean up vehicles. The moment the power had come back on, radios had started broadcasting stay at home orders to everyone who could hear it and the word had gotten out quickly. The people had been so shaken that most had adhered to the orders.

The news reports, although sporadic so far, were saying that in many larger cities and towns there were those who were either taking advantage of the situation by looting and robbing or just going out because they could. People who had not been on the road when it had happened still had operating vehicles, and his had been parked happily in his driveway at the time.

He had been surprised when the emergency broadcast system had announced that batteries were now working again. Most home computers were still nonfunctional due to data loss, as they hadn't had any shielding, but large corporations and government agencies still had working computers due to earlier shielding protocols based on the worry about EMP warfare.

One of the mysteries in all of this was how cell phones continued to work, as they were just small portable computers that happened to provide communication. Most apps on phones still weren't working, but for reasons no one could explain the basic operations of phone calls and texting still seemed to be functioning.

He arrived at the National Guard Armory. The military had recalled every retiree and former soldier to help out in the crisis, giving them active duty status for the duration. So, once again he left his home to do his duty and this time he had to leave his wife by herself. Since the kids had all left on their own adventures, he and Donna had been comfortable together, traveling to visit old friends from their army days and seeing a bit of the world they hadn't had a chance to do before.

Donna stayed busy, volunteering in the community and with their church, and always had one project or another going on to help someone who needed it. She was an accomplished seamstress, crafter, and baker, and he was so proud of her. He had asked her from time to time if she wanted a job outside the home and she answered happily that she had never had any desire to do anything outside her home to make money and she kept busy enough without that, "thank you very much".

He grinned every time he thought about her, even after all these years.

He pulled into the parking lot in an area reserved for officers and high ranking enlisted men. He had achieved the rank of Command Sargent Major in his military career. He could have easily been an officer, but he told people who asked why he didn't, "I'm just a hands-on kind of guy" and left it at that.

He was greeted in the reception area by a pink cheeked corporal with a clipboard. For some soldiers, this was as close as they ever got to a weapon outside of basic training. But the army would be in utter chaos without the clerks who kept it all organized. Clerks, cooks and medics were the backbone of a fighting army and the leadership of the military knew it very well.

"Command Sargent Major Japhet, please go to the command center at the end of the hallway. The meeting will begin at 0800."

He nodded and arrived at the meeting before most of the rest had assembled. It was a quirk of his to never be at an appointment later than fifteen minutes before it was supposed to start. It had driven his family crazy, but he felt strongly that punctuality was a sign of respect for the time of the people you were meeting with and a matter of integrity for him.

The meeting was a fairly straightforward thing as military meetings went. This wasn't a discussion. It was intended to give out assignments and clarify any of the fine points of each person's responsibilities if necessary.

Ed was given command of a small battalion that was going to be clearing the highways in about a 10-mile radius of the city limits. When they completed that task, they would be assigned to a unit outside the area. Each battalion was covering a different type of disaster relief, including medical teams, running soup kitchens, and creating emergency housing for those who had been displaced. The battalion he was in charge of was an engineer's battalion with access to heavy machinery necessary to remove vehicles from the road and repair any damage to the road itself.

They would be accompanied by a small team of combat medics in case there were any unrecovered bodies from the wreckage.

The one reason they could even do this operation was that batteries now worked again. Scientists had reported a mysterious power wave that had happened simultaneously worldwide. They seemed to think the two events were connected but were unable to explain either one.

At this point, Ed didn't really care all that much. He had always told his kids to do the work that was in front of them, and that was how he operated. He didn't want to remain ignorant of events, but he also didn't want to dwell on the things he had no control over. Once a thing had happened, and when you were dealing with the aftermath of something like this, the best plan was to simply get to work at whatever you could do and let someone else worry about the things you couldn't do.

He called Donna before he set out to brief his battalion to let her know he had arrived safely and to tell her it was going to be a very long day, grateful for the reestablishment of communication, mystery or not.

"Guess what? Jenny called! She was checking to see if we were all right. I told her we were fine. It was so good to hear her voice. She said to tell you not to work too hard. That's what your troops are for."

It had been a standing joke amongst them, but they all knew that Command Sargent Major or not, he would roll up his sleeves and get to work right alongside his men when it was necessary.

"I'm glad you got to talk to her. How's that job of hers coming along?

"She says they have power and finally got cell phone coverage, so she'll be able to get back to work after she helps them make sure they didn't lose any data in all of this."

"That's our Jenny. She does her duty."

"You taught them well, Ed."

"WE taught them well, Donna. I think you had a little bit of a hand in their raising, as I recall."

They both laughed at this and then signed off with an "I love you."

She had been crystal clear from the beginning of their relationship that saying I love you to one another was important. She didn't ask much of him and after a while of being a bit embarrassed about it in a public place he had finally decided that it wouldn't hurt his men to know that he loved his wife.

He arrived at the training ground where his men had assembled. On other training grounds within earshot, he could hear the sounds of other troops assembling and being given their orders. He wasn't one for rousing speeches.

"You all know why we're here. Thank you for answering the call to duty. Let's do our job. Your platoon leaders have their orders. We will assign two platoons to every sector with appropriate equipment. I will be coordinating the work schedule. You each should have a day's rations with you and any tools you require in your packs. Each section will also have medics assigned for body recovery and any injuries. But we don't want to distract them, so there will be no injuries. Am I right?"

"YES, Command Sargent Major!" They thundered in unison.

"Then let's do this thing. Company dismissed!"

They immediately went to their assigned areas to assemble and move the equipment. Ed got up into the passenger side of the cab of a Dusenhalf that would carry troops to the worksite. The young Sargent driving the vehicle nodded and waited until the bang-bang of a flat hand on the side of the truck indicated all were aboard and ready to leave.

The convoy left within fifteen minutes, having prepared everything before they had gotten into formation on the training grounds. It was very apparent where they would be working. Vehicles weren't only scattered all over the road, but there was broken windshield glass all over the highway. These roads weren't as highly traveled as in many large cities and the blackout didn't happen during "rush hour", but the damage was enough to be going on with.

His men immediately went to work, and he was proud of the way they systematically worked as a team. Civilians had enough on their hands taking care of the many injured people and making arrangements for children orphaned by the disaster, not to mention property damage. Who knew a power outage could cause so much destruction and loss of lives?

The sound of large machinery working was nearly overwhelming, and yet he heard her voice instantly.

"Dad? It's Jenny."

He looked around, confused. He could see no one, and...how could she have gotten here? There were no planes in the air until further notice. "Jenny?" he hollered in a random direction.

"You don't have to yell. Just think what you want to say, and I will hear you."

"What? How are you doing this? Am I finally losing it? They say as you get older..."

Her warm mental laugh was disconcerting and yet comforting in a way.

"I can't tell you. Let's just say that there are more things in heaven and earth, Dad, than are dreamt of in your philosophy. I've always wanted to use that one on you..."

"OK, so let's say I'm not losing my marbles and you can't tell me how you're doing this. What is this all about?"

"It's about you doing what I already knew I'd find you doing. It's about you knowing that this might not be the end of it and I can't tell you how I know this. It's especially about you knowing that none of the governments of Earth are responsible for this.

I can't tell you much more than that, and I don't want to worry you or mom, but you need to know that there are good guys working on the problem and Earth is being protected. But even with all of that, please make sure that when you are done cleaning up this mess that you make your usual preparations without alarming Mom. Nothing may come of it, but if it does, it will help me to stay focused, if I know you are as safe and prepared as you can be."

"You aren't ghostwriting at all, are you?"

"Got it in one, Dad. But don't tell Mom. I know she can be as tough as nails when she needs to, but I'd just as soon not worry her unless she needs to be worried. OK?"

"I agree. Let's not worry her if we don't have to. I'll take your advice under consideration. Does this thingy work two ways? Can I contact you this way from my end?"

"Sorry Dad. No. But I'll stay in touch as often as I can, I promise."

"OK, Jenny. You know your mom and I miss you, right? I love you."

"I love you too Dad."

And then she was gone, and he had work to do.

Chapter 33: Behind the Mask

Sam saluted the guard at the gates of the fortress. Finally, she had made her way to the capitol. She waved the courier message before the guard's face when he asked her business. "For the Marshall, Sargent; his eyes only."

"What do you hear from out there?" the guard asked before waving her in.

"It's crazy. Someone or something is creating havoc and destruction. No one knows how or why, but they have it in for the military; makes a soldier almost want to ditch the uniform. Whole battalions decimated right where they stand. But I'd better get this to the Marshall, or I won't have to worry about getting killed by this creature or whatever it is, because he'll have my hide if I don't get it to him right away."

The guard nodded and turned his gaze back to the busy street before him, already dismissing her as if she weren't even there. This suited her purposes just fine. She wanted to be as invisible as possible here. She had something special planned for this group and wanted it to be a surprise. She liked surprises as long as they were on somebody else.

She chuckled to herself. She was worn out and needed sleep and time to plan. There were messenger barracks in the keep, and it would give her a chance to orient herself and give herself the best chance of success.

She handed the message to the Marshall. She had managed a simple bit of forgery to alter the message slightly. Basically, it said that they needed help at the farthest city away she could think of a name for. The message was a cry for help because the Mayor was dead, and people were dying and please to send help right away. It was signed by a citizen totally made up out of whole cloth by Sam and marked "Urgent".

The Marshall scowled at the message without dismissing Sam. "Another one," he said shaking his head. It was all Sam could do not to smile. She could well imagine the number of these types of messages he had received in the past several days. She had been very busy indeed.

"Well, there'll be no reply. I'll pass this on to the guys who make these kinds of decisions. Glad it's not me. I imagine you're tired and could use some feeding up."

He handed her a voucher for food and lodging with the garrison in their "guest quarters" which basically meant a large room with a few score beds in it and a shared privy. She thanked him and left to make herself comfortable.

Sure enough, it was only a large barracks room. Most of the beds were unoccupied and there was a place at the end of the bed to insert the lodging half of her voucher to claim the cot as her own. Next to the bed was a footlocker. No one was there, so she made herself at home.

It was common for traveling soldiers pretty much anywhere else to provide their own locks, but these were seldom used in the Insenium. The penalty for stealing was death. The concept of a prison was foreign to them. People knew the rules. If they chose not to obey them, they didn't belong in Inseni society. That meant removal, not free meals and housing. The executions were always public, but they were few, as these people were conditioned to not even think in that direction.

She stowed her belongings in the trunk, kicked off her boots and got as comfortable as she could, still in her uniform. It didn't take long for her to go to sleep.

When she awoke later in the day, she realized she was famished. She rearranged her hair, put her boots back on and wandered out to the mess hall. She found it easily drawn by the aromas of cooking food. Although Inseni didn't go out of their way to make fancy dishes, the food was always tasty enough and stuck to your ribs. Sam thought wryly that if she spent much more time on this wretched planet, it was going to ruin her girlish figure. Not that her Norgoth persona had much of a figure to be concerned about. Norgoth were mostly built tall and solid, no curves worth mentioning.

She sat down at a random table next to another female soldier. The woman didn't even look up. She just continued to stare at her plate, shoveling the hearty stew into her mouth as if she hadn't eaten in weeks. That suited Sam just fine. She plowed into her own meal in silence. The woman next to her finished and took her tray back to the area designed to collect them.

Sam finished and after putting her tray into the collection bin wandered out to have a look around.

The fortress had open areas around the main buildings, unlike the towering self-contained community on her home planet. Of course, this planet was in a stable orbit around a healthy sun, so they had plants and scenery worth looking at and didn't have to restrain population due to limited resources as the Fleistians did.

Sam had never explored her planet much beyond going to the Groga encampment. She had heard there were mountains somewhere, but the mountains were as barren as the plains and Sam only knew about them from her instructors.

In the courtyards surrounding what passed for a palace here were garden plots and herb gardens, but no statuary or decorative plants. Every building was all edges and right angles and all the same color. The only thing that differentiated one building from another was the simple lettered signs which hung over each door.

Various military personnel, servants and those who appeared to be dignitaries moved purposefully about the grounds. Occasionally a few would stop to talk. Norgoths weren't supposed to "gossip". It was considered counter-productive, a sin in the opinion of the Overlord of the Grand Insenium.

But they were definitely passing the latest news about the depredations of the mysterious stranger among them, looking occasionally over their shoulders to see if anyone was looking.

"Someone told me the creature shot lasers from its eyes!"

"No, it used a bomb. Nothing else could have caused so much death at once."

"I heard they are hunting the creature with master hunters from all over. They will bring its head back and post it on the fortress walls!"

"All I know is that I'm glad I retired from the military already. I don't see how they are going to defeat the creature."

Sam walked by trying to hide a grin. It was satisfying to see that even in the capitol she had sown fear and misinformation. She noted the appearance of one of the servants and stepping into a deserted space between buildings, assumed the persona changing the features slightly. She had discovered that a good disguise didn't have to be a huge difference from the person you copied. Small differences, hair color, a difference in the length of a hem or adding freckles or a mole seemed to work just as well as radical changes.

She walked into one of the larger buildings as if she knew where she was going. The sign above the door said, "Necessaries"; the Norgoth version of the word hospitality. Sam found it amusing that this was also the British word for toilets.

She strode down the main hallway to a large room. Standing at a table laden with what appeared to be unfolded laundry was a hard-looking woman, her hair woven into a simple braid that she had wound around her head. She stopped folding the rough towel in her hands and put both hands on her hips.

"What are you doing here?" she asked, looking Sam up and down, obviously unimpressed.

"I was told you needed some help," Sam said simply, meeting her eyes, but not projecting any kind of challenge.

"Hmmph. Well, it's about time. You can start on the linens," pointing to a pile at the end of the table.

It was obvious someone had already started folding, which was good. Sam supposed there was a limited number of ways to fold a sheet, but she wanted to be sure to not stand out by not knowing how to do such an apparently simple thing.

She began folding, allowing the woman to see her hard at work. The woman nodded and went back to folding towels.

"New here?" the woman asked, not looking up from the towel she was folding.

"Yes. I lived with my sister in Ankal until the 'creature' came through and killed all those soldiers. I didn't stay around. I'd always wanted to visit the capitol, and my brother-in-law knew someone on the staff here and sent me with a recommendation. I hope I can stay. I would like to do something that is worthwhile, and this might be the best place to start."

"My name is Jolla," the woman said, stacking yet another towel on the large stack before her.

"Kinney," Sam said.

"Well, help me get this laundry folded and put away, and I'll see what else I can find to keep you busy. There's never a shortage of work here. Once we have a few other chores done, I'll take you on my delivery rounds. We deliver towels and bedding to the maids and body servants every day about this time. It lets them do their work before everyone returns to their rooms after supper."

Sam nodded and kept folding. She would make herself invaluable here and move up from where she was until she reached her goal. This was a perfect position to gather the intel she needed to pull off her little plan.

After all, no one paid attention to a servant or guarded their tongue in their presence. "The help" were invisible to the powerful. She wasn't afraid of a little work, and she knew from experience how to ingratiate herself to someone and make them think they had a valued employee or...a best friend.

Her lips pursed at that thought. Yes, she was very good at that. She hoped Jolla didn't see her wipe a tear that ran down her cheek. She wiped it away and picked up another sheet to fold.

Chapter 34: On the March

B urt stretched when he rose from the mat on the floor of his tent. Opening the tent flap, he peered about. There, at her post was Mynn. She waved cheerfully at him, suppressing a yawn.

"It's all quiet here," she sent. *"I think I hear Jenny and Chidwi stirring in there. Do you need to use the jacks, or can I take off?"*

"I'm good for now. Get some breakfast and do what you need to do. Tarafau will be around in a bit to check on Jenny and I'll get some relief at that point, as he always has a few Groga soldiers trailing behind these days."

"And Freia should be around with Jenny's breakfast in a bit as well. Grephan is pretty much always with her. I don't think Jenny will lack for protection."

She headed off to her tent to collect her toiletries. There were primitive bathing facilities available, and Burt had noticed that "the girls" never failed to take advantage of them. They always looked what his dad would have called "strack", a military term for a soldier whose uniform and presentation was impeccable.

He went over to the spot beside the tent door, pulled a camp stool out of his MDP and had a seat. He could hear a conversation between Jenny and Lizziebot about the various contacts she had made through the night. He knew she got a certain amount of sleep when she did her nighttime dream visits, but he couldn't help but notice that Jenny seldom looked completely rested on the nights she did this, which these days was nearly every night.

They had all chided her about this, but he had noticed that Jenny wasn't as malleable as she had seemed when he had first met her. She was growing into her responsibilities quickly and took them seriously. It was one of the things he admired about her, but he had also noticed that she was from time to time a little snippy for the first couple hours after she got up in the morning.

Since they had gotten on the road toward the area that Jenny had insisted was the primary strategic point for a battle with the Norgoth, they had traveled long hours, quitting just before it got dark to set up the camp and getting up soon after sunrise to eat and pack and get back on the road again.

The Groga commanders had insisted that Jenny continue to ride in the hover car to preserve her strength. The car would hold six passengers fairly comfortably. But Jenny seldom got any rest while they traveled. If she wasn't relaying communications to and from various Alliance partners, she was consulting with one or more of the Groga captains.

Her hair had continued to grow out, but not enough that she could tie it back in her usual ponytail. The curls framed her face and those amazing eyes of hers. It bothered her. She kept pushing it away from her face, a gesture that was very appealing for some reason.

The conversation in the tent broke off and Jenny ducked under the tent flap. "Good morning, Burt. Did you sleep well?" she asked brightly. He could tell she didn't feel as bright as she sounded, but he ignored it. Jenny had very firmly informed her entourage that they needed to stop telling her how tired she looked and how she should be getting more rest. "I'll sleep when this is over," she had said with a wry twist of her mouth.

So, they had agreed, but whenever they could they took steps to be sure she didn't have to do more than she needed to. Burt knew he had been instructed not to coddle her, but he reasoned that every general had aides-de-camp and Jenny shouldn't be any different. She would have done everything herself if they allowed that to happen. He and the girls simply formed a gentle conspiracy to make things as easy as they could for her without it being obvious. He was sure, however, that she noticed and chose not to say anything. It was a necessary pretense where both sides got what they needed.

"Good morning, Jenny. Good morning, Chidwi."

"Good morning, Burt," Chidwi sent cheerfully. In Chidwi's case, Burt didn't think the Linkling was overly tired. He knew she actually did sleep next to Jenny every night, but she also seemed to nod off on Jenny's shoulder during the long rides in the hover car. He'd had a friend like that. Didn't matter what the conveyance, if he wasn't driving, he would soon be snoring softly once the motor revved up. Of course, the hover car made no sound worth thinking about, but it was probably as much the scenery drifting by as the sound of the engine, Burt thought.

"So, what's the plan for today?"

"More of the same, I'm afraid. We need to get to the valley as quick as we can. Whose turn is it to ride today?"

"I think it is Nona's turn. She would rather walk, she says, and not surprising with those long legs of hers, but the other two insisted that she take her turn like the rest of us."

The hover car was escorted on the outside by Burt and whichever of the two of her bodyguards who were on outside guard that day. In addition, Tarafau, Anwhal and Grephan covered the opposite side of the car. The car moved at a walking pace, driven by Lizziebot, which amazed the Groga to no end.

At the front and back of the car were a platoon of troopers. It seemed that whatever Jenny had about her that attracted others to her and made them want to help her also worked on the Groga. Every one of the Groga soldiers could be counted on to give their own life to protect Jenny and Chidwi.

This was certainly a comfort, but Burt was painfully aware of the kind of numbers they would potentially face when the Norgoth decided to take their revenge on the unfaithful Groga. He had been grateful for the continual contact he had available to him through BaaGah and the Mookookie spy network that was operating so clandestinely in the five Insenium worlds the Norgoth had unwittingly escorted them to.

Burt had been astounded by the mental pictures the Mookookie relayed of troop numbers and equipment of the Norgoth on the various Insenium worlds. It appeared that the Groga had truly been a fraction of the manpower they had available.

Evidently, the raids they had been conducting throughout the multiverse were peripheral to the scope of all of the worlds in other dimensions they had already conquered and there were still Groga in the Norgoth's employ who knew nothing about the defection of their fellows.

Burt knew about the plans developing in the Alliance as well and, in his opinion, they would need every single nuance and detail of every single plan to carry this off.

The offensive Jenny was planning with the Groga leaders was brilliant, and the timing of each of the different attacks was being carefully coordinated from Sanglarka. They had to be careful that only a handful knew the entirety of the plans, as the Norgoth seemed to know more than they had thought at first about what was going on with the Alliance.

This made Burt suspicious that they still might have an enemy agent among them. He knew for a fact it wasn't Guaray who was working in medical research in a secluded area of the Alliance headquarters city and had no contact with anything remotely resembling tactics, strategy or anything else relating to this war. Burt also believed Guaray when he said he didn't know of any other operatives of the Insenium among them.

This made sense, and this type of organization was careful to let no agent know anything more than what they needed to know to do their job. Burt's training at the Alliance had included the study of many different cultures and their past histories. There were none of them that didn't have some history of war and tyranny, some farther back than others and some, who still lived, like Earth, in a state of turmoil, with wars and rumors of wars.

At present, the Alliance had taken every report of numbers and locations of Norgoth troops they had received from their Mookookie agents seriously. There were several different plans, depending on the planet and war machine they faced. Obviously the Mookookie, regardless of their own numbers, could still only give a limited report based on where their unknowing hosts had transported them.

Tarafau strode up, his usual entourage of Generals and Daringi in tow with his daughter Elizabeth walking beside him.

"Let's get some breakfast. The Groga are packing up the main part of the camp, but the mess tent is still open."

Jenny grinned at him and Elizabeth. *"I'm starving, let's hurry."*

The subtext of that interaction made Burt smile. She wasn't going to give in to the exhaustion he had seen when she first exited the tent. She had nearly as good facial control as he did now. You had to really catch her off guard to get even a hint of what was going on behind those beautiful blue eyes.

So, Burt folded his stool and put it back into his MDP. They faced another day on the march, but they were close, and he had a lot to think about. As he marched alongside the hover car with Mynn and Myra, he would be going over the numbers and reports again, the miniscule earphone that connected to the tablet in the big hip pocket of his cammies constantly updating him with the latest reports from all over the Alliance. It was one of the things he loved about being an Agent of the Alliance. His status gave him pretty much unlimited access to any information he needed, any time he needed it, as long as there was a network to connect to.

In the mess tent they sat and chatted about nothing consequential, teasing and laughing together as comrades in arms are wont to do. In the grimmest circumstances, there are still things that can be amusing, even if the humor can be a bit dark from time to time.

They ate quickly, eager to get more miles in before the sun went down. They generally ate on the march for lunch, only pausing a few times a day for hygiene breaks and to replenish water supplies at a local spring or river. Burt was happy to see that despite any of their other failings, the Groga had kept their rivers and streams pristine. After all they had thought about the Groga before actually meeting them and learning about them, it surprised him how many admirable qualities they had. Jenny had been right.

By the time the mess tent was down, the rest of the camp was nearly all packed. The Groga were careful to be sure they left no trace of themselves wherever they camped. Not to hide their trail as much as their own respect for the land and any who might come behind them.

They escorted Jenny to the hover car where Anwhal and Tarafau helped Jenny in. Immediately Jenny unpacked Lizziebot from her MDP. The hover cars could steer themselves, of course, simply plot in your destination. However, to make sure the car kept pace with those who surrounded it on foot, Bob had given Lizziebot another upgrade. It was amazing to Burt how he could do this across dimensions as long as there was an Alliance communication satellite in the general area. The satellites got their signal through a gateway.

They had established an Alliance temporary portal. One of Bob's cute little space drones had launched the tiny, nearly imperceptible communication satellite. The Alliance gate had been sealed enough to be sure no one could get through it, but not so much that a communication stream couldn't get through. They didn't use the gate for physical transport. They had the Daringi for that, and the system worked well. The Groga, once they had gotten over the shock of it, had approved.

As he walked, he interspersed his study of the reports with joshing with the girls and the others who stood honor guard and thinking deeply about what he had learned from the reports he had been scanning. The information and statistics were interesting, but useless until someone put them into context with what they were trying to do.

As he thought about that, he continued to think about Jenny. He had a strong feeling that there was a part of her plan she might be holding back. As honest as she tended to be, she still maintained some secrets, maybe not even intentionally. There was just more going on inside that beautiful head of hers than anyone suspected.

The days on the Groga home world were long, but the weather in this part of the country was balmy, perfect walking weather. Nevertheless, at the end of a long day of marching, they were glad to set up camp, eat and retire to get some sleep.

"We'll be to the valley in another day," Jenny informed him before they said goodnight. "I don't think we'll be fighting right away. Brendan seems to think they'll try an attack from space before they access the portal, which they think is secreted in the valley. The Groga have known about it for a long time, but had paid it no mind, as it was almost never used. It is their strong belief that if the Insenium try a ground assault, it will be through that portal.

So far, the strategy is still to use the valley as a really big trap. We will allow them to deploy fully before we make any move or even let them know we're here. There is a small forest to the east of the valley, opposite from the portal. Are you still prepared to do your part?"

"Of course, even if I don't like it a tiny single bit." Burt hoped he didn't sound sullen, but anything that put Jenny in danger was not OK with him.

Jenny laughed and his heart melted. "I promise you it will work out. Please, let's not go through this again." She sobered up a little. "I know there is always a risk, but my dad taught me to never order your troops to do something you wouldn't be willing to do yourself."

Burt just nodded. He didn't want to rehash this with her. He had already had his say on the matter. But Jenny insisted that her part of the plan couldn't be done by anyone else, so there it was.

He had first watch tonight, so he pulled his little stool out of his MDP again and pulled out his whittling. He was getting pretty good at it, he thought.

Next morning, they set off again. The marching order was pretty much the same, with Mynn taking duty inside the hover car this time. The trail was getting steeper as they approached the pass between the small mountains that surrounded the valley. As they emerged from the pass, the path was surrounded by trees.

They appeared to be ancient, towering like the sequoias he so loved at home. They were similar to deciduous trees, but Anwhal had told him they were evergreens. Their broad leaves reminded him somewhat of a philodendron plant his mother had kept in the picture window of their living room when he was a kid. As a result, they only saw small patches of sunlight as they walked along.

The path had narrowed quite a bit, so the soldiers ahead and behind Jenny's car had closed ranks at a command from Anwhal. He was proud of his troops and knew they would perform every command with diligence and exactness. He knew he could count on their discipline and prompt execution.

Finally, the command came floating back from the front of the procession to halt. It was passed back from one platoon to the next until it reached them. It continued to be passed back through the several ranks behind them. Anwhal had explained that they had done training exercises in this area in the past, so the troops would know exactly what to do when they got there.

They had paused just prior to the opening that led out into the valley. They would be camping under the protection and seclusion of the forest until their scouts noticed the Norgoth coming out of the portal.

Once they emerged, they would wait until they were pretty sure they were all assembled before following through with the rest of the plan.

Burt wasn't afraid, but he felt the adrenalin begin to pump him up. Waiting was never fun, and he certainly wasn't looking forward to this one. He hoped the Great Inseni didn't take their "own sweet time" about it.

Chapter 35: Like Shooting Swamp-Rats

B rendan watched the screen on the bridge of his ship. Sure enough, the scouts had been accurate. Three ships, slightly larger than his had entered their visual range. They had been tracking them for an hour or so when they had entered the Groga solar system. Turns out there must be a space portal in this system, which was how they had discovered the planet they had relocated the Groga to a few hundred years before. It wasn't close, but it was reasonable to assume that one of the reasons they located the Groga on this particular planet was that it also had some natural portals. Only two as far as the Groga commanders were aware.

There were no Groga on his ship. He received all of his intel from Jenny and her Mookookie agents via her amazing ability. That girl was fair dinkum in his opinion. When he was her age, he was flying for the Australian air corps, but he hadn't had a tenth of the responsibility that circumstances had put on her. She stood up to it, even when she was not confident that she could. Like the rest of the team, he worried about her, but they had been given instructions to not coddle her.

In his humble opinion, the girl hadn't had a moment of coddling from the beginning, but what did he know? He was just a space jockey. A SPACE jockey! He knew that a grin at this time would seem out of place, but he still couldn't believe this opportunity had come his way.

And now he had an enemy fleet bearing down on their position, or at least near their position. Their fleet had been completely shielded by one of the moons that orbited the planet so far. He would have given a lot to see the enemy commander's face when they realized that this wasn't just going to be some destroy and run mission. The fleet commander's voice came over the intercom. "Ready all ships; like we planned."

"Battle stations!" Brendan sent to his crew. He could visualize each of them in their respective places. *"This is not a drill! Repeat: This is NOT a drill!"*

As the enemy fleet came into view, he noted that they didn't seem as sleek as the Alliance ships, so perhaps their technology wasn't quite as advanced as they had feared. Of course, you couldn't judge a book, or a ship, by its cover. The outside of the ship wasn't nearly as important as the inside. They knew little to nothing about the construction or weapons of the ships they would soon be facing, but he was hoping that Bob's contribution would make the difference, regardless.

As his pilot maneuvered them into position, he knew that on the flight deck his crew was arming their dastardly little surprises, a huge fleet of them, by the time they combined with those on the other ships in the fleet. Bob's research into the full capabilities of the MDPs had made it possible and Brendan was glad to have him on the team as it was important not to have a major gun battle with the enemy if they could help it.

Rather, Bob had created a three stage system based on their earlier exploits in the Amazon jungle, fighting the Groga. If it worked, they would be saved a lot of potential casualties and damage to their fleet.

It required two sets of specialized drones camouflaged for use in the darkness of space equipped with some dastardly alien tech that would extend the amount of damage they could do. Add to that Bob's clever little flying bots, and this should be interesting to say the least. Bob had combined his own ideas with the tech the Alliance already had available, and Brendan expected the results to be impressive.

Mix that Yankee ingenuity with the devious minds of the tactical team and they had more than a few nasty surprises for the incoming fleet.

As the Inseni fleet neared, he considered all of the drills they had done while waiting behind this little moon. His crew was well trained, and they had cut their response time significantly along with the other ships in the fleet. They had one more ship than the Inseni fleet that now approached, but the Commander of the Alliance fleet had told them not to judge the situation by numbers, but to stick to the agreed upon strategy.

Burt would have called the strategy "prestidigitation", "Now you see it now you don't."

The first ship moved into place, directly in the path of the oncoming fleet. "Hailing alien fleet. Stand down and we won't fire upon you," the ship broadcast on all known frequencies.

They knew full and well that the Insenium would find this humorous, if not insulting. One puny ship against their noble fleet? How ludicrous. The enemy ship fired some sort of energy weapon, but the little ship was well prepared for this. They energized the hull, and the blast was repelled, although Brendan was sure it probably shook the ship, stabilizers or not. It was all he could do to be still, but for this to work the fleet had to come a bit closer.

The ships moved closer and the ship at the front of the formation fired again. Again, the shields held, but that was his signal. *"NOW!"*

At first it didn't seem like anything happened, but Brendan knew better. The first wave of nearly invisible drones had been released from all four ships. They did better than they had expected, actually making contact with the ships' hulls. The hulls were shielded similarly to their own ships and it looked as if the weak little attack had failed. The drones that had struck the hulls of the ships floated away, seemingly disabled.

They released the second wave. This wave didn't attempt to touch the hulls. The ships were now targeting them with an energy weapon that looked like it was a lower frequency than the one they had fired at the ship that had been left out for bait. However, these little drones were fast and agile. Only a computer programmed to follow them at high speed and anticipate their multiple dives and turns could have hit many of them.

They fired constantly, strafing the outsides of the enemy ships, doing their job to weaken the hull and draw enemy fire.

While the enemy had been distracted by the first two waves, what they didn't see were the flying attack robots that had been sneaking up from behind. They targeted the weapons that were firing nearly uselessly at the little drones. Too late, the enemy ships' captains realized their dilemma.

The first wave had not intended to dent their ships at all like the little nuisances they seemed to be. They had actually deposited nanobots on the hull, which had two functions, to weaken the metal of the hull with microscopic holes drilled by miniscule lasers. Secondly, like the nanobots they called "Burt's bugs", these burrowed into the hull to track the ships and to continue to do small amounts of damage to the hull and the equipment inside the ships over time.

As their plan had anticipated, when their enemy realized their weapons were being destroyed by the robots, they attempted to turn and run, only to be confronted by Brendan's ship and the two other ships of their fleet.

"Stand fast! Prepare to be boarded!" was broadcast on all frequencies. There was no answer from the enemy ships, but they suddenly spun vertically and shot away at high speed, assuming the fleet which was larger than their own and undamaged would chase them and destroy them.

And they did follow them for a time and then slowly let them put more and more distance between them. They had accomplished two objectives. The Groga planet was defended and they now could track the ships back to their main base, collecting data the whole time while making it necessary for the enemy ships to take time for repairs.

The success of this strategy would mean that the Norgoth would likely now pursue their attack via the portals on the planet, and only one of them was working. Mission accomplished.

Chapter 36: If Not Now, When?

Waiting again. One of Jenny's least favorite things. The Groga soldiers with their Daringi trainers went about the camp as if they weren't on the verge of a major offensive that could change the lives of everyone they held dear for such a long time to come.

If they were successful, they would be able to pursue their lives free from the tyranny that had plagued them for centuries. If they were not successful, it was assured that the Insenium would not leave them alone to do much of anything and, if possible, they would see the Groga wiped from existence.

And yet, if they were feeling the pressure of all of this, it wasn't evident in any of their behaviors. Jenny had to do calming exercises several times a day. She knew and had reported to the tactical council that Brendan's fleet had succeeded in their tactic to prevent destruction from space, at least for now.

At this point it would be up to the forces the Groga had assembled to pull off her own plan. Chidwi was with her always, perched quietly on her shoulder, soothing her, and crooning occasionally as Linklings were wont to do.

The forest where they had camped was vast and easily accommodated their numbers. The scouts continued to report no movement near the gate, which was to be expected as it would take time for the wounded ships to make their way home and report to their superiors of their wretched failure. A lot would depend now on the decision the Overlord Gall would make. She was fairly certain he wouldn't let the matter drop.

That left pretty much only two possibilities. Either they would try again with a larger fleet, a contingency the Alliance had prepared for, or they would send hordes of Norgoth soldiers through the portal who would assume they could simply stomp across the planet slaughtering as they went. She doubted they would be taking slaves or prisoners. Their mandate would be simple: Annihilate the Groga as a people.

She made a point to walk the perimeter of the camp and participate in public mealtimes and any other gatherings in the camp. She didn't want the soldiers to think of her as some sort of high lady or celebrity. She wanted to just be one of the thousands on this very large team.

At first she had only wanted to bring a small force, but Tarafau and the Groga commanders had convinced her that the effect would be much more dramatic if there were more of them and they needed that moment of drama for Jenny to carry out her part of the plan. Everything depended on her. She was the lynchpin and if she failed, the consequences would be bloody and terrible.

The larger numbers also served as a backup for Jenny's plan. If she failed, there was no question that there would be a violent and bloody battle here today.

Groga greeted her and Chidwi solemnly as she passed, no longer bowing as they had done in the past. She had been firm with them that this was not only unnecessary...she found it disturbing. When the word had gotten out, they simply treated her with respect, to her relief. Chidwi seemed to take every bit of it in stride. She nodded and waved to them and crooned a joyous song with no words. But every person who heard it walked away with a lighter heart.

She was slightly amazed with the lack of niggling and contention among the Groga troops. These had been trained by Anwhal who deemed every soul worthy of respect and had taught that to his soldiers. Not that there weren't occasional disagreements, but these were generally resolved quickly and peacefully, usually between the two parties on their own and only occasionally with the mediation of one of their commanders.

She was not alone, of course. Not ever. Her usual entourage rotated in and out, but she was never without at least half a dozen attendants. In the long run, however, they would not be able to protect her from some things. One of which were her own thoughts. But only a trusted few understood what she was about to do, and those had given her the courtesy of their trust. She was aware that none of them liked it but had agreed with her that it was one of a short list of options and the one least likely to create significant casualties among their own army.

She wouldn't have even begun to conceive of it if it hadn't been for the research and discoveries of Bob and the Science and Technology team and the things she had learned from Gariel and the Strategy and Tactics team. She also had to credit Lova and Arvid and her mental discipline tutors, Lova, Miriha, Elizabeth, Amenia, Liliath, and, of course, Chidwi.

She considered that she had become a group project, starting with her parents, Aunt Lizzie and then every single person she had met since becoming a Guardian. Even Sam had played a part in strengthening her and preparing her for this as much as she hated to admit it.

She mentally shook her head as she did every time she thought of Sam. She no longer felt anger when she thought of her, only a wistful sadness. She had loved Sam as a close friend, nearly like a sister. Her own sister had been an adult when she was in elementary school and had felt more like an aunt than anything. When you added to that the fact that she lived two states away, it meant that Jenny usually only saw her during family celebrations.

Sam, on the other hand, had been an intrinsic part of her life for over six years. She still mourned her loss, as if Sam had died. She harbored no illusions that it could ever be that way again.

She consoled herself with the realization of how many amazing people were in her life now and the strong conviction that she could trust each of them with her heart.

Her heart. She really didn't want her thoughts to head in that direction. She had never connected strongly to any of the people she had dated, so what was this thing with Burt? She looked to the right out of the corner of her eye and there he was, jauntily acknowledging the people they passed with his trademark grin and a wave. Everyone assumed he was the chief of her bodyguards and, as far as it went, this was true. As a Dimensional Alliance agent, he definitely outranked any of her "girls" and Elizabeth accepted his leadership without any qualms.

She wasn't sure how that had happened. The situation had pretty much evolved from Burt being a lone wolf, assigned to various missions requiring canny diplomacy and the ability to blend in wherever he went. Now he seemed at least semi-permanently assigned to caring for Jenny. Elizabeth had confided to her when she had wondered about it aloud in her presence that Burt had not asked for the assignment, but they had been given their orders by Liliath.

Now she was around him nearly constantly. He could be the most annoying person, especially when he was so often right. To be fair, he nearly never corrected her unless he felt strongly about it, especially in public, but she had noticed his gentle manipulation when he wanted to steer her toward his own opinion. However, she could see that he and she might have some pretty spectacular arguments in the future.

The future. The future? Was there one and what would it look like? Perhaps in a few days the whole argument in her head would be a moot point. How did she really feel about him? Part of her mind shied away from the question, but she realized that it had been a topic of her inner thoughts far too much lately when she should have been focusing on other things.

Perhaps it was time for another "date" by the little crystalline pool by the Merced River. He had told her once that when this was all over he would take her there, and she admitted that a part of her heart yearned for that moment. Liliath had told her once, "Jenny, you are far too guarded with your heart. You will lose something precious if you don't let the things go that are holding you back. You know what they are if you are willing to face them."

Was this the time to be thinking of that?

She heard her mom's voice in her head: "If not now, when?"

She heard herself say to her entourage, to her own surprise. *"I think I could use some rest before all of this comes together. I am sure I can depend on you to wake me if it is necessary?"*

She could see the surprise on their faces. She had been up to sparring recently and had been walking without her staff for nearly a week. She had stopped taking naps farther back than that unless it was to do deep communication as part of her responsibilities for the Alliance that had to be completely secure.

Burt looked at her, his eyes wide. *"Jenny wanting to rest? How is this possible?"*

She punched him in the arm...hard.

"OW! What was that for?"

"For being you. Wake me in about two hours if I don't wake on my own."

"Yes, your highness," he sent with a flourishing bow, as if he wore a long cape.

"Fine. I have work to do, unlike some of the layabouts I know."

"Well, I for one will be 'laying about' the entrance of your tent."

All of this was said good naturedly, as they often did with one another. Jenny thought the banter made time together a lot easier. She had been afraid it would be really awkward after his blatant declaration of love what seemed like ages ago. And it had been, at first. But when Jenny had let him know that she didn't have the time or energy to think about that, he had resumed his usual cocky air and it hadn't seemed to dent their friendship.

She sighed as she returned to the cool inside of her tent and settled onto the floor in her mental workout position. She didn't actually plan to go to sleep, but to check in with her various communication touch points, and one other thing.

She slipped easily into that mental state that allowed her to do this thing that still amazed and humbled her. Why she had been chosen for her role in all of this and why in the world she had been given these mental abilities that appeared to be so rare, she couldn't begin to fathom.

She checked in with each of her assigned touch points, received each report, touching base with Liliath last. She gave her report and moved on. There was one more thing on her to do list today.

She entered her mental fortress with a bit of misgiving. She wasn't sure where she would find the help she needed. She didn't notice any new buildings, which often happened when she had a unique issue to deal with or when she was trying to resolve an issue. She could have had Amenia, Elizabeth, or even Liliath to escort her and instruct her, but this was personal.

One by one she rejected the different buildings on the town square. The majestic mansion was still there, as yet unexplored, but she still didn't have any desire to go there. This usually happened when the building she was looking at wasn't the one she needed to visit. The only building left was the hospital. But she wasn't sick, was she? And yet, she found herself drawn to the building.

The curvy receptionist sat at her post in the empty waiting room.

"How may I help you today?" she asked in that detached manner that most receptionists tended to put on.

"I'm not sure..." Jenny began.

The receptionist wrote on a little clipboard. "Confused." It wasn't a question, but an observation.

"A little, but..." Jenny tried again, but the receptionist interrupted before she could speak.

"You need to see the counselor, please follow me."

Jenny shrugged and followed. What else could she do?

Once again, the receptionist put a file into a slot beside a door in the hallway. She waved Jenny inside and left with, "Someone will be in to see you in a moment."

So, Jenny sat on the examination chair, putting her feet up and leaning back.

There was a quick rap-rap on the door and into the room stepped... her mom?

"So, Jenny, I understand you are feeling confused about something and need to talk to someone."

"Mom?"

"Do you have a problem with that?"

"Uh, no, not really. I just expected...actually, I'm not sure what I expected."

"So, what are you confused about?" her mom said, seating herself on the doctor's examining stool.

"Well, it's about Burt... and me."

"Ah, boy problems. I wondered when this would finally come up. I was beginning to get worried."

Jenny shook her head. Talking to her mom about boys, she felt like she was 16 again.

"OK, so I think it's more than that and it's complicated."

"It always is sweetie, especially when things start to get serious. So, what is confusing you about Burt? He seems like a nice enough young man to me."

Jenny started at this. But then she remembered that this was an invention of her mind, so of course this version of her mom would know about Burt and her entire situation. In a way this was nice, she had missed her mom so much. Even if this wasn't the real thing, it felt enough like it to be comforting.

"So, the thing is, that everything is so crazy right now and we don't know what's about to happen. Does it make sense to start a serious relationship with everything that's going on?...What if one of us dies?"

"Oh, my dear Jenny; remember your history. Inevitably during and after a war, more babies are born. Young people make the choice to be together and declare their commitment to one another, not in spite of war, but because of it. Your grandmother was one of these. She and your grandfather were married right after he was called up for the draft. The only time they had together before he went to war were short furloughs.

Mom set up a household and kept it waiting for him. She had your Uncle Leroy while he was away at war. Their commitment to one another never wavered. They both knew very clearly that in times of war one of them might pass while they were apart. This didn't stop them from making that commitment."

"But what if both of you are in the middle of the conflict?"

"All the more reason for you to make a choice; not in haste and not as a last resort, but...do you love him, Jenny?"

There was a long pause. Did she? Was that the strong feeling she had for him?

"How can I tell, Mom? I've never felt like this before."

"You thought he died once. How did that make you feel?"

"Now you sound like a counselor. Hmm. I thought I was permanently broken. Like my heart would stop. The pain was nearly physical, worse than the wound in my head."

"So, why do you think that was?"

"Oh, mom, what you are saying is that this should be obvious to me."

"Not necessarily, but do you ever recall feeling such strong emotions regarding any of those you dated in high school or college?"

"Aarrgh! No, not a single one. Oh Mom, what am I going to do?" Tears began to trickle down her cheeks, and she wondered if she was also crying in her tent outside her mind.

"You will think of something," her mom replied with a twinkle in her eyes.

Jenny sighed. This was too real. Her mom was always so logical, calm, and kind. She was exactly the person she had needed to talk to. She wondered if, on some level, she had actually communicated with her mom. She felt Chidwi squeeze her shoulders with her tiny, gentle hands.

The tent melted into view. Her cheeks were wet, but she felt so much better. "You'll think of something," lingered in her thoughts. She would, but for now she still had work to do.

When she arose from her cot and went outside, Burt, true to his word, was lounging apparently carefree on his camp stool. "Any news?" he asked, his brow furrowed. Jenny wondered if her care showed on her face.

"Nothing more than we already know. Everyone has completed their preparations. Now it's just a waiting game."

"Yeah, I hate waiting."

They both laughed, as Jenny had said the exact same thing more than once.

"So, it's lunch time, ready to get some grub?"

"Sure...lead on, kind sir." And Jenny gave a royal nod of her head as if to a courtier. After all, two could play at that game.

Chidwi stayed on Jenny's shoulder, feather light and quiet. From time to time she would put a soft hand on Jenny's cheek, and Jenny realized how comforting that was. That slight touch said so much. How could she bring Burt into a serious relationship, however, with Chidwi her constant companion? She realized she hadn't consulted Chidwi about that possibility, another question for later.

As they approached the mess tent, a mental call went out, freezing everyone in their place. *"The portal has been breached! They come!"*

Chapter 37: They Come!

J enny and Burt turned from the mess tent and instead made their way to the command tent. Tarafau, the leaders of the Groga and her bodyguards were there, and Elizabeth appeared as out of thin air behind her.

Tarafau stood and those inside the tent quietened quickly. *"It is time. You all have your assignments. Remember, no one is to show themselves until I give the signal, which will only happen when they cease to come through the portal. They don't know we're here, and they mustn't know until the time is right. They will think themselves alone and with the leisure to assemble and prepare. This is vital to our plan. Prepare your units. I have sent word to the Daringi reinforcements. Burt, are the Mookookie ready to play their part?"*

BaaGah appeared suddenly atop Burt's wrist, which sagged slightly at first at the quick response by the little Mookookie.

"BaaGah and Mookookie friends all are ready, Mr. Tarafau, sir. We know what to do."

Jenny had never heard him sound so serious. The little Mookookie and his fellows were generally a cheery bunch, taking most everything in their stride, including their part in the rebellion on Krim against the Inseni.

Burt grinned at the little guy. From the time that Burt had fed the little creature in that dark cell, he and BaaGah had been "buddies". Come to think of it, this wasn't much different than, her relationship to Chidwi. Why did this have to be so complicated? Then she chided herself for such apparently frivolous thoughts in the current situation. "Pay attention!" she told herself sternly.

She wondered if any of the others had any thoughts besides focusing directly on the task at hand. Another random thought.

"Focus!" she adjured herself and fell immediately into her breathing patterns without another thought.

"*Do any of you have any questions?*" Tarafau was saying. What had she missed? She didn't dare raise her hand and request he repeat himself. "*Then you are dismissed to your duties. Wait for the order. Until then, be vigilant and relax in the short time we may have. Now that we have done all we can, worry is counterproductive. We can ask no more of any of you than for you to carry out your part.*"

The rest of them strode purposefully out of the tent, looking neither to the right or left. Tarafau came to Jenny and her entourage. "*I know you are all ready and prepared. Do not allow yourselves to be startled or dismayed. Simply do exactly what we discussed. Jenny gave us the final piece to this puzzle. Obey her and don't stop until you have followed your instructions to the letter.*"

They all nodded, their faces somber. Jenny was proud of them as none of them looked worried, only determined. She knew she could count on them to do their part.

They went to the staging area. There was nothing to assemble. Each of them had assembled their necessary weapons and tools long before now. Each of the companies was led by a Groga-ha and a Daringi. Each Daringi also wore an MDP. Bob's research into the MDPs had been invaluable in putting this plan together, and now they would test just a fraction of that research.

She stood at the front of her group which included her bodyguards, Elizabeth on her right hand, a company of Groga with their Daringi trainer and the Groga-ha who was in charge of them and, of course, Burt, on her left hand. Finally, Tarafau came to stand beside her.

"*I'm ready,*" she sent to him. "*I just wish these Inseni Norgoths would get a move on.*"

"*Sit and prepare,*" he sent back to her and handed her, out of his MDP a camp chair. "*I would prefer the troops didn't see you sitting on the ground,*" he added with a wry touch to his mind voice.

Jenny sat and immediately fell into a deep meditative state. She called to her mind the vision of a being of light, armored, and armed with a sword that cast a glow around her as far as her mental eyes could see. In this place she was standing high on a pedestal and could see infinitely far away.

Her focus was on one single thing. Gone were her distractions and concerns. Gone were her insecurities. For this time, until her task was done, she wasn't just Jenny. She was the guardian of more than an interdimensional gateway. She was more than the Gatekeeper of the Dimensional Alliance. She was the gatekeeper of truth, of right, of all that was vital for the growth and progression of every being, everywhere.

Not a God or anything like that. Not a queen. She was so much more than that and yet, so much less. She was a servant, humbled by the vastness of her task, but confident that she was capable of protecting these beings who had become precious to her and perhaps, as a result, she would aid the Alliance in protecting them all.

She was ready. But she hung in this energizing state until finally, who knows how much later, she heard Tarafau enter her mind with a gentle send, *"come back to us, Jenny. It is time."*

The world before her faded into view and she stood. Tarafau restored the stool to his MDP. Quietly she and her entourage moved from under the beautiful canopy into the light, the Groga troops on rank following quietly behind them. The light behind them meant the Norgoth would be facing into the light during this confrontation, one more advantage for the Groga.

There were no battle horns blown...that might come later. There were no shouts or loud noises of any kind. The troops had been given specific instructions not to walk in step, but to behave as if they were sneaking up on a beast in the forest. So, there was very little noise as the army of the Groga and their allies moved into the light.

Jenny didn't gasp as she realized the numbers they were facing. Apparently the Norgoth were taking no chances. Their intent was clear. With that number of troops, they could completely destroy every Groga on the planet.

The Norgoth army had assembled before their commanders, apparently for some kind of briefing. The commanders had their backs to the Groga army.

Finally, as they approached to within about a couple football field lengths from the Norgoth army, she noticed some of the troops start to move from their position of attention. Many of them were pointing toward the Groga and calling to their commanders urgently.

When their commanders finally turned to look, the look on their faces, even from this far away, was almost comical. It was exactly the effect Jenny had been hoping for, shock and confusion. She could almost see the question marks above their heads. How had the Groga known? How had they assembled an army to confront them so quickly? What should they do now?

Their army had assembled for a briefing and didn't appear to be armed, which was part of the strategy Tarafau and the generals had discussed. Surprise was going to be key. This was only one battle among many, but it might play a vital part if they could pull it off.

The Norgoths had assembled quite a distance from the portal they had emerged from, and now Jenny saw a soldier begin to sprint toward the portal after a sharp order had issued from one of the commanders in a voice that carried even to where Jenny stood.

Where she stood, she began to feel the presence of the image she had created for herself for what she was about to do. As always, visualization was important. In this one thing she could not fail. In this one thing she would do her part regardless of the consequences.

Tarafau turned to Jenny. *"Give the command when you are ready, but hurry. That soldier must not reach the portal."*

"There is just one thing I need to do," she sent back.

Then she turned to Burt. Aloud, she said to him, "Do you still love me?"

"I, um, of course, yes. Um, is this the time?"

"Long past the time; shut up and kiss me."

And he did, thoroughly.

Catching her breath, she said to Tarafau, *"I'm ready. Let's do this."*

"Mookookie ready?"

"Ready!" they roared in her head. Immediately a Mookookie was perched on the shoulder of every soldier, every Groga-ha and every member of their army.

"Daringi, are you ready?"

"Ready!"

And Jenny began to glow; at least that is how they would describe it to her later. Straddling her neck, Chidwi had a hand firmly planted on either side of her head. The Norgoth sprinting toward the portal was about 50 yards away. Jenny felt the light building and building inside of her heart. She had to wait until the crescendo.

The Norgoth was 30 yards away, 25, 15, 10...

"NOW!"

Just one word that summed it all up for her. One powerful word. It burst from her mind and heart with the power of an exploding sun.

"FREEDOM!"

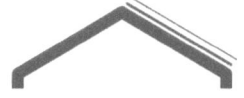

Chapter 38: Points of View

Jenny wasn't sure what to expect as an aftermath of the shout, at least not from her standpoint. There was no one alive that she was aware of who had ever done it. She had only been told secondhand stories about this particular mental ability. Those who had done it in the past had never written about the experience, and her instructors had not had anything else to go by.

So, she was frankly surprised to find herself on the winding path of Miriha's beautiful garden. "Did I die?" she wondered aloud. "Have I 'transitioned' to the next dimension?"

"Of course not, Jenny; but you are unconscious in the other place. Would you like to see what you just did?" It was Miriha in flowing robes and flowers wound into her braid.

"I would. This was the part of the plan I wasn't so sure about. There were a few on the council who opposed it, but I really felt strongly about it. The Groga need to see the full impact of what we are doing, and it is important to not just talk about freedom and choice, but to practice it."

"Well said, Jenny," and she beckoned for Jenny to follow her to the decorative stone bench beside the crystal pool. The bench should have been hard and cold, but it was warmed by a sun Jenny couldn't quite see and somehow it didn't feel hard. Of course, she was not there in her physical body, so this part made sense.

They sat for a moment in silence looking into the pool with no fish and not a single ripple, although a pleasant warm gentle breeze always seemed to be blowing here.

Then, the surface of the pond changed from reflecting the sky and their faces to something much like a television screen. They were looking down onto the large valley she had just left, at least mentally. Jenny gasped. The massive Norgoth army was lying on the ground as if blown there by hurricane-force winds. Like little toy soldiers strewn by the casual hand of a bored player, not a single one was standing. Behind the place they had assembled, their tents and stacks of supplies seemed untouched and undisturbed.

"Are they dead?" and despite herself, Jenny felt tears welling up in her eyes. These were the enemy. How could she possibly be feeling compassion for them right now?

"They are all unconscious, but no real damage has been done to them other than an occasional bump on the head where they landed on a rock. It is exactly as you had planned."

The next thing Jenny noticed were the people moving forward, each with a Mookookie on their shoulder.

Groga soldiers were searching the bodies of the Norgoth soldiers. Although it looked like they were looting the bodies, as was common on a battlefield after a victory, this was all part of the plan. Nothing would be left to them that could be used as a weapon. The rest, trinkets, and other things a soldier might carry with them were left on them.

Then the Groga would grab a Norgoth by the shoulders and sit him up, still unconscious, and a Daringi would bend and touch their MDP to the top of the head of each Norgoth soldier. One by one they disappeared into the MDP.

This process would take a long time to complete, but it would be so much better than the alternative. The idea of slaughtering the helpless in their sleep for the convenience of their conquerors was appalling to Jenny. She would never have used the shout if that was the only possibility.

She found that when she refocused on a particular part of the scene before her that it immediately zoomed in to the specifics of that part of the vast field she surveyed. The people went from looking like tiny action figures to the point where she could see faces and details. She shifted her gaze to the small cluster of people halfway down the field. She knew who they were before they came into focus. These were those of her entourage. Burt and Tarafau knelt on either side of her. Her bodyguards and Elizabeth surrounded the place where she laid on the battlefield, their backs to her each facing in a different direction.

"Can I hear what they are saying?" she asked Miriha.

"It's easiest to do that by focusing on a certain person, one you know well. Because of your close connection, you can experience the scene from their point of view and hear what they hear, although you will not be able to communicate," Miriha replied.

Jenny concentrated on Burt. She knew she had dealt him a big shock just before it all blew up. And it served him right, she thought with a touch of smugness.

Elizabeth had turned to Tarafau, evidently in response to something he had asked her. "She is in a deep meditative state," Elizabeth was saying. "As far as I can tell, everything is normal about her. She can't communicate with us in this state, as she explained when she told us what she wanted to do. But I can see no damage physically or mentally."

Tarafau nodded, looking directly into Burt's eyes. "You need not worry for Jenny. We don't know how long she will be like this. I will return her and Elizabeth to Ungoli to be tended by her and Amenia. She will be in good hands."

"I understand," Burt said softly. "And I know I would probably be useless there, but I don't know if I can bear wondering about her. What should I do?"

Tarafau laid one hand on Burt's shoulder, nodded to Elizabeth, and the scene faded from view. Now they were in Amenia's house. Tarafau and Burt lifted Jenny onto a pile of cushions that had been laid out in the large family room-kitchen area where most socializing happened in their home. Amenia nodded approvingly.

"We have her usual bedroom ready for her, but I want to have her where things are happening, to surround her with the voices and sounds she is familiar with. We will put her into her bed at night. Chidwi will see to her then and knows how to get our attention when needed. She will never be alone while she is unconscious in our home, Burt," she told him in her quiet but authoritative voice. Amenia was a leader in her own right in her community and a certified healer and used to taking charge.

In their culture healers didn't heal only physical injuries, but mental and emotional ones as well. Jenny had learned from their interactions the last time she was there just how much Amenia was respected by her fellow Daringi.

Elizabeth now put a hand on Burt's shoulder to get his attention and nodded toward Chidwi. "She isn't agitated or upset, which she would have been if Jenny was anything other than alright. You needn't worry, Burt. You can continue with your work."

Burt was embarrassed by all of this attention. Most people took it for granted that he was ok, and he never gave them any reason to think otherwise. He preferred going unnoticed. It was a survival instinct born of years of experience at what he did best. He only drew attention to himself when it was absolutely necessary for the completion of his current mission.

Right now, he had no mission. Their planning had not gone much beyond the task at hand. It had been assumed that he would simply go to Alliance headquarters and get his next assignment, but he had known from the beginning of this wild scheme that this would never happen. Right now, as far as he was concerned Jenny was his mission.

"No thank you, Elizabeth. I can sleep on the floor if there isn't another place for me, and I know Jenny is being well taken care of, but my place is here now. I've done my part. Done it and done it and done it. Right now, there is only one thing I can think of and I would be useless in the field. My primary skill is to show no emotion I don't want people to see and be 100% focused on the mission at hand. I couldn't do that now and in my current state I might do more harm than good."

Tarafau nodded. "You all have this well in hand then?" Three heads nodded at once. "So, I will be off to finish what we started. Be safe and feel my love," he concluded to Amenia and Elizabeth. "I will have no worry where Jenny is concerned. She could be in no safer hands."

He hugged his wife and daughter and patted Chidwi gently on the head who was sitting beside Jenny's unconscious body, both tiny hands holding Jenny's slack one as she crooned softly.

Jenny quickly changed focus to Tarafau, not wishing to dwell longer on this scene.

The battlefield came into view immediately from Tarafau's point of view. He strode forward, checking on one after another of his troops and consulting with the Groga generals. So far everything was proceeding as they had planned. All weapons were being removed. Soon Daringi would begin depositing the unconscious Norgoth onto a planet in an unpopulated dimension. The planet itself had no gates.

The exploratory teams of the Dimensional Alliance continued to discover new dimensions through random natural gates. Most of the gateway planets into a dimension were populated, potentially by some species wandering through the gate by accident, getting stuck there and then populating the area.

But from time to time they found a gateway planet that was apparently uninhabited. Most of them were oxygen rich. When they found such a planet, a team would go to work exploring the solar system of the planet to see if there were inhabited or habitable planets in the system.

In this particular case, there were three habitable planets in the solar system, but none of them had any discernable life beyond plant and animal life. The council had chosen the planet farthest from the gate planet to establish the Norgoths who survived this war.

They had left basic tools, temporary shelter, rations, and medical supplies in several areas throughout the planet. The thought was to separate the Norgoth into colonial areas so as not to deplete local resources and hopefully to prevent some of the conflict that might ensue as factions developed and contentions began, as they inevitably would in such a warlike culture.

Tarafau had admired Jenny's reverence for life and was grateful this option was open to them. The only other alternative would have been to exterminate the Norgoth. There would still be many deaths. Not all of the battles would be as clean as this one had been. They had no idea if Jenny would ever be able to use this ability again and what it would do to her to use it more than once if it were even possible.

He went to the designated assembly area. They had set up a table for each Daringi to check in before taking the MDP with specific numbers of Norgoth to the various settlement areas.

This was a huge and detailed task, as there were thousands of Norgoth here. Jenny had been concerned that there would be this huge number of male Norgoth with no potential mates for colonization, but as it turned out, about a fourth of the Norgoth soldiers appeared to be female. Theoretically, eventually the numbers would even out, but for now it was what they had.

According to reports Jenny had seen, when they had explored the planet they were using for the settlement, they had noticed a healthy balance of herbivores vs predators. It would initially put the Norgoth in a certain amount of danger while they established themselves.

Tarafau had expressed the opinion that the sheer numbers of the Norgoth arriving so precipitously would discourage any of the wildlife from coming too close to do any large scale damage and this was still a better option than large scale euthanasia.

All in all, Tarafau mused, it was probably better than they deserved, but there it was. Part of this exercise was to teach the Groga by example that killing wasn't the only solution to a problem. Jenny had not wanted to start them on their new path with a bloody battle, and fortunately her plan had worked. Had it not, for any reason, they had been prepared to fight it out, but the results would have been devastating on both sides.

So, he checked in with the sergeant at the desk and was passed the coordinates in the mysterious way the Daringi did that. Even Jenny, sitting now in his mind, couldn't discern how that happened. She had been so excited when Elizabeth had displayed that talent, for the potential it had for the resolution of this struggle with the Inseni.

Something startling just occurred to Jenny, as she watched this all play out. She hadn't seen a single one of the big-eyed Inseni, Peril's people since this fight with the Norgoth Inseni had begun. She couldn't help but wonder what had happened to them and shuddered slightly.

While it was true that the intentions of their leader had been malignant, that didn't mean the common people had deserved any ill treatment. The revolution had been a necessary thing, but she didn't want to focus on what might have happened to the Inseni who had survived it.

Tarafau faded out of the battlefield to an unfamiliar landscape. It was pleasant, gently rolling hills covered with grasses, wildflowers, occasional leafy trees, and some scrubby little bushes here and there. Not far from where Tarafau stood, there was a little stream chuckling along in its rocky bed. The area he was facing had several large field tents erected, and a fenced in storage area filled with crates of varying sizes.

From the information they had extracted from the Norgoth who had invaded the Puerto Rico gate compound, Alliance scholars had been able to get a crude understanding of the Norgoth language. On the outside of each crate was an inventory of sorts printed in dark ink in the Norgoth language on each container and, for the ones that required instructions, packing slips had been included inside each box.

Alliance troopers, transported there earlier by Daringi soldiers, were busy at work erecting more of the field tents. Each one would accommodate a hundred cots. It would be a little cramped, but Tarafau figured he could live with their discomfort.

"What do the medics say about their condition?" Tarafau asked another sergeant at an almost identical desk stationed at the edge of the compound.

"As far as they can tell, none of the Norgoths were badly harmed. There will be some bumps and scratches from where they all fell over, but nothing serious. They will survive," he said in a dry tone.

Tarafau nodded and entered the closest barracks tent. Row upon row of sleeping figures laid out, each on a separate cot. They didn't look so fierce with their faces slack and their breathing quiet. All was well, but he didn't want to be there when they woke up. What would they remember about their confrontation with the Dimensional Alliance Gatekeeper?

When Jenny had commanded "Now!" every Mookookie had instantly shielded every ear of every one of their soldiers, including little Chidwi. They had done a variation on the shielding they did to the body in combat situations. But the difference this time was that instead of going inside the spaces of a garment, they had somehow manipulated those retractable appendages of theirs to fit seamlessly over the ears of each individual in the Groga force. Tarafau still wasn't clear whether that involved them merging with the spaces on the actual faces of each of them and honestly didn't want to think about what that might mean.

He went back out to the desk sergeant and asked him, "Do the medics have any idea as to how long they will stay in this state? I want to be absolutely sure that all Dimensional Alliance personnel, Daringi and Groga are off planet well before that happens."

"The medics have put a device into the first tent that was filled with Norgoth. It monitors breathing patterns and heart rhythms. It should be able to give us a warning about an hour before they come back to consciousness. We are prepared to get off within 15 minutes of that alarm, or whenever we have finished installing our 'guests' into their accommodations, whichever comes first."

Tarafau nodded. "I want hourly reports. Have you assigned a courier?"

"Yes, Tarafau. All is as you requested."

"Thank you, sergeant. I'll only be returning if you need me. For now, I have to get back to the Groga planet to finalize things there."

He did a similar check in with all 10 different settlements and found all satisfactory.

As he faded back to the battlefield, Jenny noticed that much had been accomplished while they had been gone. The field had been cleared of about a third of the unconscious Norgoth and the Groga were assiduously continuing their task, each with a Daringi trainer absorbing one soldier after another. From Tarafau's point of view, if you didn't look at details, it looked as if the soldiers were just melting out of existence.

Jenny could see her plan was working as well as she could have expected. She knew the Groga still had a long journey ahead of them, and she might even have a part in that at some point. For now, she faded out of Tarafau's consciousness and back to the beautiful garden and the crystal pool.

"Would you like to see what else has been set into motion?" Miriha asked. "Remember, your part in the plan was just one small corner, albeit an important one."

"Yes, I would. I know the rest probably won't have had it go as smoothly as we did. It almost feels like cheating that I could use my ability in this way."

"Not cheating, just good use of resources."

"You sound like my dad."

"Ah, yes. I like your dad." Miriha replied with a twinkle in her eyes.

"Wait! You know my dad?"

"Of course. May I remind you that Lizzie and I monitored you for a long time before she decided on you to take her position? Had you not measured up, someone else would have ended up in that little house on Infinity Loop."

Jenny sighed. She had often tried to look back and remember what she had been up to those years she was observed intently by her aunt and Miriha, trying to think of what embarrassing things they might know about her.

"OK, so who do we need to check in on next?"

Liliath wasn't in the council room. She didn't even appear to be anywhere Jenny recognized. She stood on a ledge at the side of a tall hill. Before her were assembled something that made Jenny gasp.

Dragons! Thousands of them! Large ones, small ones, and several sizes in between; the range of colors was like a rainbow gone nuclear. Liliath trumpeted a sound Jenny had never heard from her before. It was like an entire brass band on one clear note. The stirring of wings and all other movements ceased. Every reptilian head was focused entirely on Liliath with such concentration that Jenny was intimidated by the sheer force of it.

"My dear ones; the time has come! Each of you has been chosen for your dedication and your battle prowess. It has been ages since anything like this has been required of us, but we know why we joined the Alliance in the first place. Every dimension is contributing something.

We will contribute our powers and the ability to fly. The planet we have been assigned is rocky and not easily accessible to those who only have their feet to rely on. The Norgoth on this planet are strongly fortified, and it is a main training and deployment center according to intel from our Mookookie friends.

Your squadron leaders each have the entire plan and what part your squadron will play in it. You have been briefed by them. Pay attention. The outcome of this battle could shift quickly if the Norgoth have any surprises for us.

I wish I could be with you, but necessity dictates I must play my part while you play yours. Thank you for your service and your courage. My blessings and the blessings of He Who Created All Things go with you into battle and will return with you when you come home."

Once again, she trumpeted, and the entire dragon legion trumpeted back. Jenny was surprised the very planet didn't vibrate with it. The dragons were on their way. The Norgoth would be having a bad time of it on that planet, Jenny was sure.

She faded back to the little pool. "They were majestic. Thank you for showing me this. I wish I could have taken a photo. If I were an artist, this would be a picture worth painting. Where do we go next?"

"I think you should see this. I warn you, although what you just saw was impressive, this is not as pleasant."

She was looking over a vast city on a planet with a violet sky. She was on a ridge. An alliance trooper approached and saluted. "General Gariel, we are ready."

Jenny made another mental sigh. They had discussed in council that they couldn't do like the Insenium tried to do to the Groga and just annihilate them from space. It would have been a simple solution, although it might have entailed some space battles, but still would have created much less casualties among Alliance troops. It finally came down to what Jenny had already learned. Soldiers were soldiers and expected to die in battle at some point, but they all had families who were not necessarily soldiers.

The majority of the members of the Alliance were of the mindset that it was not right to punish the innocent. Most of the beings that populated the various Inseni planets were just beings pursuing their day-to-day lives. They had been conditioned since birth that the philosophy of enforced societal order was how things should be. The people themselves had not conceived the plan to dominate the multiverse. So, it was up to the Alliance to see to it that they were able to pursue their own lives and philosophies as long as they didn't try to force them on others.

Therefore, it was back to ground warfare, hitting all of the military bases they could find. This was a war of attrition. If the Insenium didn't have the forces necessary to prosecute an interdimensional war, it would buy the Alliance time to figure out how far the Insenium had spread into other dimensions and whenever possible, free the people from that tyranny.

It would be a long term commitment and would require more intel and more planning to make it happen. In the meantime, they would create so much chaos and deplete the Inseni armed forces to the point that they wouldn't threaten any additional dimensions any time soon.

She knew Gariel was an experienced commander and she could count on him to fight using smart tactics to preserve as many of his troops as he could. Jenny had been told that Bob had been preparing some fairly nasty surprises to help the Alliance armies, along with the help of Xao Ting and the rest of the science team.

Bob had confided in her that he would never have considered building these weapons if it hadn't been for the desperate nature of their mission. However, like Gariel and the rest of the Alliance leadership, he had created all of them with the hope that, in the long run, it would mean fewer casualties than contemporary Earth weapons were intended to inflict.

Gariel gave a mental command: *"Move out! Take your positions! Prepare the first wave!"*

Jenny pondered this. First wave? Of what?

About a hundred Alliance troopers stood at the forefront of the troops, massed beside and behind Gariel. They each raised a hand into the air and from each of them poured hundreds of drones, each the size of a large paper kite, but that's where the similarity ended. They didn't float. They zoomed.

Jenny had seen documentaries of locust swarms darkening a sky as far as the eyes could see. This was much like that. En masse, they descended on the apparently unsuspecting city. From the watchtowers, however, alarms began to sound. Blaster shots fired from the city walls, but so far the drones were out of the effective range of the shooters.

Jenny also knew these drones were shielded, but the brilliant part about this part of the operation was that it didn't matter if any of them were hit. There were several modifications of these little drones that made them effective weapons long after they were downed. Inevitably the Norgoth would forage the downed drones and unknown to them, some of the new versions of Burt's bugs would be released at the first touch of anyone with Norgoth DNA.

They never did discover the purpose of the Norgoth raid on the Puerto Rico compound, but the DNA they collected from the prisoners had been invaluable in so many phases of the various attacks that would happen this day. The tacticians had all agreed that a coordinated attack all at once would be the most effective.

So, on four other planets in addition to the events at the Groga planet, the main concentrations of Inseni forces would be attacked. Each contingent was assigned a different planet, and each planet required different tactics for differing terrains.

The intel they had collected had mentioned four main planets within this dimension that were important based on the high concentration of military forces. They also had hinted that there were other colonies in dimensions they had not yet pinpointed. In addition, there was a space station that housed their space fleet in orbit around the main planet, Xatal, where Gall resided.

As she watched through Gariel's eyes, the drones zoomed closer and closer to the city. At this point the Norgoth on the walls had all they could do to keep firing as the drones were firing back. Not at the Norgoth themselves, but at the wall supports just below their feet. In many places parts of the walls where they had all been standing had crumbled beneath them, sending them to fall the several stories below to land on whatever was below them that Gariel couldn't see from this vantage point.

"Wave two!" Gariel sent again.

Once again the troopers raised their arms. Shrieking out of the MDPs was a different kind of drone, and they were faster than the previous wave. Not quite a rocket or missile, but they were shaped like the paper airplanes teen boys often made when they wanted them to fly fast and high. They were almost dagger-like. They had nearly caught up with the other drones when they began to wail, a high pitched, eerie sound.

Jenny actually smiled. This particular component actually came straight out of a favorite Bible story about the walls of Jericho. The sound was irritating, but not injurious to the ears. It was designed to start vibrating every solid structure in the city. Anything that wasn't very strongly built would eventually shake to pieces. Like with the city of Jericho, the second wave caught up to the city and began to circle the city around and around, like wolves circling their prey.

In the meantime, the first wave of drones was flying over the city, spraying some kind of light mist as they went. Jenny knew this was a concoction of Xao Ting's meant to make the people disoriented and slow their reaction time.

As soon as the spraying had stopped, the first wave of drones joined the second wave that was still wailing, its plaintive vibrating cry circling the city.

They flew below the second wave, protecting their loud friends from blaster fire. As a result, a number of them were downed, although Jenny noticed the shots of the Norgoth were getting fewer and less accurate over time.

The walls of the fortress were beginning to topple in places. The entrance which hadn't been closed when the attack began so suddenly was now only partially blocked by one gate. The other hung haphazardly from its hinges, which was disconcerting considering that even from this distance Jenny could tell they were massive. Open, the gateway would allow a full platoon to march in ten soldiers across.

As she watched, she noticed ranks of soldiers forming behind the broken door. They knew they were vulnerable now and were preparing a defense. Jenny knew that the Alliance troopers wouldn't take any more risks than they needed to. Their enemy had been softened up and, it was likely they had more than one trick up their uniform sleeves, especially those who wore MDPs.

She knew that the tactically sound thing to do was to wait for the Norgoths to come streaming out of the gate and pick them off with their blasters as they emerged from the door. The Norgoths also realized they were now vulnerable behind the walls that had seemed so safe only moments before.

Now the first wave of drones broke from the circular formation and once again began firing on the Norgoth troops below. There was return fire, but the drones were too fast, and the accuracy and speed of the gunmen had been compromised due to Xao Ting's concoction, and they missed more often than not.

This was something that had probably never happened to them before, being attacked in their own fortress. They generally fought on their own terms, and Jenny knew that their commanders were probably scrambling at the moment, devising a strategy for this different form of warfare.

Suddenly a different type of fire started shooting up from below and behind the walls at the drones. The beam was more like what Brendan had reported in his space battle above the Groga planet. The beams were wider and more constant rather than a single shot, more like a constant stream.

One by one the drones began to come down over the heads of the Norgoth in the city. Jenny was sad to see the fruits of Bob's labor disintegrating under the barrage of this new weapon and concerned that this same weapon could be turned on human beings as well.

"Bots away!" Gariel sent out in a mental bellow.

Out of the MDPs came a literal army of Bob's bots. But they didn't have the pleasant appearance of Lizziebot and Fidget. These were larger, for one thing. They could fly and they were armed to the teeth.

The air was full of thousands of them in only a few minutes. The Norgoth were still dealing with the drones that continued to dodge the deadly fire of the new weapon. The bots had some interesting camouflage, and they were hard to see unless the light hit them just right. They were completely silent and how Bob had managed that was beyond Jenny. He had obviously been given help from the Alliance scientists in the creation of these deadly little wonders.

Now that the bots were moving forward, Gariel gave one final command, "*Attack formations forward!*"

Jenny could see the strategy unfolding here. First the drones with their annoyances as effective as they were; not really fearsome, although she was sure there had been some casualties and there was definitely a lot of damage to the huge city. In some places plumes of smoke rose from inside the city, so they had that to deal with as well. Now the drones would cover the main attack by Gariel's troops.

With enough drones and bots, they could have probably destroyed the entire city without the loss of a single Alliance trooper. But bots and drones couldn't differentiate between enemies and non-combatants with any accuracy. They could only follow their programming. One of the primary reasons for this particular strategy was to limit civilian casualties. Their main objective was simply to stop the Insenium military machine before they could invade any more domains.

Once again Jenny could appreciate the objectives and ethics of the Dimensional Alliance. Protecting the members of the Alliance was important, but all lives were precious in their eyes. They wouldn't put one more being in danger than was absolutely necessary on either side.

So Gariel and his men charged, descending from their hilltop. Intel said they were up against thousands of Norgoth soldiers in this particular training base. Of the ground battles that would be fought, this was a primary target. The other forces were coordinated from this base. Although there were military bases scattered across the capitol planet of the Great Insenium, this planet had only one purpose, the training of soldiers and launching of attack after attack on unsuspecting and unprepared dimensions.

The good news is that Gariel's forces were also huge. Jenny had heard her father tell of massive battles in the history of Earth, but it didn't prepare her for the real thing. Now she was charging with Gariel riding in his mind, blaster in hand. In the science fiction films Jenny had watched so avidly as a kid, the blasters never ran out of power, but Jenny knew that energy weapons, like projectile weapons, had a limited use.

Bob had explained to her that although Alliance science was well advanced from anything Earth had developed, a small portable weapon could still only go so far on whatever power source they employed. What would happen when they had depleted the power of their weapons or fighting in close quarters required a shift in the weaponry they used or the battle descended into one on one, weapon to weapon, hand to hand fighting?

This wasn't going to be a siege. Gariel had deliberately made that impossible by destroying the walls around the city, so the Norgoth soldiers were pouring out of the now completely open gates. The noise was deafening. War cries from the Norgoth filled the air and the zap of blasters and the cries of those downed or dying ascended with a cacophony like nothing Jenny had ever experienced.

Gariel's troops didn't yell as they charged. Under the cover of the bots they had simply run forward, not even firing until the first Norgoth noticed the new peril. They engaged with quiet ferocity, focusing entirely on the task at hand. There was no hate in their faces, unlike their enemy. These men were here to do a job, nothing else.

In all the chaos, Jenny still remembered that day in the Amazon jungle when Gariel had addressed his troops: "*We are the shield of the dimensional gateways. There will be no welcoming victory parades for us. We serve those who do not know us and who may never realize the sacrifice each of us have chosen to make for their protection.*" He had told her that they would prefer to never have to harm another being, but that they also could not allow the bullies of the multiverse to harm the weak and helpless. They served and were consummate professionals at what they did.

As the clash of the two armies ensued, Jenny could see the difference clearly. Fighting had already switched from blasters to clubs, swords and other weapons Jenny could not identify. Gariel had switched out his blaster for his staff from his MDP and was applying his ample skill with vigor, cracking heads, shattering kneecaps, and breaking bones.

He was lightning fast, and Jenny realized she could never remember Gariel fighting with Arvid. That would have been a match to remember.

Jenny couldn't see much from Gariel's perspective at this point and so, not really understanding how she did it, she "zoomed out" to see the broader picture. The battleground looked like someone had kicked an anthill. There were no longer any clear demarcations between the two armies. Bots still moved forward, firing from their energy weapons at the Norgoth who had mounted what was left of the walls of the fortress. But they could no longer fire into the masses of battling soldiers without potentially harming their own troops.

Suddenly from the gates emerged a few hundred of what Jenny could have only described as trolls. They were a dozen feet tall and built like professional wrestlers. They held huge clubs that appeared to have been molded from metal, spikes protruding from the end at every angle.

Jenny wanted to cry out a warning to the Alliance forces, but it was not possible. This viewing was exactly that, a viewing, not the two-way communication Jenny had become used to. But the bots had focused in on the trolls before Gariel's troops were even aware of them, targets that stood out from the crowd.

Unfortunately, their energy weapons appeared to have only a slight effect, somewhat like biting wasps. It was almost like these beings had a shell, much like a snail Jenny had discovered when doing a paper in college about endangered species. The scaly foot snail actually created an overlay of their natural shell and armored extensions of iron that they ingested from the deep sea hydrothermal vents in the Indian Ocean.

These massive beings seemed nearly indestructible. When they swung their intimidating clubs in huge sweeps they didn't seem too particular about who they hit or what they destroyed. Jenny decided that for such a huge creature, they hadn't been supplied with a brain to match. This random element only increased the chaos on the battlefield.

Gariel or one of his commanders must have given a new command to the drones that were left, because they stopped targeting the soldiers left on the walls. Instead, they focused on the new menace. Now each of the trolls was swarmed by the wave one and wave two drones, firing at them over and over again.

The trolls now swung their massive clubs in vain at the drones that zipped in and out around them, often passing inches from their faces. One troll actually smashed himself in the face, trying to swat the drones out of his way.

With this distraction Jenny could see that for now the trolls were not the menace they had originally appeared, but only a few of them were down at this point.

She also noticed that the Norgoths were beginning to tire. Evidently it took a while for their systems to metabolize the drugs Xao Ting had put in that spray early on in the battle. Their ferocity was definitely diminishing, and their coordination was clearly inhibited.

Gariel's troops stepped up their efforts, encouraged by their progress. Bodies were everywhere, covering the ground to the point that the soldiers on both sides had one more obstacle to overcome. More and more often someone would trip over a dead or unconscious soldier.

Jenny couldn't imagine how any of them kept track of much of the battle. Gariel had led a group of his soldiers up to a rise at the edge of the battlefield. From there, he could observe and issue commands.

The trolls' numbers were diminishing, although there were still a few dozen of them standing. But the number of drones was less as well. In the meantime, the bots had also surrounded the trolls, continually pelting them with laser blasts.

Jenny faded back to Miriha's little pool. "Have you experienced a battle like this before? How long will this go on?"

"I remember the Groga wars, in my role as the gatekeeper, but I was never as directly involved as you have been in actual combat. My role was more about helping with planning and coordinating resources. My skills are different than yours, but comparable. I, for instance, never had the necessity of using the shout although I knew someone who had.

As far as the length of the conflict, I seem to recall that Gariel and others warned you that this wouldn't be as straightforward as their previous encounters with the enemy.

Even once the Alliance forces are victorious, there will be many months of work to clean up this mess. The focus will shift from battle to rebuilding on both sides. The goal and the hope, for now, is to be sure that the rebuilding on the part of the Norgoth is more about rebuilding their culture than rebuilding their armies.

But, to answer the intent of your question, based on what I've seen and our past conflicts, this particular battle could last several days, depending on how many soldiers have been held in reserve inside the city itself. Gariel's troops must take the command center in the city, a vital part of their mission. The intel they will gain there will be invaluable going forward."

Jenny considered this. "According to the reports I collected before the confrontation on the Groga planet, there will be reinforcements to Gariel's troops on the way in a few hours, to allow the current troops to pull back and rest. Since I can do nothing about the situation as it stands, I would like to see how Liliath's squadrons are faring."

"You realize that you don't have any personal connection with any of the dragons in any of the squadrons? Fortunately, I do. The main commander, Dryselli, is known to me. I can help you make that connection. As before, he will be unaware of you and in this case, you will not be able to hear his thoughts, but you will experience the battle through his eyes. Will that work for you?"

"Thank you, Miriha. Do you think you could teach me that trick sometime?"

"Ah, Jenny, there is much ahead of you. Before you transition to the dimension beyond, you will accumulate so much more than I ever aspired to, but perhaps I will share some new ideas about your abilities from time to time."

She smiled gently at Jenny, the smile of a proud teacher for a prized student.

"Then let's see what is happening on the second Inseni planet."

Dryselli perched on the peak of a mountain, but it was puny compared to the mountains of his home world. However, this was a world that could have been made for his species, mountains, and large rocks everywhere. He had done a flyover and now was waiting. Jenny had loved the feeling of soaring over the jagged saw-toothed range. There in a valley similar to the one in Sanglarka, but not as lush, was their target. Jenny got the feeling the Norgoth in the city didn't look up much. None of the soldiers milling around there even glanced once toward the skies.

So, they knew nothing of what was to descend upon them. Once, during one of their training sessions, Liliath had told her of her kindred and some of their history. There was a reason people feared dragons. Not so much because they were cruel or because of their size, but because of a special mental talent possessed by all mature dragons; fear. They could project it like a message from a bullhorn, but instead of hearing it, it vibrated into the emotional center of those within range. It was primarily a defensive mechanism.

Dragons were, in general, gentle creatures. They were meat eaters, but only hunted at need. Warfare had been eliminated among their own kind for time beyond memory. But nature had equipped them with weapons, whether they chose to use them or not.

Jenny hadn't been in on all of the strategy planning sessions, but she knew that every dimension had contributed something toward the long term success of this mission. She also knew that the Alani could be formidable when they chose to.

She had watched Liliath get herself under control more than once. The one thing she hadn't learned to control was the tiny trickle of smoke that emitted from her nostrils when she was agitated. Jenny knew that if it hadn't been for Liliath's amazing mental control, there would have been scorch marks on the walls of the private council chamber in many places.

What would they be like unleashed? Her family had thrilled to tales of dragons as her mom had read aloud from fantasy classics, such as The Hobbit when Jenny was a child. On the bookshelf in her home were every single book in the Dragonriders of Pern series, and Jenny had read every single one of them more than once.

Getting to know Liliath had been one of the most surprising and delightful aspects of her life as a Guardian and Gatekeeper of the Alliance.

She was seeing this all through the eyes of a dragon. Even with the urgency of the situation and her fear for these creatures she had grown to respect, and even, in Liliath's case, to love, she couldn't help but thrill at the thought.

Suddenly her stomach lurched as Dryselli launched himself off of the peak. From his peripheral vision, Jenny could see a squadron ranked beside and behind him. But it wasn't just one squadron. Circling the valley, from every surrounding peak, hundreds of squadrons were launching. This would be a slaughter!

She noticed that the tiny humans who had been casually going about their business were casual no more. They scattered, running about like mice in a box under the gaze of a hungry cat, but there was nowhere for them to go. Then Jenny realized they had still not looked up. This was the power of fear, unreasoning panic. They didn't know what they were afraid of. Even the flocks of animals penned in various places throughout the city were bleating and huddling together with nowhere to go and no idea where the danger was coming from.

Into this well of fear the dragons descended. They were flaming, but not at the scattering Norgoths. They were flaming the battlements surrounding the city, most specifically the watchtowers. Their Mookookie agents had been very specific about this compound. At its center was the command center of all the Norgoth forces. In this command center were the plans for every assault, every incursion they had made. If they could scatter the soldiers and take the command center, they would be able to transfer all the records and data contained therein to Alliance Headquarters.

This valuable information would give them the roadmap for the next stage of ridding the multiverse of the inimical plans of the Great Insenium. Jenny remembered that Liliath had cautioned them all that this assault was only the first stage of a running battle that could take a very long time, perhaps beyond the lifetimes of the Earthlings who were at the center of all of it now.

As they descended, they leveled out and circled the city, continually flaming the walls. The Norgoth were still running around in a panic, but a few stalwarts had begun to shoot back with blasters, although sporadically and haphazardly. Jenny could almost feel sorry for them because she knew that the majority of them had been brainwashed to believe in the Inseni cause of order in the multiverse.

Nevertheless, she realized it was a lot like the enemy soldiers of the world wars. They fought because they were told to fight. They went where their leaders pointed them. That didn't mean that they should have been allowed to destroy the freedom and safety of the rest of the world. Brainwashed or not, the allies of that time fought them and many on both sides lost their lives. This was no different. Freedom and the right to choose were seldom without a price of one kind or another.

As the dragons circled the fortress, they continued their descent until they finally settled on the walls. Suddenly the Norgoth stopped running around. The edges of the city were on fire and it ran unchecked.

Jenny realized that Dryselli must have sent them a command in mindspeech. She imagined it was probably as simple as, "If you continue to fight us, we will burn this entire city to ashes. Drop your weapons and put out the fires before they spread," since this was exactly what happened. The soldiers and other citizens stopped shooting at the draconic host and turned instead to rescuing their city from the flames.

Dryselli and his squadrons then landed inside the walls. Dryselli and several of his officers extended their arms, which Jenny now realized displayed MDPs. From the MDPs, poured a small army of Bob's bots. These dispersed throughout the city, apparently to do two things; to oversee the Norgoth now fighting multiple blazes surrounding the city and to search for the command post the Mookookie had described. Indeed, suddenly there was a group of a couple dozen Mookookie who had sprouted legs and were leading the robots to the center of town.

The citizens of the town recoiled in nearly as much fear of the Mookookie as the draconic host. The Insenium had thought of the Mookookie as rodents, but these were different. Their long legs and big feet sprouted directly from their body heads. Their arms were waving the bots forward and their wide mouths were open, showing their long rows of teeth. Jenny had to admit; in this mode, they actually looked intimidating. All of this was done in complete silence from Jenny's side, but she could imagine the screams and shouts of these people who now felt they had woken up to a nightmare.

Jenny knew, or thought she knew, that the Mookookie wouldn't harm them, but you would never have known this from the terrified expressions and the tears streaming down many faces.

As Dryselli followed the bot squadron and their Mookookie guides, he looked from side to side. The other dragons had remained perched on the areas of the walls that were not yet being consumed by flame.

There was a fair likelihood he wouldn't be able to get through the command center doors, but he needed to be there to give specific orders about the disposition of the various things they might find there. Out of his MDP he manifested an Alliance tablet which looked more like a cell phone in his clawed hand. Suddenly he could see via the tablet screen through the eyes of one of the bots as they moved forward.

They finally arrived at a large building, as the Mookookie had told them, in the center of the town. Like all Inseni cities, the buildings in the city were plain and undecorated. This building was the same, only much larger than any they had encountered through the city.

It was a single story, with unadorned windows and a single entrance, a double door. The Mookookie and the bots entered the building, the bot that was connected to the tablet going ahead of the others. Jenny got the idea that Dryselli was giving specific instructions as the bots went methodically through the various rooms.

They encountered a few Norgoth who initially took out their blasters. The Mookookie simply faded into the closest adjacent wall or the floor, leaving the bots to raise their blaster equipped arms. However, no shots were fired on either side.

Although she couldn't hear it, she got the feeling that Dryselli had issued the same mental command as he had with the army outside. The Norgoth dropped their weapons, which the bots ignored. The Mookookie however went behind like a cleanup crew, picking up the weapons and EATING them!

They finally came upon a room that was very much like every situation room Jenny had encountered so far in her adventures; large tables spaced around the room with maps and charts and several Norgoth who were probably generals of their army, as well as a handful of regular soldiers who were probably clerks.

Jenny could see their mouths moving and could imagine they were shouting at the bots. Then several Mookookie entered from behind the bots, and faces now reflected shock, confusion, and anger. Again, weapons were drawn but never fired. Again, she imagined the draconic mental voice commanding they release their weapons. And again, weapons dropped and then jaws dropped as the Mookookie promptly swallowed them.

The bots went from Norgoth to Norgoth, binding them with a flexible plastic that when applied, shrunk to the diameter of their wrists. The Norgoth were seated, until the last one, potentially their leader, shouted something at them, disdain clear on his face. He attempted to grab the robotic arms extended toward him with the binders. However, a Mookookie grabbed him from behind and extended his arms in such a way as to completely encircle him. The Norgoth officer rolled his eyes and growled something in his language that, of course, Jenny couldn't hear.

She faded back to Miriha and the pool. "Looks like our draconic friends have the situation well under control. Who knew when Burt fed his little 'buddy' that they would be so useful and helpful in so many ways?"

Miriha smiled that somewhat mysterious smile of hers, but simply nodded without comment.

"I know these battles have not been without cost to the Alliance forces, but would you say it is going well? I have no way of judging."

Miriha didn't answer right away. She looked at Jenny thoughtfully. "I think it is a good beginning. As you know, these are mostly just a holding action. No matter how successful or unsuccessful we are in the individual battles fought today, the true story will be told in how the Alliance follows through.

Regardless of good intentions, there are still those who will continue to suffer from the original Inseni incursions in their dimension. Consider that for many of them, they have lived for generations under this tyranny.

Had they not invaded my home; the Alliance would still have been blissfully unaware of the danger presented by these beings, and the Great Insenium would have continued to spread dominion and terror, potentially unchecked.

For now, we must be content with the progress we are making. We haven't yet begun to pay the full cost for what the Great Insenium has done, and the losses of the Alliance are miniscule compared to the suffering of the victims of this plan to dominate the multiverse. It is important to understand this without allowing yourself to feel insignificant. Every being plays their part."

Jenny nodded. However, she couldn't help but feel that her contribution was pretty minor. Of course, this wouldn't stop her from trying, but it was easy to feel overwhelmed. But even in her favorite fantasy novels, the wizard's magic didn't solve everything. As it was put in one of her favorite books, "The enemy has magic too." She had her equivalent to magic in the science that had made so much possible, but the enemy had science too.

She sighed. Miriha stood. "Come, Jenny. Let us take a walk through the garden. I find it helps me to think and consider deeply. For now, there is nothing you can do to change what is about to happen. Let it rest. Soon you will return to your unconscious body. Let us use the time to do what we can do. You know you can trust the others to do their best, which is all anyone can ever do."

Chapter 39: The Enemy Has Science Too

It was a relief to see Mervin and the Alliance Science Team again. They were loudly making over Ignatius on the special lab perch they had all created for him. Bob had wanted to leave Ignatius in the care of the Earth Science and Technology Team, but Ignatius had insisted. *"Am I not your lab assistant? How can I help you if I am not with you?"*

Bob hadn't known what to say to this. He had explained they wouldn't be staying in the lab, but finally conceded the point, as there would be people to care for him in the Alliance lab as well as at Adelle's lab.

"Are you ready, Merv? Timing is important, as you know. Did you get my last notes?" Bob hadn't really realized how much they had depended on Jenny's mental gifts until she wasn't able to perform her communication duties.

They had been warned that as part of the strategy for securing the Groga planet, Jenny would be out of commission for an undetermined amount of time. Tarafau had popped in at Sanglarka to apprise the teams of Jenny's condition and that she was being safely and assiduously cared for by his family and Burt.

Bob had often entertained a notion about the two of them as he observed their interactions, and Burt had confirmed it in a private conversation before he had left to attend her on the Groga planet. Bob thought of Burt as a friend and he knew Burt would never deliberately do anything to harm Jenny, but he wondered whether Jenny returned those feelings. Burt had expressed that he was willing to wait for her and Bob had let the matter drop. They were both adults and had to make their own choices.

But for now, he had his own issues to deal with. The team had discussed wardrobe, of all things. Merv had stood firm on the issue when Bob had ventured the idea that camouflage would be best; "Absolutely not. I want them to know who they are dealing with. And besides, they're gonna see us coming anyway, right?"

Bob had agreed reluctantly, so everyone was now in their traditional uniform, jeans, assorted t-shirts, sneakers, and white lab coats.

"We got your notes and we're ready. MDPs are loaded and Liliath will see us off through the gate. Ignatius, are you coming?"

"Definitely not," Bob said at the same time that Ignatius said, "Ready!"

Bob rolled his eyes. "I thought we had an agreement, Ignatius," he sighed.

"Assuming all goes according to plan, he shouldn't be in any real danger," Merv cut in, "And if there is real danger, how well would Ignatius fare without his Bob?"

"My Bob," Ignatius agreed.

Bob shook his head. "OK, I'm overruled." He reached for his shoulder perch and strapped it on over his lab coat. The last thing he needed was claw marks on his shoulder while he was dealing with the oncoming hoards.

They then rode the elevator to the gateroom, where Liliath was waiting. *"I must say, this is the most unusual invading army I've ever seen,"* she sent. *"They are in for a bit of a surprise, I do believe."* There was definitely amusement in her mental tone and Merv acted out putting his thumbs under imaginary suspenders. *"Yes, Mum. Our devious plan is to make them laugh themselves to death."*

"Then I believe you will be successful," she retorted. *"So off with you now. Bring me back a souvenir, will you?"*

Bob was incessantly surprised at the banter that went back and forth between Merv and Liliath. In his wildest imaginings he never considered the concept of a dragon with a sense of humor.

She opened the gateway and, they stepped through to Sanglarka. The Alliance had set up a way station there with a contingent of Tarafau's people to transport individuals to the various coordinates supplied by the Mookookie agents.

It was a glorious crisp day in Sanglarka, and Bob shivered slightly in his flimsy lab coat. He would have preferred a jacket. Nevertheless, they wouldn't be there long, as the assigned Daringi were waiting for them. A hand was laid on the shoulders of each of the scientists and at a nod from Mervin, Sanglarka faded from sight to be replaced by the crown of a large hill. Their objective was over the top of the hill in a shallow valley, a science lab and manufacturing plant for the Great Insenium.

"Thanks, mates," Merv said to their Daringi couriers, and all but one of them immediately faded from view. The remaining Daringi stood at parade rest. His job was to fetch his fellows when it was time to leave. He would station himself directly behind Merv to await that command.

In preparation for this assault, they had minutely studied every report; from those of the Mookookie to the original reports by Burt when he was on the planet they had thought was the capitol of the Insenium.

Burt had been given the opportunity to view the projects of their scientists, known by the Inseni as "wizards". During his tour he had been shown many things. After the rebellion, those scientists had begun to work directly with the Alliance Science Team, revealing the existence of this private base, devoted to the science of war. They had revealed that this facility was on the verge of producing a particularly heinous weapon which, if they succeeded in putting it into production, would potentially mean that any planet and any force rallied against the Inseni wouldn't stand a chance.

Each of them readied themselves. In each MDP were components of their plan, but the Inseni scientists would literally not know what hit them. The majority of their plan had to do with what Burt often called, "prestidigitation"; his favorite word for sleight of hand and deceptions that kept you looking in one direction while the real threat was taking place out of your sight.

Bob wished he could take a video of what was about to happen to share with Burt at a later time. Every single scientist on the team had given input into this project.

His team included Mervin, Argent, Clarice, Inle, Rayard and Alwin from the Alliance lab as well as Xao Ting. As serious as the situation was and considering the fact that most of them had never served in the military, they were surprisingly calm.

"OK, folks, let's get some attention from the sciency guys in the lab. If the pattern for the Great Insenium holds true, they are probably slaves recruited for their minds rather than their brawn. If we can help it, we don't want to harm any of them, or at least not permanently, but we can't allow their diabolical project to move forward another inch. Ready?"

They all nodded, and Ignatius chirped, "Ready!"

They topped the rise and gazed out at the valley. Their intel didn't say exactly what might be protecting this base, but they hoped they were ready for whatever they would throw at them. However, first they were going to do a little throwing of their own.

They stood there erect and not attempting to be subtle about it. First, Argent raised both hands above his head. In each hand was a one inch high cube with a red button on it. With an uncharacteristic grin, he simultaneously pushed both buttons. Two things happened immediately. A recording of a marching band playing "The Stars and Stripes Forever" at full volume blasted out as a bright laser-type light show blazed out from behind the group.

From below it would have looked like the sun was rising from the wrong direction, only this was ablaze with every bright color in the spectrum. There they stood in all their nerdy glory with as blatant an announcement of their presence as they could have contrived.

As soon as Argent had pushed his buttons, Rayard held up both arms and out of his MDPs poured a fleet of about thirty flying saucers each around twelve feet in diameter, moving high over the valley. These were also lighted up with a rotating red light that ran around the edges of each saucer and a blue flashing dome, like an oversized police car light bar.

Bob and Merv held out their MDPs and sent dozens of drones. They had deliberately made the buzz of each drone as loud as they were able. Therefore, they sounded like an army of extremely large angry wasps.

Clarice, Inle and Alwen held out their arms and a squadron of flying bots zoomed out, keeping pace with the drones. By now the entire sky was alight with various technological marvels. They weren't finished yet, but this was to get their attention and decoy any military personnel that might be housed in the complex.

The base looked like every other Inseni city, to put it kindly, boring. The only exception was an oval shaped dome well back from the entrance to the city, but plainly visible as it was the tallest building in sight. This seemed like their obvious target; as this was the production facility, but it wasn't their primary concern. According to Mookookie intel, there was a smallish building that wasn't much bigger than Bob's workshop on earth. The exterior of the building was somewhat shabby.

This smaller building was the lab. It was the most likely place for the scientists to store their reports and project journals. Although they would indeed want to shut down production of weapons, their true goal was to eliminate the lab. By getting everyone's attention, they were hopeful that the scientists would come out of that building to gawk at the unusual phenomenon, since part of their plan included destroying that building.

Bob realized there were definitely Norgoth troops on the base as some of the drones came under fire. The "flying saucers" were too high for regular weapons to reach them. This was part of the testing, part of the mission. They wanted to see if the Norgoth had any planetary "big guns" to use. This would be helpful for future missions, especially if the aircraft happened to be manned.

The entire crew was now fully engaged in commanding their airborne fleet. There was a game controller in every hand. "Leave it to a bunch of geeks to turn war into a video game," Bob thought with a smirk. They had made themselves the initial target with their lights and music blaring away, but unless the enemy was able to pound through their various fleets, they were potentially pretty safe, as Merv had intimated.

All of their mechs were weaponized and the saucers had an especially nasty surprise for the city's inhabitants who were now milling around. He noticed that some actually appeared to be taking photos or video of the incursion. "Curiosity is the essential qualification of every scientist," he thought, shaking his head.

The drones were dive-bombing crowds of on-lookers as well as the soldiers. An occasional drone was hit and as it careened down to the ground, it made the wailing sound that young boys playing army had been making for over a hundred years. Bob had insisted on adding it to the program; one more distraction for their enemy.

Bots were firing, but only at armed soldiers. These bots had been the last ones to come off the assembly line, and they had a special new feature. Each of them had a sensor to allow them to discern the one difference between combatants and civilians.

One of the Inseni scientists had told them that the scientists weren't allowed to carry any kind of weapon, nor were civilians. So, the bots only fired at those who were apparently carrying weapons.

The Mookookie, when they had landed on the planet in the spaces of the clothing of the soldiers they had attached to during the revolution, had spread themselves out as instructed, to be able to oversee every aspect of the operations on the planets they had been inadvertently transported to.

At this point, they were awaiting a command from Chortle, who was riding as a shield over Bob's chest. Each of the scientists on his team had a Mookookie shield and they all felt the better for it. Of course, there was that weapon they had been told about. It hadn't been made clear what it was supposed to do or how it worked, but Xao Ting had come up with a theory.

As a result, he had come up with something he called a "weapon smasher". According to the review of the device by Merv's team, it had been pronounced "beyond brilliant".

On Bob's part, he just wanted to get in, disable the weapon and destroy the scientist's notes and journals and get back out of there. The presence of the big Daringi youth behind them was comforting, to say the least. Bob had seen his share of combat and didn't want any part in it anymore. Nothing but the most urgent need to protect the weak and downtrodden could have brought him once again into this role.

They had designed their plan to do the most damage possible to the weapons production and development facilities and do the least possible damage to the beings who lived and worked there. Soldiers were necessary casualties, and they had chosen their profession and knew the risks.

Their drone population was declining, so Bob pocketed his controller and sent another squadron out of his MDP. From the standpoint of the defenders, it would look as if they came out of nowhere, loudly buzzing nuisances.

Intel indicated the Norgoth troops were sparse on the ground at this particular facility. They used a desert place on the other side of the hills surrounding the valley for their base, only keeping a small contingent within the technology base. One squadron of drones and bots had already been sent ahead on a 'seek and destroy' mission to the military base in the valley.

He picked his controller back up, but paused as Merv sent, *"Now, Rayard!"*

Rayard, who had been controlling the saucers, now brought them much lower, within firing distance, but by this time the soldiers were so engaged with the drones, Bob didn't think they even noticed them. After all, the saucers had just been hovering out of range the whole time and unlike the angrily buzzing drones, they were silent. Bob loved that he had been given the opportunity to work with "dastardly alien tech" to help assemble this tactical team.

Merv and his team had gleefully copied Burt and Bob's idea for the flying saucers used in the raid in the Amazon basin and improved on them. The original had just been a covering contrived to be fitted over camouflaged drones, and the only reason the Groga had bought the ruse was because it was so unexpected.

But these babies were packed with some interesting additional features, such as silent running mode and a hidden compartment with a trap door under the carriage of the saucer. Now, as they hovered lower and lower, Rayard gave Bob an evil grin and a wink, his wild curly mop of red hair giving him the appearance of the classic "mad scientist". He pressed a button on his controller and nodded toward the saucers, which had positioned themselves evenly around the compound.

Suddenly the trap doors opened, an apparatus much like a fire hose now protruding from the belly of each. From each of the hoses spewed a highly sticky substance. Bob didn't know if they had decided to use maple syrup as he and Burt had done, but whatever it was, it was gooey. By the time the crowds milling around in the city realized there was a problem, it was too late and most of them were doused thoroughly with the gooey stuff.

The team couldn't help themselves. Every one of them burst out spontaneously with hearty laughter. Some of their various flying things wobbled slightly in flight until they possessed themselves again. Now the people were running around with their arms extended as if they wanted to fly away. Actually, Bob was sure it was to keep their arms from sticking to their sides. This should keep them busy for a while.

In the meantime, Bob sent to Chortle, *"Mookookies ready?"*

"Ready, boss."

Chortle had picked that up from Fidget and so, "boss" it was.

"Mookookie now!" was all Chortle broadcast, but Bob knew what was happening even though he couldn't see it. The previous instructions to their Mookookie agents had been to sneak into the production facility at night. Before that, they had all taken upon themselves to multiply to the point that there were about a dozen Mookookie for every human on the base.

At this very moment they had begun to eat. Thousands of Mookookie were eating every piece of equipment, every tool and all of the supplies and anything that had been produced in the factory. They didn't try to eat anything completely, simply taking a bite here and there to make what they were eating completely dysfunctional.

Chortle had tried to explain to Bob that what they did with things like metal, paper and other nonfood like things was to break the bonds of the atoms of those things which produced usable energy for the Mookookie much like the calories of food made energy in human beings. Their understanding of the "spaces" and their ability to see between the spaces and the miniscule atomic structure of things around them, gave them some pretty scary abilities that Bob was only recently beginning to understand.

It was easy to underestimate them with their nearly comic appearance, and easy-going and enthusiastic personalities. But the Alliance had gained a powerful new ally the day Burt had first fed BaaGah.

Xao Ting was as animated as Aliki or Leland by this point, bouncing slightly on the balls of his feet, his face a picture of anticipation. Bob could never remember him being anything but stoic and calm, but he could understand. This was his moment, and it was a pass or fail test.

They had done many tests with the prototype of the device Xao Ting had envisioned. All tests in every environment and situation had been successful, but they knew from the beginning that a change in environment or situation or if the device failed to reach its target, changed the odds of success.

"Now?" Xao Ting sent, his eyebrows up and his face a picture of eager anticipation.

Merv nodded in agreement. *"Now."*

From Xao Ting's MDP emerged another drone. This drone was a vehicle for the tiny device Xao Ting called his "weapon smasher". It was a variation on an EMP pulse that would disable not only the energy source for a weapon, but also would scramble any computer code that controlled the weapon. Unlike an EMP, this did not require a huge explosion to be effective, and it only affected weaponry in a specific radius. Bob had been utterly amazed, as it was definitely not "dastardly alien tech", but purely of Earth design that required an understanding of physics he would have never expected from his friend.

When Xao Ting had described the concept and how he thought they could accomplish it, the team had enthusiastically gone right to work while Bob was working on MDP science, the enhanced drones, and the upgrade on the bots and nano bots.

The drone hovered for a moment while Xao Ting adjusted the radius settings on his controller. Then, under cover of all of the confusion that reigned on the base below them, it glided silently to the top of the production facility, landing almost daintily on the dome roof. Once it was at a full stop, it dropped its load. The tiny device had four stages. The first was to drill through the roof. The second was to drop through the hole it had drilled onto any surface in the facility. Then it was to run its program, with the hoped for result that any powered weapons in the facility would be destroyed within the radius Xao Ting had set. Finally, it would self-destruct to ensure that no evidence of the device lingered for the surviving scientists to analyze and in that process do even more damage to the facility it had landed in.

The Mookookie, on their part of the mission, had been instructed to stay away from the center of the facility at this point to prevent any injuries.

The controller in his hand beeped and Xao Ting grinned. *"Done,"* he said simply.

The team sent up a vocal cheer. While it was true, they couldn't know how successful the device had been, the completion of that task meant they were nearly done with their mission.

At a signal from Merv, all of the drones descended on the lab behind the dome in a strafing formation four drones wide. Each was in continual rapid fire mode. Lines of fire were drawn across the roof of the lab and in a few minutes, they started to see large gouts of flame springing up.

The base was now in complete chaos and it was time to go. Merv waved at the Daringi who faded out and almost immediately his transport team reappeared, laying a hand on each shoulder. They left behind the drones, bots, and saucers, which had each been programmed to self-destruct when the end of mission signal was sent. Bob sighed as they faded back to Sanglarka. It had been a wrench to leave all of that beautiful tech and it would have been spectacular to see them all explode at once, but they had completed their mission and only time would tell how successful it had been. At the very least, they had ensured that it would be a long time before any weapons were manufactured there.

The Mookookie had been given instructions to go into the spaces to protect themselves and to be prepared for Chortle's signal to assemble at a prearranged meeting place to be taken back to Krim, so they would be as safe as possible while the Alliance wrapped up the primary assault.

Bob watched his exultant team celebrating with enthusiasm and telling the tale of the assault of the sciency guys to anyone who would stand still long enough to listen. It had been a good day, but Bob exchanged knowing looks with Merv. There was no way of knowing whether any of the other assaults had been successful. Merv had immediately sent a report to headquarters where they would now give the go ahead for the space fleet to go to work. "Good luck, Brendan," Burt thought. "Live long..."

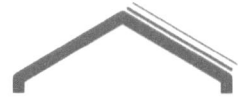

Chapter 40: Chariots of Fire

B rendan checked one last time with every battle station on his ship. Bob had worked tirelessly with Juan's team on the MDP science that would make their strategy today possible.

Bob had created a map of the coordinates of all the known MDPs with the help of the Mookookies, the Nanoites and the Daringi, which meant a person didn't have to use a gate to send supplies or troops to anyone who wore an MDP. Brendan wondered why the Alliance had neglected to realize that the place inside an MDP was an actual physical place with an actual location in dimensional space time.

With the help of the Nanoites, the inner environments of all the MDPs had been optimized for oxygen breathing creatures. The Daringi, paired with Mookookie had confirmed the coordinates of each MDP. The Mookookie would give the Daringi the coordinates, and then the Daringi would confirm by transporting directly into the MDP coordinate without any physical contact with an MDP armband.

They had found that the Daringi could transport from within one MDP directly into any other MDP they had the coordinates for, and that they could carry an MDP armband into any other MDP without any complications. Brendan admired the courage of these testers, as anything could have happened, including destruction of the MDP, the person, and the Nanoites who lived there.

So, they had created a delivery system, combining what Juan and his team were doing, collecting all the necessary resources and equipment using MDPs much like an additional gate network.

The resources were simply transferred to an MDP at one end, as usual. The person wearing that MDP would enter an MDP in any other place in the multiverse with the help of a Daringi guide.

Once in the destination MDP, they would relay a message via the Mookookie, who could communicate from inside an MDP to a Mookookie at the destination who would notify the MDP wearer at that end.

The MDP wearer would invoke the MDP to bring the delivery person out of the MDP and then the delivery person could empty the equipment, resources, or troops to the new destination.

Brendan couldn't get his head around how people thought up these things, but he was grateful for it. He knew what his ship could do, but the engineers did the real magic. Brendan's job was simply to keep his crew working at top efficiency. He was a firm believer in getting the best possible people for your team; trusting them to do their jobs and to be brilliant at what they did. He had a great crew. They all knew their jobs and were good at them.

Commanders commanded, as one of his trainers in the Royal Australian Air Force was fond of saying. His job was to see to it that they stuck to the plan agreed on by the joint commanders of the Dimensional Alliance Space Fleet.

They honestly didn't know as much as they would have liked about the space station and the space fleet of the Great Insenium, but they knew enough to prepare for every imaginable possibility. In a situation like this, there was no such thing as over preparation.

The same four ships that had protected the Groga planet had done whatever repairs they needed and were assembled once again behind a large asteroid. When they revealed themselves to the space station, they would appear to be pretty pathetic compared to the number of warships surrounding it.

The camouflaged drone they had sent to scan the station had noted a fleet of about fifty ships, give or take, as ships were constantly leaving and arriving similar to a large airport. The majority of those coming and going were transport or cargo ships, but that still left a combat fleet of around twenty ships, and they had no idea if there were more hanging out in space and within rescue distance.

The enemy would only see three of the four in the initial contact, a meager show of force for certain. But they left the fourth ship safely behind the asteroid, a crucial part of their strategy.

The last thing they needed was a cavalry charge by enemy ships held in reserve. There was no way of knowing yet what their capabilities were, whether they had smaller fighters in their launch bays, or weaponry their intel couldn't have accounted for. All in all, it was a chancy business, but the Alliance fleet had a few surprises literally up their sleeves.

Even now the launch bays on the Alliance ships were on high alert to respond instantly with their little surprise. That element of surprise was the one thing they had in their favor after the three seemingly puny ships had lured the Inseni fleet away from the space station.

The comm unit on his command chair blinked red. It was time.

Three of the assembled fleet maneuvered in unison from behind the asteroid close enough to the space station that they would be seen on any instruments they had for tracking incoming ships. Brendan doubted that the Inseni considered this more than for the purposes of tracking their own fleet, as they had no enemies in their Galaxy. But they had been noticed.

A broadcast on all frequencies went out from the Admiral's con. "Attention Inseni space station. Surrender now to the might of the Dimensional Alliance and none will be harmed."

The "fair warning" was actually part of their strategy. They didn't expect any such surrender by their enemy, but the blatant challenge obviously got their attention. Several of their warships pulled out of docking bays and zoomed toward them. Obviously, they didn't think three measly ships was much of a threat.

As they had done at the Groga home world, they sent out a swarm of armed space drones toward the oncoming ships. Let them think what they would about that. Much like a giant swatting mosquitos, the ships began to fire on the drones with their minor weaponry. The drones were fast and more maneuverable, so many of them actually got through, once again planting the little nanobots on the hulls of the ships. Of course, it would take time for them to do their damage, but it was a start. It had distracted the enemy ships for stage two of their plan.

Each of the launch bays now disgorged slightly smaller versions of the ships in their tiny fleet which had been stored in MDPs awaiting this part of the plan. All were fully crewed and ready for battle. It was like a magician pulling several rabbits out of a hat, since within moments after those emerged, three more ships joined those...and then another three and then another three. In a matter of minutes, their fleet no longer looked so harmless.

In the meantime, evidently a call for help had gone out to the space station. Several more ships now flew toward the Alliance's quickly multiplying fleet, but the Alliance ships were just beginning.

Out of the launch bays of the smaller ships flew individual fighter planes, about the size of the fighter jet Brendan had flown in his Air Force service on Earth. Brendan knew that there were around forty of these fighters assigned to emerge from each of the smaller ships, which now numbered at a few dozen and more continued to come.

Brendan blessed Bob and his MDP research for this seemingly impossible stunt.

The fighter ships immediately began to engage the enemy. And Brendan's ship continued to send out the relatively tiny drones as part of the attack. It was as if they had surrounded each of the enemy fleet with a swarm of bees along with an intimidating flock of large angry eagles. Zipping in and out, it was nearly impossible for the enemy ships to know on which of the flying menaces to focus their attack.

More enemy ships poured off of the space station. The Alliance now faced a fleet of nearly two dozen enemy ships, but by now the enemy faced an Alliance fleet of a few dozen ships of varying sizes and capabilities, not counting the swarms of fighters and drones.

The battle that ensued was not without its danger or fatalities. More than one Alliance fighter ship was either damaged or destroyed. The large Alliance attack vessels had taken minor damage, but shields were holding.

As part of the plan, they allowed their enemies to believe they were slowly retreating, farther and farther from the space station. In the meantime, their attack formation became slowly bowl like, drawing the Inseni fleet farther and farther into their midst. Additional ships and drones continued to emerge from the launch bays. This was a bit risky as there was a bigger chance that a stray shot might miss an enemy ship and instead hit an Alliance ship. But it also made it much harder for the Inseni ships to get behind the Alliance fleet.

At one point, in the heat of the battle, Brendan began to wonder if all of their preparations were going to be enough. The Inseni were mostly planet busters, more suited to conquer those on the ground than a dog fight with equal or superior forces in space. But the Alliance force had not been used for combat in living memory. The only reason they had any experienced commanders now was because the Alliance had recruited commanders such as Brendan, who had flight and combat experience on their own planets.

There was an abundance of "dastardly alien tech" in the ships, and the MDP delivery system meant that they had nearly unlimited supplies and equipment available. There was even a "hospital ship" that could receive a damaged ship into an MDP and get the repairs they needed to return to the battle. This definitely gave them an edge, but the Inseni captains were holding out remarkably against the numbers the Alliance had been able to put into the field, and now small agile fighter ships began to emerge from the Inseni's launch bays.

Alliance ships tried to pick them off one by one as they came out, but they didn't get enough of them to prevent the Inseni from evening the odds somewhat.

Now the fighter pilots had two things to worry about, the battle ships and the fighter ships. Dogfights ensued with ferocity on both sides. It was time. They were fully engaged and far enough away from the space station to implement the second stage of the mission.

The fourth ship would, at this moment, be cruising from behind the asteroid and heading for the space station to destroy it. Without the station, the enemy fleet would be greatly hampered, unable to do repairs, refuel or restock their ships. Unless they had a technology unknown by the Alliance, it was unlikely they could land easily on a planet from space.

This would mean there would be one less destructive arm of the Great Insenium that Gall and his minions would have at their disposal.

From where they were now fighting, the space station was a small glowing dot in a sky filled with stars. Brendan's tactical officer was directing the shipboard weapons crew, and his team was directing the drones and the fighter ships. The launch bay continued to pour out new drones at irregularly spaced intervals. Brendan wasn't entirely sure how many they had at their disposal, but he was grateful Bob had started production of these soon after he had been given the go ahead by the Alliance Chief Council.

They had engaged several off-dimension factories that had been cranking them out day and night ever since. As a result, part of what Juan's team was doing was constantly replenishing the fleets of them waiting in the MDPs issued to Brendan's launch bay crew.

Most of the drones were pre-programmed to recognize Alliance ships and to only fire on anything that was "not Alliance". Not all the drones were autonomous, however. Many of the drones were also being directly manipulated by pilots stationed inside the ship based on the strategy put forth by the fleet officers' tactical plan.

Brendan continued to watch the view screen, squinting to see the little dot of light. It was already at maximum magnification, so he couldn't zoom in any closer. There was a lot to keep track of, but his team was on top of it. They had drilled so hard over the last few months that Brendan sometimes felt a little extraneous. So he watched.

Occasionally his view was obscured by the flashes of light caused by a direct hit on one side or the other, but he kept focused on the tiny light. He knew he couldn't see the fourth ship approaching, and he wondered what defenses the space station had, if any.

He didn't like working with as little intel as they had on this situation, but he trusted everyone to do their best. The destruction of the space station was crucial. By now the approaching ship would have disgorged a number of smaller ships as the first three had done, and they were a small fleet bearing down on the station. But a small fleet of camouflaged drones that had issued from each of the approaching ships were the real menace. Each of them was actually a small but powerful bomb.

They would attach themselves to vulnerable areas of the hull of the station and explode simultaneously. This should even be visible from this far away. As before, the fleet of spaceships was simply a red herring, intended to draw attention away from the real danger.

Nearby, the battle raged on. Brendan knew that the real test of their fleet hadn't come yet. They still didn't know if the cavalry was on the way and their instructions were that even if they destroyed all the enemy ships, they were to remain in place for at least 24 hours to be sure there weren't more ships out there.

And there it was! The tiny light burst into a bright corona like a very miniature exploding sun. The bridge crew cheered, and Brendan was sure that the others would have celebrated as well, if it weren't for the fact that they were still in the heat of an intense battle for survival.

Now the commander of the fleet sent a message on all frequencies: "Attention Inseni fleet! Your space station has been destroyed. We regret the necessity, but your government has given us few options to protect ourselves. We now demand your surrender before we summon our reserves. As you have seen, our resources are vast and your fleet is diminished. Surrender and you will be treated fairly."

There was no reply, so the Alliance fleet continued to fire. As planned, the ships that had destroyed the space station were now closing fast on their position. The enemy fleet had been effectively surrounded.

Afterwards, Brenden would never be able to quite say what happened. All of the Inseni ships went silent. Perhaps they were going to surrender after all? But no...Brendan's ship was rocked suddenly by the huge blast created when every single Inseni ship exploded. The Alliance ships careened out of control into the blackness of space. The battle was over, but they weren't out of danger yet.

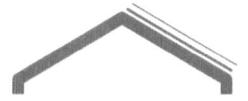

Chapter 41: Reflections

The walk around Miriha's garden had refreshed Jenny, as she and Miriha had discussed the implications of what they had seen so far. When they had returned to the pool, Jenny had requested to check in at Sanglarka, the main base for her team. A goodly number were out there risking their lives and in the situation room at the lodge Jenny knew that Lova and Arvid would be anxiously watching for reports to come in.

Miriha had reminded Jenny that she would not be able to communicate directly.

"I don't really care about that right now. They know where my unconscious body is. I just thought maybe we could get a broader picture of what the outcomes have been so far with our people."

"Very well," Miriha said, patting the stone seat beside her. "Let us reach out."

She took Jenny's hand and nodded toward the crystal pool.

Immediately a picture formed. She was riding along with Lova and could hear Arvid reading aloud from a report: "Gariel has reported in with a surprising outcome to their assault on the main training camp of the Norgoth. As you know, they took some heavy casualties, but they finally defeated the Norgoth who surrendered the training base and the surrounding city.

As they rounded up the citizens to sort out the civilians from the military and to prepare to transport the Norgoth military to the new colony, they heard an interesting report. Scouts were sent to verify.

When they returned to the camp, they had with them the mayor of a slave village that lay through a narrow valley that formed a pass behind the training city. The slave village had been created as a farming community to provide food for the military base.

Get this...this farming community was made up of the people from Miriha's village. Tarafau must be notified! He had sworn he would return her people to their home. From this report, it appears that most of them survived the Groga attack on their village and were transported to this remote planet to serve the Norgoth."

Lova clapped her hands, tears dripping down her face. "Oh, Arvid! I had lost hope that he would ever see that promise fulfilled. Good news indeed. I mourn for the loss of our Alliance comrades in this battle, but if there was ever anything that would ameliorate it, this would be it. Thank the Creator of All Things."

Arvid bowed his head briefly in agreement and reverence.

Jenny looked away from the pool momentarily. Miriha had her hands clasped to her heart, looking upward, and Jenny knew that she too was thanking the Creator of All Things for the rescue of her people. She decided not to interrupt that communion and instead returned her gaze to the pool. Arvid was saying:

"According to Liliath, a number of Daringi have been assigned to begin transporting Miriha's people to their planet, bypassing the gateway. When Jenny recovers, she can unseal the gateway. We will send volunteers to help them reestablish themselves.

After these main assaults are completed and the gate is re-established, we will want to choose a new guardian for their gate," he continued. "That is the end of this report, except to say that all is proceeding peacefully. The rest of the former slaves will be given possession of the planet after Gariel's troops have surveyed it to be sure there is no further danger to them from the Norgoth."

"But is there a potential danger from space?" Lova asked, wiping her eyes.

Arvid shifted uncomfortably in his seat. Evidently a crying woman was difficult for him to deal with, so he immediately answered her question, pretending he hadn't noticed.

"I think not, considering Brendan's report."

"How did that turn out?" she asked, sniffling.

"It's hard to say, the report cuts off in mid-sentence, but from what I can gather, they were successful in destroying the space station and were holding their own against the enemy fleet. Then, something about 'self-destruct' on the enemy ships. We haven't heard from any of the fleet since then. But I retain hope."

Lova nodded somberly. She had dried her tears and had calmed herself. The breathing exercises Lova had taught Jenny and which all of the agents and guardians of the Alliance practiced along with their physical exercise and self-defense were used more than just for protection.

"They are well equipped and competent," she agreed. "I expect they will come out of it better than their enemies appear to have done.

What about the Science and Technology team? I was very much against them going into a combat situation, but Bob had already proven himself in the Brazil campaign and had been in the military. Not all the scientists on that team had combat experience, however."

"They are returned safe and whole to Alliance Headquarters. Bob says that after they have been debriefed, he will take great pleasure in coming back to us for a good meal and the telling of the tale." And Arvid grinned wickedly. "I understand that "dastardly alien tech" won the day. They're all feeling a bit smug about the whole thing if I understand it correctly."

Lova smiled and nodded.

"Oh, and a report that came in while we were eating lunch," Arvid said swiping to a new page on the tablet in his lap. "This one applies to Earth."

"How so?" Lova said, leaning forward. Her brows were puckered with concern. "Not more about the blackout? And I thought we quashed that incursion into the Puerto Rico gate. Is there something I didn't know about?"

"Oh, this is much more interesting. Earth is digging out surprisingly well from the fallout resulting from the blackout. And Luz and her team did indeed contain the Norgoth, and after their interrogation, we sent them to the Norgoth colony, but this involves the Groga."

"The WHAT? How could they affect us now? They are either on their own home world or under the thumbs of the Insenium. What does that have to do with Earth?"

"Do you recall the Groga we had housed in that little facility in the U.S.? Well, the Council decided that now that the Groga home world is pacified and the Norgoth have been, um...discouraged from bothering them ever again, the Alliance decided it was time to wake the Groga held in the facility who have been sleeping like the little beauties they are, attended by competent medical personnel.

As part of that process, they were transferred to Alliance Headquarters by some helpful Daringi before bringing them back to consciousness. Several Groga leaders were on hand to greet them as they were awakened. They explained the current situation and offered them a choice, either return to the service of the Insenium or retire to the Groga home world.

Without exception, they all chose to go home. One of them, however, the Groga-ha of the forces in the swamp, cried out as the Daringi entered the infirmary: 'Please STOP! You must find it! It will destroy them!'

When asked to explain what he meant by that, he told them that the reason they were in that swamp was to monitor something (he didn't know what) that had been placed on the moon of Earth. He told them it was set on a timer to go off and he was to monitor Earth communications to be sure they didn't launch another moon exploration venture before that happened. If they had, it was his job to communicate to the Brazil contingency to notify the Fleistians, so the Fleistians could notify the Insenium.

It turns out that the device that caused the power blackouts on Earth was planted there by the Insenium as far back as 3 years ago. However, by the time the timer went off and the thing created the blackout, they were focused elsewhere. The blackout was to have preceded a full on invasion by the Insenium."

Lova sat there, her eyes wide, obviously dumbfounded. Then she straightened and went straight to the core of it.

"What about the main Insenium planet? How long before we can mount an assault on Gall himself?"

"When all the teams have been debriefed and intel collected from the various raids, we will plan that assault with the entire force. However, we have been getting some rather confusing reports from the Mookookie spies among them. It appears that something odd is happening on the planet that the Mookookie aren't quite sure how to describe; something about spaces being torn and bad guys blowing up. It almost sounds like a civil war of some sort."

"And so, we wait."

With that, Jenny disconnected, and the crystal pool went blank, reflecting only the garden foliage and the violet blue sky above her and Miriha.

Miriha had composed herself. She held out both hands to Jenny.

"We have much to be grateful for in all of this. I would take time now to celebrate, but there is one more thing you need to see. This will be uncomfortable for you, but it is important. We will do this a little differently. We are going to do something we never do without permission. In this case, however, permission would be a moot point. Do you trust me?"

Jenny was taken aback. Trust her?

"Of course, I trust you, Miriha. You have never lied to me nor would you lead me astray."

"We are going to enter someone's mind. We will have no power to do anything but experience what they are experiencing. We will be able to hear their thoughts and feel what they feel. We cannot communicate, and we cannot influence them in any way. A choice is about to be made and it is vital that what happens next be entirely by that individual's choice. Do you understand?"

"Not entirely, but I do trust you, Miriha. Let's do this."

Suddenly what she was seeing in the pool wasn't through her own eyes, as usual, but this time she could hear the thoughts of...

Chapter 42: The Cost of Redemption

Sam stood in a line of servants. The chatelaine of the fortress was a tall, stout, stern woman; her hair wound around her square face in a thick braid, her clothing grey and simple as were all clothing worn in the Great Insenium Empire. This didn't really bother Sam much, as she had grown up with monotone clothing, but at least there had been some actual style to her personal wardrobe.

But today she wasn't Sam. She was Kinney, a servant of the court. Her long mousy hair was knotted at the nape of her neck and her face was plain. She was built like all Norgoth, solid and strong. She had managed to work her way up in the ranks of the servants very quickly by showing diligence and alacrity and going out of her way to be especially helpful. She knew how servants were supposed to behave, she had plenty of her own...she USED to have plenty of her own, at any rate. She had simply pictured in her mind the chief of her family's servants and went to work to be that person.

This little assembly happened daily as the chatelaine made the assignments for the day; mostly it was pretty routine. She inspected each servant like a general with her troops. Invisible specks of lint were flicked away, and collars were tweaked. When she was satisfied, or at least as satisfied as she ever got, she stood before them, calling their names and issuing their assignments.

When she got to Sam, she gave a nod of approval...a rare thing. "Kinney, you have been promoted to the inner court. You will be serving Overlord Gall and his staff. You will report to Sir Nanion. You may leave."

At last! This was the assignment she had been working for. She had done so many distasteful and demeaning chores without a murmur, executing each command with exactness. She had bowed and scraped and kowtowed with an outward appearance of humility and obedience.

However, she knew that this assignment was not considered a reward for excellence. It was a test and a dangerous one. Gall had a tendency to go through servants at an alarming rate; alarming because any servants that didn't meet his approval were disintegrated.

Sam had heard about his dramatic disposal of that high and mighty do-gooder, Burt. Onlookers reported that fire had shot from his hands and Burt had exploded in a rain of sparks. But after serving in the fortress, Sam knew it was no exotic superpower. He had a simple device that fit into the palm of his hand. The strap that held it on was elaborate and to the uninformed looked like a fine decorative armband. When he activated it, he appeared to have mystical destructive powers, so much for appearances.

As she walked down a long hallway that led to the throne room, she considered what she was about to do. She was so tired, so very, very tired. It had all been too much. She had stomped across this vile planet, destroying battalion after battalion of Gall's troops. She knew she could have continued for several more weeks, if she had wanted to destroy them all, but she estimated she had destroyed nearly half of the Inseni forces inhabiting this planet. It would have to do.

She had heard that people often reviewed the course of their lives at times like these. As she did so, she realized that her life hadn't been all that remarkable until she had been assigned to her mission on Earth.

Earthlings were so strange; all of the colors, the music, the art and their wild adventures. Her first assignment to induce Guaray to kill the India gate guardian hadn't been much fun, but bullying the man had been well within her skill set.

At the time, it hadn't occurred to her that the taking of a human life meant much of anything. She had hidden around a corner of the little alleyway near a booth selling amazing, colorful scarves. She had watched the woman go down. The little dart with the potent poison did its job quickly. As soon as she had hit the ground, she had stiffened, spasmed, and lay there conscious for only long enough for her to transfer her key to Guaray, because she thought he had come to rescue her. Pitiful.

Her second mission had been a lot more fun. Now that they had a spy among the guardians, it was easy to get intel about the each of them and their various tasks. Guaray had told them that Lizzie was a close friend of the Gatekeeper, their ultimate target, so Sam had set about gaining her trust.

Playing Marie had been a little bit boring, if she was honest with herself, but she was consoled with the knowledge that she was playing Lizzie for a fool. Lizzie was old and seemingly gullible. She bought it all; the garden club meetings, the root beer and cookies out on the patio, the shopping trips, every bit of it.

At one point she had been certain that Lizzie was warming to her to the point that she might even choose her to be her successor as guardian of the Los Angeles gate. Her hopes had been dashed, however, when Lizzie started going on and on about her niece; the brilliant writer, how kind she was, her great potential, her spirit of adventure, blah-blah-blah...

She finally decided she wouldn't accomplish her mission this way. So, she changed persona and became Sam, the one mask that had suited her so much that she still considered herself to be the young, tall, quirky, fun person who became Jenny's BFF.

College life had been a blast. The opportunity to learn in such a relaxing atmosphere, compared to schooling in Fleist, was so much fun. She had begun a semester behind Jenny, but by taking some extra credit hours she quickly caught up. By the end of Sam's first semester at the university, she and Jenny had decided to get a little apartment off campus. Those were days she could never forget.

She had to be careful. She really did grow to care for Jenny, something she had been warned against. "Don't allow yourself to become maudlin and soft," her mother had scolded before she had been sent through the Brazil portal at the beginning of her first mission. "Remember that these Earthlings are no better than vermin. A time will come when we will own them and all they have, if you are faithful to your assignment."

But it was difficult, immersed as she was in Earth culture with an amenable companion, to remember why she was there over the long term. She had been as excited as Jenny when she had been chosen Valedictorian for their graduating class and proud of her. She had seen the effort Jenny had not only put into her classes, but in establishing herself as a well-respected ghost-blogger by the end of their junior year.

She had loved their monthly excursions with their hiking club and had become friends with most of the members of the club, for although she had had companions while she was growing up, they had never been friends. The idea of multiple friends had been a foreign concept to her. Those were times when it had been very hard to remember why she was there.

She had continued to correspond with Lizzie the entire time she was working on Jenny. She sent pictures of Marie working in her garden and long chatty letters about her new neighbors and how very much she missed their time together. Then one day, Lizzie had told her that she wouldn't be able to correspond for a while because she would be in the hospital. This was exciting news...or was it? It had been what she had been waiting for, after all.

Lizzie had always been unusually healthy for an Earthling of her age but, as Marie, Sam had managed to plant a slow-acting virulent disease in the cookies or brownies Marie constantly brought to their little forays into the garden of Lizzie's house that built up over time. Lizzie would probably still be cranking along if it wasn't for that.

When she had gotten hired on at the television station near Jenny's little studio apartment, she had been elated. Looking as normal as possible was important, and on Earth people all had employment of one sort or another, even if it was panhandling. The station was a place to do some real growing and to perfect her persona to the point that she began to believe it. Engoza was quickly becoming a distant memory.

She had been surprised that Jenny was clueless as to her aunt's situation, but it had often puzzled her why Lizzie hadn't made any attempt to get closer to her favorite niece. She had finally decided that Lizzie had known that Jenny was not only clever, but observant, and might have caught on to Lizzie's true occupation before it was time.

So, Sam had been appropriately surprised and sympathetic when Jenny got the message that her aunt had died, and could she please attend a reading of her aunt's will with a certain attorney?

But more than feeling for Jenny, she also realized that things were about to change between them, and it surprised her that she actually felt regretful about it. Wasn't this why she had come to Earth in the first place? She should be excited and happy about this. It meant she was coming close to the time when she could complete her mission and return home to Fleist.

All that she had done to the young woman who had been her friend now came flooding back to her in waves of regret and guilt. Mission or not, how could she have done all of those things to someone who had never said an unkind word in her hearing? She had even blamed her people's deaths on Jenny without any real reason to do so.

How could it all have gone so wrong? How had her parents not seen through the wily words of Gall and his minions? How had they leashed their people to this tyrannical despot?

Jenny had been right. And now there was a price to be paid and none left but Sam to pay it. And she would do it, not as Engoza, but as Sam, a saucy, flippant Earthling who liked bright colors, Earth music and art and hiking in the wilderness with friends. She would do it as Jenny's somewhat deceitful, wicked friend. Could Jenny ever forgive her? Would she even know?

Regardless, she must do what must be done. She straightened her shoulders as she approached the double doors that led to the throne room. All of these thoughts that had rushed through her mind had happened in that fateful walk down the long hallway that led to her destination.

As she approached the guard at the door she thought determinedly, "Mother? Father? You will be avenged. Jenny? I am still your BFF, even if you can never again be mine."

The guard acknowledged her with a lazy wave of the hand, indicating she should enter.

As she opened the door, she realized that this room was huge. At the far end, on a low dais, Gall sprawled on a surprisingly elaborate throne in rich dark green robes so dark as to be nearly black. His head was bald and polished to a glaring shine. He wore no crown. One large electric green eye stared haughtily at the Norgoth kneeling before him.

"Another one? How does this continue to happen? Why can't you catch this menace? It is a single being, as I understand it. How is he doing this? How is it that you cannot catch or destroy one single...puny...nuisance?!" As he said each of those last words, he hammered a huge fist on the arm of the throne so hard that the dais actually shook.

"My Great Lord, I was not there. I simply am the courier for the message," the Norgoth said, his voice trembling and his head bowed even lower than before.

"Well, messenger, here is your payment!"

He raised his hand and in the center of the palm was a glowing oval, like a brilliant gem attached by straps leading to an ornate armband. The man, looking up raised his hands before his face in a feeble attempt to deny his fate. A thin column of red light poured from Gall's hand, and the messenger exploded in sparks that shimmered and turned to black ash.

Gall turned to a male servant standing off to one side. "Clean up that mess and send it to his commander with a note to stop sending me messenger boys to do a man's job."

Then he noted Sam standing quietly nearby. "Come here, wench. Clean this up," he said, pointing to an overturned cup that had spilled its contents when he had pounded the arm of the throne. The little table it stood on was at his elbow to keep his cup at easy reach.

"Yes, Great Lord," she said mildly, stepping forward and taking a white cloth from the pocket of her apron.

She stepped up onto the dais, but by this time he had all but forgotten she was there, which suited her well.

"Redemption!" she cried as she threw herself across the gap between them and wrapped her arms tightly around his neck. She poured every bit of sorrow and anger and hate she had been building up within her in her march across this wretched planet, and with all her heart she directed it into the small space between them before he could even blink in surprise. Light exploded...and then there was blessed darkness.

Later, when the Mookookie who had not been destroyed in the blast reported to the Alliance, they described a crater about 2 miles across that took in the entire fortress and a large part of the capitol city. The ashes from the explosion were still in the air over a week later, and everything that survived the blast was covered in them.

But Jenny knew nothing of this. When she came back to herself with tears streaming down her face, she realized she was no longer in Miriha's beautiful garden. She was on a chaise near the grove of trees in the park-like area in Tarafau's back yard, Chidwi's tiny hands brushing the tears from her cheeks.

"Welcome back to us, dear Jenny." And she crooned her soft healing and comforting song.

On a chair beside her, Burt sprung up, grabbing her hand in his. His hands were warm and the light in his eyes said all that needed to be said.

"Oh, Burt!" she cried, and he took her into his arms, the one place where she could heal from what she had just witnessed.

"I've got you, Jenny. And I'm keeping you," he declared. "Cry if you must. I am here."

Epilogue:

Miriha watched with a tender heart as Jenny faded from her view, back to her body and the waiting arms of her true love. From across the garden she heard the sobs of the one she had been expecting.

She found her in a heap in an alcove surrounded by blossoming trees. She had resumed her Sam persona, and Miriha felt that this would be the form she chose from now on. Tall and a bit lanky with a cap of auburn curls, she lay on the grass shaking and shivering as if from intense cold.

Miriha knew that this would pass, but for now, she was where she needed to be as she transitioned to the next stage in her progression. She went to her and knelt beside her, laying one hand on her back that shook with sobs. This was a good thing. Crying often released negative energy and cleared the way for eventual joy.

Sam looked up at her, her face streaked with tears.

"Who are you? Where am I?" It was a plea, as if from a small child lost in an unfamiliar place.

"I am Miriha and you are in my garden."

"But I died! I intended to die! I want to forget forever!"

"Yes, you died. But death is such a subjective thing. In the mortal stage of our existence, we can only see it from one side. But the end of life from the standpoint of mortality is an illusion and you are not finished, Sam."

"How do you know my name? And I do want to be finished! I do! I don't want to remember all of the terrible things I did. The whole idea was to finish Gall and pay for my life choices. How could anyone ever forgive me for any of this? There is no future for me but the torture of knowing what I have done and cannot take back."

"Ah, Sam, I know it is all hard to take in, but the pain will pass. You have much to learn and I have been chosen to be your guide and mentor as you move on. Your final act was that of ultimate repentance, and because of you, the Alliance has bettered their chances to rid the multiverse of evil. For now, come with me. We will walk in the garden and chat for a bit. Then I have something to show you that will make you feel somewhat better."

So, they walked, Sam asking her questions and Miriha answering those she could. As they did so, a growing warmth and peace began to surround them both.

In Miriha's garden time passed differently than in other places in the multiverse, sometimes running faster and sometimes slower as need required.

As they talked, understanding began to dawn in Sam's eyes. Miriha could see the pain beginning to recede. Miriha explained to her that, although her intentions had not been benign, that much of what she had done had strengthened Jenny and taught her many valuable lessons. It didn't lessen the wrongness of her actions, but that in the scope of what was happening, her actions had been expected.

She would yet have to come to terms with much of what she had chosen to do, but Miriha had explained that such repentance was not only possible but encouraged. She had been born into an environment that had taught her incorrect principles, but in the end her desires had been for redemption and that was one desire that was always honored.

Miriha explained to her that she still had a long road ahead of her, but if she chose to, she could change the trajectory of her path and arrive in a much better place as a much better person.

Sam did not argue. She asked respectful questions, and Miriha knew she was being genuine. No one could successfully lie to her or to themselves in this place.

Finally, she led Sam to the little stone bench by the crystal pool.

"Time has passed in the existence you knew before you came here. More time than you can understand until you have mastered the concept that time isn't what you've been taught by previous experience. I want to show you something that may bring you peace."

She gestured for Sam to sit beside her.

"You will be seeing this through another's eyes. You will not be able to hear their thoughts, but you will hear and see everything they hear and see. This experience is crucial to your healing."

Sam simply nodded and turned to look into the pool.

She was in Jenny's backyard, arranging some flowers beside a trellis covered in blossoms. Beyond the trellis was a grassy space in front of a small dais. Behind her was the patio and as she turned she noted the black cat dabbling his paw in the koi pond with his two new kitty friends. She smiled and walked through the French doors, past the dining room and down the hall to Jenny's bedroom.

Jenny stood before a long mirror as her older sister fussed with the arrangement of the short train behind a simple but elegant wedding gown.

"I believe I have never seen you look so beautiful!" and, hearing the familiar voice, Sam recognized that the person she was "riding along with" was Jenny's mom. She had met her many times in the past and had found herself guiltily wishing that she had been her own mom.

As she stood just behind Jenny's shoulder looking at her daughter in the mirror, Sam saw that she had aged somewhat since the last time Sam had visited with Jenny during their college days.

"Oh mom! You have to say that. I don't see much difference." Jenny's hair was slightly shorter than she usually wore it, but the frame of honey colored curls suited her face. There was definitely something different about her, something Sam couldn't quite put her finger on. Not somber, but not as light-hearted as she had been.

"Well, you ARE beautiful, right Sara?"

The sister who Sam had only met once before, grinned. "No, mom, Jenny's right. You DO have to say that, but she is more than beautiful. She has the proper glow for a bride to be and she looks regal, in my humble opinion, as official big sister and maid of honor."

"Does George have the groom well in hand? I understand that he and your dad are giving the groom 'The Talk'." And she chuckled at this.

"Big brother has him properly cowed, I think, although that one seems like a guy who is not easily intimidated. Besides, I like him. I think Jenny made a good choice."

Jenny blushed. "Can you two stop talking about me as if I wasn't here?"

Her mom and sister laughed uproariously.

Jenny twitched the skirt of her gown and turned to face them, "How much longer?"

"Well, considering that you only invited a few, who should be arriving any minute now, we should be able to start in about fifteen minutes."

Jenny turned back to the mirror. It amused Sam that she was spending so much care on her appearance. The Jenny she knew despised mirrors, only looking into one long enough to check her hair or brush her teeth before running out the door.

The doorbell rang. Jenny's mom opened the door to see a group of people led by Bob. "Ah Bob! Welcome. Come in! You must introduce me to your friends."

Bob was dressed in a suit and tie, and the rest were also dressed for a wedding.

"Donna, these are Jenny's friends from her work. This is Lova, Brendan, Mervin, Xao Ting, Adelle, Dhakira, Juan, Luz, Aliki, Leland, Mustapha, Leonora, Megan and Arvid," he said, pointing to each as he introduced them.

"It is so nice to meet you all. Please follow me to the backyard. We didn't have a big enough wedding party to have ushers, so I guess I get the honor.

They all followed her to the folding chairs arranged in a semi-circle around the trellis arch. As they were seated, she turned the wedding prelude music playlist on, and the doorbell rang again. She bustled to the front door. It was the minister here to perform the ceremony.

Donna went to the guest room that doubled as Jenny's home office. George, Ed, and Burt were all standing there chatting quietly.

"It's time," she said. "The minister is here. George and Burt need to go out to take their places by him. Ed, come with me to get your daughter."

The three men nodded obediently. Sam knew that Donna was the organizer in Jenny's family, and she could be firm when the situation required it.

Ed put his arm around his wife and the two of them went to Jenny's room. "Get ready to lead them out as soon as the wedding march begins to play. Jenny, grab your father's arm. It's time."

She then hustled out to sit in the chairs reserved for her and her husband and on her way pushed the button that would play the wedding march. Burt and George were standing on either side of the minister who stood on the dais. Neither looked nervous. Weren't new grooms supposed to look nervous?

As the march began to play all of the guests stood and turned toward the French doors. First came Sara, then Jenny two paces behind, clutching the arm of her grinning father and looking amazing.

As they arrived where Burt was standing, looking in awe at Jenny, Ed placed Jenny's hand in Burt's and retreated to stand beside his wife. The minister gave the signal for them to be seated.

The ceremony was simple, and when the two of them turned to one another to exchange rings, Sam found tears running down her face. As best friend, Sam would have been the one holding Jenny's bouquet, but it seemed appropriate that the brother and sister who had spent so little time with Jenny when she was little could have this honor.

Then, as the minister pronounced the final words, "I now pronounce you man and wife," something strange happened. The effect was entrancing. Suddenly the scene zoomed to Jenny's and Burt's faces, looking raptly into one another's eyes. This portrait began to multiply behind them in an infinity mirror effect reproducing over and over again, getting smaller and smaller until it became impossible to see the details, then it was gone and once again she was peering through a cloud of tears into the calm little crystal pool.

"Eternity is more than an illusion of the imagination," Miriha said, putting her arms around Sam's shaking shoulders. "There is still much in their future and in yours. Let us begin."

The End of the Foundational Trilogy for
The Dimensional Alliance series...Or is it?

It is definitely not the end of the series. We will add several groups of books to continue to add to the multiverse we only touch on lightly in the first three books over time. The fourth book "Ripples of Infinity" will be published spring of 2021. Also, in the works us a Bob and Merv series where they go searching for the origins of the Dimensional Alliance Gate Network.

If you loved Infinity on Fire and The House on Infinity Loop, please take a moment and do a review:

Or any social media groups or book clubs you may participate in. This helps me know how best to continue to provide good reading for you, my audience, and it will be greatly appreciated.

If you can't get enough of The Dimensional Alliance and want to know more about the characters, not to mention giveaways, events, release dates of new books in the series and much more, you can get a free monthly story by joining the free Dimensional Alliance Stories Club at:

http://storiesclub.dimensionalallianceheadquarters.com/.

For news about upcoming books, audio books, contests, giveaways and fan gear, <u>visit my fan page on Facebook:</u> <u>The Dimensional Alliance – Fan Gate</u>

About the author:

B onnie K.T. Dillabough

At 16 years old I started having a recurring dream that pestered me most of my life. Time and time again I would discuss the dream with people I thought were wiser than me and time and time again the repeated answer came, "No idea. I've never heard of such a thing."

At age 63 after having the dream once again I decided that maybe if I wrote it down it might leave me alone. I did so and filed it on my desktop, but didn't think of it again until I started hanging out with published authors.

Mercedes S. Lackey told me at one point, when I confessed I had often considered writing a book, "Put your butt in the chair and write!" It was some of the best advice I had ever gotten.

In search of material to write about I stumbled upon that dusty text file about my dream and the rest is history. From it came the science fiction - fantasy series "The Dimensional Alliance" beginning with "The House on Infinity Loop". Now, at the launch of "The Infinite Publishing Alliance, I find myself grateful for the events leading up to setting myself upon this path.

To my readers: Never give up on your dream. The first book in this series was published two weeks before my 64th birthday. It is never too late. There are many more to come.

Don't miss out!

Visit the website below and you can sign up to receive emails whenever Bonnie K.T. Dillabough publishes a new book. There's no charge and no obligation.

https://books2read.com/r/B-A-ZNYK-GWJLB

BOOKS 2 READ

Connecting independent readers to independent writers.

Also by Bonnie K.T. Dillabough

The Dimensional Alliance 2nd edition
The House on Infinity Loop
Infinity on Fire
Mirrors of Infinity

Watch for more at https://dimensionalallianceheadquarters.com.

www.ingramcontent.com/pod-product-compliance
Lightning Source LLC
Chambersburg PA
CBHW051601100726
47898CB00001B/179